DARK LORD OF THE NIGHT

DARK DESTINIES, BOOK 2

S.K. RYDER

Dark Lord of the Night
Dark Destinies, Book 2

Copyright © 2024 by S.K. Ryder

Ancient Hunger
A Dark Destinies Tale

Copyright © 2019 by S.K. Ryder

Published by Hidden Worlds Press
Cover design by 100 Covers

All rights reserved.

No portion of this publication may be reproduced, distributed, or transmitted in any form or by any means, electronic or manual, without the prior written permission of the publisher or author, except for the use of brief quotations in a book review. For permission requests, contact the author.

This is a work of fiction. All characters, organizations, places, and events are a product of the author's imagination, and any resemblance to actual persons (living or deceased), places, or events is coincidental.

1st edition: October 2017
2nd edition: January 2024

Paperback ISBN: 979-8-9893855-3-9
eBook ISBN: 979-8-9893855-2-2

hiddenworldspress.com

I

The Oracle

From the moment Dominique Marchant crawled out of the dune at sunset, Serge, already up and waiting for him, had been on a cheerful, prattling roll. Tonight, they would hunt together as that rarest of all blood-drinker social structures, a team. The only question that remained was where.

Until it wasn't.

"Blood-child, I crave the flavors of Miami. The spices are unmatched on this side of the continent, and we haven't been there in...in..." Serge's enthusiastic chatter faded away. As did the mood of light-hearted anticipation.

Dominique didn't need to look to know his friend and mentor had gone statue-still behind him. He could almost feel those glassy eyes drill holes into his skull. Though he pretended not to notice, the back of his neck crawled. Instead, he finished releasing the lock on the shed behind the beach cottage he shared with the human Cassidy, the feline Eddie, and, sometimes, the maybe-clairvoyant vampire Serge.

"Miami is too far tonight. I don't want to be gone that long," Dominique said, hanging up the lock on a hook just inside the door. "There should be plenty of Latin flavors in Fort Lauderdale for you." *Please let this be it,* he thought, already knowing it wasn't, and determined not to let his friend's eccentricities derail him. As hollowed out by hunger as he was, he had little patience left.

Dominique scanned the shed's dark interior. The usual smells of engine grease and dank brine hung in the air. No signs of human intrusion, no trace of hunters. But there was a small, new pile of sand in one corner where something had dug under the edge of the sheet metal wall. Tiny tracks led away from the excavation, and a soft clicking noise came from underneath the cover fastened over his motorcycle—a cover that now sported a new hole. "*Merde.*"

The cover came off in a whoosh, revealing the sleek, black BMW bike beneath, along with a passenger. The crab, half the size of his hand, reared up on the seat, pincers extended and open, ready to inflict damage...or reach for the handlebars. Any other night, he might have laughed. Picking up the creature by its carapace, he handed it to Serge who had traipsed in after him. "Take this outside and be quick. We need to be on our way."

Serge didn't move.

Dominique reluctantly looked up from inspecting the bike for additional hitchhikers. There he was, the madman he hadn't seen in months, frozen still and staring at him with glistening round eyes while the crab mountaineered up his ragged shirtsleeve. Serge was lost in his visions, seeing what only he could see: Dominique's immediate future supposedly, his ultimate fate maybe, chaos most certainly. Hard to know, really. Serge never explained himself in terms that made sense.

No, you are not doing this to me, vieux fou. *Not tonight.* With a determined flick of his wrist, Dominique zipped up his black leather jacket, then snatched up the helmet and wedged it over his head. Grabbing the handlebars, he collapsed the kickstand. "Fort Lauderdale, then?"

The would-be oracle blinked his great brown eyes as if waking from a dream, but his child-like exuberance was gone, replaced by fatalistic gloom. The crab, now on his shoulder, explored the tangled curls springing around his broad face. "Yes," Serge said quietly and shuffled his bare feet out the door. "It's time you were gone, blood-child."

Dominique's turn to pause. Serge never passed up an opportunity to ride—or "surf"—the back of the bike. Whatever Serge had seen or imagined just now rattled him into a quiet daze that was, if possible, even more unsettling than the wide-eyed stare.

No, I don't have time for this, Dominique admonished himself and resolutely pushed the bike outside. "I'm hungry, old fool. Don't play your games with me tonight."

"Games," Serge murmured and retrieved the crab from inside his shirt collar. "It's the night for them, yes." His bushy brows bunched together. "And hunger, too. Like no other."

"What—"

"Go and see what will be." He gave the agitated crab a pat. It promptly whacked his grubby finger. Serge didn't seem to notice. "I will be busy here with this little one."

"There is not much blood in that," Dominique said, trying for a far lighter tone than he felt. Serge just looked at him.

This was bad. Beyond bad. Serge, three hundred years old and onetime pirate, was many things—quietly fatalistic wasn't one of them. Dominique gave only the most grudging credence to his friend's powers of clairvoyance, but right now, if not for the hunger raking his gut, he would have been tempted to put the bike back in the shed and crawl into Cassidy's arms. The words were out of his mouth before he could stop himself. "What did you see?"

"What do I ever see?"

Dominique shook his head. Riddles, of course. "My 'destiny' awaits again? Is that it? And you don't want to 'meddle' with 'what must be?' So, you will stay here and play with the crab?"

This, at last, brought the familiar gab-toothed smile. "See? You know all." The crab in question was now clamped onto the side of his hand. Serge pulled it off and studied the waving pincers. "She will need some persuading, this one."

Cursing below his breath, Dominique straddled the bike and pulled on his gloves. Why did he bother? Why did he let the unhinged babbling get under his skin like this? Nothing good ever came from that. "You will be the end of me."

"No, blood-child, no end for you. A beginning," Serge intoned solemnly.

This was more than Serge had ever shared about his supposed glimpses into the future, which had an unnerving way of coming to pass in twisted, inconvenient, and often perilous ways. Dominique was reluctantly reassured by the positive spin on this one. At least until Serge spoke again.

"If you are strong enough, blood-child. Only if you are strong enough."

2

A Hunger Like No Other

Over the past few months, Dominique had let the officers patrolling the southern-most portion of I-95 pull him over without protest. Then, once he was face-to-face with them, he convinced them that a motorcycle pushing two hundred miles per hour was nothing out of the ordinary. Just a glitch in their radar units, a trick of the light in their eyes.

Which was why he remained unchallenged now, twenty minutes after leaving the cottage, as he hunched over the bullet-shaped bike and pushed the engine until it screamed. He darted through traffic, hurtled between semis, and left other bikers swerving in his wake. The occasional fool even tried to race him, which never ended well for the fool.

The ghost of anxiety, however, had no trouble keeping up.

Dominique muttered curses into his helmet. Of course, he would do "what will be." In fact, what *must* be tonight was for him to feed on terror to appease the beast that defined his existence as a youngling vampire. If he waited much longer, he would make corpses, and he was in no mood to dispose of those, much less explain them to Cassidy.

But with Serge, "what will be" was never that obvious, and cold foreboding soaked the November night. The faster he could conclude his business and return to Cassidy's arms, the better.

He took the next available exit ramp.

Within moments, new tension rode his shoulders. This was still well north of the urban jungles of Fort Lauderdale, his intended hunting ground tonight. Would that stop whatever disaster supposedly awaited him? Or put him squarely in its path?

And would he be "strong enough?"

"Idiot," he cursed, trying to shake Serge's words out of his skull. He had to focus on the hunt. Everything else, lunatic blood-drinkers included, would have to wait.

The exit deposited him into a neighborhood far past its prime. Fissured sidewalks, squalid apartments, shuttered retailers, and a dingy strip club lined the street, the last blasting a palpitating beat from a speaker. Three prostitutes plied their trade on one corner while a junkie huddled on the other. Farther down, a dealer conferenced with the driver of a gleaming Mercedes sedan.

In his chest, the beast slithered awake. Add one hungry vampire to this cauldron of debauchery.

He stopped long enough to pull off his helmet and set it in the compartment beneath the shotgun seat. To locate the perfect meal, he needed to see, smell, and hear without obstructions. He also shook out his overgrown ebony hair. This softened the sharp lines of his face and the lean cut of his body, lending him an air of pampered vulnerability—or bait.

A group of young men, heavily inked with gang insignia, loitered by a convenience store. Dominique felt their callous eyes on him as he passed, assessing him and his ride, his black motorcycle leathers and silver-studded boots, cataloging him as friend, foe, or mark. He slowed to see if they would climb into their tricked-out Chevy and follow him. They didn't. No matter; there would be others in less public places.

At the end of a cul-de-sac, he swung through the parking lot of a two-story motel. I boarded several windows, others lit up bright. A handful of cars occupied the lot, some of them pricey and therefore promising indicators of the type of prey he favored.

"Hey, you look like someone who wants to party," a youngish male voice called out to him.

Dominique pulled up in front of a tall, skinny man with cornrow hair and bright eyes. A too baggy and too well-worn, black jacket—reeking of noxious substances—hung off the man's narrow shoulders. A sizable diamond stud sparkled in one ear. "I do," Dominique confirmed as he assessed the stranger's thin craw. Not much more blood than Serge's crab, but an acceptable appetizer.

"Well, you've come to the right place, my man. We've got it all right here." "All" included a long list of synthetic and prescription intoxicants which he rattled off at a brisk clip, concluding with a wave at the motel behind him, "And, of course, only the classiest girls."

Dominique cocked his head, focusing on the muffled sounds of a struggle in one of the upstairs rooms.

Misinterpreting the lack of reaction, the dealing pimp elaborated. "We also cater to a wide variety of specialized interests. Just let me know what you're looking for."

A scream emerged from the upstairs ruckus. Female. Frightened. Too muted for anyone but Dominique to hear.

"*Merde.*" He parked the motorcycle. Catching the pimp's attention, he laced his voice with persuasion and ordered him to not leave the bike's side. If he couldn't afford the time to secure it, he could at least post a guard.

Seconds later, he knocked at the door concealing the altercation. The barest whisper of blood shimmered in the night, but the door opened before he realized the disastrous implication.

He almost didn't notice the doughy white man standing before him, wearing a straw sombrero, cowboy boots, barrel belly—and nothing else. The stink of lust was drowned out by the metallic tang of blood and fear, and the man's demands for an explanation faded beneath his hammering heartbeat.

A ravenous frenzy shrieked in Dominique's head. The only thing he could do was the last thing he wanted to do—stand still. Perfectly still.

As long as he stood still, no one would die.

"Did you hear me? Get lost. I paid for the full hour," the barrel belly said.

Yes, Dominique should get lost. The faster the better. But that girl on the bed could not. She was sprawled face down and naked, her wrists bound behind her back. Blood welled from a gash and coated her buttocks. She turned her head toward the door, and he saw blood smearing her face as well. She couldn't have been more than seventeen, if that, and she reeked of fear.

Sweet, irresistible fear.

His control slipped as the beast reared up. His vision shifted, making the blood glitter and her veins glow through her earthy-blue aura. A gaping maw of hunger opened in his gut.

The girl's voice shook in bumpy English and rapid Spanish as she begged for help from the vampire, who craved only to tear open her jugular.

Barrel belly laughed. "She's worth every penny. You go tell Dex."

Dominique put his hand out to stop the door slamming on him and closed his eyes. "*Aidez-moi, mon amour,*" he whispered. Conjuring Cassidy in his mind, he focused on the memory of her absolute faith in him. If he did the unthinkable here, he could never face her again. And without her, he was nothing more than a bloodthirsty, youngling vampire. Without her, he had no tether to humanity and no reason to care about the lives he may or may not take.

Without Cassidy…Dominique was lost.

What he did here now would determine the rest of his existence, whether this was centuries—or hours.

The beast retreated. His vision normalized. He looked up and edged his voice with compulsion. "Your hour is up. Now shut up and sit down."

Outrage colored the naked man's puffy face. His mouth worked, opening and closing like a goldfish, but he remained obediently silent as he staggered backward and dropped. Missing the chair he aimed for, he crashed to the floor with a grunt and a fart. The sombrero slipped forward to cover his eyes.

Dominique cut the girl's hands free with the bloodied knife lying beside her. When he inhaled to speak, he concentrated on the other smells in the room—mildew and dried vomit—while hunger pulled at his veins.

"Do you have a safe place to go?" he asked in Spanish, his tone terse.

She nodded, shaking and sniffling with relief. "*Mi tía.*"

"Get dressed."

While she pulled on a Lycra sheath dress that struggled to cover her bottom, he located her client's wallet and removed the handful of hundreds it contained. These he handed to the girl. She clutched the money to her breast, together with a faux fur bolero jacket and her faux leather purse.

"Go to your aunt." Pitching his voice into its most persuasive form, he added, "Whatever your reason for being here, it no longer exists. You will never come back. You never saw me."

Her eyes became unfocused as they slid away from him, not seeing him, forgetting him. Without a word, she left, taking the temptation with her.

Barrel belly hoisted his bulk off the floor. "What the fuck do you think you're doing? Where do you get off telling me what to do and then give away my money on top of it?" He flung the sombrero on the bed. "Do you have any idea who I am?"

Dominique inhaled deeply, feeding on the outrage as much as he would feed on the fear and the blood.

The blood. The air was thick with the girl's blood.

"You are a man with a blood fetish?" he ventured without quite facing his imminent meal.

"Hey, I paid Dex plenty for something special," the man insisted, stabbing a finger toward him. He looked ridiculous wearing nothing but boots, but he behaved as though dressed in a suit and tie. "Dex is gonna hear about this, you little fuck. You're messing with his best customer. Who the hell do you think you are, anyway?"

Dominique's vampire senses surged. A raw, brutal need seized his body from his extending canines all the way down to his toes.

The beast unchained.

"I am a man with a blood fetish," he said, his voice no longer passing for human. Turning to the prey, his hunger sharpened further at the sight of the plump veins. They formed a pulsing web of light beneath the leathery skin. "And you appear to have plenty."

The first hint of apprehension narrowed the man's small eyes. "What? No. You can't..."

Dominique prowled closer. His eyes were solid black now, his fangs obvious, and the flesh tightening around his bones lent him the skeletal appearance of a vampire at his most dangerous.

The prey stumbled backward, brow furrowed in confused outrage. "What the *fuck* was in those pills Dex gave me?" He pushed the heels of both hands into his eyes. When he looked up to find the grim reaper—as Cassidy had dubbed Dominique's alter ego—still hovering, he clutched at his chest. "My God."

Dominique sucked at the air. Sweat. Shock. Surprise. No fear. He snarled his impatience. *Know me!* screamed the beast. *Know me! Fear me! Drench your blood in terror!*

He took a menacing step closer. "Justice has come for you."

"Oh God, oh God, oh my fucking God," the man wheezed, face turning flour pale as a stink of panic sloughed off his clammy body. The mattress squeaked in protest as he dropped onto it and hunched his shoulders. His stubby fingers clawed at his sternum as though trying to pry through his ribs and grip his heart in a fist—the heart Dominique heard struggling with desperate, walloping thumps.

"*Non.*" Dominique rushed forward and leaned into the prey's face. "No no *no*, do not die, you piece of shit," he growled.

Wide, watery eyes locked with the empty black pools of Dominique's true self. The man's ruddy face went slack with wonder. His jaw worked, tried to form words, but only a breathless groan emerged. Then he sagged across the bed—

Dead.

The beast released Dominique in an astonished instant. With the toe of his boot, he prodded at a dangling leg. Nothing.

"*Merde.*" So much for a speedy hunt and making no bodies.

He raked the long fingers of both hands through his hair. So close. He had denied himself the innocent in favor of this deviant, and now he didn't even have that.

His vampire-self raged with disappointment, but calmed a little when he recalled the pimp waiting for him downstairs. That one didn't seem like a heart attack looking for a reason.

Trembling with the effort to maintain what little control he had left, Dominique barely remembered to pocket the knife and pull down the sleeve of his leather jacket to operate the door handle. He also wiped the spot where his hand had held the door earlier. Officially deceased as he was, his fingerprints had no business showing up in a police report.

He found his bike where he left it, untouched but also un-guarded. The compulsion had worn off in record time, which was about right, considering how the evening was going so far. Was this what Serge had seen for him? He had been strong enough to resist the temptation of the girl, and the fatality had been beyond his control—well, mostly—so his future was supposedly set. Or would be, assuming he could get his teeth into some live prey soon.

A low grunt caught his attention from the dark recesses of a breezeway. Growling to himself in agitation, he stalked to-ward what he hoped was the wayward bike guard—his new prey—who was presumably named Dex.

He rounded a corner and froze mid-step, no longer caring about the pimp's name or anything else.

The miscreant he had compelled stood propped up against a leaking ice-maker with his pants and boxers pooled around his ankles and his head thrown back, mouth open with shallow, panting gasps. A woman cleaved to him, her pale, delicate hand working his cock, her face buried in his neck.

Feeding.

Dominique stared at this apparition, this female glowing with a vampire's cold, bright aura, and knew a flash of primal fear. If he had not sensed her presence before now, it was because she hadn't wanted him to sense it. She probably chose Dex for her meal to force Dominique to discover her in just this way—feeding and vulnerable.

These were not the actions of a blood-drinker concerned for her safety. This had all the markings of a trap, possibly a lethal one.

He tried to catch her scent and caught everything but. A miasma of cloying perfume, urgent sex, and heated blood assaulted him like a blow to the head, the gut, and the groin, all at once. Inhuman lust exploded in every cell of his body.

She lifted her head and pinned him with the empty, jet-black eyes of her vampire beast. The tip of her tongue mopped the shimmering blood from her full lips, and Dominique's groin grew tight. His own beast screeched with need.

The pimp thrust his hips a little, weak and moaning. She latched onto his throat again.

Dominique's world collapsed with stunning speed. Only this moment remained, only this hunger clamoring for satisfaction as helplessly as that man begged for her touch, heedless of the death coming for him. Watching with preternatural stillness, Dominique imagined those strong fingers stroking his own needy shaft, and could almost taste the prey's warm skin beneath his tingling lips and the slick blood sliding down his parched gullet. Nothing else mattered. Nothing except plunging his fangs into that vein and drinking until the prey's ecstasy became his own.

The moment he darted forward, mouth agape, the pimp shuddered and cried out. Then he wilted into Dominique's arms.

Dead.

For a long moment, he stood there with his burden, disappointed beyond all reason, before letting the body drop to the stained concrete floor.

The female was gone.

He leaned against the wall, stared at the corpse, and tried to make sense of what happened. No blood on his tongue or in his belly. His teeth had not found their mark. The relief he felt was reluctant at best.

The female vampire stood across from him, dabbing lipstick to her rosebud mouth and smoothing her short, platinum-blond hair. No hint of blood marred her snowy skin or the brief, metallic-green dress hugging her petite, voluptuous curves. He sought her scent again and found the heady floral aroma of a blood-drinker older than him, though not by much. Decades rather than centuries separated them. She was no true threat to him—if he kept his wits about him.

Which he had not.

Nausea pinched the back of his throat when he realized she could have easily killed him while he tangled in the fevered web she spun. This was why vampires hunted alone. Feeding made them vulnerable.

He pushed off the wall. "Who are you? What do you want?"

She tucked her mirror and lipstick into a small clutch that matched her dress and stiletto shoes, and regarded him with enormous, innocent green eyes. "I hope you won't be this slow next time."

The implication that there might be a next time was only half as shocking as the fact that she proclaimed it in the flawless French of his Caribbean island home of St. Barth.

"Who are you?" he asked again, making no attempt to hide his astonishment.

The smile curving her polished mouth made his flesh crawl for all it promised to conceal. "Perhaps we will discuss such things another time." Her smoky voice hinted at far more than conversation. "But for now, be a darling and clean this up, won't you?"

Before he could form a reply, she was gone, leaving him alone in the dark with the dead pimp.

And a hunger unlike any he had ever known.

3

Night Rituals

An hour before dawn, Dominique pushed the bike back into the shed. A chill fog had rolled in from the sea, spreading over the land the way black ice spread under his ribs. He shouldn't have come back here, not tonight. Not knowing what Cassidy would expect of him. But staying away was impossible. He would always be drawn to her, she who knew him as no other. She was the keeper of his soul and the source of his humanity—both of which he had come dangerously close to losing tonight.

After camouflaging the other vampire's leavings as a more mundane death, he had pushed countless pushers, pimps, and petty criminals into incoherent terror. Somehow, they all walked away, a little paler, remembering nothing, and compelled to confess every crime that ever crossed their minds at the nearest police station. Their blood warmed his belly and lulled the beast into contentment.

It did nothing for his peace of mind.

In the back downstairs bedroom, he stripped out of the leathers and boots, and spent only enough time in the shower to rinse away any remaining traces of the hunt. After a moment's hesitation, he pulled on a T-shirt and a pair of gym pants before ghosting up the stairs and into the main bedroom.

The woman in the bed made a shapeless lump beneath a blue and yellow comforter, only a riot of russet curls visible in the pillows at the top. He stayed by the door and watched her sleep in the diffuse glow of a nightlight from the adjoining bathroom. Her scent permeated the damp air that squeezed past the aged window frames. Like honeyed nuts, rich and deep, the aroma was distinctly Cassidy, a balm to his frayed nerves.

He closed his eyes, savoring, listening to the drowsy cadence of her heart, half hoping she wouldn't wake up. Then he heard the sheets rustle and opened his eyes again to meet her deep blue gaze over the comforter's edge. Her hair, shoulder length and unruly with humidity, framed her heart-shaped face like a lion's mane. Despite himself, he smiled.

"That must have been some hunt," she said. No judgment. Only understanding. She knew him so well, it was a given that his late return to her side was not by choice.

He slipped beneath the covers without meaning to, knowing he shouldn't, knowing he courted heartache just being in her presence. She wriggled close, a warm weight nestling against his side, and he curled one arm around her. "It was, *chérie*. Quite the hunt."

Her hand caressed the shirt covering his chest, silently questioning its presence. "Show me."

His canines tingled, preparing to elongate and do what she was really asking—pierce her skin, taste her glorious blood, and re-ignite a rare telepathic link between them. It was a miraculous bond, an intimacy that allowed her to survive being his human lover, but it was not without danger. Renew it too often, and they risked triggering her transformation into a blood-drinker. Not often enough, and the beast considered her prey again. Every two weeks was the middle ground they had settled on, and they made an ecstatic, passion-fueled ritual of it.

This was supposed to be that night. This was supposed to be that moment...

Dominique's thoughts flashed back to the scenes she would see and experience if their minds reunited. The pimp, the female vampire. Her ruthless seduction, his unholy reaction. The hunger that still simmered despite all the blood and terror he had consumed since.

His jaw tightened, locking away his eager teeth. She could not learn these things. At least not until he had made sense of them and brought them under control. They were more than a betrayal of their intimate relationship. This new lust to feed on sexual passion to the death was too close to how she almost died only a six months ago at the hands of another blood-drinker. For all that she understood about him...there would be no understanding this.

Her hand slid up his shoulder, a thumb brushing the spot on his neck he would normally lance on hers. He shivered. "It's almost dawn."

Ignoring his flimsy excuse, she shifted closer and seared a kiss against the pulse below his jawbone. He felt her mouth all the way down to his toes and plenty of places in between. A deep, involuntary breath filled him, saturating his senses with her warmth and...smoke?

Dominique stilled as alarms shrieked in the back of his skull. Breathing again, slowly this time, he focused. Burning cedar? Or his imagination playing on his fears? But it was gone. Nothing in this air but salty seas, winter winds, and the woman in his arms offering the gift of her blood, her mind, and her body.

Something heavy landed on the mattress, startling them both. Eddie, an enormous black-and-white Maine Coon cat, marched across the lumpy comforter toward them. The cat had long avoided Dominique, respecting the vampire as the superior predator. Eddie's willingness to approach him was a recent and much welcomed development.

Cassidy sighed. "Oh, Eddie. Not now."

Eddie head-butted her scrunched-up face and then gave Dominique's nose a thorough sniff. Any other night, he would have been elated at this sign of trust and acceptance from his little predator brother. All he felt now was an inexplicable anger. With the tips of his fangs showing, he snarled at the cat. Saucer-eyed and flat-eared, Eddie bolted backward as though blown by a wind. He thumped off the foot of the bed with an uncharacteristic lack of grace and bolted out the door.

Cassidy sat up. "Okay, that's it. What is going on with you? What the hell happened out there?"

Dominique studied the motionless ceiling fan. "I'm not sure."

"What do you mean, you're not sure? Who did you kill? Anyone I know?"

"*Non.* Nobody you know." Though that would have been so much simpler to explain.

A small fold creased the skin above her freckled nose. "But someone did die?"

He told her in French.

"I get the 'bastard' part, but not the rest," she said, her words clipped with agitation. Her lack of comprehension of his native language was yet another sign that their minds were currently far from one.

"He died before I ever touched him," he clarified. "Apparently, I scared him to death."

She stared at him. The corner of her mouth twitched before she gave a small cough that sounded suspiciously like a stifled chortle. "Oh. Really. I can't imagine how that might have happened."

He shot her a sour look.

"Your alter ego must have been terribly disappointed, poor baby."

"Beside himself," he muttered. He couldn't meet her eyes anymore.

After a brief silence, she said, "But that's not what you don't want to show me, is it? That's not why you won't have my blood." The disappointment in her voice scratched at his heart, but he remained still and silent. "You know better than that. I know you do. There is nothing you could have done that you can't share with me. Or that you haven't already shared with me." She cupped his face in one hand, her fingers grazing against the stubble shadowing his cheeks. "I'm here for you, my love, always. No matter what. We're a team, remember?"

A well-spring of uncertainty opened within him. His whole body ached with his need for her. How could he exist without being part of her? How could he exist without her love?

How could he exist with her knowing about this dark new hunger?

He gathered her into his arms and buried his face in her hair. In a harsh, emotion-chocked whisper, he said, "I made you a solemn promise that I will be by your side as long as you will have me. On my eternal life, this is an oath I will not betray." And he would do nothing to motivate her not to have him. Nothing at all. "But I need time. Just a little time to...think about some things. On my own."

"Vampire things?" she wondered against his chest.

He loosened his hold far enough to meet her eyes, making no effort to hide his hunger for her, nor his love, or his gratitude. "*Oui.*"

"Don't I know all about those by now?"

"Perhaps too much," he admitted. How she stayed sane knowing all she did about his world mystified him.

Her eyes glistened, but her voice remained steady. "I see." She inclined her head in a tiny gesture of surrender. "All right. Maybe I should think about some human things. For a change."

He kissed her, tasting her resignation and disappointment—and feeling the hope in her tender response. Always hope. "*J'taime,* Cassie," he murmured, pressing his forehead against hers. "I am yours. No matter what happens, I am yours. Never forget that."

She nodded, wordless. They lay together, cocooned in an alien silence they had not known since before he first tasted her blood. He would have killed her then, if not for Serge.

Dominique's thoughts reluctantly returned to the blood-drinker pirate who had saved both their lives twice over since that night, acted as his guide, and was his only friend. Serge teetered on the edge of madness more often than not, claiming to see futures unfold in the blood he drank, and sometimes even in the auras of others. Like earlier tonight, when he had looked through Dominique into another reality. A "night for games", he proclaimed, and so it had been. Vampire games. The sort Dominique wanted no part of but couldn't seem to escape.

The crushing weight of the sun rolled over him. By the time it mounted the horizon, both he and Serge—whom he heard impatiently pacing the yard below—would be buried deep beneath the dunes. Staying in the house during the day when they were unconscious was not an option—not with a vampire hunter lying in wait for them.

He lingered over a parting kiss with Cassidy as he did every morning and slid out from under the comforter, taking care not to expose her to the chill air. She shimmied into the spot he had vacated and snuggled her face in his pillow. What he wouldn't give not to have to leave her now.

"You should talk to Serge," she said when he was almost at the door. He knew what she would say next, yet her words—the words he dared not even think—still shot apprehension up his back. "Whatever happened to you tonight...maybe it's part of the prophecy."

4

ULTERIOR MOTIVES

Cassidy Chandler, coordinator of the *Orchard Beach Gazette's* brand new Digital Services division, had barely set foot into the office when she needed the day to be over.

No, that wasn't right. She needed it to be over since the moment the sun had come up.

After a night fretting over Dominique's whereabouts and his refusal to complete their ritual, she reeled with both lack of sleep and a ragged sense of loss. As her link with him faded, she felt increasingly adrift, with land in sight, but no way to get to it until he tossed her the lifeline of their re-ignited bond. Afterward, his presence always hummed in her heart like a taut wire, even during the day.

Not today. Today she was untethered.

The usual "good mornings" floated after her, along with a larger than usual number of speculative glances. Rumors still swirled about how she, a penniless rookie, could break her engagement to the son of the *Gazette's* most influential patron and somehow end up with a promotion. Cassidy didn't make sense to her coworkers. Some days, she didn't even make sense to herself. Like today.

The only genuinely friendly smile in the place was Larry's. The large, semi-retired court-reporter who had been her champion from day one, handed her a steaming mug of coffee, along with a warning. "Brace yourself, kiddo. There's someone waiting for you."

Cassidy turned toward her office—one of only three with a door—and nearly dropped the coffee. Sure enough, through the window that separated her office from the central cubicle bullpen, she could see the close-cropped head of the man sitting in her visitor chair. She closed her eyes. *I really* need this day to be over.

"He was waiting outside when Jan opened the door this morning," a disembodied female voice said. A second later, Brandi's head—every blond hair flawlessly in place—popped up above the cubicle wall. She lowered her voice. "It's so sweet how he's still pining for you."

Cassidy gave the resident gossip columnist an incredulous look. "You don't give up, do you?"

"On the feisty reporter and the billionaire heir? Oh, honey, that story's going to have legs for years."

"Good God." Her stomach dropped a notch. Yes, that was what it looked like. Not only had she been given the juicy promotion after breaking her engagement with Jackson Striker—correctly implying he had pulled strings for her—she had also accepted the position—erroneously implying she still had feelings for him. That she might need the money or want the experience didn't seem to register with people like Brandi. Nor would they have a clue about Jackson's true motives.

"So, are you going to give him another chance?" The woman's eyes glittered with eagerness; the whiff of a scoop hung in the air. "What's happening with you two lovebirds?"

Cassidy leaned in, mimicking the conspiratorial attitude. "Nothing that's fit to print." At least not in the society pages. Police blotter, maybe.

"Oh, c'mon."

While Larry chuckled, Cassidy summoned what fight she had left and headed for her office. She didn't even want to know Jackson's reasons—as though she couldn't guess—for showing up here and throwing fuel on the gossip fires. The faster she could kick him out, the better.

By the time she burst into her office, Cassidy was in full battle mode. She dumped her carryall at the base of her desk and set down the mug hard enough to send coffee sloshing over the rim. Her nostrils flared when she caught his painfully familiar scent of masculine citrus and bright sunshine.

"Whatever it is you want, I'm not interested."

"Good morning, Cass," Jackson said as he jumped up from the visitor chair, the perfect gentleman except for the patronizing tone. "You look hassled. Rough night?"

"My nights are none of your business," she countered with a glare. Then she spotted Brandi outside, right behind him, cell phone at the ready, paparazzi mode engaged. Cassidy stabbed a finger in her direction. "Oh no, you don't."

Jackson turned. "Hey. Private conversation here," he barked.

Brandi put up her hands and retreated. "Sorry," she mouthed unconvincingly.

"That's all I need," he grumbled as he went to shut the door. "More coverage in the social pages."

"It must suck being so well-known when you're living such a lie."

He looked her up and down, assessing, his six-foot-four frame making the office feel even smaller than it was. Cassidy straightened to her full five and a half feet and wished she'd gone for the heels and a blazer today instead of her long-neglected boots and sweater.

Jackson appeared oblivious to the chill. In his polo shirt and crisp shorts, his tanned, muscular arms and legs were on full display. Vigorous youth, rugged charm, mind-boggling wealth...Jackson Striker was all that. In every way, he appeared to be the polar opposite of the dark and enigmatic Dominique Marchant.

Cassidy knew better.

Jackson and Dominique had one crucial thing in common: they were both killers. But while Dominique, the vampire, wrestled with agonized guilt over what he had done, Jackson, the vampire hunter, destroyed lives with the cold calculation of an exterminator.

His smile was just this side of condescending. "It's great to see you up and about during the day."

"Oh? Would you cut off my head, too, if I weren't? Or are your uncle's methods more your speed now? Have you roasted anyone alive lately?"

His expression soured. "Easy, babe. I didn't come here to pick a fight."

"Too bad. I'm in a mood." She shoved up the sleeves of her sweater and propped her hands on her hips.

"I can see that." His bright gray eyes narrowed. "Trouble in moonlit paradise?"

"You need to leave."

"Okay, okay, sorry." He backed up a step and ducked his head. The polished charm she had once fallen in love with surfaced as if on command. "I really didn't come here to fight."

"Then why are you here?"

"Well, actually—" He scratched his clean-shaven jaw, shrugged.

"I'm aging here. Out with it and go."

"Right. Well, I was wondering what you're doing for Thanksgiving next week."

"For Thanksgiving?" she said, dumbfounded.

"Yeah. Thanksgiving. I was hoping you and Sam might like to come have dinner with us. If you're not busy."

God help her, he looked like he meant it. "Why?"

"What? I can't invite my ex and my sister over for a holiday dinner?"

"Your ex wants nothing to do with you, and your sister hasn't spoken to you since you decapitated someone right in front of her."

"Right." He rubbed the back of his neck, then toyed with the thin silver chain suspending two small St. Christopher medallions around his neck. Her eyes caught on the stumps that remained of two of his fingers, casualties of a hunt gone unthinkably wrong. "Look, I know how it is, but, well...oh for fuck's sake, Cass, don't make this hard. My mom is on my case about making up with Sam, and I really need her to come to this dinner. Will you talk to her? I think she'll join if you come."

"Your poor mother still doesn't have a clue what's going on with her own family, does she?" He just looked at her, mouth flat. "Unbelievable," Cassidy said on a stunned exhalation. Of all the people he could ask to help him keep up this charade, she had to rank at the very bottom, if not lower. His pained expression notwithstanding, something here felt beyond wrong.

Something else very wrong presently opened the door. Jim Lawley's grinning face appeared. "Good morning, Sunshine. Got a minute?"

Since the only person she wanted to deal with less than the veteran newsman was settling back into the visitor chair, this answer was obvious.

"Of course, Jim. Come in." She ignored Jackson's glower, sat down, and pulled a legal pad from a drawer. During her first weeks on the job, Jim had been very vocal about his resentment for her. In his eyes, she was the clueless new J-school grad who had landed her then-entry-level job only because her then-fiancé was the son of the *Gazette's* most generous investor.

That was then.

Now he appeared in her office every morning with a long-stemmed red rose twirling in his fingers. Giving Jackson only a faint acknowledgment, he tucked the bloom into the vase on her desk where all the others he had recently delivered stood at various states of attention. Their dusty sweet scent permeated the air. Petals dripped from one of the oldest, like ruby splatters of blood.

"A token of eternal devotion."

She pulled her face into a tight smile.

When she caught Jackson's hard scowl, she sobered. "What have you got for me today, Jim?"

"I'm working on a series about the rise of overdose deaths right here in Orchard Beach," he began, and detailed sources and findings with grim delight. There would also be a digital exclusive for her about the police response.

She made notes and mentally shuffled scheduled posts. "I appreciate it, Jim, but...aren't you going out of town tomorrow?"

"For my cousin's wedding in New York, yes. Don't worry," he intoned, lifting a reassuring hand, "I'll have it to you by end of day today." He retreated toward the exit, steps bouncing. "Carry on," he told Jackson before closing the door behind himself.

Jackson frowned at the door, then the vase of roses. He swung a finger between the two. "Is this the same Jim who said he was going to 'bury' you? Professionally?"

She sucked on her lower lip and folded her hands on the desk, waiting for the inevitable conclusion.

"He had a visit from your resident bloodsucker, didn't he?"

"Why are you even asking?"

"Cassidy. That guy's compelled out of his fucking gourd."

"Only where I am concerned. He's still a son of a bitch to everyone else." Which caused speculations of an entirely different sort she didn't even want to contemplate.

"And he brings you flowers." Jackson smirked. "Nice."

She clutched her hands tighter, fighting the urge to move the vase out of his reach. The roses Jim delivered were Dominique's way of reaching her during the day when they couldn't be together.

Jackson leaned back in the chair, legs wide. "So, you know that there are people in your life that don't act of their own free will because of the company you keep, right?"

"And your point is?"

"More of a question. If you know he's compelled, why don't you think you are, too?"

"Oh, not this again."

"Yes, *this*. It's always *this* with me. Your well-being is, and always has been, my top concern, Cass. Even before you got sucked into my reality."

"Well, I've been living in *your reality*"—she made air quotes around the term—"for months now, and as you can see"—indicating herself with both hands—"I'm doing just fine. Dominique is no threat to me."

He leaned forward, his tone hushed and urgent. "You only think that. It's what he wants you to believe. Cass, listen—"

She threw up her hands and pushed her open palms toward him. "Oh my God. Can you just please leave already? I. Am. Not. Compelled."

Their eyes locked, the sudden silence tense enough to scoop with a spoon. In his jaw, a muscle twitched.

"Fine. Prove it. Prove you're not compelled."

"Seriously? Me being here, working my day job, having this conversation isn't proof enough?"

"Nick...Dominique is one of the strongest we've ever seen. Whatever hold he's got on you is deep and complicated. So, no. It's not enough."

Beyond deep, she thought. *But not at all complicated.* She had tried to explain their connection to Jackson once, to make him understand that not every vampire was like the monster that had slaughtered his twin brother. It had been like shouting at a wall.

She suddenly felt tired, longing again for the day to be over. "Maybe I don't care what you believe, Jack. Maybe I just want you to leave us alone."

"Maybe you're being evasive."

Cassidy huffed out an at-the-end-of-her-rope sigh. "How can I prove something to you that you don't want to believe?"

"Simple. Come to Thanksgiving dinner next week and bring Sam."

"You're joking."

"No. A holiday dinner is a totally human experience. No vampire would care for it, but it might do you a world of good. Remind you of what you're turning your back on."

"Oh, right. Your mom would think we're back together, I'd make you stammer an explanation of why we're not, and your father would plot to poison my plate while I'd be swiping the carving knife so I can defend myself against your uncle when he pulls a gun on me again on my way to the powder room. Yeah, that sounds about like the real human Thanksgiving I just can't wait to experience."

He flashed a grin of pure wickedness. "Now *that* sounds way more fun than last year's dinner. Except you wouldn't have to worry about Uncle Garrett. He's out of town on—"

"Still hiding from Dominique? Or off killing someone?"

"My mom knows we're purely platonic now—"

"Platonic enemies, right."

"And my father is seeing reason."

"Oh, do tell."

Jackson became grim. "Cassidy. I know there's hope for you, or you wouldn't still be alive, much less looking as good as you do." He swept her with an almost suggestive appraisal. She didn't react. He cleared his throat. "My father is finally coming around to that, and he wants to help you as much as I do. You're human, for God's sake. How can we not?"

She stared at him, though in her mind she saw again the horrific abuse Dominique had endured at Garrett Striker's hands, the manipulation she had fallen victim to from Jackson, the bullet that had almost killed her. She shook off a shiver.

"Um. No. I'll pass. Of my own free will, thank you."

"Would it change anything if I said that if you come over and have dinner with us, it would be so unprecedented that we'd have no choice but to be open to the idea that maybe, just maybe, Dominique really is...different?" To his credit, the vampire hunter's face cringed only mildly with discomfort at these words.

She considered the possibility of a truce between Dominique and the Strikers for all of three seconds before realizing that the vampire didn't need one. As long as he could hide during the day, he knew how to avoid the Strikers at night as well.

"But if you tell me no," Jackson continued, "that can only mean you're compelled and he is, in fact, the lying, bloodsucking demon I know him to be."

Cassidy rolled her eyes. "Why? Because you think Dominique would never let me go to such a dinner?"

"You tell me. Would he?"

"Dominique doesn't tell me what to do, but he would..." She broke off as the realization slammed home. There was only one reason Jackson Striker did anything. With a bitter smile, she nodded and finished her thought. "...follow me. Of course. You're counting on me wanting to prove my point and Dominique following me to your house because you know he would never trust you. I bet you've got some fancy new trap all ready to go for him there. Am I right?"

Jackson said nothing. But the way his mouth paled and face turned dark red told her all she needed to know. She could only manage a hissing whisper. "And you call *him* a lying demon?"

He slid to the edge of his seat. "I'm trying to save your life."

She got up and leaned across the desk. "You're trying to use me, you lying, cheating, manipulative son of a bitch. You're trying to con me into helping you lure the most important person in my life to his death. Again. *How dare you?*"

"*He* is the one who's manipulating *you*, Cassidy." Jackson pounded a finger into her notepad for emphasis. "I know you can't see that right now, but—"

"What I see is you telling me that killing the man I love is doing me a freaking favor."

"Nice. Okay. Believe what you want." He burst from the chair and marched to the door. Halfway there, he turned back, and it was like she had never seen him before. All pretense dropped away and a man far older and more cunning than her twenty-four-year-old ex-fiancé stood before her. "You're a game to him, Cassidy, nothing more. Eventually he'll remember that you're mortal and he's not and what that really means. You're prey to him. If you're lucky—if he has even an ounce of compassion in that black heart of his—he'll move on. More likely he'll kill you. Or worse, he'll turn you, in which case you'll become our target, and there will be no mercy. That's your future, Cassidy Chandler. That and nothing else."

Her jaw dropped as tremors of nameless shock rattled her body. Had he really just threatened her life?

Apparently realizing he had crossed a line, Jackson's tone shifted yet again. "I'm sorry, babe. I really do only want to help—"

"Get. Out." The words emerged in a raspy whisper.

He raised a placating hand. "Fine. Okay." He turned toward the door, turned back. "I'm here for you. Any time, anywhere. Please believe at least that, Cass. Remember it in your heart, for when you figure out I'm right. If it's not too late."

She could only stare at him, adrift in an emotional storm.

With a brief nod, Jackson strode out her office door and through the cubicle farm, looking neither left nor right. Heads popped up and swiveled to follow him and glance at her. God only knew what anyone might have heard. Nothing fit to print, certainly.

Not that Cassidy cared. She wasn't there anymore. She was back in her bedroom a few short hours ago and saw Dominique walking out another door. Dominique, who hid from the light of day, who was not human.

And whom she no longer felt in her heart.

5

It Begins

"**Y**ou don't think I'd make a good vampire?"

It was the first thing Dominique heard over the rumbling surf after cautiously excavating himself from the dune. His movements were slow and fluid to make no noise, to not give himself away while he was still halfway under the spell of the setting sun. For all he knew, Jackson Striker could have stood over this very spot, a sword in hand, ready to separate his head from his body.

"That is not for you," a gruff voice that was not Jackson's countered.

"So, you don't see me getting turned in my future?"

"No."

"Why not?"

Sand still pouring out of his shirt and pants, Dominique merged with the shadows, maintaining his stealth as he neared the cottage adjoining his and Cassidy's home. A small Hobie sailboat lay against the dune, secured to a cabbage palm. Hoisting the single sail as though it were tissue paper was Serge who, being far older and stronger, woke earlier than Dominique.

The woman perched on one pontoon patiently waited for an answer as she hunched deeper into her sweatshirt against the cool gusts blowing off the sea. Her long, golden hair hung in a thick braid over one shoulder.

Just the sight of her raised Dominique's ire. Samantha Reynolds was half-sister to Jackson Striker, heir to a centuries-old vampire-hunting legacy. Though she adored her brother, when she discovered his true mission, she had moved out of the Striker family mansion and rented this cottage adjoining Cassidy's. She claimed to want to get away from the secretive Striker clan her mother had married into, distance herself from the cold-blooded murder practiced by her brother and step-uncle. That the cold-blooded murder had been committed against other cold-blooded murderers—one of which had killed another brother of hers—did not seem to factor into her reasoning.

By all appearances, she was one of the purest, most guileless souls Dominique had ever encountered. Still, he wouldn't have tolerated this potential spy anywhere near him if not for Serge. Serge fed from her and knew her mind, and Samantha was the sun around which the old pirate's dark moon cheerfully orbited. Too smitten by her undiluted personality, Serge didn't compel her, not even a little. If anything, she had bewitched him.

Occasionally, like now, this made for awkward turns of conversation.

"Serge, why not?" she prodded when the sail was secured and the old blood-drinker still didn't speak.

He folded his stocky legs and sat on the trampoline beside her. "You don't want to be like us, golden one. You would not survive."

"Maybe I should be the judge of that."

"No one who desires this lives long after having their wish granted." Serge spoke with the grave sincerity he usually reserved for his shapeless prophecies, but there was nothing vague about these words and no uncertainty about his demeanor. He leaned toward the human woman and made grand, authoritative gestures as he elaborated. "What they expect never matches reality. Only those chosen by a wise old one, often against their will, learn to survive the night for any length of time." He shrugged. "Usually."

"Like you were chosen?"

He grunted and scooted back to fuss with the boat's rudders. "Not much wisdom there. But he was old."

She considered this. "Dominique's sire was old."

In the shadows, Dominique became corpse-still, like prey in a predator's presence. He could almost smell Kambyses's cedar smoke essence streaming in the wind, even glanced at the sea, half-expecting to spot the shadowy bulk of his sire's floating lair.

"Yes. Old. Very old." Serge tested the hinge of a rudder, secured it back into place. "No one would have known better how to choose a new blood-child."

Dominique's eyes narrowed. The lunatic sounded more certain of himself than usual.

"And he chose magnificently," she said.

Serge stretched out on his back beneath the gently flapping sail and sighed his contentment. "Yes. Yes, he did."

She stroked his wild, curling hair and kissed his forehead. "I don't want it. I promise I don't." The pirate's grubby bare toes curled with pleasure and, possibly, restraint. Their relationship was a platonic one and could be nothing more. Not if she was to continue breathing.

"Are you ever going to take this thing out?" she said, getting up. "Or will you just be sailing the dune?"

"I need time to get to know my vessel."

Samantha snorted, and Dominique stifled a similar reaction. Serge may have been a seafarer in his mortal life, but several near-drownings had taught him to fear water the way other things feared fire. That, as a vampire, he didn't need to breathe meant nothing in the face of his terror at being unable to float, much less swim. The sailboat was a gift from Samantha to help him conquer his phobia—when he was ready, which at this rate, might take a decade or two.

"All right, you do that. But I hear a cup of hot chocolate calling my name." She pulled up her hoodie and headed toward her cottage. "When you're ready, I found a new pirate movie I think you'll like."

She was barely out of sight when Dominique took her still-warm place on the smooth pontoon. "What do you *truly* know of the miscreant that spawned me?"

Serge kept his eyes closed and grinned. "Greetings, blood-child. So impatient tonight."

"I want a straight answer out of you," Dominique snapped. "For once, I want to hear all that you think you know."

"Not yet."

"*Not yet?* What does that mean?"

Serge sat up as though spring-powered at the hips. "The prophecy will not be rushed. You will know what you need to when you need to know it. Not before. I cannot interfere. I *must* not interfere. You know this."

Dominique let out a sound of pure frustration. "I should have killed you when I had the chance."

"And without me, you would have also killed the sweet Cassidy. Then where would we be?" He shook his head. "Everything is and will be as it must."

"Is it? So what happened to me last night was supposed to happen?"

Serge studied Dominique, his enormous chocolate eyes going eerily out of focus, seeing futures unfold. What Dominique used to shrug off as the antics of an unhinged mind now sent shivers galloping down his arms.

"So it begins." Serge nodded to himself. "You have met her."

"Who is she?" Dominique demanded in a terse whisper, as though the green-eyed she-demon already lurked in the shadows.

"A harbinger."

"Of—"

In an instant, Serge had Dominique by the scruff and pulled him so close their noses pressed together. "Your destiny," he whispered, his cool, wet-forest breath brushing Dominique's cheek. Two heartbeats later, he let go. And cackled.

Unnerved, Dominique jumped up and moved out of Serge's easy reach.

"You claim my destiny is tied to Cassidy. This doesn't concern her and it never will." Even if it meant not drinking from her, not maintaining their bond, and altering their relationship, perhaps for a while, perhaps forever, perhaps beyond mending. He would not expose her to this dark new twist of his hunger or, worse, risk having her fall prey to it.

"Yes, it does concern her. It is your destiny to face what comes for you. It is hers to face it by your side."

Dominique bared his emerging fangs and growled a challenge to the fates. "*Jamais.* Never."

The old vampire's eyes glistened with sudden and uncharacteristic moisture. "If you deny her, blood-child...I shall forever mourn you both."

6

ANOTHER WAY

*I*f you're lucky, he'll move on.

Jackson's loathsome words would not leave her. No matter how busy she kept herself, they echoed in the back of her head like a drumbeat, rattled her soul, and cut into her confidence.

If you're lucky, he'll move on.

People always moved on and out of Cassidy's life. Some by betrayal, as Jackson had, others, like her father, because he couldn't handle the reality of the incurable disease that claimed her mother. There had never been close family to rely on, and friends soon faded away too, busy with lives that bore no resemblance to her responsibility-packed existence. By the time she started college and met Jackson, she was determined to charge at life solo. He persuaded her to give him a chance anyway. She barely lived to regret it.

Then again, if not for Jackson, she wouldn't have met Dominique. And Dominique was the only one she trusted never to betray her.

At least until last night.

If you're lucky, he'll move on.

She sucked in a breath between clamped teeth and scrubbed both hands over her face. No, Dominique would figure it out, whatever *it* was. When he was ready to face this new demon, she would be ready to face it with him. For all that Jackson knew about vampires, he knew nothing about Dominique.

Something pushed at her side with small, sharp-clawed hands. Eddie. The enormous cat lay wedged between her and the back of the sofa she had passed out on when she got home and exhaustion finally caught up to her. His green eyes were slits of warning, clearly displeased with her anxiety.

"I'm sorry, buddy. Go back to sleep," she said and scratched his shaggy head until a contended purr rumbled to life.

With her free hand, she checked her phone. No messages, and sunset had been an hour ago. Around her, the house was quiet and empty.

Before her thoughts could spiral again, she carefully separated from the cat, got up, and padded to the kitchen. Her mushroom and cheese omelet dinner was almost ready when she heard the front door open.

"*Salut,*" she said without turning around.

"*Bon soir, mon amour,*" Dominique replied, his voice as tender as his words.

She bit her lip to keep from running into his arms. His wintery scent enveloped her as he came closer, making her dizzy with a longing that transcended the merely physical.

He moved to the counter next to her and busied himself cutting up the ingredients she had laid out for a salad. "How was your day?"

"Complicated," she allowed. The confusion still swirled, though not so thick now that he was by her side, and the tang of peppers and onions began to overpower his intoxicating fragrance.

"What happened?"

Cassidy smiled through her bitterness. Now, there was a question they never asked each other. They didn't need to. Not when their bond was intact.

She shook her head a little. "Nothing I want to talk about."

The knife dicing a cucumber stilled. Then he was behind her, solid as a wall, his powerful arms gently coming around her. With a deep sigh, she leaned against him, feeling safe for the first time in twenty-four hours.

He kissed her temple, drawing her closer. She turned her head to press a cheek against his sand-dusted shoulder and bare her neck to him. No, she wouldn't ask again, much less beg. But neither could she tell him in words what only emotion could convey—her uncertainty, her longing…her love.

His breath caressed her skin as he savored her aroma, making her shiver with anticipation of those razor-sharp teeth sliding into her flesh. They didn't. Instead, he whispered in her ear. "Come ride with me tonight."

It took a moment for the words to penetrate her disappointment. "Ride with you on your bike?"

"*Oui.*"

Her whole body stiffened. "You want me to go hunting with you?" That was his usual reason for taking the bike out. She had experienced the worst of him in his memories *and* with her own eyes. There was no point in witnessing more. Especially now, when there was no telepathic link between them to keep her safe when he became aroused.

"No. I had enough of that to keep me for a while."

"Then where would we go?"

"Anywhere you want. Just you and me and the night."

Where Cassidy wanted to go, no motorcycle was required, but she bit off that thought before it could leave her tongue. This was Dominique trying something new—being with her without being in her head—and she would give it a chance. Anything was better than spending another night wondering what was going on with him.

She shut off the stove and poked at the somewhat overdone omelet. It would keep for breakfast.

"You can take me to dinner. We could talk."

"Excellent." He released her to pull a storage container out of the cabinet and began piling the salad ingredients into it. His gold-flecked hazel eyes sparkled as he lapsed into French, his go-to language when he got excited. His relief at not having to bite her was painfully obvious.

She tried to follow his words. Without a direct connection to his mind, her comprehension of French was dicey, but *"bistro français"* was clear enough.

"Cuban," she interrupted. "There's a new Cuban place in Jupiter that's getting rave reviews."

He hesitated before nodding. "Your wish is my command, *chérie.* Cuban, it is."

So much for being compelled, she thought as she went upstairs to get dressed. *Too bad Jackson isn't here to see it.*

Traveling south had not been in Dominique's plans, much less with Cassidy in tow. South was where the other vampire hunted, and he had no intention of crossing paths with her again, much less expose Cassidy to a threat of that magnitude.

This possibility ate at him all the way down the highway, even as he reveled in the feel of her clinging to his back. He matched his speed with prevailing traffic, but couldn't resist the occasional artful swerve that made her gasp and giggle inside her helmet.

At the restaurant, he ordered for them in Spanish. When the food arrived, he left his own small plate of *papas rellenas* untouched while she demolished her order of *bistec empanizado*.

No other blood-drinkers lurked among the boisterous crowd, allowing him to focus solely on her. She wore his favorite sweater, no doubt a conscious decision on her part. It was a thin, muted blue garment that was as seductive to the touch as it was to the eye, leaving as it did, one sun-kissed shoulder invitingly bare. Last time she had worn it, he'd been unable to maintain a coherent thought in his head until he nuzzled into her neck and...

No. That wouldn't happen tonight. It *could* not.

He took pains to keep his eyes away from her shoulder and concentrated instead on her voice. They spoke as they had not in a while, about their pasts and aspirations, delighting in the challenge of translating into actual words what they both already knew emotionally and from shared memories.

Cassidy reaffirmed her intention of making a success of her position at the *Gazette* for the next year or two and then use the experience to qualify for opportunities elsewhere. Where didn't matter to Dominique. Where she went, he would go. Keeping her safe was his top priority, closely followed by reversing his own cursed condition, slim as that possibility was.

Neither one of them mentioned the prophecy.

Though they talked and laughed like any other couple there, the sense of loss over their bond haunted them. She gamely followed his lead and didn't mention it, but she couldn't hide the flashes of sadness in her eyes. He felt it, too. Mutual sorrow lingered where a live wire of connection should have crackled.

Back at the cottage, on the front porch, she thanked him for a "delightful evening" with a gentle kiss that quickly turned passionate. He melted into her yielding mouth as deeply as he longed to melt into her body, her blood, her very soul, and she met him with staggering desperation. His hunger sharpened into a fine steel blade slicing through his heart and emerged in a soft, throbbing growl.

Encouraged, she slid an inquisitive hand down his back and took brazen hold of his buttocks. The memory of another hand working another part of another body exploded in his mind. In an instant, his pure yearning for her twisted into every degenerate lust roused by that kill, a seething depravity demanding satisfaction.

Somehow, he stopped himself from bolting out of her arms, withdrawing instead with profound regret.

"Would you like to come in?" Her voice was smoky with desire. "For a nightcap?" She tucked her shoulder-length hair behind one ear and inclined her head toward the door.

The pulse ticking in her neck drew his attention without mercy. As did the sound of blood rushing in her veins, and the knowledge of the tantalizing sweater she wore beneath her jacket.

"Not a good idea," he said quietly. If he stepped through that door, not taking her up on her invitation would be impossible. His teeth would find their mark, he would merge with her, and she would know this new vile appetite. After that, she wouldn't want to be in the same house with him, much less the same bed.

Her hands sunk into the pockets of her jacket. "Still haven't figured it out, have you?"

"No. Not yet." Maybe never. Could they exist like this after the intimacies they had shared? Or would she consider it yet another abandonment in her life? But wasn't what he was saving her from worse? Or was he just delaying the inevitable, and he would lose her either way?

They stood shrouded in darkness, the silence between them filling with an intrepid cricket and the ocean's mumbling.

Finally, she drew a shaky breath. "I love you, Dominique, and I miss you more than words can say."

He bowed his head but said nothing. She held his heart in her hands. She was why he dared to hope, and the reason he lived at all. For this, there were no words. There were only the tears sliding down his face.

Cassidy entered the cottage, her steps hesitant, and closed the door with a soft click.

"*Et je te manque,*" he whispered. "And I you."

7

BLIND SPOTS

When Dominique announced he would go out alone for a while on Friday night, Cassidy's emotions waffled between regret and relief. Despite having taken her out in grand style for several nights in a row, emotionally he had pulled away so far by now that being near him was torture. He didn't even enter the cottage—at least not while she was awake. Every morning, she found Eddie cowering under the bed, letting her know the vampire had recently lingered in the room.

While she was grateful for his efforts, they couldn't make up for the widening chasm between them. He felt it too—she could see it in his bleak eyes—but did nothing. Whatever his reasons for not sharing his mind with her, by now they had taken on cataclysmic, world-ending proportions in her imagination and stoked her mounting anxiety.

Not long after he left, she couldn't sit still any longer and walked down the lane to Samantha's cottage. Serge opened the door before she even knocked. With his tousled, caramel-streaked hair, Hawaiian shirt and board shorts, he would have been the epitome of a hippie surfer if not for the hideous way the bright colors clashed with his supernaturally pale skin. They did, however, perfectly compliment his cheerful demeanor.

He ushered her inside what was essentially a mirror of her own cottage, but vastly more updated. Plush new furniture filled the living room to one side of the front door. On the other, modern appliances sparkled in the granite-festooned kitchen. Spotless white tile covered the floor throughout.

"Great timing," Samantha greeted as she put down her phone. "I just ordered pizza."

Cassidy frowned. "You don't eat pizza."

"But you do, right? Veggie pizza I can handle."

"Thanks," she murmured. Serge must have been watching her and alerted Samantha to get the comfort food organized. So much for forgetting her problems for a while.

She kept the conversation light and trivial, but once the food arrived, she realized her attempts at distracting herself were doomed. Serge took delivery of the pizza and handed it to Samantha. Then he dropped all human pretensions. In a voice vibrating with power, he ordered the delivery boy to present a vein. The young man's color bordered on ashen by the time Serge—now well-fed—sent him on his way with a cheerful slap on the shoulder and a generous cash tip.

"I'm liking this century," Serge declared cheerfully as he waved Samantha's smartphone. "So much bounty to be summoned with such ease." His tongue mopped a smear of blood off his lips as he returned to the sofa and resumed watching a black-and-white swashbuckling adventure film.

"Sam, you're creating a monster," Cassidy said under her breath.

Samantha pulled a fragrant cheese-oozing slice onto her plate. "Taming," she corrected with a gentle smile.

Proving her brother wrong was probably closer to the truth. Serge had been Jackson's first kill, and would have stayed that

way if not for Samantha's swift intervention. The old pirate
had been her devoted shadow ever since.

By the end of her first slice, Cassidy gave up. She spilled
the whole sad tale of her troubles with the vampire in her
life.

Her friend listened, concern furrowing her delicate brow.
"That doesn't sound like Dominique."

"Tell me about it." She lifted the lid and pulled another
gooey helping out of the box.

"My guess would be that he's just trying to protect you
from something."

"That makes no sense." Last time Dominique had tried
that, they both had almost died. He knew better. "I'm on
intimate terms with his alter ego. I'm never safer than when
our link is strong."

Samantha looked away and took a long drink of lemonade.

"Sorry," Cassidy murmured. Her telepathic bond with
Dominique was a sore spot for Samantha, whose relationship with Serge, no matter how solid, would never be more
than a shadow of what Cassidy and Dominique enjoyed.

When Dominique allowed it.

"Then maybe it's not you he's protecting," Samantha
speculated.

"How do you mean?"

"It might be your relationship he wants to save."

This gave Cassidy pause, but then she shook her head. "I
don't see how. It feels more like he's trying to destroy it."

Samantha glanced over her shoulder at Serge, who appeared oblivious to their conversation but surely followed
every word. "Then I'm guessing. I don't know."

"But I bet Serge does," Cassidy said, watching the lounging
vampire for any hint of a reaction. There was none. She ex-

changed a look with Samantha, who put a hand on her arm and gave an encouraging squeeze.

"Don't worry, sweetie. As long as you two are together, nothing can harm either of you. He is smart enough to figure that out. You'll see."

"I hope you're right. And I hope he figures it out soon."

A sharp knock at the door made both women jump. They looked to Serge, who hadn't moved. "Who is it?" Samantha whispered.

Serge muted the already indistinct sound of his movie and gave them a doleful look. "Go and see."

"Oh great," Cassidy muttered. "More ominous mysteries."

The knock repeated, strong enough to rattle the door on its hinges. Samantha approached it as though venturing into a tiger's den. What she found glowering on the other side wasn't far off.

"Dominique?"

His gaze darted past her, first finding Serge on the sofa, then Cassidy at the kitchen counter.

"What can I do for you?" Shock strained Samantha's voice. Dominique avoided her like he avoided daylight. He rarely came near her home. And he never knocked on her door.

"Cassidy?"

"Yes, of course." She stepped aside. "Come in."

Dominique entered the room, a vision to behold in his full black leather regalia, all effortless grace and leashed power, bristling with agitation. He came to a halt five feet away from Cassidy. The heart-stopping scowl on his face hardened. No doubt he would have preferred to speak to her privately, but without their link, that wouldn't be happening here.

Nor was Cassidy particularly inspired to leave with him just now.

"You're back early," she said, breaking the awkward silence. "What happened?"

"I almost fell into Jackson's latest trap." His tone was clipped and his French accent thick as a stew.

Samantha smothered a gasp behind one hand.

Cassidy slid off the barstool. "What? Where? How?"

"*La maison...euh...*Jim Lawley's home has been made into a trap for me," he declared, hands gesturing to encompass the room as though it might harbor a similar threat. "If not for the smell of new paint, I would not have noticed the changes and would now sit in a silver-lined *cage*, awaiting my tormentor's twisted pleasure."

She grabbed the counter edge for support. No, this couldn't be happening. Not again.

He took two more steps toward her and leaned in close. "*Sais-tu...*do you know anything about this?"

"Me? Are you insane? Why would you think that?"

"You are the only one who knows I go to see that useless man and why." He glanced at Samantha, who had paled by several shades. "Or should I ask my tormentor's sister?"

"I have no idea what you're talking about," the sister sputtered.

Serge still hadn't moved from his nest of sofa pillows, though he watched them all with a strange, far-away stare that gave Cassidy chills. He didn't watch *them* so much, she knew, as he watched the possible future events being triggered by this very moment.

"Jim Lawley is out of town. Has been since Tuesday." On a more sarcastic note, Cassidy added, "But you'd know that if you had bitten me when you were supposed to."

Another five or ten seconds, then the outrage drained from his face. "Why did you not tell me this?"

"I'm sorry. Jim's personal plans aren't a priority for me right now. Want to guess why that might be?"

Shoulders slumping, he shoved the fingers of both hands through his disheveled hair. "*D'accord.* But what about Jackson? How would he know I might be there?"

It took her only a second to make the connection. Then her stomach fisted with anger. "That manipulative, opportunistic, freaking bastard."

Everybody looked at her, expectant, but she hesitated. This was a conversation she hadn't intended to have in words, much less with witnesses. But whatever.

"He came to see me on Monday, and he saw Jim acting at his compelled finest. He put two and two together. There was no point in denying anything."

Dominique's eyes rounded, incredulous.

With mounting disgust, she recalled one more thing. "He also heard Jim talk about going out of town. Son of a bitch."

"Jackson Striker contacted you? And you did not tell me this either?"

Cassidy crossed her arms. "I really didn't think you'd want to hear about that while we were out on our dates. Or about the colorful things he had to say about you, of which there were plenty."

He leaned one hand on the cold granite countertop beside her. "*Merde.*"

"Exactly."

"Jackson is not going to give up," Samantha said with a disappointed shake of her head. "Please be careful, Dominique."

Cassidy saw the subtle tension running through him and recognized it for the hostile annoyance it was. He was moments away from snarling at Jackson's sister outright—or worse.

The oracle on the sofa chose that moment to speak. "What must be, will be." Dominique shot Serge a murderous glare that was acknowledged with a careless shrug. "You know what you have to do, blood-child."

In the silence that followed, the tension in the room folded back on itself and doubled, then quadrupled. They all knew what Dominique had to do—to be whole, to survive.

When he turned to Cassidy, the hunger and desperation pooling in his darkening eyes stilled her breath and made the blood roar in her ears. Would he bite her now? Right here? Merging their souls? Even succumbing to the delirious passion that would follow? In front of witnesses?

So be it. Witnesses be damned, she decided and raised her chin, exposing more of her neck, daring him.

Several more seconds ticked by. Then the darkness ebbed from his eyes. He gently cupped the back of her head and pressed his forehead to hers, silently urging her to understand.

"*Je t'aime*," he said, his voice hoarse with ache. "I love you. Never doubt it."

And then he was gone.

8

TROUBLE YOU SO

Dominique opened the bike's throttle and roared out onto A1A.

This was intolerable, this being near her but not being part of her, being sick with longing for her even as the guilty cravings churned his gut. This was his new definition of hell.

That look in Cassidy's eyes, the set of her jaw, had nearly unhinged him. She was his beloved blue-eyed lioness in full battle mode, fighting for their relationship despite his unthinkable accusation. How much farther could he push her before she truly conspired with Jackson to put him out of his misery?

And would that maybe be for the better after all?

A sickening sense of familiar hopelessness crushed him, making his body feel too small for his insides, for his emotions. He slowed the bike. Where was he going? Why? What was the point of anything if he didn't have Cassidy to keep him grounded and sane?

The beast stirred with displeasure. To his alter ego—the pure vampire essence of him—there was no problem that couldn't be solved with a good, terror-fueled blood-letting. Especially when, like now, he was hungry.

The lot he pulled into belonged to the Conch House, a popular waterfront restaurant, and the car by which he stopped—and which had drawn him there, he realized—was a white, high-performance Audi sports coupe. He stared at the license plate number his photographic memory so clearly recalled.

For once, destiny had not found him. He had found it.

He parked the bike and circled the building on foot, following the thickening aromas of grilled beef and seafood, and staying in the shadows until he reached the back deck, which overlooked the beach. If this was yet another trap set by the man sworn to destroy him, it was an unlikely one. There were too many escape routes here, no possibility of cages crashing from the awnings or leaping through the splintered wooden floors. Also, the place teemed with potential witnesses enjoying classical jazz, glasses of fine wine, and plates of gourmet delights.

Nor would Jackson Striker use himself as bait. Yet, there he was, at a table on the far, uncovered side of the deck, long past sunset. Jackson didn't like being there; Dominique could tell from the tight, squared shoulders and the way the man's hooded eyes scanned the crowd.

He focused his hearing to catch Jackson's words over the restaurant's bustle. The girl with him was pretty in a boring, faultless sort of way. Even her long, artfully highlighted hair was ruler straight.

"Your turn," she said. "Tell me something about yourself no one else knows."

Jackson laughed, bashful, and Dominique's lips pulled into a sneer. The hunter's secrets were nothing this girl would ever know.

"I don't know, Avery. It's only our first date."

"Yeah, we're getting to know each other. So spill, and I'll tell you something about me."

"Well. Okay. I...well, I sleep in the nude."

"*Pathétique*," Dominique muttered.

Avery giggled. "Oh, c'mon. Like I wouldn't have figured that out before the end of the night."

"Oh, would you?" Jackson's grin grew lecherous.

Outrage seized Dominique out of nowhere. Neither he nor Cassidy cared what this man did or with whom, as long as it didn't involve killing vampires. But this was not the Jackson Striker she had once given her heart and body to. How easy was it for this superficial man to hook up with the first girl to throw herself at him? After years with Cassidy who was worth a hundred of this inane tramp? Or was this one really the first? Had he cheated on Cassidy? Had she ever meant anything to him? Just how long had this *salaud* been manipulating her?

Dominique flowed over the rail like a ghost and flitted between the tables so fast as to be invisible in the muted light. He reappeared in a crouch behind Avery's chair and hovered there to relish the undiluted shock claiming Jackson's face. Locking his gaze with the hunter's, Dominique spoke at the girl's ear in his spookiest voice. "He kills vampires."

By the time she spun around, he was gone. "What the...did you hear that?"

From his new hiding place, deep inside the restaurant, Dominique watched Jackson try to keep it together with only marginal success. It took a full minute before the hunter had regained his composure and several more to convince his date that he had seen and heard nothing. She shifted in her seat, dubious, but seemed to think better of making herself appear a complete lunatic by insisting otherwise.

When their food arrived, Jackson excused himself and made for the men's room at a brisk clip. Dominique followed, maintaining his guard for any sign of deception.

Jackson hunched over a sink and splashed water on his face. He paid no heed to the door opening and didn't know a vampire had entered until he looked into the mirror—and froze.

"Do I trouble you so, *cher?*" Dominique wondered, a seductive purr in his voice.

Jackson said nothing, didn't move. In the mirror, his cold, bright eyes blasted Dominique with rage.

Jackson could resist verbal compulsions. It would take a bite and plenty of serum to manipulate him, but even then, the compulsion would be tentative and temporary. The hate that fueled him would not be subdued. If anything, it would only burn brighter if Dominique so much as touched him. There was no point in going that route. Unless he meant to kill him.

"Relax," Dominique said. "My pledge to Cassidy stands. You are safe from me, you worthless piece of shit."

Jackson turned to face him. Water dripped off his reddening face and soaked his shirt collar. His fists clenched by his side. "Then what the *fuck* are you doing here?"

Good question. Leaning against a stall partition, Dominique hooked his thumbs into his pockets and mustered a reluctant smile. "You should know that I am aware of your updates to Jim Lawley's home. I won't be visiting with him again."

Only the slightest shock registered on Jackson's face.

"If he makes Cassidy's days unpleasant again now, she can blame you, *non?*" He watched the other man's throat bob and fantasized about ripping it open.

"Maybe you should let her fight her own battles. Get out of her head and—"

The door swung open. A bulky, middle-aged man in an expensive blue blazer took in the scene and seemed to consider the wisdom of being anywhere near them. His need apparently outweighed his sense of dread as he gave them a small nod, averted his eyes and made use of a urinal.

Dominique's smile widened. "*Pardon*," he told Jackson. "My dinner has arrived."

An instant later, he was behind the stranger, pushed the head aside, and drove his fangs home. He allowed himself only three deep swallows of blood. By then, the prey was oblivious, convinced he had a crick in his neck, and relished his piss. Dominique shuddered a little as he withdrew. He hungered for so much more. Instead, he sealed the wounds into neat, tiny scars with a swipe of his tongue, and stepped back. The prey ignored them, concluded his business, and washed his hands.

Jackson stared at Dominique with an expression of stunned disbelief. There was a small flashlight in his hand, unlit and about to slip from his fingers. It was a miniature version of the full-spectrum light guns that had once charred Dominique to the bone. Why hadn't the hunter used it? Not that it mattered; its feeble light would have been little more than annoying.

"*Au revoir*," Dominique said, inclining his head, and followed his erstwhile meal out the door.

With a sense of grim satisfaction, he continued his travels. His impromptu demonstration of stealth feeding was unlikely to change Jackson's mind about wanting to end him, but he hoped it had at least planted a small seed of doubt. Not all blood-drinkers were the murderous demons the Strikers believed them to be.

Only most of them.

Including the mysterious female who vexed him. She was old enough to feed without taking lives, yet she chose to kill. Perhaps he should have told Jackson about her and let the hunter eliminate the problem?

He dismissed that thought almost as quickly as it occurred to him. That wouldn't free him of the temptation she represented. No, he had to deal with her himself. It was the only way. The sooner the better.

Twenty-five minutes later, he was back in the neighborhood where she had found him before. It was quiet for a Friday night, owing to the threat of rain rumbling in the distance. He removed and stowed his helmet, freeing his senses to the night. Ozone rode the cool breeze, trying but failing to scrub the air of decay, drugs, and cheap perfume.

Two hours later, he was almost resigned to not confronting her tonight, when he caught a hint of sweet gardenia. Heading into the rising wind, he found the out-of-place odor again.

There. Just ahead, walking in the shadows of a row of warehouses, invisible to human eyes. To his sensitive eyes, she glowed blue-white. Another life force bobbed not far ahead of her, this one red and human.

She waited for him to roll to a stop, planting his boots on the pavement to either side. "Ah, *bon soir, chéri*," she cooed and continued in French. "I knew you would be back. And what magnificent timing." She put a hand on his leather-clad arm. Her fangs were out, her eyes black. Beneath a long, open fur coat, she also wore black leather, though not the kind intended for riding motorcycles. "Are you ready to have some fun tonight?"

Her touch and the insinuating tone sent an unwelcome shiver up his back. He ruthlessly tamped it down. "I am ready to know who you are, *madame*."

She smiled as if bemused by his bluntness. "You may call me Bijou."

"And what is it you want from me, Bijou?"

"Me? Want from you?" Her eyes reverted to green, her round, porcelain-doll face arranging itself into the picture of innocence. "You are the one who is seeking me out, are you not?" She touched one long, deceptively delicate fingernail to his cheek. "Do I trouble you so, *cher*?"

A flash of disorientation struck him at her words, virtually the same ones he had spoken to Jackson only hours ago. "I need you to explain your presence in my territory."

"Tsk, tsk. Territories. You know there is no such thing."

True enough. Not officially, anyway. Unofficially, vampires were often sticklers about maintaining their charades in the places they settled. Others, especially younglings, coming in and leaving obvious bodies in unfortunate places was punishable by everything from eviction to execution.

In theory, being the younger of them, Dominique had neither the right nor the ability to order her away, much less kill her.

In practice, this had never stopped him before from doing either.

"We should get to know each other," Bijou said, tilting her head in invitation. "Come." When he didn't move, she shrugged and continued walking. Up ahead, the red aura had stopped. A flicker of lightning revealed it to be a male. A gust of wind brought the tangy spice of his anxiety.

Uneasy anticipation quivered along Dominique's nerves, a promise of both danger and ecstasy. He parked the bike and followed her at a distance, his steps reluctant, telling himself he had to uncover her true nature, learn her intentions, and her weaknesses.

The young man, her compelled prey, was expecting her. When she walked past him and rounded a corner, he trailed after her, their footfalls lost in a crack of thunder.

Dominique hesitated. He knew what he'd find if he went farther, knew that he should wait for her to finish her feeding. Better yet would be to turn around and leave. But he had ventured too far into this hell of temptation. The only way out now was through.

Bracing himself, he turned into the narrow alley that had swallowed them. As before, she seasoned her meal with sexual arousal. The musky stink of rut, the mad thumping of the human heart, the coppery smell of blood—all this he had expected. It strained his self-control to the point of agony, but he could watch without losing all reason.

What he hadn't expected was to find her on her knees, appearing at first glance to be servicing him with her mouth. Instead, she was tapping into a vein at his groin, leaving her meal's bare throat unmarked and begging to be claimed. But it was the prey's rapturous face that was most unexpected of all. It was...familiar.

Dominique's mouth fell open, and there was no stopping his lethal teeth lengthening. The young man clawing at the brick wall in an ecstatic fever, bleeding out into Bijou's greedy mouth was a little younger, a little darker, and much more poorly dressed, but in every other way—the cut of the square jaw, the tilt of the eyes, his muscular height—could have been Jackson Striker.

And then he was.

Dominique's body throbbed with the sound of crashing thunder and Jackson's panting moans. He grabbed the short hair and yanked it back to expose more of the thick neck, and trembled with the effort to savor every moment of opening the plump vein. Only a few swallows, that was all. He would need no more to make his point that he maintained control.

Within a gulp and a half, his serum reached Jackson's mind. There, the erotic fantasies Bijou spun for their shared feed seized him without warning or mercy, reducing him to a quivering, moaning mass of primal need. Long minutes later, or maybe only seconds, a shudder rattled the prey's limbs. The visions contracted into nothingness. The heart stumbled to a halt.

Dominique leaned against the wall. Every nerve in his body thrummed with mindless satisfaction.

Bijou snuggled up to his side as rain began to patter down around them. "You liked that, *non*?"

Not sure why, but aware that he should, he opened his eyes to lazy slits and made a cursory attempt to dislodge her. She didn't budge and nipped at his lower lip. "We should do this more often."

This? What *this*? What had they done? Reason reasserting itself, he shook her off and surveyed the scene. To his relief, both of them were still fully clothed, but pseudo-Jackson lay slumped in a heap, his jeans caught around his ankles.

Dead.

What they had done was kill him.

Dominique screwed his eyes shut and shook his head. No, not *they*. He, Dominique, had killed this man by taking part in a feed he could have stopped, but didn't. Hadn't even considered stopping it.

Memories flooded him. Another night, not so long ago. He had come out of a blood swoon much like this to find his lover dead beneath him. Then, as now, his mouth was still wet with her bloi

He clutched at his belly as it heaved in a way it had not since his mortal days. A stream of blood shot out of his gorge and splattered across the corpse. Limbs shaking, he leaned against the wall. What a lie he was living. This is what he truly was: a brutal, bloodthirsty demon.

Just as Jackson believed.

The rain came harder now, sluicing down his face and reaching long, icy fingers into his collar and between his shoulder blades. The vomited blood spread around his boots.

"What a shame," she said, hunching into her coat and sounding somewhere between disappointed and resigned.

"How dare you?" he demanded in a guttural snarl, but by the time he spun around to confront her, she was gone.

And in the torrential downpour, so was her scent.

9

Thanksgiving

Samantha's first call went to voice mail. The second was picked up after the fourth ring. "Ready?" she asked.

A long groan. Then, "What time is it?"

"Five-thirty on a gorgeous Thanksgiving morning."

"Oh my God. You were serious."

"You won't regret this, Cass. Besides, you're awake now, and what else are you going to do?"

The silence on the other end told her she had stepped in it. Big time. There was nothing Cassidy would be doing this time of day, not lately anyway. "Sorry. I didn't mean—"

"I'll be there." The line went dead.

Samantha put the phone down and berated herself for letting her enthusiasm make her forget what was going on with her friend. It was hard, though. Thanksgiving was her favorite holiday, and Cassidy was as close to family as she could celebrate with.

The best part about the holiday wasn't the turkey dinner—she was a devout vegetarian—or the pie—she shunned sugar—and definitely not the football—too violent. It was this—her very own predawn pranayama and meditation ritual to reflect on the blessings in her life, something she felt Cassidy desperately needed this year.

She exhaled, releasing the unwelcome tension with a mental image of hands opening to the universe. "What must be, will be," she chanted softly. This was her mantra since Serge had come into her life.

On her way to the beach, she passed her immortal pirate prince lazing on his landed vessel, staring up into the hazy night sky. She kissed his cheek and continued on her way. Because he drank from her, he knew her mind, and he would know where she was going and why. She still marveled at the magic of him.

Only a sliver of gray was visible on the eastern horizon, and a half-moon struggled to illuminate the roiling surf through wispy fingers of fog. A small flashlight helped her avoid driftwood and stones in the sand, but there was enough natural light to see the lone silhouette against the ocean's soft glitter. The figure moved rhythmically, freezing in deliberate poses, handling what looked like a sword with stunning coordination.

Dominique Marchant.

Great. Much as she would have liked it to be otherwise between them, the idea of meeting the youngling vampire alone on a dark beach inspired a fair amount of anxiety. Still, he was nothing if not mesmerizing. Also, Serge was only a thought away, and she wouldn't delude herself into thinking that Dominique didn't already know she stood there, gawking.

Such was life with vampires.

She drew her meditation shawl more tightly around her shoulders and continued to the spot where the dune curved a little to make a flat area sheltered from the wind. That location turned out to be a front-row seat to Dominique's doings. This would be no end of distracting for her, and probably intolerable for Cassidy, whom Dominique had been avoiding all week. She kept walking, searching for another spot, when Dominique materialized before her. Her heart leapt onto her tongue, and she staggered back several steps.

His lean-muscled torso and arms gleamed in the weak light. She couldn't see his eyes through the wind-tousled shock of hair falling across his forehead, but she could feel them skewer her well enough. Which made her think of his teeth piercing her skin. They never had. Nor were they likely to. Serge, as the older, stronger vampire, had laid some sort of unspoken claim to her. Not that this dissuaded her from daydreaming about the titillating possibilities—none of which were about to materialize.

"What is it you want?" Dominique snapped.

She raised both hands in a placating gesture. "I'm looking for a place to meditate. I didn't know you were out here." For good measure, she added, "And, no, I'm not spying on you." Before she could stop herself, she finished with, "Drink from me and see for yourself."

She heard him inhale, no doubt reading her scent. Her cheeks warmed. Would he take her up on her reckless offer?

He didn't.

Nor did he leave. In fact, a moment later, he folded his legs and sat on his heels in the sand, the *bokken*, a wooden practice sword, across his lap. "I could have killed your brother last weekend," he said, his tone now wistful.

Feeling somewhere between disappointed and relieved, she relaxed. Not what a girl wanted to hear from a vampire, but also not a surprise. "I can't say I blame you. That trap he set at Jim's—"

"*Non.* You misunderstand. He was foolish, and I had an actual opportunity to kill him."

"Oh."

"I did not."

She swallowed hard, mouth suddenly gone dry. Jackson had cornered her just two days ago after a yoga class, so she knew he was all right and still brimming with anti-vampire vitriol. More than usual, now that she thought of it.

"I may regret it yet," Dominique said with a sigh.

It was the closest thing to a relaxed, honest exchange she ever had with the temperamental Frenchman. Serge was convinced Dominique was destined to be legendary, and she had no cause to doubt him. But right now, all she saw was someone caught in a struggle that threatened to destroy him.

She settled into the sand beside him. "What's going on with you? It's not just Jackson, is it?"

"No." He paused. "I would gladly have ten of him than one of what I do have."

"Can you tell—?"

"No."

"Okay. Are you telling Serge?"

"Does Serge need to be told anything?"

"Good point." She thought for a moment. "Would you like to join us for meditation?"

He swiveled his head toward her in silent inquiry. She licked her lips and tucked stray hairs behind one ear, then told him of her Thanksgiving ritual, which was now getting delayed and curtailed, though not in a bad way. She often thought of herself as a bridge between the forces of light and dark in the world, and never had she sensed this more strongly than at this moment. "Maybe if you can empty your mind and find stillness, the answers you seek will come to you."

"Empty my mind?" He scoffed. "I might as well try to empty the sea with a spoon."

"Well, yes. It can be daunting, even for humans, but there are ways. Yoga is one of them." She felt the instructor in her rise to the occasion. "We can train the mind to concentrate by taking and holding a pose that challenges us. This forces our minds to empty and focus on the present moment and the sensations in our bodies." Her impromptu pupil's attentive silence encouraged her. "Physically, is there anything that's a challenge for you? Anything that would force you to really concentrate?"

He seemed to consider this. After a moment, he said, "I don't know."

She considered her options. Downward dog? Tree pose? Headstand? She could already see the vampire yawn. She shrugged off her shawl and ignored the cool, damp air penetrating the light sweater and yoga pants she wore. "Okay. Let's try this then."

She placed her forearms on the ground, shoulder-width apart and hands splayed wide, inhaled, and kicked up into an exhilarating peacock pose. Heat rushed through her body as she focused on maintaining balance on her forearms while explaining the fine points of what she was doing.

Beside her, the sand crunched. Glancing sideways, she saw him assuming the same pose. He made it look so elegant, beyond effortless. Thankfully, he didn't yawn.

"Okay then. Moving on to scorpion," she said and slowly curled her back, feeling her way through stiff morning muscles. It took a while, but eventually she felt the soles of her feet connect with the back of her head. Her entire body hummed with light and energy, harmony and peace. She was vaguely aware of the vampire by her side mirroring her. "And now we concentrate on breathing into all the sensations in the body."

"I don't breathe," he said.

That jolted her out of her burgeoning bliss. Uncurling, she plopped out of the pose, sat on her heels, and waited for the dizziness to pass. He stayed as he was, the most flawless scorpion in forearm balance she had ever witnessed. Not a wobble in sight. Only his hair and exercise pants moved in the stirring air. He could have been a statue.

"Is there anything you do unconsciously that you could try to focus on? Take control of?"

Silence stretched. She waited. Finally, he flexed his arms, and, maintaining the pose, lifted into a handstand. She stopped breathing.

"Hunger," he said, sounding distracted as he floated his feet to the ground behind him, forming an arch. From there, he stood up as if gravity didn't apply to him. He came to sit beside her again. "There is always the hunger."

"I see." She turned to reach for her shawl. "I suppose you could equate that with drawing breath, which is a hunger for—"

The vampire was gone.

She looked around, bewildered. "What did I say?"

A faint sound caught her ear. A woman wailing? She couldn't be sure. But there was no mistaking the hysterical shriek that followed.

"Get away from me!"

10

A MATTER OF TRUST

Dominique found Cassidy slumped on the front porch of their cottage, gut-wrenching sobs and keening shaking her body. Clutched in her arms was...

"*Mon Dieu.*"

The smell of fresh blood obscured the creature's familiar scent, but the shaggy, black fur was unmistakable. He rushed forward, reaching for her. "What happened?"

She jerked upright, unaware of him until that moment. Her eyes brimmed with grief—and flashed with rage. "Get away from me!"

Disoriented, he froze where he was.

"I said, don't touch me, you fucking bastard!" she shrieked, possessed by grief, spittle flying from her snarling lips.

Dominique couldn't even begin to fathom what was happening, or why she would attack him like this. It was as if he had fallen into a twisted alternate reality where confusion swirled in the night as thick as the scent of blood.

"*Get away from me!*" she screamed again, startling him into stumbling backwards as though slapped.

Serge appeared beside him, Samantha in his arms. He unceremoniously deposited her on her feet.

"Whoa, what happened?" she said, staggering a little as she pushed wind-blown hair out of her face and eyes. When she spotted Cassidy, she rushed to her friend's side. "Oh, sweetie, what's going on?"

"Sam, look! Look what he did," Cassidy wailed and placed the bundle of fur in a shaft of light falling from the open door.

Eddie's body wasn't quite limp anymore. His death wasn't immediately recent, but it was clearly violent. His clouding eyes were frozen in a sightless stare, his jaw agape. She pushed the huge, unresisting paws apart to reveal his belly...and a raw, gaping hole.

Samantha gasped. "Oh, noooo."

Cassidy more than sobbed; she howled. Anguish contorted her face and curled her body into a fetal ball. Dominique closed his eyes, fighting to regain his balance between wanting to comfort her, knowing she wouldn't permit it, and his own ache at seeing the mutilated carcass of a creature he thought of as his little predator brother.

"Dominique, how could you?" Samantha hissed.

His eyes snapped open. "What?"

Serge muttered under his breath in a language Dominique didn't know.

"Look at this damage! Who but a vampire would do such a thing? And it sure as hell wasn't Serge!"

The fog finally lifted from his brain, revealing a whole new level of horror. "*Moi, non.* I did not do this. Eddie is...was dear to me."

Cassidy looked up, her swollen face wet and splotchy. "Which is why you purposely scared the shit out of him last week and haven't looked at him since."

"No, I—"

"What's he ever done to you? If you were that hungry, you should have gone hunting for something your own size, or—*God forbid*—even come to me. You didn't h-have to…k-kill…Eddie." Her spike of fury disintegrated into sobbing, hiccupping, and inconsolable misery.

He shook his head in denial and disbelief. "No, no, no." He took the three steps required to reach the two huddled women and dropped to his knees. Flattening both hands against his chest, he tried again. "I did not do this. You know this. You know *me. You know!*"

Cassidy bolted to her feet, hands curling into fists at her sides. "I *know*? Hell, no, I don't know! You won't let me know anything about you anymore. You're too busy being a vampire, doing God-knows-what and fuck your humanity. Fuck us." She was shaking now. "Why the hell are you even still here? I'm done with this. I'm done with you. You hear me? Done!"

He stared up at her, as helpless as he had ever been, awash in shock and agony.

"Your destiny will not be denied, blood-child," Serge said quietly. "You know what you must do."

Did he? He certainly knew what he wanted to do—take her into his arms, drink from her, flow into her mind. Show her the truth of what he had actually done rather than what she only imagined.

"No," he whispered, getting up. That could not happen.

Cassidy stooped to retrieve Eddie's body and turned toward the door.

"Wait," he said, grabbing at her elbow with the tips of his fingers. "Whether or not you believe me, I did not do this. But someone did, and for all our sake, I need to know who."

"Get. Your hand. *Off* me."

Samantha took up position beside Cassidy, her eyes—bright blue and suddenly hard as her brother's—running him through where he stood. "You heard her."

Dominique moved his hand from Cassidy to the feline body in her arms. So soft, like silk brushing his fingertips. His heart dropped to his knees. He had never touched the little brother like this while he lived. Bending forward, he inhaled. The killer's scent was well masked in the animal fur and ragged wound, but it was there. Something sweet, floral...

Gardenia.

He took several quick steps back and spun around, all his senses stretching to their limits. No other trace of her drifted in the night. No vampire aura glowed in the shadows. In the east, the sky glowed pale gray. By now, she must be near her sanctuary and miles away.

Serge took an assessing sniff of the body and gave a soft growl. "It is she then?"

"It is her," Dominique confirmed as fear slid into his gut. She had been here—in his lair—while he was distracted, grappling with the demons she had set loose in him. While Cassidy slept upstairs, defenseless.

Bijou would have been in the house to find Eddie, and could have just as easily left Cassidy's drained and broken corpse on the front porch for him to find.

The realization made him gasp.

Cassidy sneered with disgust. "You're taking a page out of Jackson's book now and blaming someone else? Fuck off. Both of you."

"No, wait," Samantha said, stopping Cassidy from retreating. "She? She, who?"

Serge looked between Samantha and Dominique, imploring him to speak up, but he couldn't. The horror of knowing how close she had come to dying blanked his mind and robbed him of speech.

"There is another blood-drinker," Serge offered, fidgeting. "She has been driving Dominique mad."

"She?" Cassidy said, and Dominique's heart clenched against his ribs. Acid dripped from her tongue. "Well, that explains everything now, doesn't it? Obviously, Jackson was right when he said you'd get tired of me. What's it to be then? You walk away? Turn me?"

"*Mon Dieu, non!*"

"So you'll kill me then? Good to know."

"No!" Shock reverberated in his bones. Jackson, that piece of filth, had lost no time cultivating her fears and doubts. Pain and contempt blazed in her eyes—pain of his betrayal, contempt for what he was. Jackson could not have landed a cleaner blow had he slashed Dominique's throat.

"Cass, no. Hear them out. There has to be a reason."

"Oh please, Sam. It's obvious." She thrust her chin toward Dominique. "He's having way too much fun screwing a vamp bitch to even think about the silly little human girl anymore."

Dominique tried to catch the pieces of his battered heart before they disappeared into the void opening up beneath his feet. He reached out, but stopped himself from touching her. "Cassie, *mon amour,* I beg you, listen to me. Yes, there is another who has found me, and she is torturing me with demonic games. Games that have nothing to do with you and must *never* have anything to do with you. Not because I'm hiding indiscretions; I'm trying to protect you from her. Because I love you. Because you mean everything to me. You are the best part of me. Cassidy...I don't exist without you."

Fresh tears pooled in her eyes, and he felt his own sting. "I want to believe you, Dominique, but—" She glanced down at

The answer sat propped against the lamp on the nightstand. He snatched up the envelope emblazoned with his name in elegant cursive script and tore it open. The velvet green card inside held a silver-inscribed invitation.

"Club Bijou," he read, incredulous, and flipped the card over. A West Palm Beach address. Too easy.

Dangerously easy.

As he got into his leathers and secured the boots on his feet, his mind sifted through the possibilities. She would expect him. Taking her up on the invitation was the surest way of locating her. Also, the surest way of walking into a trap.

Either way, he would be prepared.

Hung up in the center of one wall was a *daisho* set of sixteenth-century samurai swords. He retrieved them reverently, feeling the weight of their history balance in his hands. Sinuous dragons circled the ebony scabbards and brass hand guards. Their tiny golden brothers lay embedded in the hilts' wrapping, waiting to lend their mythic powers to the bearer. A gift from his once dearest friend, they had been merely decorative collector items during his mortal days. During his immortal nights, these blades had become indispensable tools of survival. And the dragons—symbols of wisdom and cunning—served as his frequent reminders that he was more than a creature of raw strength and impulse.

He slung them across his back cross-wise so that one hilt was accessible over each shoulder. Feeling them settle against his back calmed him, helped him focus on the task ahead.

The card, he tucked into the inside pocket of his jacket. He would be on guard, but he would proceed. He couldn't afford not to.

Club Bijou was a converted two-story storefront on Clematis Street, the glittering hub of West Palm Beach nightlife. Most establishments were closed for the Thanksgiving holiday, but Club Bijou was lit up in a garish red as though dipped in fresh blood. Mesmeric music throbbed from deep within.

Two bulky, grim-faced men in suits, their eyes hidden behind dark glasses, flanked the double brass doors. A velvet rope blocked access, but they unlatched this from time to time for a trickle of patrons. When Dominique approached, one of the men held up his hand. "I'm sorry, sir. You can't bring in weapons."

Dominique pitched his voice into its more persuasive registers. "Yes. I can."

The human bouncer raised a brow. "No, sir. You can't," said his partner.

Taken aback, Dominique tried again with more force. The reaction was slower, but the brutes still refused the compulsion...because someone had already compelled them, he realized. Someone formidable.

Unease crawled under his skin. Just how strong was this Bijou? Or were there others here? How foolish would it be to confront her—them?—without his weapons? He glanced up the front of the building, seeking a place to leave the swords where they might still be accessible, and found instead a still figure silhouetted in the smoked upstairs windows. He didn't need to see the face to know who was watching him. So much for the element of surprise.

He blurred away. Twenty seconds later, he was back, minus the blades, which now lay tucked away on the roof of a neighboring restaurant. One of the recalcitrant bouncers scrutinized the invitation Dominique presented, nodded his approval, and unhooked the velvet rope to the golden doors encrusted with imitation gemstones.

The club's ground floor was a restaurant and bar filled with small tables and booths. Engraved slabs of glass glowing with green light served as partitions, making the whole interior feel like an algae-infested underwater venue. A "Closed for Thanksgiving" sign hung at the hostess station, but a handful of humans hunched at the bar, their attention glued to the game on the flat-screen. The chandelier hanging over the reception area clinked with the thumping music upstairs.

Bijou waited for him at the foot of a curved, translucent stairway. A black leather mini dress appeared to be painted onto the porcelain canvas of her skin. Stiletto-heeled boots rose to her thighs. She regarded him with eyes like cold emeralds set in white satin. Her petite mouth pouted. "Do you bring weapons to all your social engagements?"

"I like to be prepared," he countered, every sense keyed for clues about her intentions.

The smell of gardenia swamped him. It was a strange, too sweet scent, and he wondered if he read it correctly. Blood-drinkers could estimate each other's age and abilities on a scale that followed the progression of time in the natural world. The ice and snow of winter belonged to the newly turned, like himself. Serge's mossy aroma heralded the beginning of summer and several centuries gone. Somewhere in between there was spring, a time of sweet grasses and flowers, presumably like Bijou. Or so he believed. Given the power of the compulsion on the bouncers outside, he was no longer so sure.

"So you come prepared to kill your own kind? A little extreme, *non*?"

Several replies crowded his tongue. He swallowed them all. Betraying the extent of his fury would put her on guard and lose him whatever advantage he still had. While she considered his silence, he calculated the odds of shattering the glass steps and using a sharp edge to rid her of her head. Then she laughed, shattering his concentration instead.

"Ah, *mon petit chéri*. You are adorable. So young. So fresh. So serious." She fanned herself with one hand, which came to rest on the skin above her lush bosom. "Come now. Bijou knows just what you need to relax." Turning, she moved up the stairs, her boot heels clacking in a leisurely rhythm. Despite himself, his eyes clung to her backside, which swayed in undeniable invitation.

When she cast him a blatantly seductive look over one shoulder, the urge to pounce and crack her head open against the nearest wall nearly overwhelmed him. Instead, he schooled his face into casual amusement. Deception was not his weapon of choice, but he knew how to wield it as well as any blood-drinker. "I may have misjudged you."

"Oh, but you have." She graced him with a smile that dazzled with promises.

He followed her up the stairs close enough to crowd her but not touch her. "Tell me this…Bijou." He purred her name. "How did you find me?"

She laughed again, a deep and confident sound, and turned toward him on the top landing. "You fascinate me. How could I not?"

Dominique allowed his hunger to show in his face as he peered down at her, his gaze lingering on her glossy rosebud mouth. "How do I fascinate you? Tell me."

As he intended, she mistook his murderous intentions for something else entirely. Her teeth caught at her lower lip, and unguarded lust flickered in her darkening eyes. Her voice was husky with want. "You should know. Don't I fascinate you, *Monsieur* Dominique Marchant?"

"Endlessly, *madame*."

She leaned toward him as though she might kiss him, but then backed away and opened another door. A blast of syncopated music surged out, along with a cloud of sultry air reeking of alcohol, sweat, and illicit smoke—but no blood.

Silhouettes moved in the pulsating light. Men and women gyrated, entranced, on a central dance floor. More lounged on scattered settees, alone or in clumps, some swathed in smoke. Waitresses in tiny dresses circulated between them. Human, all of them. All of them prey.

Vertigo gripped him. His control, so resolute only moments before, teetered on the brink of crumbling. Trying to distract himself from the sensory overload, he turned to the only thing here that mattered, the blood-drinker, Bijou. "This is your place?"

"It is. Do you like it?"

More like hit over the head with it. He hoped his grimace would pass for a smile. "It has its charms."

She led him around the periphery of the room. As they passed through an area of deeper shadows, he spotted two men and a woman writhing together, all of them nude, all of them beautiful. He hesitated, surprised not so much by the scene as by his reaction to it, his sharp desire to...join them. His body hungered for their adoring touch. His heart lusted for their passion-spiced blood.

"I permit only the most palatable to enjoy themselves here," Bijou explained. She took his arm and pressed close to his side as she shepherded him away. "Think of this as my personal wine cellar, stocked with only the finest vintages."

He inhaled her syrupy aroma to smother the smell of sex, though this did nothing to clear his head. "Yet you hunt in the gutters."

"But of course. A girl cannot live on wine alone."

"And corpses would be inconvenient here."

"Leftovers? Oh, yes. Very. *Venez.* Come. Sit, *chéri,* and be welcome. Enjoy." She gestured toward a settee occupied by a languorous young woman in a strappy top and an abbreviated skirt. The girl's hooded eyes lit up with interest as they raked over him.

Bijou reclined into the opposite seat where a muscular, dark-skinned man sporting an impressive wealth of dreadlocks welcomed her with a suggestive caress.

Ignoring the girl, Dominique sat by Bijou's feet and closed one hand around her ankle. "I'm more interested in you."

Bijou eyed the girl. "Yes, she is a little boring compared to me, isn't she? How about—" She reached up to stroke the male's jaw. With a dreamy smile, he lifted his chin and shut his eyes in obvious anticipation. "He is my favorite. For you...I would be willing to share."

He held her gaze as he let his hand travel up the length of one long boot before resting it at the top edge, allowing only his fingertips to brush the bare skin of her thigh. Her canines lengthened, emerging between glistening parted lips, and Dominique wondered what her blood would taste like. Then he refocused.

"Would you? Am I truly so special?"

"*Mais bien sûr,*" she murmured, barely audible over the sensual beat. But of course.

His hand moved higher, tantalizing. "Why?"

"Because you are splendid." She paused before adding, "And because you could be magnificent. If you let me show you the way."

She took his wandering hand and pressed it to one of her breasts, which bulged from the plunging leather neckline. Those breasts were supernaturally stunning, he had to admit.

Again his attention drifted. Again he forced himself to remember he was there to rip open her throat, not feel her up. Though at this rate, if he didn't do it soon, he might not.

"And which way is that, *chérie*?" he asked.

"Oh, you poor child." She stroked his cheek. "No one ever taught you how to be what you are, did they? I can do that for you." Her finger trailed along his jaw. "I can show you the way..." Down his neck and inside the collar of his jacket. "...and answer all your questions." A nail scraped his Adam's apple.

He couldn't quite stifle a shiver. Unwelcome anticipation almost overpowered the ominous sense that something sinister lurked just beyond his comprehension.

Her voice was thick with promise. "That is what I want of you, *mon petit vampire*. To watch you become all that you are meant to be."

Something about her scent. It wasn't right. But the thought vanished as quickly as it appeared when the earthy smell of blood burst into his awareness. It was the human's. There was a fresh wound on his wrist, which he offered to Dominique. The blood welled and glittered in his enhanced vision, captivating him.

Out of the corner of his eye, Dominique saw Bijou smile, serene and confident, and had a fleeting sense of a trap closing around him. She knew he would do her bidding without protest—even kill for her again. It was true, and it didn't matter.

Hunger in all its forms seized him. With his last shred of reason, he recalled Samantha's suggestion and focused on this craving that defined him, blocking out all else, tried to direct it, command it to only taste, not to savage. He would lick the wound and seal it, savor the flavor, and eliminate the unbearable temptation.

The moment his tongue touched the blood, he knew he had made a fatal mistake. The moment after that, he didn't know why. Then the concoction of drugs and serum in the man's veins cast him into dreamy oblivion, and he no longer cared.

Dominique didn't remember who he was, much less where, until ecstasy shuddered through his body and emerged in a hoarse cry. He was sprawling on the settee, his head pillowed on the human's lap. His jacket and pants were undone, his shirt torn, and his hands were claws that dug into the full hips of the woman straddling him, riding him with abandon.

Using him.

Suspended between shock and delight, he watched Bijou's rapturous face as she rocked against him a few more times. Those extraordinary breasts bopped and spilled from her dress, which was hiked up over her hips. She arched and moaned in orgasmic bliss.

The man's dark hands roamed over Dominique's bare breast and hard belly with great care, as though studying a piece of art by feel. The tenderness in that touch instantly brought Cassidy to mind along with the sharp prick of guilt—and the certain knowledge that he would never feed from her again, never be part of her again. Not after this.

After all the battles he had waged with himself over this, all he felt now was relief. The decision was made, his path set. He would let the girl go to live the human life she deserved, and he would be his true self. He was done fighting.

Bijou smiled down at him. Her fangs retracted, and her eyes cleared to their luminous green. A strange light shone in them. "I was right. You *are* magnificent."

"As are you." He meant it, but something still troubled him. Something...something about her scent.

She swatted away the human's hands and lay down on Dominique's chest. It was triumph he saw in her gaze as she settled her chin on her folded hands and watched him at close range. Smug triumph, he realized, but the twinge of disquiet he felt was fleeting. Given how hard he had fought her before seeing reason, she was justified in celebrating her victory.

"And now?" he prompted.

"Join me."

She said more, but he no longer heard her. Her breath against his face was steeped in blood: vampire blood.

His blood.

She had fed from him.

Her serum was in his body.

His thoughts were not his own.

Which is why he didn't allow them.

Reacting instantly, he flung her to the ground and pinned her there, slamming his forearm against her throat. Her eyes bulged with shock, caught by surprise despite being able to read and manipulate his mind now.

He let his rage rise. "How dare you!"

Bijou gasped a little, trying to draw breath to answer or scold or command. An overpowering urge to release her seized him. Dominique fought it the way he fought the beast—with a bargain. He would release her, but on his terms.

"How dare you feed from me, *salope!*" He snarled into her gaping face before pushing her head aside, his fangs sliding free. If she could plunder his thoughts, he could plunder hers.

The moment he would have struck was the moment he found himself thrown back with a violence he would not have believed her capable of, not given her age. Or the age he believed she was. Which was not her age at all. The taste of the human's blood had told him so because it contained large quantities of her serum, and there was not a hint of spring to be found in that.

"That is enough," she said, standing over him. Her command cut through the music, cut through his mind, and threatened to cut through his will. "Either accept what is, or suffer the consequences."

He secured his pants as he got up. Taking a page from the book of Jackson, he drowned his true emotion, his fear—and the nagging compulsion to submit—in a storm of fiery indignation.

"You are not strong enough," he growled.

"Bien au contraire. You belong to me now."

Those words.... His entire body rang like a struck gong with the memory of the last time he heard them. Back then he didn't know what they meant, what nightmares they implied. Now he did.

Without a conscious decision to do so, Dominique hurled himself at the nearest window. It exploded on impact, and a hundred razor edges sliced his clothes and skin as he flew past, out into the night. In a cascade of glittering shards, he bounced off a passing SUV's roof. Tires screeched and the stink of hot rubber rose as he dropped to the asphalt and rolled into the path of a neon purple sports car. One tire caught his boot; the wet crack of bone followed. He barely saved his knee from shattering, too, by scrambling away despite the blinding pain in his foot.

Within seconds, the agony dulled. By then he was already moving down the sidewalk, bloodied and tattered, teeth grinding with resolve, hobbling at first, running moments later, away from the mental pull trying to reel him back to her side—and back into the past.

12

Leap of Faith

Eddie was a cat, Cassidy told herself as she stared out the window at the bougainvillea beneath which she and Samantha had made his grave. A big, lovable, opinionated lug of a cat that had died too young and in terror rather than in her loving arms at the end of a long and happy life, but...a cat. What was that, really, compared to watching her mother's lingering death in the clutches of an aggressive cancer? At least Eddie had died quickly.

And yet, grief flooded her from every direction. Grief, not just for Eddie, but also for the family she once had and thought she might have again; for the dreams that had disappeared with the people she'd lost; and for—she closed her eyes and let the tears come—Dominique. For what they had shared, the forever bond that had disintegrated in a matter of months, along with her hard-fought-for sense of security.

Down the hall, the toilet flushed, and Cassidy quickly swiped at her wet cheeks. Samantha had all but moved in to dote on her, feed her, distract her, and no doubt surreptitiously monitor her sanity.

When Samantha returned to the living room, the worry wrinkle between her brows deepened again. Cassidy forced a smile. "Just a spell. I'll be fine."

"Okay, sweetie. I'll make us some snacks. Or would you prefer soup? Or a sandwich?" she added hopefully. Cassidy had barely touched food in two days.

"Just snacks is fine."

"Coming right up." She headed for the kitchen. "Why don't you pick the next movie?"

Cassidy glanced at the streaming remote. They had watched two films already this afternoon. Or was it three? She couldn't remember any of them. The action just blurred past without meaning. Suddenly, she felt exhausted. "You know what, Sam? If you don't mind, I think I'll just go lie down."

Samantha's head popped around the edge of the fridge to give her a probing look. "But of course. You go upstairs. I'll make some lavender mint tea and bring it up in a bit with some biscuits."

Cassidy wanted to argue, but then realized she didn't have the energy. "Thanks." Halfway up the stairs, she sensed a feline presence by her feet and looked down. Eddie wasn't there. He never would be again. She grabbed the banister rail and battled a fresh surge of grief. *Oh, Eddie.*

A sharp knock at the door made her flinch.

"I'll get that," Samantha called.

Cassidy clutched the rail with both hands now. It was dusk out. Soon, the vampires would surface. In fact, one already had.

Samantha opened the door. "Hi, sweetie. You're up early tonight."

Cassidy checked the windows. There was still plenty of light in the sky, the sun barely down.

Serge squinted and squirmed in his paler-than-usual skin. Sand dusted his face and drizzled out of his clothes and hair with every movement. He must have crawled out of his den only seconds ago and come straight here.

Her heart sank. *Oh, that can't be good.*

"Come with me," he told Cassidy without preamble.

"I really don't—"

"Come with me now."

She clomped back down the stairs. "Compulsion? Really?"

"Dominique needs you."

The fog of apathy lifted a little. Knowing better than to ask for details, she took a sweater off the hooks behind the door and stuffed her feet into a pair of canvas slip-ons.

Ordering Samantha to stay put, Serge grabbed Cassidy's hand and hustled her out the door, toward the dune.

She stumbled along behind him until a rock smashed her toe and dislodged a shoe. "Ow! Try to remember I'm only—" She finished with a squawk as Serge swept her up in his arms and literally made the world go away in a blurring rush of wind and night.

Seconds later, he put her back down and handed her the shoe. Bewildered, she put it back on and looked around at a wild stretch of beach about a mile north of the cottage, where the salty wind was even more blustery. She hugged herself and was glad for her fleecy sweat pants and top.

Serge stood and stared at a spot in the dune where the shrubby ground cover was half buried as though hit by a small tornado.

"What's happening, Serge?"

He didn't answer right away, eyes now studying the darkening sky. "He'll wake soon. Then he will need you."

She peered at the disturbed area. "Oh. Wait. I'm not sure this is a good idea."

"It's not." Leaning in close and lowering his voice, he added, "But it is what must be, sweet one." With that, he was gone.

"Great. Just...great."

Cassidy sat on a driftwood log, hunched into her sweater, and wondered what Serge imagined she could do here. Deep as Dominique's wounds were, as long as he wouldn't let her in, she was powerless to help him. If anything, she had probably added to the scars on his psyche with her initial reaction to Eddie's murder. But damn it, he had pushed her away, and she had no idea what was going on with him. What was she supposed to think?

Several minutes ticked by. The last of the day faded from the sky, replaced by ever more stars. She slipped off the log to sit in the sand, trying to shelter against the increasing bite of the wind. "You up yet? It's getting cold out here."

Nothing. She wished she had grabbed a flashlight along with the sweater.

"If you don't come out, I'll start digging you out just so I can warm up."

A soft hiss rose over the rumbling surf. It took her a moment to recognize the sound of sand shifting at high speed. She couldn't be sure in the faint light, but the spot Serge had indicated now boiled like a cauldron of quicksand. Shadows appeared, which solidified into hands and arms, a head, a torso. A body.

Dominique stood before her, a still column of darkness. She couldn't see his face, but his hands gleamed in the starlight. The wind blew sand off him in torrents and carried his winter cold scent.

He wore all his leathers and boots.

Her stomach clenched.

"What are you doing here?" he said, his tone remote.

"You went to see her, didn't you."

He turned away from her. She got up and rubbed her arms against the shivers wracking her body. Not all were on account of the chill air. "But you didn't kill her."

His silence told her everything. As did the fact that he hadn't bothered to change out of his gear before he sought shelter for the day. To say nothing of not visiting with her. Not that he had done this lately, either. Wherever his head was, it wasn't here.

"You didn't kill her," she repeated to herself.

"No. I did not."

"Well, then. I g-guess this is it." Her teeth clacked with the tremors shaking her limbs. "You've made your decision." She scanned the inky darkness, the stars in the immense, black sky. No lights. No hint of home, warmth, or safety. Anxious fists squeezed her lungs.

"There was no choice about it."

"Oh, right. No, I'm sure there wasn't. You're fine k-killing vampires that want to kill you, but this one you c-can't bring yourself to put down. I'm not s-stupid, Dominique. I can imagine why."

"You can imagine nothing," he snapped.

"Sorry. My bad. Just the s-stupid little human t-talking here. God only knows why Serge thought I had to be here to *help* you. Just take me b-back to the house and—" She couldn't finish the sentence. She couldn't tell him to leave any more than she could tear out her own heart. He wouldn't be here if he had given up on his humanity—or her—but it was close. He balanced at the edge of a precipice, and she would not—could not—push him over.

His shadowy form moved closer. "I do need your help, Cassidy."

She shivered, waiting for him to collect his thoughts.

"I don't want to be the—" He shook his head. "I don't want to be what she wants me to be."

"So don't."

"It's not so simple."

"What—" She stopped. Dominique was ruled by his emotions, especially love—in all its forms. "You...you s-slept with her?"

"Sleep had nothing to do with it." He paused before adding more quietly, "Not really."

She bit down a fresh wave of disappointment, even jealousy, before anger seized her with a fiery heat all its own. There was no way she could compete with an inhuman lover, but there was far more to her relationship with Dominique than sex. So much that they treasured, and which had drained away on account of a vampire bitch who turned his head inside out. Were she to appear right then and there, Cassidy would have ripped her head off with her bare hands—or at least made a decent attempt at it before getting herself killed.

She took a deep, gasping breath that sounded more like the sob she had hoped to swallow. Wet, wintry air soaked her lungs. "How could you have let this happen?"

"*Let* this happen? I had no choice about it."

"No choice? Really? Explain it to me. Right now. Just tell me. Everything."

He scrubbed both hands across his face. How she wished she could see his eyes. Or sense his mind.

"She is stronger than I knew. Stronger even than Serge."

"You've killed worse."

"*Oui.* But none of them has ever deceived me like this. She altered her scent to make herself appear less of a threat. I was curious, and I let my guard down." A passionate refrain followed in French, accompanied by a gesture of helpless disgust.

Finally, he shook himself hard, spraying sand in every direction, and then sat on the driftwood log beside her. "She is toying with me. She could have killed me half a dozen times by now."

Cassidy hoisted herself back onto the log and pressed her hands between her knees. "What were you curious about?"

"Blood-drinker things."

"Tell me."

"You wouldn't—"

"You let me be the judge of what I can or can't understand. I need to know what—" She heaved another involuntary sob. "I need to understand what is tearing us apart, because it's tearing apart my sanity. Dominique, please. If you can't show me, then tell me. I don't care how. But please don't disappear without an explanation. If nothing else, you owe me that."

He looked at her for a small eternity. She refused to avert her gaze and surrender. She refused to give up on him, on them. It was getting damn cold out here in more ways than one, but hell was a long way from freezing over.

When he spoke, he sounded as miserable as she felt. "It was a beautiful dream, what we had, but I think we both knew it could not last."

"That's not an explanation."

"*Chère*. I am a blood-drinker. A monster."

"We've been through this. Stop hedging, damn you."

"Your life is in danger every moment you spend with me."

"You would never hurt—"

Suddenly, he was in her face, his nose smashing against hers. "I might. I would. I have."

She pressed even closer, placed her frozen hands against his icy cheeks. "You would not. You love me."

"I kill what I love," he whispered. "One way or another, everything I love...I kill."

She touched her lips to his and inhaled deeply. Calm settled over her, along with absolute certainty. There was only one way out of this. "Well then," she said, preparing to leap into the abyss with him. "Don't stop now."

He struck so fast, if she hadn't expected it, she would have missed the actual moment his teeth found her neck. A deep, potent bite, devoid of tenderness, and packing a massive quantity of serum. It reached her brain an instant later. After that, reality as she knew it vanished.

She didn't have to reach for his mind; it rolled over her like a tsunami of rage, bitterness, and guilt. Her own anger, frustration, and sorrow rose to meet it. For one dark moment, he intended to take her life and rid himself of all that was still human in him. Then her soul touched his, and they were one again, a single being inhabiting two bodies, defining each other like light and shadow, each incapable of existing without the other.

Shock at what he had almost done ricocheted through them both. Shaking, their minds merging, they clung together in the uneasy night. Still he tried to conceal what happened, but he might as well have tried to hide a ravaged corpse in a leaky paper bag. Blood and guts oozed out everywhere.

So be it, he thought at her, his arms coming around her more tightly. *If I am to lose you, let it be honestly.*

13

ENOUGH

Dominique threw open his mind, sparing her nothing. Not that he could have. She had but to want him to remember, and he did, and she knew.

The lust-fueled daze. The erotic brutality. His willing participation.

His hunger for more.

With a long moan, she collapsed against him, buffeted by his emotional storms and memories. As her mind struggled to comprehend the worst of his blood-drinker instincts with her human understanding, he scooped her up and delivered her back to the cottage.

Samantha took one look at them and opted to return to her own home without comment. Gently, he placed Cassidy on the old wicker sofa in the living room, propped her head up with accent pillows, and sat on the cool tile floor beside her. Holding her hand, fingers twined, he kept their link as strong as she needed it to be.

Minutes passed. She drifted from horrified shock to dazed realization and finally surfaced with a gasp. In her mind, his memory of Bijou astride him still played in lecherous detail, and he sensed her pushing it away—pushing *him* away—fighting to regain a sense of her singular self. Her hand shook as she pulled it from his grasp.

He withdrew, granting her wish for distance, and sat with his head down, arms draped over his knees, waiting for whatever fate would decide to pile on him now.

"Do you think it was enough?" she wondered, sounding hollow.

He brushed against her mind just enough to understand what she meant. After escaping Bijou, he had done all he could to dilute her serum and her power over him by drinking from every vein he could find until the attached body threatened to falter. But was it enough? Had he washed her from his body, if not his memories?

"I don't know."

"You should probably get some more then."

He looked up to see her staring at the ceiling, her face as empty as her tone. Her thoughts, however, roiled. He could hear them like distant thunder.

"Why am I never enough, Dominique?"

"You are more than enough, *chérie*." He turned to kneel beside her and resisted the urge to reach for her hand. She needed to be separate right now. Maybe he did, too. "Never doubt it. Bijou manipulated me. You know this."

She gave him a wretched look. "You know I don't give a rat's ass about that bitch. She basically roofied you. I'm glad you don't remember more than you do." Her fingers curled in her sweatshirt. "I know I can't compete with a vampire sex pot, but—"

"It is she who cannot compete with you."

Her throat bobbed on a hard swallow. "That's not what I meant. Dominique, why couldn't you trust me? After all we've been through, all that I know about you? No, I don't like what's happening to you one bit, and I wouldn't have liked it any better two weeks ago. But at least I could have been there for you, helped you figure this out before it got to this point. Before you"—she swallowed a gasp, recalling the kill he had shared *by choice* with Bijou—"had to live with the consequences."

"You know why. I can't bear the thought of losing you."

"Keeping things from me is only going to make that more likely," she said with a weary sigh. When he remained quiet, she pushed herself into a seated position. "Maybe you're right. Maybe all this really is too much for me. Too much vampire reality for my poor human brain."

Despair roiled through him. He tried to subdue it, but it washed into her awareness like a rogue wave.

"No, Dominique. I'm not giving up on you. As long as you choose to be here and not with her, the human in you is stronger than the vampire. Of that I have no doubt."

"You are the human in me," he whispered. "My love for you will always be stronger than the darkness that calls me."

"And yet, when it really matters, you don't trust me. I'm not enough." *Again.*

Her silent addendum might as well have been a physical blow. He had vowed to never desert her as so many others had. And yet...he had.

She was right. Falling under Bijou's spell was not the worst of what he'd done.

This was.

"*Mon amour,* listen to me. I'm done keeping things from you. If I can't have faith in you—if I have to exist in fear of losing you—I will be lost whether you stay or go." He carefully placed his hand on hers, giving her an opportunity to pull away. She didn't, and the hum of their mental bond deepened into the caress of souls.

You are enough for me, Cassie amour. *For as long as you will have me. No matter what.*

14

EMOTIONALLY CHARGED

When Cassidy arrived at the Conch House, Jackson was already seated in a booth against the far wall, well away from the other patrons, who, on this glorious Saturday after Thanksgiving, preferred the outside deck overlooking the ocean.

"Thanks for seeing me on such short notice," she said, slipping into the seat across from him.

"I always have time for you, Cass."

She twisted her lips in irony. "If I didn't know what you were really after, I might even be flattered."

"Hope you don't mind. I ordered your drink for you." He gestured at the tall glass of dark soda, the straw sticking in it still capped with paper. She nudged it aside.

"I don't drink that anymore."

"Since when?"

"Since I know what all is in it." She did her best to sound like she spoke only of the standard soda contents and not whatever she half-suspected he had added. "Is that fresh-brewed?"

His mouth pulling into a thin line, he pushed his iced tea toward her. He had already drunk two inches off the top. "Thanks."

A waitress came to take their order. A fried calamari appetizer was all Cassidy asked for. She didn't intend to eat much of it. Jackson could round out his gourmet burger with it after she left.

"So. How was your Thanksgiving?" he prompted after the server departed and she remained quiet.

"We lost Eddie." The words were out before she could stop them.

"What do you mean 'lost?' Did he run off?"

She shook her head.

"He died?"

Nod.

"How?"

"Long story. Just thought you'd like to know. You seemed to like him." She busied her hands with her napkin.

His gaze narrowed. "I see."

"What?"

"Someone made a snack out of him."

She opened her mouth to deny it, but couldn't. Lying was Jackson's talent, not hers. His lips grew paper thin and just as white.

"Not anyone you know," she finally said.

"There's *another* one living with you now?"

"God, no."

He leaned forward and spoke in a low snarl. "When are you and Sam going to realize what's going on here? Does one of you have to die before the other decides that having homicidal maniacs for roommates is a bad idea? For someone who claims she isn't compelled you're sure acting like you are."

"This was a mistake." She grabbed her bag and was halfway off her seat when he grabbed her wrist.

"I'm sorry. I'm sorry, babe. Please." He let go of her and sat back. "Stay and tell me what I can do for you, and I promise I'll shut up."

She sat reluctantly. "I won't tell you anything that'll help you kill anyone."

He gestured "that's okay," but kept his mouth shut as promised.

Cassidy sucked down half the iced tea. Jackson waited. She fidgeted with the straw. "Well, this is awkward."

Still he said nothing.

"I decided to see you only this morning...after sunrise. Dominique doesn't know I'm here. He has nothing to do with it. And I'm definitely not compelled."

He motioned her to continue; the chunky Rolex rattled on his wrist as he did.

She frowned. "You're even more annoying when you don't say anything, you know that?"

"I'm listening. Carefully."

"Okay, well, I need you to start talking about what you and or the Foundation may know about...um..."

"Yes?"

"Er—erotic feeding."

His brows shot up. "Don't you have actual vampires you could ask about that?"

"Actual vampires are a bit of a mixed bag. Not the norm, I'm pretty sure. Either of them."

"If they drink blood, they're as normal as they get."

"Humor me. Tell me what you know."

He pulled a hunk of bread from the loaf sitting on the table, tore into it with his teeth, and chewed as though there were no conversation happening at all. Cassidy's turn to wait.

"They feed on emotion as much as blood," he began, gesturing with the bread. "Fear is one of the most potent. They lose control when they sense that. Which, of course, you know."

She nodded. "No fear" was her motto for a reason.

"Anger isn't so irresistible."

"Which is why you use it to distract them."

He shrugged one shoulder. "It's a last-ditch defense mechanism, yes."

"Is that why you fly off the handle at the drop of any given hat? You've trained yourself to be angry at the first sign of a threat?"

He looked like he might want to fly off that handle again right now. His jaw muscles worked as he ground his teeth, his fingers playing with the half-eaten piece of bread. "Do you want me to answer your question or not?"

"Please. Continue."

Before he did, he grabbed the iced tea and lowered the level in the glass another inch. "They most enjoy emotions that reflect how they see themselves."

"Huh?"

"Emotions that are about them, their prey's reaction to them. Few people like making others angry, so a human who is angry with the bloodsucker attacking him won't have the right emotional flavor, if you will. They won't 'taste' so satisfying. But when someone is terrified enough to shit themselves, they're feeding an ego that thinks it's the most terrifying thing ever."

"Huh. That makes a terrifying kind of sense."

"Cocky bastards. I know."

"Yes. But also...no."

The waitress was back with the calamari appetizer, and Jackson shoved the bread he held into his mouth, stuffing down whatever retort he was on the verge of hurling. She pushed the deep-fried plate in his direction. "Here. You look hungrier than I am."

"Go ahead. Charge to their defense. I can't wait to hear what you have to say now."

She folded her hands in front of her. "Not all the vampires I've met are full of themselves. For instance, Serge is the epitome of a charming bungler who has kept to himself for centuries."

"Centuries. Nice. That must make for quite the body count."

"I'm not saying he never killed. God knows, he can scare the crap out of someone if he wants to. It's just not his thing." She leaned forward, emphatic. "Jack, his idea of a satisfying meal is compelling drug dealers to find religion."

"Charming. So what's your point?"

"My point is you can't lump them all together. Not all of them let their alter egos call the shots."

"Alter egos?"

"Yes. The, you know, vampire part of them."

"Their true selves. Yes, I get it."

"I'm not sure you do."

"If there is any part of them that needs to feed on terror, then what they are is something that needs to be exterminated." He popped a calamari ring into his mouth and chewed for a moment. "It's an instinct. Reason has nothing to do with it. With time and practice, they can curb it to a point, but the lust for emotionally charged blood never subsides.

"Which brings us back to your original question." Jackson emphasized his words by gesturing with another crispy ring. "Erotic feeding is feeding on lust. On the ego-feeding scale, being an object of desire is right up there with being feared. Either provides a power rush they can't resist."

Her mental gears tumbled and clicked. Lust and terror: interchangeable in the eyes of the beast. Good to know. If Dominique could master one, he could master the other. The thought made her smile.

"You're not hearing anything I'm saying, are you?"

"On the contrary, Jackson. I hear everything you're saying, and then some." She reached for a piece of calamari. "Whether I want to or not."

"I see." He played with the straw for a moment. "So, why do you want to know about erotic feeding?"

She hesitated a moment too long before shrugging. "The topic came up."

"Oh? In casual conversation?"

"Well—" Heat bloomed in her cheeks as she recalled Dominique's recent memories. "It's hard to explain."

"God damn it, Cass," he hissed and took hold of her hand. "You're playing with your *life* here. Don't you see that?"

"Jack—"

"Well, isn't this cozy?"

They looked up at a woman glaring accusations down at them. Tall, ridiculously skinny, and draped in Prada and Gucci and perfectly behaved long, straight hair, she could have stepped off the cover of *Vogue* and right onto Cassidy's short list of least favorite people.

Jackson let go of Cassidy's hand and sat back, his face shuttering. "Avery. What are you doing here?"

Cassidy looked between them, curious. The woman's eyes narrowed at her. "My friends and I are here for lunch before we get back to the shopping you stood me up for." She glanced back at three women by the entrance, their attentions glued to the scene. "And what's your excuse?"

"Avery, this is—"

"I know who it is. Your former fiancée. What I want to know is: what are you doing here with her?"

"You know, that tone doesn't work with him," Cassidy offered. In fact, Jackson already turned irritated colors.

"I'm not talking to you. As my fiancé, he owes me an explanation." Avery waved her hand toward Cassidy, making it impossible to miss the enormous pink diamond rock on her finger, the Striker family engagement ring. One of Dominique's memories was of him spying on Jackson and this woman only last week—on their first date.

Cassidy exhaled sharply. "Wow, you move fast."

"And you're too late. Jackson? What's going on here?"

Cassidy spoke first. "Is this your uncle's idea of an 'acceptable bride for the heir?'" That had been only one of many of Garrett Striker's objections to Cassidy.

"Cass—"

"Oh, please. Like he could marry someone as common as you."

"Avery, stop. Right now," Jackson said, holding up a warning finger. "Cassidy and I are still friends. She needed advice about an investment she wants to make. It's time-sensitive, so we're meeting on short notice. I'm sorry if I didn't have time to clarify that earlier."

Cassidy stared at him. She knew the man could lie, but this was a whole new level of instant spin. "Now that's terrifying."

The look he gave her could have split logs.

"Oh, an investment, is it? What in?" Avery was having none of it. Smart girl.

Cassidy collected her bag and scooted out of the booth. "A relationship," she said. "He's helping me save a most uncommon relationship. Aren't you, babe?"

He looked like a bomb fuse in want of a flame.

"Well, I'll leave you two class acts to it then. But Jackson, this one's sharp. You'll need to be careful with your cloak and dagger work around her."

"Excuse me?" Avery said.

"Oh, didn't he tell you? Working at Striker Capital is only his day job. At night…he kills vampires."

Cassidy took a moment to relish the stunned silence from the booth and the startled recognition on Avery's flawless face. It's what Dominique had whispered in this woman's ear, forcing Jackson to gaslight her into doubting her own mind.

When Avery's expression turned from shock to doubt, Cassidy dismissed the comment with a small wave. "Sorry. Private joke. But just between us girls?" She lowered her voice into the realm of conspiracy. "Don't trust him. Not for a second."

"Just between us girls? You've outstayed your welcome."

With a shrug, Cassidy brushed past her. "Don't say I didn't warn you."

She had walked three paces when an idea struck her. Spinning round on a boot heel, she snapped her fingers. "Oh, Jackson, before I forget. You should check out Club Bijou down on Clematis and talk to the owner. She's only available after dark, though. FYI."

15

Hidden Things

Before Dominique swung onto his bike, swords slung across his back, he and Cassidy lingered over a kiss. It was the first time he had touched her in a week and a half. By unhappy mutual agreement, he kept his distance while there was any risk of Bijou turning him against her again.

A week had passed before his nemesis summoned him. He resisted the silent command for several nights more, using the time to drink all the surreptitious blood he could catch and sharpening his powers of concentration by practicing kata and meditation.

As Bijou's influence over him diminished, her impatience only intensified. Denying her much longer risked her showing up at his door again, which is where Dominique drew the line. He refused to be cornered in his lair and put Cassidy—and, yes, even Samantha—in any more danger than they already were.

We should run.

With their link, too, fading, he heard Cassidy's thoughts as though through a fog. Touched by how confidently she included herself in that plot, Dominique deepened the kiss until she melted in his arms. For him, she would run with him, hide with him, leave her newly stable life for that of a hunted animal.

But this he could not ask of her.

Bijou is not my sire, mon amour. *She is a threat I have to face and defeat, and I have to do it tonight.*

"This is the night," Serge had solemnly told him as he fussed with his little boat's sail earlier, tying and retying the same knots over and over. "What must be, will be. Tonight." His expression said "what must be" might well involve Dominique being staked out in the morning sun.

A shiver raced through Cassidy, and he held her closer. "Don't let Serge's drama trouble you," he whispered. "I will do what I must, and that will be the end of that."

She touched the faint stubble on his cheek and locked her quiet, ocean-blue gaze with his. "I don't care what happens tonight, Dominique, so long as you come back to me as fast as you possibly can. Promise me."

He ran a fingertip down the bridge of her freckled nose. *"Je te promets, mon amour.* I promise." He would not fail.

He *could* not fail.

Club Bijou was shuttered, courtesy of the Striker Foundation, which had followed up on Cassidy's tip. They had failed, of course, since Bijou, tapped into his mind as she was right now, learned of the ploy the moment he did.

The glittering streets teemed with mortals enjoying the holiday lights, and the cool air dripped with food and perfume, but not blood or blood-drinkers. Yet that sensation of being tugged, albeit weak, still haunted him. She wasn't far.

A causeway took him to the island of Palm Beach. Imposing gates and immaculate box hedges concealed elegant driveways to palatial homes bristling with state-of-the-art security systems. While no blood-drinker would risk hunting here, one of these grand mansions concealed a well-fortified lair.

A prickle up the back of his neck urged him to turn onto a driveway where the gates stood open. At its end sprawled a château that, if not for the ring of illuminated palm trees, could have been a transplant straight out of the French countryside, complete with a steepled roof-line and cast-iron fixtures.

Dominique silenced the bike, pulled off his helmet, and studied the façade for the best place to enter—or exit in a hurry. Carefully keeping his thoughts to an absolute minimum, he considered one of the dark upstairs windows when the ruby-red door swung open. A tall, slender young woman in a floor-length white gown emerged from the dim interior. Dark red hair fell across her bare shoulders in lustrous waves. A Grecian goddess incarnate—except that she was human.

Her smile was tentative, but not shy. "Monsieur Marchant? You're expected. Please come in."

He hesitated, thrown by this surprising stranger. But as a human, it hardly mattered who she was in this house. He buried his questions and stepped inside.

In the two-story, oval-shaped foyer, a semi-nude stone figure ruled from atop a Greek column. Aphrodite, he guessed, given the sultry look with which she greeted new arrivals. Two sweeping staircases hugged the room's curved sides, meeting at a landing opposite the entrance. Sconces cast dramatic slashes of light down the dull black walls, illuminating tiny alabaster statues on small pedestals. Beneath his black boots, the white floor gleamed like polished ice.

"My name is Monica Sol," the woman said, closing the door. "It's great to meet you finally. I've heard so much about you."

He glanced at her sharply.

Her cheeks bloomed pink as her gaze dropped. "Come."

Dominique followed her up the marble stairs, keeping his steps silent, straining his senses past the click of her heels and pounding of her heart. A soft mustiness hung in the air, and a whiff of sandalwood trailed in the redhead's wake. Somewhere in the house, someone moaned.

They turned past an impressive set of mahogany doors with intricate ironwork, and continued down a wide hallway before stopping at another, less ornate set of double-doors. Dominique could smell the sex ooze past the seams, even before he heard a woman's moan followed by a man's groan. Monica reached for the handles when he pushed her aside and slammed the doors open.

The scene inside was sadly predictable. An oversize bed covered in red satin sheets and five entwined bodies of various ethnicities. One man glanced in his direction before deeming him uninteresting in light of another male's passionate attentions.

As before, the temptation to join them seized him, but within seconds he had pried it loose and let it drain away, powerless. An instinct, nothing more. A desire to feed the beast's ego, not himself. He intended to be in the arms of the woman he loved before the night was done, and she would more than appease every part of him. Someday he might consider thanking Jackson for that priceless explanation of his alter ego.

Beside him, Monica bowed and murmured, "My apologies, mistress."

Bijou waved a dismissive hand, and the Grecian goddess scurried away. She lounged on a red velvet settee facing the tableau on the bed. Behind her, gossamer curtains moved in the breezes coming through open balcony doors. The room was as opulent as the rest of the house was sparse, an eclectic cross between European royalty and Middle Eastern harem.

"I'm so pleased you could make it tonight, *cher*. Dinner is almost ready."

He took in her translucent black lingerie, the knowing smirk—and the fresh-cut wood flavor of her true scent—and opted for distraction. "What is this? Are you bored with your wine cellar?"

The corners of her mouth tensed. "This is so much more private, don't you think?" She moved one of her bare feet along the shin of her other leg, but he kept his eyes locked on hers. "I would have called you much sooner if not for some very pesky humans, making my existence difficult. I see that you have spent the time"—he could feel her probing his mental barriers—"being difficult as well." She heaved a dramatic sigh. "And your weapons again. Silly child. Don't you know by now that—"

He yanked the *wakizashi* sword out of its scabbard. The curved blade flashed at superhuman speeds. Shredded upholstery and a cloud of stuffing were the result.

"Be gentle with that. It is an antique."

Spinning around, he found her on the bed, reclining amidst the languid bodies.

"So impulsive. I can't decide if I like that about you." Spreading her hands over the nude humans, she added, "Would you like to try again?"

His teeth ground together, every muscle tensing. He wanted to see her dead, but not at the risk of turning her "vintages" into carnage. Bijou was too fast for him to be surgical about his attacks. In fact, she was too fast for him, period.

Taking his time, he pulled the longer *katana* from its scabbard as well and advanced on her across a thick, blood-red rug. She didn't even flinch as he snapped the *katana's* tip against her neck and held the other blade in position to catch any attack she might mount, any movement she might make away from the humans. With a low growl, he said, "You do not threaten me and my family and expect to live."

Bijou touched one fingertip to the razor-sharp edge. It came away with a minor cut, which she licked with care. Her eyes smoldered, as did her words. "I hope you realize that the reverse is also true."

An instant later, she was gone.

The human woman who found her breasts at the end of his sword grew round-eyed with shock. He fought to subdue his own disorientation. He had seen little more than a ripple of Bijou's movement and no sense of direction. So she still had her hooks deep enough in him to addle his perceptions. Not even the two-thousand-year-old Roman he battled last summer had been this fast.

"You seem to forget that you belong to me," Bijou said, all pretense at seduction and condescension stripped from her inhuman voice.

He spun to face her. "Never."

She stood behind the butchered settee, her hands out of view, holding something that clinked and rattled. "We all belong to someone, Dominique. The sooner you accept this, the better for everyone."

A chill prickled the back of his neck before he even knew why. His name. She had used it the first time they met—but he had never told her what it was. Something monumental was happening here, something just beyond his awareness. He stood at the edge of an invisible chasm. One step in the wrong direction and he would plunge in.

Or maybe he was already falling.

With a powerful, lightning-fast movement, Bijou tossed a hailstorm into the air. He barely had time to recognize the sound as chains before they snapped outward and vanished into a whirling shroud of steel. They droned around her as she moved, hands and arms blurring. The ends must have been weighted and sharpened; where they collided with lamps and furniture, glass exploded, wood splintered and fabric ripped.

Dominique had never seen anything like it, but he wasn't about to run into it with nothing but a pair of swords. He took several steps back. She lunged, and the chains leapt at him. First one sword, then the other tore from his hands. Something whistled past his face. He heard the crunch of bone and tasted blood on the back of his tongue. His vision blurred with the pain of a shattered nose.

He staggered back until his legs collided with the bed and he tumbled in. Four of the vintages scrambled away. The fifth lay pinned beneath him—the girl whose life he had spared by not taking his one and only chance to destroy Bijou.

He rolled to the side, taking her with him. Her panic-stricken face stared into his. Her eyes were sky blue, only a little lighter than Cassidy's, and he fell into them, reaching desperately for his anchor, his sanity, his strength.

The back of her head exploded in a plume of gore.

Fear colder than ice shot through him as the dead girl collapsed by his side. Not her. Not Cassidy.

But it could have been.

It would be.

If he didn't stop Bijou now.

Right now.

The beast's rage closed its claws around him. Nothing mattered but destroying this monster. He gathered the only weapon that remained to him—the preternatural power of his own terror—and flew at Bijou. Sunrise would find her in bloody pieces, even if he lay dismembered beside her.

She darted out of his way. The chains snapped and hissed ever faster. He ducked and leapt, feinted to the right, dove to the left, away, then close. Bijou moved so fast, he saw her arms and legs only as ghostly flickers.

The next weight to find its mark, like a high-caliber bullet, broke an arm. The one after that caved in the side of his ribcage and punctured a lung. As he doubled over, the chains whipped around him with crushing force. He fell, hobbled, to the ground, mindless with wrath and pain, all his limbs lashed tight.

She rolled him on his back with one small foot and fell on him. Jerking back his head by a fistful of hair, she drove her teeth into his jugular. A second later, her serum delivered a walloping punch to his mind. She released him and wiped her mouth with the back of a hand. "Stupid child."

He stared at her through the eyes of the beast, aware of nothing but the clicking crunch of his bones knitting back together. Only when she glanced away, her attention captured by he-cared-not-what, did he react. He snapped upright, ignoring the chains that cut deep into his flesh, and in the same motion slammed his fangs into her throat so hard she toppled sideways. He stayed with her, biting down, ferociously grabbing onto the muscle and sinew.

Her blood burst into his mouth, thick and redolent with outrage and the flavor of dense, dark forests. Seven or eight centuries, he guessed. Perhaps a millennium.

He reached for the truth she concealed from him, only to sense her mind disappear like smoke in a wind, allowing him nothing. An instant later, she shook him off and backhanded him hard enough to make his brain slosh inside his skull. Then she stood over him and shrieked, incoherent with black-eyed fury.

Dominique pulled his bloodied lips into a feeble smile.

Two heartbeats later, she had hurled him out into the night. As he flew, he spun out of his ties as Bijou whipped the ends of the chains. Neptune, god of the deep, awaited him with his trident in the backyard pool. Dominique went straight to the bottom and lay there, staring at the fierce, bearded face rendered in tiny mosaic stones. Two smaller splashes, and his swords drifted down to lie beside him.

His head and his world continued to spin. Disoriented, he stared at Neptune's face, the only still point. It reminded him of Serge and the lunatic pirate's babbling of grand destinies. What would the oracle have to say about this dubious turn of events? Not that it mattered.

As his body healed, the dazed fog slowly lifted from his mind. He had been bested. He should be dead. As unprepared as he was for Bijou's true age and power, he should have been an easy kill for her. In fact, she should be coming after him even now. Why didn't she? Why did she toy with him? A frisson of unease rippled over his shoulders, but he pushed it away. He still lived, his serum swam in her blood, and he knew more about her now than he did before. Next time, his odds would be better.

Next time, he decided, was now.

Crabbing along the bottom, he retrieved his weapons, moved to the edge, and climbed out as quietly as he could. Then he stood and scanned the back of the house across the wide pool. The wrap-around second-floor balcony was empty, doors open, curtains still. Except for the blood-scent hanging in the damp air, there was no hint of either vampire or humans. Nor could he feel Bijou in his mind.

A profound emptiness settled over the night like the calm before a storm. Every hair on his body rose in silent alarm. His hands tightened on the hilts as he moved the swords out to either side of him, ready to counter any attack. Balancing on the balls of his feet, he stepped back softly, his water-logged boots squelching as he pivoted. All his senses heightened to detect the smallest movement and lowest sound.

There was neither.

The silent horror that waited for him had been there all along. It melted into his awareness out of the darkness at the end of a long dock. Dominique didn't need to see the gold script on the sleek, black hull to know the mega yacht's name, to remember instantly all the nightmares he had endured aboard. There was only one.

Apokryphos.

His sire's lair...

16

WALK INTO HELL

The moment the first whiff of his sire's cedar smoke scent touched his nose, Dominique knew it was useless to run. He did anyway.

Bijou could have stopped him before he reached his bike with little effort. Kambyses could have done it with no effort at all. Neither one bothered to show themselves—though both were surely watching him gun the bike's engine down the driveway and out the gate.

They could afford to let him run. With her fresh bite on him, he was as good as tethered. She could track him down at leisure and deliver him to Kambyses wrapped in chains.

His deepest instinct was to run—the faster and farther, the better—but his need to return to his lair and Cassidy overwhelmed all else. Perhaps this was a compulsion to remain close. If so, he wouldn't fight it. Cassidy was everything.

Fragile, mortal Cassidy. Hopelessness threatened to crush him by the time he stripped and showered as if he could scrub the truth out of his pores. He had placed her in the center of a conflict neither of them could survive.

When he slipped into her bed, he wanted only to hold her and love her. And he wanted her to not wake and realize how impossible their situation had become.

She woke. He didn't touch her.

"Oh God," she said after searching his quiet demeanor. "She's still alive."

"I could not kill her."

"Could not?" The "would not" hung between them and pinched her face.

"She is too strong."

Cassidy nodded, thoughtful, and pushed sleep-tousled hair out of her face. "I see." Wheels tumbled behind her eyes. "Okay. So...wait. I've seen you put down a two-thousand-year-old vampire. Are you telling me this chick is stronger than that?"

He shook his head a little. "No, but...her master is."

"Her—" She connected the dots in a flash—and blanched. "No. Not him."

He slipped under the comforter and pulled her close. For a long while, he simply let her warmth soak into his weary body and breathed her familiar sweetness as he prepared to speak the words he never wanted to be true. "Kambyses has found me."

She tightened her hold on him.

"Bijou is only a pawn, maybe his spawn," he murmured, stroking her hair and pushing away the memory of the girl dying in his arms earlier. If Kambyses had sired Bijou with his blood—unlike Dominique, who had received only his serum—or allowed her to drink from him recently, either would explain her tremendous power, which far surpassed her age.

"She could have killed me with ease tonight, but he did not permit it. She is his to command. Even..." His thoughts spun out to the inevitable, terrifying conclusion. "Even had I finished her"—and the humans with her—"it would have made no difference." None whatsoever. "I should not have come back here."

"Here is where you belong," she said against his chest.

"Here is where he knows he can find me. If I want to escape him, I have to run as far as I can for the rest of the night, and the next, and the next thousand after that. And he..." His tongue felt numb, uncooperative. "He would still win, because I would have lost you, my humanity." What other purpose could there be for what Bijou had done?

"Then I'll come with you. We can leave right now. Just go. Anywhere. We'll figure out the details later." The resolve ringing in her voice grew with every word and almost gave him hope. Almost.

He kissed her temple, lips brushing the thin scar where a bullet had nearly killed her the last time she risked her life for him. "It's not so easy for a human to hide. He knows about you and how important you are to me, and he would find you long before he found me."

"I have the advantage. I have the day. We can use that. I could—"

"He can compel a daytime army to hunt us down."

That at last stilled her enthusiasm for half-formed escape plots. A wretched little sob escaped her. "I won't let him take you from me, Dominique. I can't."

"You won't have a choice about it, *chérie,*" he whispered. "No more than I."

She pushed out of his embrace far enough to see his eyes. "I don't understand. What are you saying?"

He caressed her cheekbone with his thumb, catching the first of her tears. "I will never be his. The only way this ends is if he lets me go, or—"

"Don't say it." She put a finger to his lips. "I won't let him take you from me. Not in any way, shape, or form."

He took her hand in his and kissed it. "I belong to you, Cassidy. Hell itself will not stand in my way. All that matters is your survival."

"Well. That settles it then." She wiped at her eyes and tucked her hair back behind her ears. "Since I can't survive without you, we have to both get through this. Together."

"Together," he repeated, smiling faintly. Fragile mortal she may be, but the spirit flashing in her eyes was that of a lioness charging to protect her pride.

"As one," she clarified with a pointed look and tilted her head to expose her neck.

Strange how he hadn't seen this coming. The one thing they both wanted tonight had been eclipsed by events. Now, tasting her, becoming one, seemed the most dangerous path of all. Though not because of Bijou. With his serum fresh in the other vampire's blood, he could sense her presence and would have some warning. Nor did he fear causing Cassidy harm, thanks to Jackson's annoyingly helpful explanation. There was no room for a greedy blood-drinker ego in her arms. Only salvation waited for him there.

No, what mattered was that being part of him now would put her squarely in the path of Kambyses, blood-drinker lust incarnate. Or was it too late already? Had he exposed her by returning here tonight? Or did it matter? Bijou had rummaged through his thoughts and memories. She and Kambyses would know how important Cassidy was to Dominique, regardless of what he did. She walked this hell with him, had done so from the beginning, and she was correct—the only way out of this was through. Together.

He watched the blood rushing beneath her skin turn into pulsing rivers of golden light. When he kissed the brightest of these just beneath her ear, she cupped his head, encouraging him, then moaned softly when he pierced her skin. Her blood swept into him, along with her soul, scouring away the filth left by Bijou. He drank more deeply from Cassidy than he had in a long time. She knew it and permitted it, trusting him without question.

They fell into a shared dream, a reality all their own. But instead of the usual jungle waterfall scene, a high mountain meadow surrounded them. A sea of grass rippled around him in an earthy, fragrant breeze, and snowy mountain peaks reared into a cobalt sky. He blinked at the sun. Joy fizzed in his veins like fine champagne in a crystal flute.

Cassidy sat and smiled at him, love and mischief shining in her eyes.

"The place we first shared," he said, recalling that first time he had bitten her—and nearly killed her.

She pulled her sleep shirt over her head and tossed it aside. It vanished before it hit the ground. Her bare body shamelessly called to his. "We first realized how much we are a part of each other here."

Oh, what a sweet shock that had been. He touched her face, felt her press her hot cheek against his palm, and knew that awe again—the wonder of her trust. "And how much more we are together."

She leaned in, brushing her nose against his, teasing. "Don't you ever forget it."

"Never," he vowed, and kissed her gently, reverently.

She briefly closed her teeth on his lower lip. "Kiss me like you mean it."

He did that—and more.

Hell would have to wait.

17

Lost and Found

Late the following afternoon, Cassidy slammed on the brakes the moment the cottage came into view. An unfamiliar gray Ford SUV sat in the driveway. Was the compelled army of Kambyses coming for her already?

She gripped the steering wheel hard, her hands going clammy with indecision. Venture forth and gather the facts? Or flee with her life and groceries and let the boys take care of this, whatever "this" was?

"Next thing you know, you'll be jumping at shadows, Chandler," she muttered. There was still time to assess the situation before things turned supernatural. Probably someone from the property management office. The joys of being a tenant.

She pulled to the curb, slung her bag over her shoulder, and got out. To demonstrate that she was busy—not to mention inconvenienced by the driveway being blocked—she grabbed as many stuffed grocery bags as she could manage. Also, the six-pack of glass-bottled Perrier water in one of these could double as a weapon if need be.

A familiar willowy figure in a white sweatshirt descended the porch steps.

"Sam? What's going on?"

"You have a visitor," she said under her breath.

Cassidy glanced at the invading vehicle. "I would have never guessed."

"Please give him a chance. He's trying. Here, let me help you with these." She grabbed for the grocery bags.

"What? No. Who is it?"

In the shadowed recesses of the porch, one of the Adirondack chairs creaked as someone got up and stepped forward.

Cassidy clutched the bags as if the flimsy plastic could grant her strength. The air rushed out of her. "You."

Tall and large-bellied, the man sported a head of dark hair, graying at the temples. A trace of apprehension flickered in his blue eyes, which were so much like her own.

"Hi, baby girl. How've you been?"

Cassidy's jaw dropped. No, this couldn't be happening. Not now. Not with everything else going on. No way, no how, not ever. Just no. "You need to leave."

He lifted his hand in a gesture of inquiry. "Is this any way to greet your father?"

"It is when I really didn't want you to find me. Ever."

"Tell me about it." He said with a chuckle. "I had to hire a PI to track you down here." He waved at the neighborhood of overgrown yards with a pinched expression that betrayed the disgust she knew he felt. If it wasn't a manicured golf course or a glittering downtown high-rise apartment, it was beneath his contempt. "Not what I expected."

"Then do feel free to go," she said and stomped up the three steps with her load. Shouldering past him, she caught a nose full of the cigarette smoke that forever permeated his clothes, and she struggled not to burst into furious tears. That stink would always be the poison with which he had killed her mother.

Samantha leapt ahead of her to open the door. Instead of locking it behind them, though, she let Cassidy's father and his evil cloud in, too.

Cassidy dumped the bags on the kitchen counter and whirled around. "I did not invite you in."

Samantha cringed, apologetic, and slipped back out the door. "I'll get the rest of your bags."

Cassidy's father, Gil Chandler, cut-throat car dealer and calculating philanderer extraordinaire, strode into the living room, a Denver Broncos windbreaker rustling around him. "Really, Cassidy. Can't you do better than this? What's with this guy you're marrying? This Jackson fellow? I mean, this place—" More dismissive gesturing at the faded rugs and comfortably worn furniture. "It's—"

"My home."

"Not permanently, I hope?"

Her nostrils flared, and her insides contracted into a hard core, preparing for battle. "What the hell do you think you're doing here?"

"I'm helping a friend. Or rather, the widow of a friend."

"Consoling a grieving widow in her bed?"

"No. No, of course not. He dropped dead of a heart attack, and she needs someone to keep his dealerships running until she can offload them."

"Oh, do tell. Was he found in a sleazy motel room, wearing nothing but cowboy boots?" she snapped, desperate to offend him into storming away. Instead, her father's eyes widened in surprise.

"How did you—no, wait. What difference does that make?"

She put a hand to her forehead and turned away. So much for her father showing up here being a complete coincidence. The world felt smaller by the moment and was clearly determined to conspire against her. "Oh. My. God."

"What?"

She turned back. "Nothing. He was a real piece of work, that one. Right up to your standards. But that still doesn't explain what you're doing here, standing in my home."

Gil's brow folded thoughtfully as he held his daughter's challenging look. "When I found out that you were just up the highway, I thought—"

"You thought wrong."

"Will you give a guy a chance to explain?"

"There's nothing to explain. Really. There's the door. Use it."

"Baby girl, I screwed up."

Her turn to be confounded. She had never heard those words come out of this man's mouth before. Ever. "What?"

Samantha eased back through the door with more bags. "He screwed up, Cass. He admits it."

Cassidy gaped at her friend. "My mother was being eaten alive by cancer thanks to *him*"—she stabbed a furious finger in his direction—"and his answer was to pack his bags and move in with the woman he was fucking. That's *way* past 'screwing up,'"

"I'm not asking you to forgive and forget," Gil said.

She whirled around to face him. "Good for you. Because hell will freeze over before either happens."

"I'm just hoping for a chance to make it up to you somehow. In person."

"There is nothing of yours I want."

He held up both hands. "Look, I get that you're angry, baby girl. I'm not proud of myself, believe me, but what's done is done. We can only go forward, and I would like us to go forward together. Or at least driving in the same general direction. What do'ya say?"

"Never." She all but snarled.

He opened his mouth to reply, but then smiled and shook his head. "All fire and vinegar. Just like your mother. Yeah, I deserve that."

Cassidy ignored Samantha's imploring look. The peacemaker would find no satisfaction here tonight. "You need to leave. Go console the widow, or, better yet, call your wife and your two bratty new kids."

"Yeah. Them." He grimaced and sucked at his lips, hands on hips. "Right. Well. You'll love this, but Kelly filed for divorce and full custody two months ago."

Cassidy didn't bother to suppress a vindictive smirk. She loved it all right, in a dark, twisted way she found impossible to feel guilty about. "Did you cheat on this one, too?"

His shoulders dropped a little, as did his gaze. "I was a fool. A weak, stupid fool." When he looked up, his eyes glistened in a way that made her want to turn away. "Your mother was the best thing that ever happened to me. I see that now. And you're the best thing I ever did. You're all I have left. You don't have to forgive me, or even like me. Just let me be near you. Let me at least get to know the beautiful, brave young woman you've become. That's all I'm asking."

She hated herself for the prickle in her eyes, for the sorrow rocking her, and told herself the emotion couldn't be hers. Somewhere in the newborn night, Dominique had awakened. His presence rippled in her awareness, absorbed her grief and rage, and reflected them back, colored by his own grief. And his regrets.

Regrets she didn't want.

"It's too late," she said. "Once she was dead, it was too late." She flicked a tear out of her eye. "Go. Please go. Leave me alone."

The door slammed open without warning. Everyone jumped, startled.

Samantha, apparently used to such entrances, recovered first. "Serge? What happened?"

The pirate vampire stood in the doorway and eyed the new arrival from hairline to trouser hem.

Gill regarded the barefoot, powder pale little man drizzling sand out of his hair with slack-jawed astonishment. "Friend of yours, baby girl?"

"My roommate," Samantha said, adding, "Serge, this is Cassidy's father."

Serge flashed a brief, gap-toothed grin. "What excellent timing," he announced and then bee-lined over to Cassidy. "Where is it?"

More sand dusted his wake, making her twitch with a need to get the broom and sweep it out together with her father. "Showers can't kill you, you know. And no. Not excellent timing. At all."

"The thing you found today. We need it."

"What thi—"

Serge's eyes darkened with impatience.

"Oh. That thing."

"Yes. The thing," Serge insisted, his tone drenched in meaning as though they had discussed this brand new "thing" a dozen times before. Why was she still surprised that he knew about it already?

She shook her head. "I didn't find it. Jackson gave it to me." More like ambushed her with it in the *Gazette's* parking lot. To, as he put it, "explain what you've gotten yourself into better than I obviously can."

Serge clapped his hands together with giddy delight, sprinkling dry seaweed in the process. "Excellent. Excellent. Where is it?"

"Jackson gave you something?" Samantha sounded apprehensive.

"Only never-ending aggravation." She dug into her bag. Serge bounced on his toes, vibrating with eagerness, but his enthusiasm wilted when she pulled out a tattered old book. It had been pilfered from Garrett Striker's private collection, if Jackson was to be believed.

Serge's face went slack.

"Well, that's what he gave me. What were you expecting?"

"A weapon, of course."

Samantha's hand went to her chest. "We need a weapon?"

Serge gave her arm a brief pat and took the book. "We will soon."

"You're such a comfort," Cassidy grumbled.

Book firmly pressed to his breast, Serge made for the door without so much as a glance at Gil. He must have seen nothing in the man's aura that was relevant to their current situation. Cassidy allowed herself a tiny sigh of relief. The last thing they needed was her father bungling around in the middle of a supernatural battle.

"Do you have a lot like that down here?" Gil wondered.

"Like what?" Samantha asked, all doe-eyed innocence. Cassidy was too surprised to respond. Gil couldn't possibly know what sort of entity he had just encountered, could he?

"You know." He twirled a finger near his temple, and she relaxed.

Samantha smiled, relieved. "Eccentrics. Yes, we do have our share."

And the next one was on his way. The thrum of Dominique's nearness swelled in her awareness moments before he opened the door. Unlike his water-terrorized mentor, Dominique had rinsed off the remnants of his sandy lair. The muscles of his bare torso and arms glistened with moisture, his ebony hair lay smooth against his head and neck, and the wet polyester gym pants hugged his hips in a way that left little to the imagination.

"Oh! Well. Wow," Samantha said, gaze first darting down, then up, and finally off into the kitchen. Color burned in her cheeks as she busied herself with the groceries again.

Dominique closed the door and looked Gil over, his expression revealing nothing.

"So. You must be Jackson," Gil said, returning the scrutiny. "Or you better be marrying my daughter if you're going to walk into her house dressed like that."

Cassidy bit her tongue to stop herself from charging to Dominique's defense. She wanted her father gone, not justify her living arrangements to him. Not that he would do anything more than scoff at the notion of soulmates, which was as close as she could explain their relationship without straying into the otherworldly.

Dominique gave her a thoughtful look before addressing her father. "I am not Jackson. Cassidy is my soul, and I am her heart. This is our home."

In the kitchen, Samantha sighed wistfully.

Cassidy bristled. *What are you doing? Stop chitchatting and make him go. Now.*

"Is that so?" Gil said, gaze narrowing.

"That is so," she said. "Jackson and I split. Now I'm with Dominique, and I'm happy. Now make me even happier and show yourself out."

"Baby girl, I—"

Dominique seized Gil's chin, forcing him to meet his eyes. "Why are you truly here?"

Her father's face relaxed as he fell under the vampire's compulsion, and Dominique released him. "Because my daughter is here. She's my family. This is where I belong."

"Don't do this, Dominique," Cassidy whispered.

His reply was a caress in her mind. *Don't you want to know the truth?*

She blinked hard, willing the tears away. The truth. As a journalist, she was its champion. The absolute honesty between her and Dominique was the bedrock of their relationship the way lies and deceit had been the basis of her father's relationship with her mother. Whatever guilt over this nibbled at Gil Chandler, it was bound to be perfunctory and fleeting.

And yet...

Dominique tilted his head. "Did you mean everything you have told your daughter tonight?"

Gil stood docile and thoughtful, hands in his windbreaker pockets. He nodded. "Every word. I should have said it long ago, but I've been too proud. I kept thinking I could move on and make a new life when I was only digging my hole deeper. Until it all collapsed on me."

"So, Kelly wised up to you," she said bitterly. "You just don't want to be alone."

"Not if I know you're out there somewhere, no."

"I can't help you. Consider this bridge burned beyond repair."

Dominique slanted her a poignant look. *There is no such thing, mon amour. Not while either of you lives.*

She hurled silent denials like lightning from her emotional storm.

He turned back to her father. "What did you hope would happen here tonight?"

"Well, I didn't think she'd welcome me with a party, but it would have been nice to at least spend some time talking." Gil cast a hopeful look in her direction. "What do you say, baby girl? I have a bag in my car. I can stay awhile."

Cassidy sucked in a mighty breath. "Absolutely not."

Dominique smiled, and she felt the warm wave of his love embrace her soul.

Then he went and ruined it.

"There is a spare bedroom upstairs," he told her father. "Make yourself comfortable."

18

The Key

Cassidy was mute with anger, even in her mind, but Dominique saw it ride her shoulders and blaze in her eyes. He had pushed her too far. Any other night, he would have chastised himself and begged her for understanding. Not tonight.

While Gil Chandler bumped his suitcase upstairs, Dominique toweled off the ocean and donned dry clothes. Then he ushered Cassidy and Samantha outside and down the street. The women walked to either side of him, one boiling, the other casting wary glances.

They were halfway to Samantha's cottage when Cassidy exploded. "How *could* you?"

Relief surged through him. Her temper he could handle, but against her silence he was powerless.

"How could you invite him to move in with us? You know what he did to my mom and me. You know how I feel. What is *wrong* with you?"

He ventured an apologetic smile. "You still need to ask?"

She threw up both hands. "No. I know why you did this. You think because you had a chummy relationship with your dad, everybody else should have one, too. What I don't understand is why you're cramming this down my throat now."

He didn't want to understand it either. His senses strained for any hint of blood-drinkers in the vicinity. No cool auras glowed in the shadows. No trace of cedar smoke drifted in the sea air. Kambyses would leave him be for the moment, but he might well be near. That creature's powers of concealment had no limits.

You may need family before all this is over, Dominique said silently, inviting her to reply in kind in case sensitive ears waited beyond his perception.

"I have no family," she spat. "He's dead to me." A moment later, he felt her recoil at her own words as she recalled that his own beloved father was literally dead and why.

She wrapped her arms around her middle. Sorrow and apology rose as the fury loosened its grip on her. *Serge seemed excited to see him.*

Which meant for once he and the oracle were in agreement. If anything took Dominique away from her, at least one blood relative—no matter how flawed—would be there for her.

Cassidy leaned against him. *Nothing is going to happen to you that won't happen to us both.*

Curling an arm around her shoulders, he pulled her closer and kissed the top of her head. *That, mon amour, is my greatest fear.*

The tension drained out of her in a rush, and she snaked an arm around his waist.

"Oh, good. You guys made up," Samantha said as they turned up her driveway. "I was starting to worry that the world had come off its axis."

"The night is young," he said, feeling grim despite his relief.

Inside Samantha's cottage, Serge sat cross-legged on the plush sofa, staring at the small book open on the coffee table before him.

Samantha sat beside him. "What did you find?"

"It's all wrong," he muttered. "This is all wrong."

Dominique sat on the table facing Serge on the side opposite Samantha. "We poor fools who don't see the future will need a little more than that."

Serge looked up, frowning. "No, this is not the future. This writing—it's wrong."

"How so?" Samantha prompted.

"This—" He gestured at the book. "This is fantasy. We are all caught by tethers, it says, connected to the one who made us and that one to the one before them and so on, forever. Lunacy."

Dominique's brows knit together. "Is it?" The words were unfamiliar, but what they described had some basis in facts as he knew them. "We have a permanent telepathic bond with our sires. Our blood sires, anyway," he amended ruefully. Kambyses had taken him to the brink of death, but the blood that finally changed him had been another's.

"You are genetically linked as well," Cassidy said. She had poured herself a glass of water and now settled into a swiveling bucket chair. "To whoever's serum infected you."

"True," Dominique said, considering. The same virus that created a telepathic link with the prey when feeding also carried the genetic payload that—once at critical mass and presented with vampire blood—transformed the host. With every new blood-drinker, the virus mutated as it fit itself into the new genome.

A few months ago, he had only the barest idea about any of this and Serge none at all. They had Jackson and his vampire hunting family's centuries of research to thank for this knowledge. Not that this was in any way useful to him. There was no pill he could take to undo the unwelcome updates to his DNA.

Serge's eyes had gone owlish. "There is nothing in here about viruses."

"I doubt they knew about things like that when this was written," Samantha offered in the soothing tone one might use for a disturbed child. "But it makes sense. The strains of the virus in a sire and their youngling must be similar enough to maintain a link—a 'tether'—between them. Right?" She looked at Dominique for confirmation. He arched a brow. Clearly, she had given this some thought. "Like children inherit traits from their parents?"

The ends of Serge's curls trembled. "But children don't die when their parents die."

The room went still.

Serge took the book and flipped the warped yellow pages. "Right here. 'The tether casts out the mortal soul and becomes the true nature of the consumer of life and rules him always. Break one tether and you shall unravel all who have sprung from it and cast them into death eternal.'" His bugging puppy-dog eyes dared anyone to argue.

"Wow," Samantha said, thoughtfully brushing her lips with two fingertips. "That's...dark."

"It is lies," he insisted.

"I don't know. You have always seemed a little 'unraveled' to me," Dominique said with a smirk he hoped would goad Serge out of his spiraling anxiety. It didn't.

"But my sire has perished, and I have not been 'cast into death eternal,' have I, blood-child?"

Samantha put a calming hand on his shoulder. "Of course not, sweetie. So you know better. Why are you getting so upset?"

"I am not upset," he shouted, even as the tips of his fangs appeared.

Dominique leaned back onto his hands and regarded his mentor. "You don't know for certain that your sire is dead, do you?"

"Of course, I do. I saw his fate the night before the fire consumed his lair."

"And you don't think he might have read that in your mind and taken precautions?"

"But—"

"And knowing his own youngling wouldn't warn him, why would he want to be anywhere near you after that?"

Serge shot to his feet. "No!"

"He abandoned you."

He blurred across the table and past Cassidy so fast, she spilled half the water left in her glass. In the dark recesses of the kitchen, he began to pace and mutter and whine under his breath. Dominique's skin crawled. He'd never seen the old one so shaken.

"Or it's all just lies, Serge," Cassidy said, flicking water off one hand. "Like you said. The book did come from Jackson. You probably shouldn't expect too much."

Dominique met her eyes. If Serge didn't at least suspect his sire had survived, he would dismiss these words with a scoff and be done with them.

But he isn't sure, she thought at him.

Which means we cannot dismiss this. It could be true. And if it was, his fate might well be bound to that of Kambyses.

Serge returned to them and stood, looking helpless, until Samantha took his hand and pulled him down on the sofa beside her.

"Can't trust my brother as far as you...well, as far as I can throw him. You know that, sweetie."

He flashed an uncertain smile, apparently willing to buy into this theory for now. Or making himself buy into it.

"I don't trust him at all," Dominique said, and picked up the book to flip through the crackling pages. The stained fabric covers smelled of ancient dust, Jackson's aftershave, and...what? He peered at the worn spine. Closely. Sniffed more deeply. "Samantha, do you have tweezers?"

"Um. Yes?"

"I need them."

"Hold on." She was halfway out of her seat when Serge blurred away and up the stairs.

"Oh," she said, sitting back down.

What is it? Cassidy asked.

Jackson's crumbs, he replied and felt her tense.

Serge returned and presented a pair of cosmetic tweezers.

"*Merci.*" Dominique poked the slender instrument into the bottom of the book's spine and fished for the incongruous smell that emanated from there. Moments later, he extracted the tiny bug.

Serge dropped into his seat, eyes narrowing. "What's this?"

"A listening device."

Samantha shook her head. "Oh, Jack."

"Of course," Cassidy said. "He does nothing without an ulterior motive."

"*Au revoir.*" Dominique crushed the device between his thumb and forefinger. Somewhere not too far away, he imagined Jackson tearing off headphones and cursing violently.

"So this was only a way for Jackson to spy on our conversations," Samantha said.

"An excuse, certainly," Dominique agreed, turning pages again. The faded, looping cursive was difficult to make out. If this was a ruse to plant a bug, it was an elaborate one, but not beyond the realm of possibility for Jackson, who had tried to plant surveillance equipment in their homes before.

He paged back to the passage that had so upset Serge. "'...casts out the mortal soul and becomes the true nature of the consumer of life and rules him always.'"

"Lies," Cassidy said. "In all the ways it matters, you're still who you were as a mortal."

Dominique rubbed his chin, and felt the acute bones of his jaw, felt his alter ego tug at the chains that confined it—most of the time. "The beast is not who I was."

"That's not your true nature."

"It is now."

Her clapped mouth shut, but not her mind. *No, it isn't.*

Because I fight it. Because you help me fight it. "You remember what I was like when you first met me?"

One of her arched brows rose higher in challenge. "An obnoxious Frenchman with a limited wardrobe?"

"And you liked that about me, *non?*" His smile faltered when she didn't take the bait. "The beast ruled me, *chérie.* It still does." For all his efforts to keep his humanity, he would always need blood, and he would always want to take it in the most violent, emotionally charged way possible. If his encounters with Bijou had taught him anything at all, it was that he would always be a slave to his instincts.

I don't care. Just because it's written in a book that looks and smells old doesn't mean it's true of you.

But it was true. He knew this, and so did she, even if, like Serge, she chose to pretend otherwise. When that bit of logic hit her, she sat forward and put her glass down on the table. "It's because of me."

"*Oui,*" he murmured. Her faith in his ability to master his darkest demons was the only reason that he could.

"What is?" Samantha asked, looking between them. Beside her, Serge stared at the parquet floor between his feet.

Cassidy propped her elbows on her knees and touched her fingertips together. A storm brewed in her mind. He caught it in their link like a first whiff of ozone on the wind. There was no stopping her. He could only watch in spellbound horror.

"You can't kill your sire. Not if there's any possibility of you"—*Dying*. She glanced at Serge—"damaging yourself."

"I can't destroy him either way. I am no match for him. No blood-drinker I have ever met would be."

Serge began to quake.

"Even if you could, it wouldn't be only *your* life you'd be risking. Is it?"

Her quiet words struck hard and fast as lightning, illuminating a new truth. Kambyses was ancient. How many had he sired? How many generations of blood-drinkers walked the Earth because of him? Thousands? Tens of thousands? More? How many of these were like Dominique and Serge? Struggling to exist night after night with the least amount of violence, clinging to whatever little joy they might have? If he destroyed Kambyses, could he cast them all into "death eternal" like some divine judge, jury, and executioner?

"*Non,*" he whispered. "Perhaps not."

"He obviously wants you for something, and he's gone to great lengths to find and manipulate you."

Dominique opened his mouth, but words would not come. Nor could he move. Or think. The sheer power of the storm about to annihilate his existence paralyzed him with dread.

"Serge, you said you foresaw me bringing home a weapon today."

When the pirate's eyes lifted to focus on her, they lit up as he, too, recognized the coming tempest. He nodded slightly, mesmerized.

"I only brought the trigger." She glanced at the book. "The weapon is..."

"No!" Dominique bellowed. Samantha and Serge flinched in unison.

Cassidy tilted her head in defiance. "Yes."

"You must have nothing to do with him. Never!"

"It's a bit late for that. Don't you think?"

Dominique's world shuddered.

"It's the prophecy," she explained. "I am the key to something momentous happening to the vampires. Something other than killing them all, or I think Serge would have just killed me that first night he saw me. Right?"

Serge made no response. He stared at her, mouth agape, lost in whatever it was he saw when he witnessed time unfold around someone.

"Okay, let's assume that's a yes. So, what better way to make that happen than to work with a powerful vampire? One that has influence over many others?"

Desperation scraped at Dominique like rusty nails. "You cannot *work* with Kambyses. He is bound by no law and has no conscience. He is unpredictable. Insane."

"You know I've seen all that in your memories. But Dominique, my love. Look what knowing me has done for you."

The room closed in on him now. Black thunder rolled in his bones. "No. You can't—"

"Kambyses is your—let's call it your serum sire, which means your so-called true nature is genetically his offspring. Whatever happens between us when you feed from me, there is a good chance it would also happen if he fed from me."

"My God, no," Samantha burst out. "You can't be serious."

"She's not," Dominique growled.

"Serge, I'm right, aren't I? If I'm the key, this has to be the way."

Serge swayed as though buffeted by an invisible wind. "You know what you have to do, sweet one."

Dominique bolted out of his seat, and in the next instant, landed a solid slap to the back of Serge's head. He yelped. Sand sprayed everywhere. "Shut up, old fool. Play with my head all you want, but not hers." Pivoting to Cassidy, he continued, "Absolutely not. I will never allow that madman to lay his claws on you. Even if I have to make a million corpses to stop him."

As his fear exploded through her, she lowered her head and clasped her hands into a white-knuckled fist before her. "Then what do you suggest? Do we run? For how long? The rest of my life? The rest of time? The world is only so big." She met his eyes again. "You need to talk to him, if nothing else. Find out what he really wants from you."

"You know I have tried."

"More than a year ago, yes. He might be more willing to discuss it now that you've proved he doesn't control you."

"There is no reasoning with him. There is only obedience or death."

"Since you're still alive, I'd say that second option is off the table. Talk to him," she added emphatically.

Dominique plowed both hands through his damp hair and clutched his shoulders. Knots bunched in the muscles beneath his fingers. "There is no point."

"I see." A sensation like a bristling hedgehog rustled through their link. "So, you're forcing me to live in the same house with my lying, manipulative father, but you won't even talk to yours, who searched the world for you?"

"He is *not* my father."

"In this life, he's the closest thing you've got to one. And you need to talk to him."

He shook his head. He couldn't even imagine such a conversation, but he knew how the attempt would end—with him in chains, literal or figurative. Or both.

She tucked her hair behind her ears, got up, and stalked around the sofa, where Serge and Samantha swiveled their heads like breathless spectators at a sporting event. Facing Dominique, her hands moving to underscore her words, she said, "Let me sum this up for you out loud, because you're so deep in these woods, I don't think you hear my thoughts anymore. You are going to go talk to Kambyses like the capable adult vampire you are, not the clueless youngling he last saw. You're going to do it tonight, and I'm going to come with you, because the closer I am to you, the more you can draw on your human strength from me."

"The more I will be distracted by worry for you." This would not happen. Could not. Not now. Not ever.

"Dominique, we do this together tonight," she said, closing the distance between them and placing a hand over his heart. The storm raged in her deep-ocean eyes—and swept him along without mercy. "Or I'll go there during the day, and tomorrow night do this my way."

19

SOL

All the way down the highway, Dominique obeyed every speed limit and traffic law. Keeping the fragile human clinging to his back safe was one reason for this, but the fragile human also recognized a delaying tactic when she saw one. Cassidy decided not to point this out. The trip was a short one, and the winter night long.

She still chafed at finding her father making himself comfortable in her living room when she returned to change for this outing. There he sat, content in XXL striped PJs and frayed slippers, while enjoying a beer, chips, and Fox News. *The moment he lights up a cigarette, he's gone,* she promised herself. No way would she put up with him polluting her airspace with his cancerous poison.

He won't, Dominique countered and showed her why in his memories: Gil Chandler was an unwitting participant in a new quit-smoking-by-compulsion program.

She leaned her helmeted head against his back. *How could you let him stay?* There was no rancor in the question now, and he wrapped her in a comforting mental embrace.

Parce que je t'aime, Cassie amour.

She sighed. *I love you, too.*

The night flowed past them for several minutes before she heard his focused thought again. *Are you still certain about this?*

Yes. No hesitation. She was certain about her intentions and certain about her safety, too. *There's another human there, this Monica Sol girl. Obviously, the vampires we're meeting have enough restraint not to kill every human on sight. I think they'll listen to reason.*

To this logic, Dominique had no comment.

Through the visor, she eyed the scabbards crossing his back. *I'm not sure that bringing these was a good idea.*

Being prepared is always a good idea.

She couldn't argue with that. She had made some preparations of her own, after all. *Nothing I plan to use,* she told him when she sensed his inquiry. *It'll all work out, you'll see. As long as we're together, we'll be all right.*

Her confidence wavered once they crossed the Intracoastal Waterway into Palm Beach, and he withdrew from their link. *Bijou is close,* was the last thing she heard before the connection drained to a low hum.

Cassidy tightened her arms around him. Maybe they should have waited until the vamp bitch's serum had left his system, when he would have been less susceptible to her will. Coming back here so soon, bringing a human with him, was piling risk upon risk.

But would Bijou have given him that time? Would Kambyses? Unlikely. Best to meet the threat head-on then, on their terms. Besides, it was too late now. They already turned into the driveway, which stretched past manicured hedges and elegant palm trees, all glowing with hidden landscape lighting. Ahead, the mansion sat, regal as a princess, watching their approach. Beneath the jagged steeples, tall windows glowed with soft interior lights.

Dominique brought them to a halt a solid twenty feet away from the front door and cut the motor. She pulled off her helmet and inhaled. Vibrant vegetation and sea spray filled her nose. No smoke, no ash.

While he finger-combed his hair and tied it at his nape with a thin leather strap, readying for the battle he expected, she stowed the helmet and their gloves. Suddenly, his hand captured hers, and he blew back into her mind like a winter wind. *This is as far as you go. Wait here for me, or use the bike to run if you have to, but do not take foolish risks. I cannot protect you against what is in this house. No one can.*

Squeezing his fingers, she held his worried gaze. *It'll be alright. And, no, I won't leave without you.*

The blood-red front door swung open without warning, and a young woman with a striking mane of bright auburn hair stepped out. She was dressed like a Grecian temple priestess, flowing white gown and all. "Back so soon," she exclaimed, smiling brightly. "He will be so pleased."

Dominique pulled his hand out of Cassidy's, withdrawing from her mind in an instant, triggering a small wave of vertigo.

"And you must be Cassidy. I've so wanted to meet you."

Cassidy smiled, instantly charmed by this strange, lively girl who lived with two exceedingly strong vampires. "Nice to meet you, too."

"Come in, come in, both of you." Monica gestured in enthusiastic welcome.

When Cassidy followed Dominique to the door, ignoring his request to stay behind, he gave her a dark look.

"Monica and I can chat while you're doing your thing," she said with a conciliatory shrug. That would keep her close, but not in the direct line of fire. A reasonable compromise, she thought. Dominique didn't look convinced, but he said nothing.

"But of course we have to talk. Do you like tea? I was just making some." Monica took Cassidy's hand and guided her inside.

Gloom permeated the palatial lobby, except for a piercing spotlight at its center. There, a bare-breasted alabaster goddess oozed sensuality from a tall pedestal. The petite woman with the platinum pixie hair coming down the sweeping staircase was the statue's living likeness. Her skin was just as white and her curves—wrapped in an emerald gown—were just as voluptuous.

Dominique stepped in front of Cassidy and growled softly. Bijou's smile became brittle, her green eyes cold and hard. "Such poor manners," she cooed. "Don't worry your handsome youngling head over this one. Had I wanted her dead, she would be."

The growl grew deeper, his eyes flashing to full black and fangs extending.

Bijou sighed dramatically. "Oh, but you are tiresome. I don't know what he sees in you." She turned away, curling a finger over her shoulder. "Come. You are expected."

His eyes reverted to normal as he gave Cassidy one last look. Then he followed that undulating backside up the stairs. She fought the urge to run after a centuries-old vampire and break her neck for what she had done to Eddie. For laying hands on Dominique. For upending their lives. Grab her, punch her, and pitch her over the railing.

Or at least slap that sneer off her face.

"Scrumptious," Monica said, sounding a little breathless.

Cassidy shook herself out of her violent daydream and turned to her human hostess. "What is?"

"Him. Dominique. He's so...dominating in spite of being so young. And so intense. What's he like to have for a master?"

"Master? He's not—" She stopped. The only control Dominique had over her—they had over each other—was love and respect. No compulsion, no enslavement. Something told her this wouldn't be understood here. It might even be used against them. "He's...he's not bad. Not bad at all."

The temple priestess smiled knowingly. Hooking her arm into Cassidy's, she steered her toward a brightly lit hallway leading into the mansion's interior. "Oh, do tell me more."

"I'm actually more interested in your mistress. Bijou, is it? She seems a little, um, edgy."

Monica laughed. "Bijou? Oh, no, she's not my mistress. My lord and I are her guests."

Cassidy's steps would have faltered if not for Monica pulling her along. "Your lord?"

"But of course. I am Sol." She enunciated her surname with care and a sweeping gesture of her hand. "S-O-L."

Cassidy stared at her. *Shit out of luck?* That about summed this up alright. If Kambyses was this woman's "master," then surely he was plugged into her head and might as well be standing in front of Cassidy already.

With a pleased smile, Monica elaborated. "It stands for 'Servant of the Lord.' As in Lord Kambyses. I'm the most trusted of his mortal aides." She leaned close, voice lowering. "I serve of my own free will. My mind is as clear as a summer sky."

Cassidy's lips twitched. "Really? Do tell me more."

20

Ancient Blood

Bijou led him straight to the double-doors with the hammered ironwork at the top of the stairs. Opening them, she stood back without comment. The room beyond glowed with the mellow, peach light of dusk or maybe dawn, giving Dominique pause. But as he advanced across plush Persian rugs, all his senses keyed, the illuminated sky mural on the recessed ceiling became obvious.

The cedar smoke scent of old power choked the air, sharp as needles in his nose. Suppressing a tremor, he scanned the room. Shelves, heavy with books, lined the back wall. To one side hung tapestries depicting gruesome battles. To the other stood a life-size relief carving of a mounted medieval warrior. Another statue—a pair of classical Greek nudes in an erotic embrace—took center stage among a scattering of ponderous, dark leather furnishings. And in the far corner, against a wall of glass black with night, stood two tall wingback chairs.

One of these, he was sure, hid the room's sole other occupant.

The door had closed behind him, leaving him alone—to *talk*—with the monster who had stolen his mortal life. His blood boiled. It took all his years of martial arts training to contain a tidal wave of emotion and narrow his awareness to this moment alone.

The moment was a long one. Nothing happened. Kambyses seemed in no rush to welcome him. Of course not. Why would he?

Bracing himself, Dominique moved deeper into the room, his creaking leathers the only sound. He rounded the chairs in a wide arc. They were empty. Yet, invisible cedars smoldered all around him.

He closed his eyes.

Nico.

More than a thought. Less than a sound. Familiar and unmistakable, his sire's pet name for him. He turned to the being who had taught him to kill.

Kambyses stood with his back to him, staring out the windows, hands in the pockets of his tailored black trousers, casual as if he had stood there all along. He probably had. His hair hung thick and straight down his back in a shimmering ebony mass that was partially gathered in a golden, ruby-adorned clip. Then there was the burgundy silk shirt with the rolled-up sleeves. It all made for a rakish air Dominique had not seen before in this creature. Gone were the drab cloaks and moping demeanor of a silent film era monster. A cosmopolitan eccentric had taken its place.

Dominique froze when he realized that his reflection was being studied in the night-black glass.

"You have returned to me," Kambyses said, his French as smooth as any of the countless other languages at his disposal. The resonant black velvet voice held a tender note that made Dominique bristle.

"No. I have not." Best to get that cleared up right away. "I have come to ask a question."

Cassidy's excitement and anticipation flickered beyond the mental barriers he maintained. No trace of apprehension in her thoughts. Perhaps there was hope yet that they weren't both doomed the moment they walked into this house.

Kambyses turned to look at him with the deep-set, unblinking gaze of a hawk. Appearing to be a man in his early forties, he wasn't handsome so much as he was striking, with an aquiline nose, prominent brows, and the bold bones of the beast just beneath his flawless skin. His generous mouth approached something that might have been an indulgent smile. "Ask."

Dominique didn't return the smile. "Why me?"

No reaction registered in the face of the ancient blood-drinker whose heart no longer beat. Dominique's own youngling heart thumped ever faster. After a full minute of this, maybe longer, he burst out, "Answer me, damn you. Why did you do this to me? What do you want from me?"

At last, a single, grudging nod. "A fair question, Nico."

One Dominique had asked—begged, pleaded, screamed—more often than he cared to recall during his first horrific months as a blood-drinker. There had never been an answer. This time looked to be no different. Though Kambyses appeared at least thoughtful as he turned, slid open a glass door, and walked outside.

Dominique debated leaving while he still could—*if* he still could. This was pointless—always had been—and yet the promise of answers loomed larger than ever.

Biting back a curse, he followed his sire onto the balcony terrace overlooking the manicured grounds and driveway. Starlight glittered on the churning sea beyond. Kambyses stood at the balustrade, looking out, a still figure made of night. Dominique stopped several steps behind him and unclenched his jaw long enough to say, "Do you think you might grant me an answer tonight?"

"The answer lies in your name," Kambyses said with a sigh. "Dominique. It suits you well."

Baffled, it took him a second to recall the meaning of his Christian name and make the connection. Then he scoffed. "You are not the 'lord' my parents intended for me to 'belong to.'"

"You are so young. Not even in your third decade," Kambyses continued as if Dominique hadn't spoken. "Can you fathom twice that much time? Or a century? Can you imagine existing for two?" He glanced over his shoulder. "Or ten?"

Dominique said nothing. This was the most this man had ever said to him—the most human he had ever appeared—and his words drew him into a world he had barely glimpsed. The world of the ancients. A world where time had no meaning.

Kambyses faced the sea again. "Empires rise and fall in moments. All the world's creatures are born, live, and die in seconds. Like mist." He made a flicking gesture with the fingers of one hand. "I lose myself in thought and a year passes." There was a long pause before he added in a whisper, "I drop into the sea and a hundred have gone."

Horrified fascination held Dominique riveted.

"Can you imagine a thousand years?" The words were just a breath. "Or five?"

He stifled a shudder at the sudden chill worming in his gut. He knew Kambyses measured his age in millennia, but this was far more than he ever imagined—or *could* imagine.

"There is no history I have not witnessed. There is no horror and no joy I have not tasted or caused. I am the only constant in a world of eternal change. Not even my children are immune. They perish at the hands of time, at the hands of mortals. Sometimes at the hands of their brothers and sisters."

"And sometimes they're made and pitted against each other by an ancient madman who no longer cares that he is toying with lives." It was a gamble to confront the ancient madman in question like this, but not much of one. He had done it before and never received a response, much less gotten killed for it.

Kambyses turned to regard Dominique's stance, his leathers, his weapons—the same blades with which he had slaughtered the younglings Kambyses had set against him in pointless battles. "They were not worthy. You are. You are the one."

Foreboding knocked at the back of Dominique's skull. Along with...excitement. "The one...what?"

Kambyses moved closer, soundless as a ghost. "I suspected it the night you left. The longer I couldn't find you, the more I hoped it might be so." He stopped barely an arm's length away, his hawk eyes bright with madness. "But I knew it for certain the night I felt your blade pass through one of my own."

A knot formed in Dominique's throat. The ancient Roman he had killed only this past summer, against all conceivable odds. The one who had threatened Cassidy. Even then, he suspected a connection between Aurelius and Kambyses and feared the consequences of his actions. There would be a price to pay. Apparently, he would pay it now. He didn't dare move.

"Aurelius was my companion for an eon, and one of the strongest. To vanquish him required great cleverness. And the strength of character and resourcefulness of one who is worthy." Kambyses's tone grew hushed. "You are that one, Nico. The clever one. You, Dominique, are my chosen one."

Every instinct told him to run. Every sense told him it was too late. "For what?"

"To be mine. Completely."

Growling, Dominique backed up several paces. "No."

"I can convince you."

"Compel me, you mean. Yes, that is what it will take to bind me to you."

"You know I never have. You will remain with me as you did before: by choice."

"Choice? My choice is to never have known you." His lips curled into a sneer. "My choice is to be rid of you for good."

Kambyses did something that startled Dominique as nothing else could have. He laughed. Amusement smoothed his rough-hewn face. "You will never be rid of me any more than you can be rid of yourself. I am part of you. Don't you feel that in your heart?"

"Only the worst part, yes," he replied with less heat than he intended. He was unaccountably disarmed by this connection, however uncomfortable, with this eternal being.

"You hear my call every time you pierce a vein, do you not?"

Know me.

The words thrummed in his bones like a struck chord. Know me. The desperate demand of the beast, full of sorrow and rage. "Know me," he whispered.

"Know me," Kambyses repeated, his smile growing thin. "The one genuine desire of every feeling thing." He closed the distance between them. "You want to know me, don't you? You hunger to know me. And through me, know yourself."

Dominique couldn't have denied it to save his life. Answers. There was nothing he wanted more. He nodded.

"Then my search has ended. You are worthy of my gift. Know me, Nico," he murmured and tilted his head, chin raised, the invitation unmistakable. "Know all of me."

Dominique smothered an involuntary gasp. Never had he known Kambyses to share his blood—and the thousands of years of time it contained. But here it was, in a quiet rope of vein lying across hard muscle, offered to him and him alone. His world reeled.

"Destiny," Serge had said. And, "You know what you have to do."

This time, Dominique didn't argue. Or hesitate.

Long bottled grief and rage drove his fangs out, drove him to fist a hand in the thick hair and yank the head back hard enough to snap a mortal neck. The prey gave no resistance. Instead, Kambyses embraced him, cupped the back of his skull, and sighed when Dominique's teeth slammed home.

Though there was no heartbeat, the blood squelched into his mouth—like lava.

Dominique tried to jerk away, but Kambyses held him closer. "Know me, Nico."

Liquid fire blistered his tongue, scorched his esophagus, and, when he choked on it, fried his sinuses and nose. An inferno ignited in his stomach and bowels. The sun roared in his veins and burned away the world.

Burned it to ashes floating in an ocean of night.

The link didn't just fade. It snuffed out like a candle—from an already dim flicker to full dark in an instant.

It's nothing, Cassidy told herself, trying to shake off the sensation of being smothered, of...something falling over her. Dominique was dealing with an ancient vampire. There was no telling what mental games he would have to play.

"What do you think is happening?" she asked Monica. They sat side-by-side on a sofa in a small, immaculate reading room overlooking the back gardens. Her eyes kept straying past the luminous pool, drawn to the dock, where, at the far end, she could just make out a deep black presence. Only a handful of utility lights revealed the enormous shadow, the nightmare of Dominique's memories made real: *Apokryphos*.

"Oh, I wouldn't know. He doesn't tell me these things," said the temple priestess as she poured more tea into their cups.

"Something is happening."

"Oh? How can you tell?"

Cassidy picked up the cup, saw the pale gold liquid inside shiver and put it back down. "I just can."

"Interesting," Monica said and helped herself to another pastry with delicate fingers.

It was nothing. Nothing for her to get involved in. Vampire things. Stay with the loopy human girl. Pick her brain. She buried her hands in her lap, fighting to still their trembling. "Um. How did you meet him? Kambyses, I mean?"

Monica beamed. "On vacation last year in San Juan. I was walking down a street, minding my own business, when he found me. My hair caught his attention, I think. I used to model it, you know." She flipped the deep-red waves over her shoulder with a dramatic shampoo-commercial-worthy shake of her head. "I took one look at him, and I just *knew* what he was. I mean, I've seen the movies. How can you not know, right? Well, I came right out and said it. 'You're a vampire.'" She giggled. "Totally threw him, poor guy."

"I bet," Cassidy murmured for the sake of politeness and trying to keep the panic at bay. Dominique knew how to handle himself around the very powerful. He would be all right. They would both be all right.

"I've been traveling with him ever since, and I'm waiting for the night that he'll turn me." Monica's eyes narrowed. "Are you okay?"

"Why?"

Monica glanced at Cassidy's hands where they were wringing, white-knuckled, in her lap like a pair of suffocating fish. Cassidy untangled them. "No. Something is wrong. I feel it."

"What do you feel?"

"Empty." The realization hit her hard enough to drive the breath out of her. She couldn't breathe for all the emptiness sucking at her innards. "Oh my God, he's killed him."

"Are you kidding? Kam's besotted with Dominique. He would never hurt him."

Besotted? Cassidy stood so fast, she bumped the coffee table, rattling the cups on their saucers. "I have to know what's going on."

"Wait. Where are you going?"

Heedless of a vamp bitch that might ambush her, she marched through the shadowy lobby, her rubber boots quiet on the glass tile floor. Monica's sandals slapped in her wake. "Cassidy, stop! You can't go up there."

"I can, and I will." She took the steps two at a time.

"No, you don't understand. We're not allowed up there without being called." Monica's legs were longer than Cassidy's. She caught up to her at the top of the stairs and grabbed her elbow hard. "Listen to me. We have no business up here. We haven't been summoned."

"So much for your trust in your lord and master, I see."

"Those are not his rules. This isn't his house."

"Bijou can go fuck herself." She circled her arm in one of the martial arts moves Dominique had taught her and shook off Monica's hold. Then she turned to face the iron-studded mahogany doors. Grabbing both handles, she shoved them open.

21

LONELY OLD MAN

Dominique opened his eyes and stared into the sky mural on the ceiling. An icy heat suffused his limbs, and his senses extended far past every limit he had ever known. It took some effort to filter out the onslaught of sounds from beyond the mansion's walls, and the miasma of smells in his vicinity. Finally, only silence remained—and sweet cedar smoke.

He sat up on the leather sofa he didn't remember lying down on. His swords lay across a nearby wingback chair. Kambyses sat in another, watching him over steepled fingers, one ankle propped on the opposite knee. "Do you see, Nico?"

Dominique nodded slowly. The impressions and emotions he had tasted in the firestorm still coated his mouth, though many details were lost to him, their depths too great for his mind to grasp. The ancient blood-drinker's consciousness swirled in his awareness like a vast, dark sea, waiting for him to dive in, explore—and disappear.

No longer was Kambyses's reluctance to share his blood a mystery. Over the millennia, his blood had grown in potency until it was more likely to kill a mortal than turn them. Or worse. The last two who survived a turning almost two thousand years ago had gone mad. In the grief-drenched memories Kambyses offered, Dominique witnessed their sanity disintegrate until they had to be destroyed. Even the ones he sired before—those who still existed—had turned away long ago, closing themselves off from the timeless chasm of his mind through distance and obscurity.

Which left Kambyses forever bereft of the profound psychic bond shared by sire and youngling. The price for his eternal power was eternal solitude.

Until now.

In Dominique, Kambyses believed he had found a blood-drinker strong enough to take his blood, share his mind, and be a true companion through the ages, one he wanted by his side willingly and without reservation.

"What of Bijou?" Dominique wondered.

Memories swirled on the surface of the dark sea. Bijou's sire was another ancient one once dear to Kambyses, but now estranged. He thought of her as troublesome family, recruited to acquaint Dominique with his true nature. They would leave her to the existence his arrival had interrupted.

"We will travel the oceans together and watch this world change through the ages." Quiet anticipation hummed in the rich voice. "We shall both see it through our eyes. Understand it in both our hearts."

Dominique had no desire to return to a life aboard *Apokryphos* and its eerily compelled mortal crew. But now that he had glimpsed the lonely old man inside the unimaginably powerful blood-drinker, he was no longer so violently opposed to being in his sire's presence. He understood the longing for companionship, could even sympathize.

To a point.

That lonely old man had caused unimaginable carnage for five millennia and harbored an unsettling lack of empathy toward anything he considered unworthy of his attention.

"Maybe we could—" Dominique's half-formed olive branch died on his lips when a commotion of female voices in the hallway rose to a level he could no longer ignore.

The door burst open, and Cassidy charged in, battle mode engaged. "Dominique? Are you okay?"

The shock of seeing her here, in the same space with his sire, rendered him momentarily senseless. How had he lost track of her and the danger she was in?

Monica rushed past Cassidy and dropped a bow so deep the ends of her hair brushed the rug. "I'm so sorry, my lord. She is being completely unreasonable."

The lonely old man vanished, replaced by the ancient vampire whose countenance revealed nothing. Even his mind shuttered against Dominique with a natural ease. Monica backed away, turned, and scurried out, closing the door behind her, no doubt at her master's silent command.

Only now did Cassidy spot Kambyses in the shadows of his seat. She blanched.

Merde, what had she done? He should have expected this, warned her not to react, no matter what. Of course, she would have sensed their link burn to cinders under the onslaught of the fire-blood. And of course she would attempt to storm to his rescue—right through the gates of hell.

Run, he begged. If she heard him, she gave no sign, her attention locked on Kambyses, the mad look in her eyes a bizarre mixture of fear and—God help them—challenge.

"This is a private conversation," Dominique said with authority, attempting to wrest control of the situation. Cassidy's eyes flashed to him, frowning. He put compulsion in his voice, prayed she would accept it. "Leave us."

The frown deepened before understanding dawned...too late.

"Stay," Kambyses said, switching to English, the compulsion quiet but powerful. He rose from his seat as though levitating, his propped up leg swinging forward to take his first step, a predator stirring to the hunt.

Dominique heard her breath catch at this nonchalant display of strength and fought the impulse to back away himself. This was the version of his sire he knew so well, the true version, and what Kambyses wanted him to become as his eternal companion. Dominique shuddered to think he had considered it, even for a moment.

But it might well be too late.

There she stood—his brave lioness, his reason for being, his last link to humanity—in the middle of the room, her eyes shiny and huge, her fingers fidgeting and heart pounding.

Stay still, mon amour. Stay calm. Do not speak. Do not think.

Kambyses walked behind her, taking in every detail. His fingertips touched the chestnut halo of her hair. His nostrils flared to drink her scent. "This is the one who is aware of you."

There was no point denying it. Pretending calm thought instead of the dread swarming up his body, Dominique got up and moved closer. Cassidy's eyes found him, apprehensive and questioning, but he focused on Kambyses, who never failed to destroy any mortal who drew his interest.

"*Oui*, she is. What does it mean?" he said, assuming the role of the curious acolyte his sire had ordained for him.

Kambyses considered him over her shoulder. He wasn't quite her height, short for a man of the modern age. Strange how Dominique had never noticed that before.

"It means nothing," he said, dismissive.

No, it wasn't nothing. Not to him. Dominique struggled to show no reaction.

Kambyses brushed the back of his fingers against Cassidy's cheek, making her face squirm. "You should not surround yourself with such petty distractions." He caressed her jaw, her neck, her frantic pulse. Her throat bobbed with a nervous swallow. "They are temporary and meaningless."

The look he slanted Dominique over her shoulder was clear. *Drink her*, it said. *Drink to the death.*

Dominique throttled his surging rage and morphed it into an arctic smile. "She amuses me."

Cassidy arched a dubious brow. She had to know what he was doing. She knew him well enough to recognize this tactic, even without being privy to his thoughts.

But she would also know the danger she was in, and—as usual—showed no intention of backing down. With a shaky breath, she squared her shoulders and pulled down the zipper of her leather jacket.

His belly churned, then flipped and punched him in the spine when he recognized the dusty-blue sweater she wore underneath. "*Non.*"

She smiled with grim determination and shrugged out of the jacket. *My turn*, her eyes said as she tossed it aside. Then she pulled at her scarf to reveal the sweater's slanted cut, which so provocatively emphasized the long column of her neck. The garment never failed to rouse Dominique's lust—as it would any blood-drinker's, Kambyses included.

The ancient vampire's gaze darkened with arousal. "Very amusing indeed."

"Is there something I can do for you? My lord?" she murmured, as if the ancient monster behind her wasn't already irrevocably enthralled by her offer.

"No, there isn't. Stop this," Dominique said. As if Cassidy could. As if Kambyses would. When Kambyses glanced at him, he added, "She is mine."

His sire paused for all of three seconds—maybe five—then he returned his attention to the expanse of silky, sun-kissed skin before him. He opened his mouth. Brutal canines appeared, laced with serum. Serum to reinforce what Dominique had already given her while taking more blood than he should have.

Assuming Kambyses intended to let her live at all.

Dominique struck with a ferocious speed that shocked even him. A fraction of a second is all it took to retrieve his *katana* and press the tip beneath Kambyses's jawbone. Blood oozed around the forged steel. The stench of smoke smothered the air.

"I said no," he said on a furious growl.

Solid black eyes burned in the ancient one's skull, and Dominique let his own beast rise.

Cassidy's human-speed perceptions took a little longer. When she realized how close the lethal blade was to her own throat, she gasped. Unthinking, she put up her hand to ward off an edge that would sever her fingers before she even knew she had touched it.

Dominique reached for her wrist—which was all the distraction Kambyses needed. A titanic force plowed into him, carrying him away in a blur. There were only flashes of his sire's dispassionate face. Wind rushed in his ears, and copper pooled in his mouth just before something hit his back with stunning force. A hammer blow to his right shoulder, then another to his left thigh, splitting his bones. He shrieked in agony, but the pain subsided into a crackling tingle almost as fast as it hit, the fire-blood already racing to repair the damage.

Kambyses stood before him, his long hair in only slight disarray. On the other side of the room, Cassidy stared in open-mouthed shock. Dominique tried to rush to her side, fetch her up and run, but he couldn't. His one arm and leg refused to move. Looking down, he saw why. The hilts of his swords protruded from them, their blades run through his flesh and bone and the carved-wood relief behind him, pinning him in place. His blood oozed and dripped, adding ice and snow to the stench of fire and ash.

He vibrated with fury. He had been here before. Immobilizing him with his own weapons was Kambyses's favorite means of disciplining him. "Is this truly your answer to everything?" he roared. "Run me through and ignore me when I ask for the slightest consideration?"

Kambyses tilted his head a tiny amount, drawing attention to the spot where he had given Dominique his vein. As he did, his mind opened to him again. *Nico. You don't even know how many questions you still have. Or how far you must still travel. I will show you the way.*

With that, Kambyses held out his hand to Cassidy. She shook her head as though to clear it and took a tentative step toward her summoner.

"Cassidy, no," Dominique commanded.

She gave him a tight smile that said she knew better than to think she had any say in what would happen next.

"It'll be all right," she said, though she sounded like she was trying to convince herself more than him. She moved across the room and slipped her fingers into Kambyses's hand as she met his gaze with a brave smile. "We haven't been introduced. I'm Cassidy Chandler. The amusing one." When there was no reaction from Kambyses, her expression faltered into heartbreaking uncertainty.

As though leading her in a dance, he guided her around until she faced away from Dominique. Her shoulders relaxed. Her heart slowed its mad gallop. She sighed, under his spell.

"Don't touch her, you miserable, filthy old piece of shit!"

Kambyses paid him no attention. Neither did Cassidy, who likely was no longer aware of anything real. She tucked her hair behind an ear and angled her head to the side, letting the bite come. The moment it did, she collapsed into his arms.

Dominique screamed his outrage, his beast well off its chain, and scrabbled against the wall like a pinned insect.

Kambyses fed only briefly. Then he let his head fall back, eyes closed, a mirror to the limp form he held in their macabre dance. The tip of his tongue appeared, relishing her blood, still bright scarlet on his lips. Then he scooped her up to hang in his arms like a string-less puppet and gazed down at her.

Whatever effect she hoped feeding from her would have on the ancient one, there was no evidence of it. Kambyses was in complete control as his prey curled against him and grasped the front of his silk shirt.

"How much more we are together. Don't you ever forget it," Cassidy mumbled against his shoulder. "Don't...forget. Never—" Her ragged gasp and moan left no doubt which memory she was reliving—what he *made* her relive.

"No!" Dominique cried. Kambyses being privy to his most intimate moments with her—all their joys and dreams, fears and desires—was like another sword running him through, this one slicing open his heart. He shook with the force of the anguish tearing at him.

With a languid sigh, Cassidy went limp, one arm dangling, jaw slack. Kambyses regarded him with profound concern, even pity. "You have much to learn, Nico."

"Hurt her and I will hunt you down and destroy you," Dominique snarled through his tears. "If it takes a thousand years and costs ten thousand lives, I will find you, and I will end you!"

"I know," Kambyses said with a thin smile. Then he walked away with his burden. The door obligingly swung open, swallowing him, taking with him Dominique's heart and soul.

The redhead, Monica, peered around the edge of the door and winced when she caught sight of him. "Ugh. What a mess."

"Release me," he ordered with the deepest compulsion he could muster, but the sound of her sandals already retreated down the stairs.

Desperation mounting, he wrapped his left hand around the hilt protruding from his right shoulder and pulled. The *katana* budged, but the moment it did, his shoulder blade broke again with a sickening, muffled crack that had him seeing stars. Hissing through the pain, he kept pulling before the bone could mend again with ferocious speed, fueled by the fire-blood. Dominique had been weak as a hatchling sparrow compared to the strength that surged through him now. Yet, it still hadn't been anywhere near enough to challenge his sire.

No matter. For Cassidy, he would do it again. As soon as he got free.

The *katana* came out only so far. His arm wasn't long enough to pull out the entire length, and grabbing the blade itself would only cost him fingers. The shorter sword skewering his thighbone prevented him from levering himself up. It was also well out of reach.

The last time Kambyses had left him like this, he didn't return to release him until dawn. This night would likely be no different. Except, this time Dominique wasn't worried about the coming day so much as he was about Cassidy.

He strained his ears for any clues about what was happening in and around the mansion. For a while, only indistinct rummaging, traffic, and footsteps reached him. Muted radio chatter was his first clue of what was about to happen. The throaty rumble of marine engines waking up confirmed it.

Apokryphos was making ready to leave.

That Kambyses would be aboard was a given. That Cassidy was with him was inevitable. That Dominique would have no way to reach them once the yacht was at sea was inescapable.

Their thousand-year battle had already begun.

The sound that exploded out of him was more than a scream. It was his soul turning inside out and flying into the room with a shattering physical presence. Furniture rattled across the floor, books shivered off shelves, and statues toppled. The wall of black glass exploded before the power of his wrath roaring into the night—promising revenge.

22

FEAR

B ijou came at dawn.

Beyond the shattered glass walls, the sky was brighter than Dominique had seen it since his mortal days. His eyes watered, but still he was conscious. His beast was anxious, but a long way from the usual blind panic. Perhaps it was the fire-blood. Or maybe he didn't care about himself anymore. Even his darkest nature quailed over the loss of Cassidy to a demonic madman.

He recognized the cadence of Bijou's heels click-clacking in the hall outside, but he didn't react when she pushed open the door. Dressed in a pale-green, floor-length satin slip, she stood, surveying the wreckage he had caused with his voice alone. "Are you quite done destroying my home?"

He didn't respond. He would burn the place to its foundation if he thought it would get him Cassidy back.

Bijou walked up to him. Her delicate nostrils twitched, taking in his altered scent. "So he gave you his vein. And this is how you repay him? Over a human?" Her round doll-like face pinched in an ugly sneer. "Stupid, stupid child."

"Get out and let me die in peace."

Her eyes narrowed as though she considered doing just that. But then she said, "That is not for me to say."

Grabbing both sword hilts at once, she yanked back with brutal force. Dominique's vision blurred as his left femur and right shoulder blade splintered in unison. He bit back the urge to scream, refusing to give her the satisfaction of seeing his pain. With an agonized grunt, he dropped to the ground. His injuries crackled, mending again with stunning speed.

Bijou dropped the bloody blades, letting them clatter on the tiles to either side of her stilettos. "You may spend the day as my guest," she said, her tone far from welcoming.

He sat up, mostly healed, though the bones in his shoulder and thigh still ached and prickled ferociously. "I would rather watch the sunrise."

She graced him with a long look that might have been grudging compassion. "I am not your enemy, you know."

"Oh? Are you not his to command, then?"

"I am. As are we all."

A shiver rippled through his innards with the coming sun. The first tendrils of fog swirled in his mind. Within ten minutes at most, its pull would suck him under. The beast had enough dawdling. Using the wood relief of the medieval warrior—now smeared with blood—for support, he stood and put weight on his leg, forcing the bone to finish healing faster. "Not me."

"Suit yourself." While he collected the swords and their scabbards, she retreated, but paused at the doorway to half-turn her head. "Know this, young one. Your sire is a man relishing his first good chase in centuries. The harder you run...the harder he will come after you."

When Dominique regained consciousness, he wondered why he was awake, even though he could still feel the sun's weight.

Then he remembered the sun groping for him with searing paws as he ran. At some point, his alter ego must have taken control and sunk him into this sandy grave.

Seconds later, he recalled the rest.

He exploded from the soggy ground under a hedge of sea grapes and violently shook the wet sand from his clothes and hair. Beneath a leaden gray sky, the ocean still shimmered in the day's last light. The dark bulk of *Apokryphos* was, of course, nowhere to be seen. Not that he expected Kambyses to make this easy for him.

Simmering with renewed rage, he tore through the seaside vegetation to retrieve his swords and raced back to Bijou's mansion. Tonight, he knew he had the strength to finish her. Apparently, so did she. The house contained not a single heartbeat, mortal or otherwise.

"*La prochaine fois,*" he promised the empty rooms on a growl. Next time. Next time, they would be more evenly matched. As long as next time was soon. His newfound abilities would weaken in a matter of days.

The bike was where he left it. It still dripped from the day's rain, but was otherwise untouched. When he pulled the helmet over his head, Cassidy's scent nearly undid him, nearly drove him over the edge into despair. But by the time he raced the bike up to Serge's lair half an hour later, he was back to unbridled fury.

Samantha burst from the door, bundled in an oversize gray sweater. "Thank God you're back. I've been worried sick all day."

"Keep worrying then," Dominique said as he pulled off the helmet.

"I...wait. Where's..." Whatever she saw in his face made her take a step back and hug herself. "Oh, God. What ha—?"

He vanished from the spot. There was no point explaining anything to someone so powerless to help.

Serge waited for him behind the cottage. He sat on a pontoon of his tiny vessel and stared at the rolling surf. The un-cleated sail flapped violently when Dominique bolted past, snatched up Serge, and pinned him to the wet sand. Serge gaped, mouth working like a landed fish amidst a dusting of beard.

"You knew this would happen, you filthy idiot," Dominique roared into his face. "You knew what danger she was in. You knew, and you let this happen!" His body tightened around his bones, and his canines lengthened. The kaleidoscope of color that was the beast's vision flared before his eyes, but with a shocking new intensity.

Serge's hands grabbed at Dominique's wrists, clawing, tearing, and pulling, but accomplishing nothing. His eyes, round and large enough to consume his face, locked on Dominique, not blinking even when a wave foamed over him. The old fool's fear of drowning apparently paled compared to the terror that seized him now: terror of Dominique. Dominique, who was suddenly the far stronger blood-drinker and could now snuff out three centuries of life in an instant.

For an ecstatic moment, he hungered to tear open the bobbing gullet and drink until nothing but an empty husk remained of his friend and mentor. *Know me!*

You hear my call every time you pierce a vein.

The memory of Kambyses's words acted like a cold slap to his face. This craving...this was his sire's will. More potent than ever perhaps, but not his.

Never his.

He released Serge. His almost-victim scrambled away as he sat and stared at his shaking hands. Hunger, rage, and helplessness pulsed through him, one after the other, over and over, until finally the cycle slowed, the beast subsided, and only Dominique remained.

Several waves broke around him, drenching him, filling his boots and leathers with water and sand. He had never felt so omnipotent. Or so vulnerable.

And...empty.

Serge was back at his boat. Soggy and trembling, he huddled in the sail's moon shadow. His bugging eyes tracked him up the beach, for once clearly focused on the present. Dominique sat on a pontoon with his back to his friend.

"Did you know what would happen? And do not tell me again that whatever will be, will be." His tone was devoid of all emotion, but the implied threat of his words was more real than any he had ever made.

Sand crunched under Serge's bare feet as he gingerly moved around the boat to Dominique's side. "Not exactly," he admitted. "I never see the details. Only the outlines, the possibilities."

"You could have warned her, stopped her. Stopped *us*. Even I believed that if it came to it, her blood...could..." He made a noise of sheer frustration. The fiberglass squeaked where his hands clamped onto the boat. "It made no difference at all. Now he has her where I have no hope of reaching her."

"What...it's...I mean—"

Dominique shot him a warning look, and Serge made a desolate little sound. "But you...you received something else you always wanted. Did you not?"

"His blood? Oh, yes. No one in their right mind should ever want five-thousand-year-old blood."

Serge recoiled, but his chin lifted a little as he sniffed for the new smoky edge in Dominique's scent. "What did you see?" His voice was barely audible with awe. When Dominique shook his head, Serge took the hint and changed the subject. "You will need that strength, blood-child," he proclaimed. "You will be glad for it."

"I already know that all this vile power is not enough against him. What can I possibly do with it to save Cassidy from whatever fate he has in store for her?"

Serge's mouth flattened as though fighting to hold back a swarm of wasps.

"You know, don't you? If my having his blood is so important, you must have seen this"—he made air quotes with one hand—"outline. And you know that without Cassidy, there is no me. Without her, there is no future for you to claim as so critical. So how do I do it? How do I save her?" He leaned closer and dropped his voice. "How do I save the peace I have only just found?"

Serge fiddled the buttons on his shirt. "That peace is gone, blood-child. That, you lost the moment you took his blood. Your destiny is now...set."

"To hunt him for a thousand years?" Dominique sneered. "Come now, oracle. You can do better than that."

Serge shrugged, first one shoulder, then the other. "I could, but—"

Dominique reached out with one hand and seized Serge by his wet collar. "No 'but!' I am done walking into one catastrophe after another in the name of your damned prophecy."

"But don't you see? Whatever I tell you will change what you do and so change everything. I'm only the witness. Not a doer."

"But don't *you* see?" Dominique mocked on a hiss and pulled Serge so close their noses almost touched. "You are the one who started it all the night you couldn't keep your filthy fangs off Cassidy. Without your interference—yes, interference," he snapped when Serge cringed "—she would not have left Jackson, and we would have never crossed paths. My destiny exists because of her and, therefore, because of you. Now finish what you started and tell me what I must do."

Serge shook as if his ribcage contained a rotor spinning off balance. "If I d-do that, you will n-never see her again."

Dominique released him with a disgusted shove, stood, and glared down at the wretched creature. "You are worse than useless."

"I can't tell you what you're not ready to hear." Serge slid off the pontoon and onto unsteady legs. "Or what you already know."

"I know nothing. Why else would I be here trying to get you to talk sense?"

Serge nodded, hesitant at first, then with more vigor. "Good. This is good. You do know that you need help."

"*Enculé!* Then help me."

"Not me. I am only the witness."

Dominique growled and took a menacing step. Serge held up a hand. "You know, blood-child. You know what you need to do. You always do."

Something in this earnest pronouncement gave him pause. Did he? True, he had no hope of finding—much less rescuing—Cassidy on his own, but if he couldn't, then no one else could either. No one, except maybe—

Dominique straightened with shock. "*Non.*"

Serge plastered his wet hair back against his skull with both hands and lifted one shoulder in a there-you-have-it shrug. "You see? You know."

"Never," Dominique hissed.

"You know what you need to do. You will find a way."

"And you know what you need to do with this useless thing, right?" He kicked the side of the little sailboat hard enough for the whole thing to bounce a foot off the ground. "Find a way, *vieux fou*," he commanded and darted away.

Dominique left the drenched leathers and sand-clogged boots on the front porch and entered his home. Lights blazed. The TV blared. The air stank of Chinese takeout. For a moment, he didn't know who the large man on the sofa was. So much had happened since he invited Cassidy's father to move in—to be there for his daughter when the inevitable happened to Dominique. Now that the unthinkable had transpired instead, the last thing he wanted to deal with was an ignorant human in his lair.

A piece of food slipped off Gil's chopsticks and plopped onto the faded automotive logo emblazoned on his white T-shirt. He swiped at it with a paper napkin as he got up, uncertainly eyeing Dominique's nakedness. To his credit, however, that was not his primary concern. "Where's my daughter?"

Dominique opened his mouth, but the impulse to compel the nuisance to leave evaporated. Sending away her father would have been an admission that Cassidy was truly gone. "She is traveling for work," he said. "She will be back as soon as she can."

"Will she now? Well, then. She might have mentioned—"

"You are alone in this house," Dominique continued, this time lacing his voice with compulsion. "No one else is here with you."

Gil blinked and looked around as if he heard a noise he couldn't place. He shook his head and sat back down, took a swig of beer from a bottle, and returned to stabbing his food with the chopsticks.

Standing there, naked and raw, Dominique sensed himself becoming invisible to more than just this one man. All he had ever treasured, the entire mortal world, seemed to move on without him. Before the emptiness could overwhelm him, he moved up the stairs into the main bedroom.

The cherry-wood bed was drenched in her honeyed-fruit smell and the memories they had made there. Her personal items—the carryall on a chair, the picture of herself with her mother on the dresser, the clothes discarded on the foot of the bed, a pair of worn sandals on the floor—all awaited her imminent return.

In the bathroom, he stepped into the roomy shower of turquoise tile, and turned on the water. They had made some memories here too, he and Cassidy.

The spray turned scalding hot against his face and scalp. He ignored it, shaking all over again with the memory of her wilted body hanging in the arms of an eternal hunger, a beast like no other. Where had it all gone so wrong? The first night he encountered Bijou? Did he still have a choice then? What was it that stopped him from confiding in Cassidy when he wanted nothing more than to be one with her? Some vague fear of something completely unjustified? A lack of trust in her?

Or in himself?

"Fool, fool, *fool*!" He pounded the heel of his hand at the slick wall and heard several tiles crack. Crack the way his world cracked—even shattered—because of his own blind stubbornness.

No, not stubbornness.

Fear, he thought and turned off the water. He lived in fear since the moment he had been turned. Fear of the sun, of his sire, of those stronger than him. Fear of losing himself. Fear of losing Cassidy.

Fear.

It dictated everything he did.

difference. Her voice shook only a little. "Your guest? I don't remember accepting an invitation."

He peered at her with one unblinking eye in which the pupil threatened to consume all the white.

She steeled herself. "Where's Dominique?" Nothing. "Did you leave him there for the sun to find?" Good God, how did she forget all this during the day and believe she was on a mere leisure cruise with Monica, her new bestie? This was one hell of a powerful compulsion. And the only reason she was aware of it now was because Kambyses permitted her to be aware.

He sat up and pushed that magnificent skein of hair away from his face. His skin was almost translucent; she could see ribbons of indigo veins spider along his jaw and temple, and wrap around his joints. Grabbing the back of his neck, he tilted his head as though stretching out a kink. The gesture was so human it startled her as much as it reassured her. Or was that him somehow compelling her again?

His mouth curved in a tiny, indulgent smile. "I prefer you like this. I wish to experience your true self."

"What have you done with Dominique?" she tried again, her true self not liking where this conversation was going.

"Nothing of consequence."

"Other than turning him into something he doesn't want to be, of course."

"He has much to learn of what he is."

"Does he? And whose fault is that?" She glared a challenge at this man who had walked the ancient world.

He sobered, and she silently congratulated herself for getting through to him, for possibly touching the human in this being as she had in Dominique. Which, of course, had been her sole reason for wanting to meet Kambyses in the first place—to have him taste her blood, join with his mind, and reintroduce him to his humanity. Given his age and presumed influence over his descendants, this had to be the way to trigger those changes Serge prophesied.

Also, it might save her life.

Had he fed from her, though? She couldn't remember. She felt no soreness on her neck and nothing in her head felt out of place. Then why the hell was she here on this yacht with him? Why was she still alive? Where was Dominique?

Unease squelched in the pit of her belly, but she refused to let it balloon and interfere with what might be a productive conversation with this extraordinary being.

When he remained quiet, she tucked her hair behind her ears and put her journalist hat firmly in place. "Will you tell me something? Why do you pursue him when he's made it so clear that he wants nothing more to do with you?"

This earned her a slight frown on the prominent brow. "You know what I am and what I can do, and yet...your only thoughts and words are of Nico. Why?"

"Is—isn't he the reason I'm here?"

"You are the reason you are here. Your...hold on him...fascinates me."

"So we're back to Dominique. Why are you so fascinated by him? He's a product of the twenty-first century. I'm sure you know older, more interesting vampires to hang out with?"

Kambyses's gaze grew unfocused as he stared past her. "None are like him." His voice sounded as mesmerized as it was mesmerizing. He appeared caught in his own dream as he continued. "Nico is the very essence of us. He is brash, yet he loves. He is courageous, but he fears. He can be brutal, and so very tender. He is...pure emotion." His voice dropped to a reverent whisper. "And I will have him. I will have his devotion. Above all, I will have his heart." The cold, black eyes locked onto hers. "You are his heart, are you not?"

A shiver rattled her as she tried to make sense of what he said. "You—you're using me to control him?"

He shook his head, a movement so slight she almost missed it. "You will help me teach him what he must know to be at peace with himself. Is that not what you wish for him?"

She could scarcely get the words out. "He is at peace. When he drinks from me."

Kambyses sounded almost bored. "A rare but unfortunate compatibility of the blood, nothing more. It shackles him to a mortal world that is beneath him now."

"Does it?" she murmured, only too aware of her own status as the only mortal in the room. What did he imagine her part in this lesson should be? As a lesser life form, her chances of survival hovered near zero, if not below—unless she made herself a heck of a lot more important to him—and fast.

Letting the sheet slide down to expose her shoulders, she moistened dry lips with the tip of her tongue and regarded him from beneath lowered lashes. "Have you ever experienced such a connection?"

He watched her, hawk-like, but said nothing.

"Have you ever been that known to anyone?"

He tilted his head. She let the cover drop all the way to her waist and leaned toward him on one arm, exposing the side of her neck with her best vein. "Have you considered that since Dominique and I have this connection, you and I might also?"

Kambyses sounded entranced. "You wish to know me? As you know him?"

"Yes." It was like sprinkling catnip before a cat. She knew she had him when his pupils expanded the rest of the way, obliterating all the whites of his eyes. The fangs emerged between full lips and his face narrowed, his flesh hewing closer to his bone as his beast rose.

No, not catnip, she decided, fighting not to recoil. More like raw meat...before a hungry tiger.

No fear, Chandler, she exhorted herself. *You can do this.* Not that there were other options short of leaping overboard. If she was to be deemed worthy of survival beyond her value as a hostage, she had to connect with this being. He would have to feed from her. She would have to know his mind.

Holding his gaze, she lay back in the pillows and arranged herself so that her neck was exposed and inviting, along with her cleavage in the red lace negligee.

Kambyses bent over her, a smothering wave of smoke and ash. She heard him inhale her scent before he scooped her up and held her tight enough to constrict her breathing. She gripped his arms, silky and hot to the touch, and tried to loosen his hold, but wriggling out of a burning trash compactor would have been easier.

Cassidy closed her eyes and fought the claustrophobic panic threatening to suck her under. *Keep it together, Chandler. A few more seconds and this will all be over.*

He murmured something in her ear in a language she didn't understand. Then those fangs pierced her skin, hard and deep.

Know me!

Kambyses struck her conscious mind like a lightning bolt shattering a moonless night. Blinded and incoherent, her thoughts staggered about, groping for the intruder.

There was nothing there.

No link, not even a whisper of one, and no control over what he showed her, what he made her experience.

She saw her blushing self in his memories when he first encountered her, heard the wet rush of her blood in his ears, smelled the raw terror Dominique tried so hard to hide. All of it stoked a raging jealousy tearing through Kambyses. Jealousy of her, this mere mortal girl who had such a hold on the chosen one.

Chosen for what? She didn't know. He didn't show her. But he did show her how he spun a dream for her that night, that he fed from her. He showed her Dominique watching, immobilized and in a helpless, murderous rage.

The virtual floor vanished beneath her feet, dropping her into a free-fall toward oblivion. She heard the ancient vampire's hoarse whisper from the fathomless depths.

Know me.

So she did. And she knew Kambyses resented her beyond all measure.

But he would not destroy her.

No, that he would leave for Dominique.

24

Hunter's Lair

"**B**aby? I think you need to come back here."

Jackson groaned under his breath. What did he have to do to keep this woman satisfied? His dick lay exhausted in his hand as he relieved himself. It was doubtful that Avery would get another rise out of him this morning, but she sounded determined to try.

"Babe?"

"Can I finish my piss?" he said more sharply than he intended. She didn't respond. He knew better than to think she was offended. Nor would it matter if she was. Money and fucking were the extent of her interests, and he provided both in spades, though he would cut back on the latter the moment she was pregnant. Heirs to secure the Striker family line were all his father and uncle asked of him these days. That and a wife who harbored no ambitions beyond marrying into a prominent family, and was as pleasing to the eye as she was dim. Uncle Garrett had selected Avery for him based on these exacting requirements.

"Can you piss faster?"

He ground his teeth and willed his bladder to slow down. He had refused to see this woman, one year his senior, for months. Then his father threatened to disown him unless he fell in line and fast. He was done waiting for Jackson to get over Cassidy, a woman who, besides being too bright for her own good, was also enslaved to a vampire and therefore lost to him.

Officially, anyway.

By some unfathomable miracle, she still lived and seemed very much herself. Sometimes he could cajole her into useful conversation. Eventually he'd get an opening to reach her, make her see reason, or, better yet, take that cunning bastard blood-sucker out of the picture entirely.

Until then, Jackson would bide his time, be vigilant, and do what he was told. Even if that meant screwing until his dick fell off with a woman who didn't give a shit about him outside his family's bank accounts and his ability to keep it up in bed. Which right now he definitely couldn't. He checked his Rolex, which she insisted he wear to bed. Ten past five in the morning.

"I need to get going," he called and flushed to drown out her renewed plea. Snatching up a discarded pair of briefs and his running shorts, he pulled them on. He didn't look at the dark-haired woman in the bed as he paced past, toward his walk-in closet. "Time for my run, babe."

"You're going to leave me here alone with him?"

He turned on the light to locate a fresh shirt. He also pocketed one of the small full-spectrum flashlights he kept stashed here. These were a required night-time precaution for more reasons than being able to see.

The indignant words didn't register until he reached for his shoes. With him? Which him? The only "him" he could think of in his suite at this time of day was Garrett. His uncle didn't much respect anyone's privacy, especially where clandestine Foundation business was concerned.

But Garrett wasn't in the house. Garrett wasn't even in the country. Or had he returned without telling anyone?

Shoes in hand, Jackson emerged into the bedroom, ready for an argument. After the bright light in the closet, the room—lit only by the soft flicker of a gas fireplace—was filled with pockets of obscurity. The bed was clear enough, though. Instead of lounging provocatively as she had earlier, Avery sat with the satin sheets drawn up over her breasts. Haughty displeasure radiated off her. Beside the bed, the balcony door stood ajar, letting in cool night air. His flesh tingled with the chill of premonition. "Leave you alone with who?"

She jerked her chin at the far corner of the room. "He says you know him."

Jackson peered into the shadows where an occasional chair contained another, perfectly still shadow.

He dropped the shoes and reached for the flashlight in his pocket. "What the fuck are you doing here?" he barked, twisting the burgeoning fear into outrage. "Avery, you need to go. Now."

Avery hesitated only a moment before scooting off the bed. With the sheet trailing behind her, she collected her clothes from the floor.

The vampire in the corner stirred. Firelight edged the acute cheekbones and long nose in gold and glinted in the unruly black hair. His attention was riveted on Avery.

"Hurry up," Jackson said. He had to get her out of there before Nick decided to show off his feeding skills again. Fuck, they couldn't afford another human caught up in Foundation business.

"I'm going, I'm going. Chill."

"You should feed her better before you breed her," the obstinate French bastard of a vampire drawled. "She is far too skinny to carry a plate of food, much less a child."

Avery spun on a heel. "Excuse me?"

"Go." When she didn't move, indignation flashing in her eyes, Jackson grabbed her arm and propelled her into the hallway toward the suite's door.

She dug in her heels. "Hey! Let go of me. What the fuck is wrong with you?"

"Sorry. I'll explain later, I promise. But go. Please, just go." While she still could.

"You better," she huffed. With one last irate look at both of them, she tossed the sheet to the ground and marched away, wearing nothing but an armful of clothes. From behind, she looked to be all of fifteen years old.

"Will you explain? Truly?" the vampire mocked.

"Shut the fuck up and get out." Jackson jerked a thumb towards the balcony door. "Right now."

"Or what? You're going to annoy me with your little light?"

His hand closed around the flashlight in his pocket. It was a decent enough defense, if used without warning, but Nick was right. To a bloodsucker who knew what it was, the burning sting would only be a momentary nuisance, because a moment is all it would take to kill whoever pointed it at him. Jackson didn't pull out the weapon, but he kept a firm grip on it. "Oh, I've got much bigger things planned for you."

"Oh, I know."

The bland acknowledgment confused Jackson for a moment. Head games again? Well, at least Jackson still had entertainment value. Good. The longer he could keep the vampire interested, the more opportunity Jackson had to finish him.

"So, what's your game tonight?" Jackson prodded. "How are you planning to scare the shit out of me this time?" When there was no response, he charged ahead. "You've got to know that showing me you can get around our defenses is only going to make us lock them down that much harder." Assuming this creature wouldn't just slaughter everyone in the house tonight. He quickly shoved aside this thought, along with the fear that came with it.

"I didn't 'get around' your defenses, *toi idiot*. I hacked them."

Jackson scoffed. "Riiight. This system isn't even on the Internet."

A smile ghosted across the vampire's face. "But your phone is, *non*?"

He glanced at the device sitting on the nightstand and felt his insides turn over. The security app tied into the primary system via local Wi-Fi, and, yes, damn him, of course the phone was on the Internet.

"You hacked...my phone." How the fuck had he missed this possibility? "Okay. You made your point. Yes, you can feed without killing if you want to. Congratulations." He made a sweeping gesture with one hand. "And, yes, you can break into my house. You're one badass vamp. Is that what you want from me? You got it. Now go."

Nick leaned forward, elbows on his thighs, and regarded Jackson with an expression of serious thought. More of him was now visible in the warm light, which made him look so deceptively human. He wore a simple black, long-sleeved V-neck shirt with jeans and scuffed running shoes. No leathers, no swords, no attitude. Nothing about him telegraphed a threat.

Jackson knew better. His grip on the little flashlight in his pocket tightened.

"I assure you I no more want to be here than you want me to be here, but I am out of options. I—" He shook his head as if in disbelief at what he was about to say. "I need...your help."

Jackson grinned. Damn, this fucker was good. "Decided to call it quits?"

Nick blinked. "What?"

"Because you know that the only thing I'll ever help you with is turning you into a pile of ash."

The future pile of ash got up and took several slow steps in Jackson's direction, his thumbs hooked into the pockets of his pants. "Tell me something. The book you gave Cassidy. It implies that if one of us is destroyed, so are all those they made and all those made by them and so on. Is this true? Have you seen this happen?"

An actual conversation? Was this guy for real? "Oh, it's true all right. Uncle Garrett has seen it happen."

Nick seemed to consider this. He rubbed his jaw, murmured something in French, and nodded. "*D'accord*. So be it." Meeting Jackson's gaze, he said, "Hunter, I give you my sire. You do with him—with us—as you wish."

For one breathless moment, Jackson believed him. Then he laughed. "You're out of your mind if you think I'd fall for that. Whatever game you're playing now, I won't be a part of it."

"This is no game." A note of frustration edged Nick's voice.

"Then why would you make such an offer?"

"For the only reason I have done anything since the night she appeared in my lair—Cassidy."

"You're not seriously telling me this is her idea."

Suddenly, the vampire was within touching distance. Impatience drew his sweeping brows together over his knife-blade nose. Too startled to think, Jackson whipped out the flashlight and beamed it at Nick's face. For a fraction of a second, the vampire's features flashed a luminous white.

Then Jackson's arm jerked back, his entire body spun on its axis, and his front slammed into the nearest wall with enough force to spill the air from his lungs. He fought for breath, only dimly aware of the screaming ligaments in his shoulder—and the bloodsucking menace crushing him in place.

A resonant growl at his ear. "Did I not say I find that annoying?"

"*Get. Off. Me.*"

The bloodsucker ran his tongue up the side of Jackson's neck, triggering a slew of horrific memories and a fresh flood of terror-induced fury. Jackson slammed his free fist into the wall and thrashed between it and the vampire. He tried to scream for help, but his burning lungs scarcely managed a hoarse wheeze. Not that anyone could have helped him. At least not in time. Come morning, they would find him like his brother, drained and dismembered.

"I should just pierce your vein, drench you with serum, and compel you senseless," the vampire said against Jackson's pulsing jugular.

Fighting to subdue the flashbacks, Jackson tried to ready himself for the attack. Physically, he lost this fight before it ever began, but mentally, there was still a lot he could do to ward off a compulsion, even if backed up with a dose of serum. Or so he hoped. It wasn't like he had much opportunity to practice that.

But instead of chomping on him, Nick spoke again, sounding weary. "Did you ever love her?"

It took Jackson a moment to focus on the words. Her...Cassidy. Of course, he loved her. And he would continue to do so for as long as there was breath in his body, which at the moment was precious little. Not that he was about to share that with a vampire fishing for an emotional response.

"What's it to you?" he croaked.

"Right now? Everything."

With that, Jackson was free and staggered off the wall. He caught his footing and gingerly tested his abused arm. Sore, but not broken.

His assailant stood halfway across the room again, thumbs back in his pockets. "My sire has found me, and I was foolish enough to think I could reason with him. I was even more foolish to allow Cassidy into his presence. He took her."

Jackson's every nerve thrilled with reluctant alarm. If he was being manipulated, he was being played by a master. But until he knew Cassidy was safe, he couldn't afford to ignore the possibility that the vampire was telling the truth. He finally managed to draw a full breath again. "Took her? Why?"

"To control me. She is interesting to him only until I either submit or flee. Then she will be dead."

Or worse, Jackson amended to himself and flexed his aching shoulder. "So why don't you run?"

"Did you miss the part where I said she would die?"

"No, I got that." He cleared his throat forcefully, hating the still somewhat strangled sound of his voice. "What I don't get is why you would care. She's human. We're expendable in your world, aren't we? God knows enough of my family has been."

Nick searched his face. "Not to all of us. Not all of them."

Something about the raw, haunted tone caught Jackson off-guard, and it wasn't a compulsion. "My God. You really are in love with her."

Nick's silence was all the confirmation he needed—and sparked a whole new kind of animosity. It was one thing to think that Nick spirited Cassidy away with supernatural charm, quite another to consider that there was a true emotional connection between them. "How's that even possible?"

A thin smile curved Nick's wide mouth. "You never fail to underestimate me, do you?"

"Fuck you."

His expression darkened. "We can discuss this some other night if you wish, but right now I need to know if you will help me locate and rescue Cassidy."

Some other night? Right. If the offer was genuine, Nick wouldn't have too many more of those. "I thought you knew where she is."

"She is on a yacht, the *Apokryphos*, which is somewhere offshore."

"A yacht. Offshore," Jackson repeated. That made sense, given what they already knew about Nick's sire and his sea-going habits, but also complicated things exponentially.

"*Oui*. At some point, *Apokryphos* will return, or I will be contacted, but I don't want to give him that much time with Cassidy. I need to get her free of him, but this vessel is as adept at hiding as her master. I have no way of locating them quickly on my own, and even if I did, I could only approach them at night."

"Which means you'd be picking a fight you can't win."

Nick closed his eyes and hung his head in unspoken agreement. They ran his vamp DNA when they had him captive this summer—before Cassidy risked her life breaking him out. There was a good reason he was such a dominant youngling. His sire was no garden-variety bloodsucker.

Jackson scratched at his chin, trying to look more casual than he felt about having an actual conversation with a creature he was sworn to kill. Unbelievable that he considered agreeing to this. Besides the chance to charge to Cassidy's rescue, the opportunity to take out an ancient one, along with all his spawn, only came along once every couple of centuries, if that. He couldn't afford to ignore this.

If he wasn't being played.

He tried not to smile as he touched the small St. Christopher medallions at his throat. He, too, knew how to play games.

"All right. You have my attention. Let's talk."

25

The Key and The Lock

The old fool had been right.

If Serge had hinted at even half of how this bizarre night would unfold, Dominique never would have started down this path. Asking Jackson Striker for help turned out to be the least of it.

Dominique was beyond incredulous when Jackson made a request of him as well—compel Avery. They found her, now dressed, in the suite's sitting room, eavesdropping on her intended husband and wavering between confusion and terror. He eased her mind with a simple command to return to bed and remember nothing unusual.

He also suggested that she rethink her relationship with the Striker heir and consider a more docile mate.

After she had gone, he tried for an amicable expression. "You're welcome?"

Jackson shook his head, his face coloring straight up to his hairline. He turned away and slipped into a pair of flip-flops by the door. "Let's go, smartass."

"Where are we going?"

"A place we can talk."

Dominique glanced back at the balcony door through which he had entered, the only exit he knew for sure was safe. Following his nemesis deep into this vampire hunting clan's fortress of a home, with little more than an hour to spare before dawn, seemed ludicrous. Had Serge mentioned this possibility, Dominique might have laughed outright.

But Serge would have been right. And Dominique wasn't laughing.

Soundless, he moved across the Italian marble floors in Jackson's wake, all his senses keyed to the quiet house, which didn't feel as defenseless as he thought it should be. By the time they arrived at a staircase of polished oak, at the end of a narrow back hallway, his apprehensions morphed into an electric prickle of outright dread. These stairs, he knew, led to a hidden, window-less room on the third floor, guarded by an electronically sealed, steel-core door. This was the Striker Foundation's inner sanctum, the core of a centuries-old operation dedicated to destroying immortals.

"You coming?" Jackson asked from halfway up the stairs.

"Why is this necessary?"

"You'll see."

"What I see is you behaving very much as you did when you trapped me in a plane," Dominique countered dryly.

"The plane you trashed, yes. I've yet to hear the end of that. I won't let you do that to this house, believe me."

He cocked his head. Wasn't going to *let* him? "Cassidy doesn't have time for us to play these games."

"So, what're you doing standing there? Let's go." Jackson ascended several more steps.

"Why?"

"Oh, for fuck's sake. Our office is where the computer is that will let me get in touch with Uncle Garrett," he explained, gesturing back and forth with both hands. "If you're going to tell us everything we need to know, you're going to do it for both of us together."

"Garrett," Dominique growled. Just the mention of the name made his flesh crawl with the remembered agony of the torture that despicable man had inflicted on him.

Jackson eyed him carefully. "What? You didn't expect me to run a raid operation by myself, did you?"

Dominique hadn't thought anything at all about the details. He'd been too desperate to find a way out for Cassidy at any price. Now that price would include having to rely on his tormentor. "*Merde.*"

"Do I detect a problem?"

"Your *uncle*"—he intoned the term with great contempt—"is a savage. I fully expect to die if you are successful, but if your uncle feels the need to sacrifice Cassidy to annihilating my sire, you know he will do just that. In which case, the result is the same no matter what I do—she will die—and I have no reason for being here, much less following you up there."

The tension that rode Jackson's shoulders seemed to ease along with the snide belligerence. "Never thought I'd say this, but I actually agree with you." His hands stopped clutching at the carved-wood rail. "But I still can't do this by myself, and if we can't convince Garrett that what you're offering is legit, he won't lift a finger to help."

Dominique watched Jackson's grip tighten on the rail again. "Do *you* believe what I'm offering is...legit?"

A grudging nod. "I do now."

Now? What had changed his mind? "What about Cassidy?"

"I will do everything I can to get her out of there in one piece and let Garrett worry about the rest."

He still didn't like it, but he felt a warm resonance of sincerity against his ear. This was the only chance Cassidy had, and he couldn't stand in its way because he feared one of the potential outcomes.

Resolved to his path, he moved up the steps.

Jackson waited for him on the landing at the top. When Dominique joined him in the tiny space, the skin on his face and hands prickled with uncomfortable heat. He lowered his head, only to have the sensation crawl down the back of his neck.

"Oh, yeah. Forgot about the light," Jackson said. "That's a full—"

Dominique jabbed his fist through the offending bulb in the low ceiling. The landing plunged into semi-darkness, and hot shards rained over them both.

"Well, it *was* a full-spectrum bulb," Jackson finished, brushing the glittering glass out of his short hair.

"I assume there will be more of them?" If there were, he'd stop right here.

The hunter pressed his thumb to a reader embedded in the wall. The red light beside it turned green with a cheerful warble. "No," he said, and pushed the door open.

The room inside, Striker Foundation headquarters, was lined with bookcases carved of solid wood and loaded with thousands of meticulously ordered volumes. Time oozed from the masses of yellowed paper and worn leather covers, and streamed out the door on a cool, dusty dry current of air. Interspersed between the stacks, covering every bare piece of wall, were portraits of regal men. Jackson shared his square-jawed, fierce-eyed countenance with most of them, his forebears.

The lights brightened. There was no hint of heat. Still, Dominique hesitated. With no other doors or windows, this room had "trap" written all over it. There was no telling what manner of devious devices it hid in the ornate furnishings and recessed lights.

Jackson waited, calm as any hunter waiting for his prey to make a fatal mistake.

Dominique kicked off his shoes. With two solid whacks, he crammed them between the frame and the door, jamming it open.

Jackson let out a sharp breath but didn't comment.

Barefoot, Dominique crossed the parquet to a massive weathered desk in the room's center. Two wide, curved displays sat at the ends, streaming data, images and snippets of video. This was the Grid, the nerve center of a world-wide network, constantly collecting and analyzing information for any clue of blood-drinker activity. God help the hapless immortal who triggered it.

"Stay back for now," Jackson directed as he sat and brought up the encrypted video app on one monitor. The call rang six times before it connected. The sleep-mussed visage of a middle-aged male wobbled into focus on the cinematic curve of the display. A rumpled, empty bed took up most of the background.

"Do you know what time it is here, kid?" Garrett Striker said by way of hello, his unshaven face scrunched up and lined with the imprints of linen wrinkles. He smoothed his dark hair over his scalp with one hand and glared at the web cam.

A soft, involuntary growl vibrated in the back of Dominique's throat at the sight of this human who made most blood-drinkers look like angels of mercy. If not for Cassidy, he would have already killed him. Though if he had, there would be no hope for her now. "All is as it must be," Serge often said, and in this case, Dominique could not disagree.

"We have a target I'll need your help with," Jackson said without preamble. "An ancient."

Garrett reached for something out of frame, slid a pair of reading glasses on his nose, and squinted down. "I didn't get any alerts from the Grid."

"We didn't get this from the Grid."

He pulled the glasses off again, suspicion now sharpening his gaze. "Where did we get it from then?"

"A one hundred percent reliable source."

"Oh. I see. This is some story that Chandler girl fed you?"

"Not exactly."

"Not at all, Jack. You know everything coming out of her mouth is suspect."

Crossing his arms, Dominique leaned against a bookshelf and watched every nuance of the exchange. He could smell the frustration seeping from the hunter.

New tension hardened Jackson's eyes and jaw. "Dominique's sire showed up, and we've got a real chance of taking him out."

"I just bet he did."

"Listen—"

"No, you listen." Garrett's fingertip grew huge on the monitor. "The only thing that youngling ghoul is interested in is drawing us out—drawing *me* out—so he can get his revenge in the nastiest possible way. He's had months to come up with a scheme because you couldn't do your goddamn job and put him down when you had the chance. And now you wake me up in the middle of the goddamn night—"

"Get over yourself. He doesn't want you anymore," Jackson broke in.

"—because you're too dim to know when you're being played."

"Will you shut up and listen? There's a human life at stake here. I believe Cassidy is in real danger from this target."

"In more danger than she has been? Hard to believe."

"She's been abducted."

Garrett blinked and sat back. "Oh, now I see. The baby vamp has been feeding you this himself, has he? Has he been feeding *from* you, too? I'm betting he's compelled the crap out of you. Go sleep it off."

Jackson threw up both hands, but his jaw clamped down on whatever colorful epithet was about to hurtle from his mouth.

"Are you two done?" Dominique said. "The night is getting old."

Garrett sat up abruptly. "Who the—"

The look Jackson shot Dominique threatened to draw blood. He turned back to his uncle. "Yes, I got this intel from Nick. No, he didn't compel me. And, no, he does not want your sorry ass. He wants to get Cassidy away from his son-of-a-bitch sire, and he can't get her without us. And I believe all that because I practically had to twist his fucking arm to convince him I wasn't about to go up against an ancient by myself. He would just as soon not see your ugly face again, and right now, I honestly can't blame him."

"Jack—" Garrett said, the single word alive with warning.

"And now he's going to spill his guts and tell us everything we need to know." Jackson got up. "Nick. Get your ass in this chair and start talking."

Dominique raised a dubious brow. This was not the sort of tone to which he responded well. But Jackson and Garrett would know this, too—and if compelled, Jackson would never speak to him like this. This young hunter was even more cunning than he had given him credit for. He correctly reasoned that if Dominique really was after Garrett and concocted Cassidy's abduction as a ruse, he would have been eager to involve Jackson's uncle, luring him out of hiding and exacting well-deserved vengeance.

Not that Dominique didn't want to exact vengeance. But for now, this was a secondary pursuit.

Twisting up a corner of his mouth in grudging respect, he sauntered to the desk and slid into the still-warm chair. He took a moment to relish the flash of horrified recognition on Garrett's blanching face. The impulse to crawl through the screen and tear this man limb from limb vibrated in his bones. Instead, he spoke mildly. "What would you like to know?"

"Jackson," Garrett yelled, leaning away from the webcam as though reading Dominique's mind.

His nephew, who sat with one hip hiked up on the edge of the desk, ducked into the frame. "Yes?"

"Are you going to do something about this?"

Jackson glanced at the door stuck open thanks to the strategically placed shoes. His lips pushed out. He shook his head. "Nope."

Dominique followed the look, then scanned the room again with his peripheral vision. There were inactive lighting fixtures recessed into the walls and ceiling that, given the room's size, seemed excessive. So it was a trap. If the door shut and those lights triggered, chances were he would be broiled alive. Dominique trusted Jackson with his life by walking in here, and now Jackson did likewise by remaining in his presence without a single defense left at his disposal.

"Have you lost all sense of—"

"Just listen to him. All we have to do is check his story out during the day."

"I have no interest in—"

"It's his sire. Don't tell me you're not itching to end that bastard and Nick right along with him."

"Listen to yourself, you idiot. What you're saying doesn't even make sense. He'll never let you put down his sire, knowing that'll kill him, too. If that's what you believe—"

"Not only me," Dominique interrupted. He was done listening to the familial bickering. They were wasting night. "I suspect thousands descend from him. You are welcome to all our blood as long as you get Cassidy out of danger."

Jackson gestured at Dominique. "Any questions?"

Garrett stared at his nephew and the blood-drinker waiting for him to come to grips with a situation all three of them would have considered inconceivable only an hour ago. When he didn't speak, Jackson volunteered all that Dominique had shared with him so far, asking clarifying questions along the way. Dominique answered as best he could about the yacht, its owner's habits, Bijou, and some details that led up to Cassidy's kidnapping. To his amazement, he and the hunter worked well together once they got past their innate hostilities and focused on the common goal of rescuing the woman they obviously both loved.

That last bit he tried not to think about. Since he wouldn't survive long enough to see her again, it didn't matter. At least she would know he gave his life for her.

"What do you think?" Jackson finished. "Are we doing this?"

Garrett still stared straight ahead, probably at Dominique on his screen, and rubbed a knuckle over his lower lip in thought. The shock and disbelief in his face had given way to something more guarded and calculating. "That depends. Does your demon sire have a name?"

Somehow, Dominique spoke the name without a trace of emotion.

"I see," Garrett said, leaning forward. "Don't suppose you know just how old this...Kambyses might be, do you?"

"He claims five-thousand years."

"Shit," Jackson whispered. His right hand fidgeted, the thumb rubbing two amputated fingers. "We knew your sire had to be old, but this—"

"Not just old," Garrett broke in. "Kambyses." He rolled the name around his mouth as though tasting a fine wine. "That's a myth name among their kind, one of several this guy has taken over the ages. The younger ones don't usually know much about it, though. Including you, I'd wager."

The small hairs all over Dominique's body rose in silent and primal warning. "I know enough, and I promise you, he is no myth."

"We never thought he was."

"Then why haven't I heard about him?" Jackson said.

"Because you're still working on getting all the facts straight, kid, and this is a character we didn't think we'd ever find." A smug smile spread across his hard face. "Kambyses isn't just 'old.' He is *the* oldest. The first one. The whole sorry lot began with him."

Dominique sat, motionless as stone, as his mind flashed back to the haunted abyss and eons of time in his sire's blood—and the utter lack of daylight in his memories.

"You're looking a little paler than usual there, Nicky," Garrett drawled. "I trust you know I'm right? And you've figured out what it means?"

He had. So had Jackson. "You mean when we take this thing out, we'll—"

"Destroy us all," Dominique whispered.

"All one hundred thirty-three thousand of you, give or take." Garrett hummed with anticipation. "Which is only the ones we know about, of course."

Dominique felt wispy, as close to fainting as he ever had. What had he done? For Cassidy, he had been willing to send thousands to their eternal deaths, himself included. Now he had irrevocably sealed the fate of them all. The hunters were on to the scent now, and while stopping Jackson would have been simple, he had no means to even reach Garrett, the far more efficient killing machine.

And what of Cassidy? She was at the center of this storm. He was doing this for her, for the slim chance that she would survive and carry with her the memory of their love.

For Cassidy, he would obliterate an entire world.

She is the key, and you are the lock. Together, you will change the world of night forever.

These were some of the first words Serge had ever said to him. Dominique had thought him mad. Now he shut his eyes and shuddered.

The old fool had been right.

26

PHANTOMS

Three days. Three fucking days.

Jackson sat strapped to his seat in the helicopter. The muscles in his jaw and neck threatened to snap with tension, and the pounding roar of the rotors flayed his nerves and thrashed his patience. Samana Cay was still ten minutes out. Dusk only another hour and a half after that, tops, and then another night for Cassidy with the most dangerous creature ever to walk the earth.

Three days.

Jackson's imagination ran wild with what all she had endured in the last four nights. His fist curled, itching to smash into something, anything.

Three days for Garrett to fly in from his South American hideout, to assemble their gear, organize their strategy—and find one lousy yacht. Between the two of them, everything but that last bit took less than a day. Finding *Apokryphos* should have been a simple matter of looking up her official tracking data, but anything named for its ability to remain hidden would, of course, not make it that easy for mere mortals to find her.

Nick had called Jackson the evening after his visit and railed at him—in both English and French—for, oddly enough, still being alive. "Are you truly so incompetent? This is over sixty meters of boat, very likely lurking very nearby. How can you not find such a thing, you imbecile?"

Normally they'd look up her AIS info and current coordinates, and be on their way. *Apokryphos* transmitted no such data. Or, if she did, falsified it. This search would take eyeballs. Coast Guard eyeballs, drone eyeballs, their eyeballs, even tourists-on-the-beach eyeballs.

"Where was all this eagerness to die when I had him in a cage?" Garrett said after the call disconnected. Jackson's uncle hadn't uttered a word during the conversation, which Jackson put on speaker for his benefit. Though nothing would have kept Garrett away from this ultimate of all hunts, he preferred his contact with their unlikely source to be as minimal as possible.

"You didn't use the right motivation. It's Cassidy he says he's willing to die for." That idea still brought him up short. Whether it was true for the vampire, would Jackson be willing to sacrifice himself for her? He liked to think he would, but...

Garrett snorted. "Right. He gave us a lead we can't afford to pass up. As long as they all end up dead, I don't care why."

They had poured over the incomplete data about *Apokryphos's* location, called in favors with patrols, and contacted Bahamian customs. There was no record anywhere of a vessel by that name or description. *Apokryphos* was a phantom.

"He may have gone straight out to sea and off the grid," Garrett said. "We may need to wait until he surfaces for Nicky. Assuming this thing exists at all, of course. We only have his word on that and your...hunch that he's telling the truth."

"I checked. Cassidy really is MIA from work and from home." Where he had found her father, of all unlikely people, believing that his daughter was out of town on business. "So I'll follow every clue we have to find her."

"Suit yourself."

Jackson kept digging through the data. This morning he finally spotted an oddity among the hundreds of vessels plying these waters, a "fishing charter" that seemed to have no interest in deep water and instead loitered around the uninhabited Samana Cay in the far eastern Bahamas. It had to be *Apokryphos*. The situation smelled right, especially after he couldn't get a hold of anyone on land connected with the mystery signal. If this wasn't the traveling lair of the legendary Kambyses, Jackson would be as incompetent as Nick proclaimed him to be.

His headphones crackled and the irritatingly cheerful voice of the pilot said in a mellow island lilt, "Coming up on Samana Cay, gentlemen."

It wasn't the Striker corporate helo they were in, but the first available flying bucket they could hire out of Nassau, an old Bell 206 Jet Ranger he hoped had a better maintenance record than its exterior suggested. The pilot, looking as battered as his transport, was in high spirits the moment he saw the brick of cash Garrett tossed at him. Nor did he question the duffel bags they insisted on hauling into the cramped passenger compartment.

Though he might have, had he known what they contained.

Garrett fitted a pistol with a full magazine and handed it to his nephew. Jackson chambered a round, confirmed the safety, and slid it into a holster strapped to his thigh. His uncle did the same. Both of them had donned Kevlar vests over their black, long-sleeved shirts. The pockets of their cargo pants were stuffed with extra ammunition, charged full-spectrum lights and vials of silver dust. Each carried knives sharp enough to sever spines.

Garrett also had a small backpack hanging off one shoulder. Jackson tried not to think about the contents, which was Garrett's idea of a weapon of last resort. There was enough C-4 in there to sink a small naval vessel in a matter of minutes. A yacht, probably in seconds. The thought made his nerves squirm. He was prepared to battle a vampire out to rip him apart, but would they really need to blow themselves up in the process?

No, it wouldn't come to that. Garrett wasn't that crazy. Right?

Jackson shook his head. This was no time to second-guess anything. He had to operate on instinct, and instinct dictated that he trust his uncle—with explosives.

He pushed the polarized sunglasses up his nose and cracked open the side window. Cool sea air blasted him as he angled for a better view. At the horizon, surrounded by dull blue water under a dull gray sky, was the dull green smear of Samana Cay, featureless and devoid of human life, remote to everything but seagulls and boats.

"And there're your friends," the pilot announced.

Jackson's heart jumped. Where? He sat up straighter and peered between the pilot and empty copilot seats out the front window. "Fuck."

Beside him, Garrett glanced up from reviewing the yacht's schematics drawn up from Nick's memory. "What have we got? The Queen Mary?"

No, this couldn't be. This just could not be. Jackson stared harder. It was. A bright white dot anchored in the island's shallow bay. A sport fisherman, maybe forty or fifty feet, sinister only to sailfish and Mahi.

"Want me to hail them, gentlemen?" the pilot inquired helpfully.

"No point," Jackson said, feeling his hands clench until the knuckles cracked. "That's not them."

Grinning, Garret shook his head and pocketed the drawing. "I knew it."

"No, you didn't. Or you would have let me fly out here by myself."

He shrugged. "Take it easy, kid. Patience is the key."

That was something Jackson had less of by the hour. "Carlos, we're leaving."

The chopper wiggled around in a hesitant turn over the island just as the sun broke through a gap in the clouds. "You sure you don't want to land here?"

"No, just turn this—wait!" Jackson tore off the sunglasses and pushed his face against the window. Something along the island's far shore, two miles away, caught the late afternoon light. Something he couldn't quite see.

A phantom.

"Carlos, head to the east shore."

Another turn, this one more enthusiastic.

"Are you going to get us home in time for dinner?" Garrett wondered, though his tone held more wariness than jest.

Jackson focused out the front window, desperately searching the dark-gray Atlantic waters, seeking one enormous shadow. He spotted the glint of bold, gold lettering first, then the much lighter teak deck as it came into view.

"Got you, you son of a bitch. Carlos, swing around. Let's take a closer look."

As they choppered several wide circles around the vessel, the hunters made note of every nuance with binoculars. Two hundred feet of ship cruised below, sleek and dark and barely there. Along her sides and across her aft, the stylized gold script announced her name to all unfortunate enough to spot her anyway.

Apokryphos.

The hidden.

"I'll be damned," Garrett muttered.

"Can we hail them?" Jackson called out to the pilot.

Over the headphones, they listened to Carlos trying to radio the yacht. It didn't respond until the third attempt. A chillingly unemotional male voice informed them they were on a leisure cruise, in no need of assistance, and receiving no guests.

"I hope you weren't expecting a welcome mat," Garrett said.

"Carlos, can you land this thing on their helipad?" The tiny space on the front deck looked tight, but clear of obstructions.

"They don't sound like—"

"Just do it. Someone on board needs help. Trust me."

Carlos swung around to eye the possibilities. "Wind is picking up. That boat is moving. It's risky, gentlemen."

"I'll spot you. Just get us close. We'll jump."

Garret raised both brows. "It's a bit late in the day for stunt work, don't you think?"

"You can go home and have dinner. I'm not letting this—*this*"—he stabbed a finger at their target—"get away. We let this go, we'll never see it again. We do this now, we retire tomorrow."

"Oh, please tell us more," Garrett said with a glance at the pilot. The man asked no questions about their trip, but at this rate, it wouldn't be much longer before he figured out bloodshed was involved.

Jackson sat back, glaring a challenge until Garrett sighed, raised his binoculars again, and became all business. A moment later, he gave the hand signal confirming that he saw no weapons pointing their way, at least not yet.

They were clear to go. He was in.

Opening the window as far as it would go, Jackson hung his head out and talked the reluctant Carlos into a wobbly approach while Garrett secured their gear.

The helo bounced in a wind gust and struck the rail with a strut. They jarred violently. The pilot fretted about lawyers he couldn't afford and called upon Jesus to run divine interference as he attempted another angle.

"Now," Jackson shouted, and they slammed to the deck, rattling every bolt in the fuselage and every bone in their bodies.

While Jackson pushed gear out the door, Garrett ordered the pilot to wait on the island and stay tuned to the radio for thirty minutes in case their plan to escape using the yacht's life boats didn't pan out. If they weren't ready to leave by then, they never would. The clock started ticking the second they set boots on *Apokryphos*. The helo hopped off the deck, leaving them crouched in its gusty backwash and dodging unsecured seat cushions. As their ride clop-clopped toward the island, silence descended, filled only by the quiet slaps and hiss of the sea against the ship's hull.

"You'd think they have people dropping in uninvited all the time," Jackson said, reaching for his gun.

Garrett stayed his hand. "Easy, Jack. Let's not look like a threat until we have to."

Looking straight back, they faced the bridge. Someone had to be watching them from behind those smoked windows. Watching them and not caring? Nick had said the crew was compelled to function as little more than automatons to operate and maintain the ship. His flesh crawled. He could almost feel the primal power envelop this vessel and everyone on it, even in the light of day.

They were about to embark on their mission when a woman rounded the outside of the bridge, wearing a black windbreaker, white palazzo pants, and a colorless smile. She walked tall and straight with confidence, her deep-red ponytail flying in the wind. "Welcome aboard *Apokryphos*."

Garrett put his hand on his gun. Their welcome committee kept her hands in her pockets, against the chill—or holding a weapon of her own? Smiling assassins were all too common in their line of work.

"You two look tense," the redhead said, following his hand's movement with her eyes. "Well, not to worry. Your travel nightmares are over." She removed her hands from her pockets to clasp them before her, empty. "I'm Monica Sol, manager of this fine vessel and the owner's representative."

"Well. Aren't you special," Garrett said, not moving his hand.

She lowered her head and blushed. "As a matter of fact, I am, yes."

"As it happens, we've dropped in to have a chat with—"

"Cassidy," Jackson broke in. "We're friends of Cassidy's."

"Right," Garrett agreed without missing a beat.

"Oh, how delightful." The hands now clapped, excited. "She'll be so happy to see you. I'm afraid she's been a little bored."

"I bet," Jackson said.

"Come, come." Monica gestured for them to follow and turned away. "You're just in time for dinner."

"Won't be staying for that," Garrett said under his breath. "Plan A."

Jackson nodded and fell in behind their hostess, whom Nick described as the least compelled mortal he had ever witnessed in his sire's presence. That made her either harmless—or the most dangerous person on the ship before sundown. Which was in another—he checked his watch—seventy-two minutes. Plenty of time.

Nervous energy tingled over his skin as they stepped through a door into the serene, spotless interior full of geometric-patterned carpets and cherry-wood paneling. Monica slipped out of her jacket and hung it in a utility closet by the door. Her white tunic bore no pockets. She was unarmed.

Garrett reached for his gun again when a blank-faced crew-member dressed entirely in black passed them on his way to the bridge. The man didn't even glance in their direction, and Jackson felt like a ghost suddenly, there but unseen and in the company of an angel. Like he was already dead. He set his jaw and shook his head. He had to stay focused on the mission. Otherwise, they were done for.

"We'll take the stairs," Garrett said, when Monica pushed the call button on an elevator. "Healthier."

"If you prefer." She entered the stairwell.

Jackson nodded to his uncle and followed, tromping with as much noise as possible. As per "Plan A," Garrett went to find another stairway farther back to take himself and his backpack two decks down to the engine room. The engine room where, according to Dominique, the miniature submarine was housed. The submarine in which Kambyses spent his oblivious days.

Monica only moved down one deck and into a short hallway. "Did we lose someone?" she said, brows rising when she stopped by a door and noticed Garrett gone.

"Hmm?" Jackson looked around and feigned innocence. "Oh, right. He needed the men's room. He'll find us. Can't really get lost on this thing, can you?"

Her smile showed the first cracks. "You'd be surprised how many people get lost on this boat."

"Cassidy?" Jackson prompted, gesturing toward the door.

"Yes, of course." She knocked. "Cassie? You have company, honey." Opening the door, she entered, Jackson on her heels.

"Cass?" The generous cabin suite with two neatly made up beds was empty. Swinging open the bathroom door, he found this deserted as well. He turned back to Monica, who hung back by the doorway, and let his defensive anger rise. "Where is she?"

The redhead's angelic demeanor vanished. "You silly boy," she chided. "What are you doing here?"

"What do you think?" he ground out, fists balling by his sides.

"I see. In that case, you should know that there is no one on this ship who isn't ready to give their life to protect my lord's interests. Currently, these interests include Cassidy Chandler."

A muted pop-pop-pop from elsewhere on the ship punctuated her last words. Jackson recognized gunfire when he heard it. So did his tour guide, who looked pleased.

"It sounds like your colleague just figured that out, too."

Jackson pulled out his own gun, but his thoughts immediately flew to the C-4 in Garrett's backpack. Could a bullet set that off?

Monica's condescending expression didn't waver. More distant gunfire reached them, making him brace for an explosion that didn't come. Instead, there was a small sound directly behind him.

Raising his weapon, he whirled around, but only made it far enough to spot a large body clad in black from the corner of his eye. *Shit!* How the fuck had he missed that guy? Why hadn't he checked the closet, too?

His racing thoughts came to an abrupt halt when something hard connected with the back of his head. Stars exploded before his eyes.

Then he saw nothing at all.

27

EDGE OF NIGHT ETERNAL

Beneath an indigo sky, which wasn't quite day nor quite night, Cassidy was breathless with exertion. "I love you. More than life itself."

Dominique, hovering over her, took her mouth with his, hard and fast, the way the rest of his body took hers. With sweet, wanton desperation, they consumed each other—body, mind, and soul—until emotion and release shuddered through her.

He cradled her in his arms afterward, rubbed the back of her neck. Her fingertips caressed his sensitive throat and strong shoulders, the taut muscles of his chest. In her thoughts, she spoke to him of her need for him, her love, her devotion. *Nothing must ever come between us again.*

"Death will come between us," he whispered in her ear.

Her fingers stilled their exploration. *Don't say that.*

"But it will, if we let it."

Let it? A frisson of apprehension scurried over her damp skin.

"You love me more than life itself?"

Words. Only words uttered in moments of mindless passion. But where had they come from? Could they be true? Would she give up life in the sun to be with him? As long as she was mortal, she was his humanity. Would he give that up to be with her literally forever? And why did he bring this up now? Weren't there more immediate things for them to worry about? Although, what they might be, she couldn't remember just now. In his mind, she saw...

Nothing.

Cassidy pushed back to search his face. "What are you trying to—" Unfamiliar face. The indigo sky was gone. She blinked, disoriented. The gentle sound of wind in long grasses morphed into a distant, grumbling hum, and the blanket she remembered was now a softly swaying bed. "What—"

It all came rushing back. Her insides crumpled into a void, sucking all the air out of her body. "You." She breathed the word. Why hadn't she noticed that smoky stench before now?

Because he owned her head. That's why.

"Do you love me?" Kambyses murmured.

"How dare you." Shaking, Cassidy extricated herself from his proximity and straightened her slip, which was rucked up to her waist. Dear God. How much of what she just experienced was real? At least he was still dressed from the waist down, though where his hands had gone on her body, she didn't want to think. But why the charade? Why trick her into believing she was with Dominique when Kambyses could just as easily make her give him what would otherwise never be his?

Her breath caught at that last thought. She looked at him over her shoulder. "Is that what you want? To be loved?"

He held her gaze for a moment longer before rolling to his back to stare at the ceiling. The thick hair fanned out around his head on the pillow. In profile, his features had a coarse beauty that was more fascinating than handsome. He spoke so quietly she had to strain to hear him. "I want the darkness to end."

"But—you need the darkness to survive, don't you?"

"Only so much of it."

Cassidy waited, inviting him to fill the silence, even though she knew how unwilling this being was to share his thoughts, even with his own younglings, much less random mortals.

But Kambyses was also aware of how there were no secrets between her and Dominique, and this seemed to be the approach he wanted to emulate now. He drew a deep breath and in his soft accent said, "When ships first traveled across this sea, I rode on one to witness the worlds beyond the horizon. We traveled peacefully for weeks beneath the stars. Until one day, while I slept, hidden in the hold—" His mouth froze, his eyes wide and unblinking.

Unease slithered in her belly.

"I woke while falling through darkness," he said, and the unease condensed into a smooth, cold stone. The memory of him feeding from her without the pleasant illusions was all too fresh. She had fallen into a blackness so thick she could feel it eddy around her and squeeze into her body. A nothingness made of water.

"Ice cold darkness. Impenetrable darkness. A darkness as I had never imagined," he continued. "I don't know how long I fell. Maybe hours. Maybe days. At last there was a bottom to it."

"You—you fell to the bottom of the deep ocean? And you survived?" She shook her head, trying to un-boggle her brain. "Sorry. Of course you would." Here was an aspect of immortality she hadn't considered—not being able to die when surely that would have been preferable to unending tortures.

The expression in his hyper-dilated eyes was unfathomable. "You know so much of these things in this age. I knew nothing. I even doubted there would ever be a bottom. There was only the cold becoming thicker and thicker. The pressure crushed even my bones. They healed, only to be crushed again. Over and over."

"How did you get back to the surface?" she asked, morbidly fascinated. He wouldn't be able to swim or float any more than Dominique would.

"I crawled."

"Crawled?"

"For a century. Maybe more."

Cassidy recoiled a little. Her mind struck dumb with shock. Kambyses gave her a small, humorless smile, acknowledging her understanding. A hundred years on the bottom of the sea, crawling in the muck and rock, through abysmal trenches and across submarine mountain ranges that put their terrestrial counterparts to shame. There would be no light there to see by except for the bio-luminescence of deep-sea creatures. Not much blood either, to say nothing of heat.

For a century.

Lifetimes.

Spent in the frozen dark.

"There was heat and some light," he said, reading her thoughts. "I crawled only sometimes. More often, the current pushed me where it would. Eventually, I came to a place where the bottom splits and boils with the fury of the gods. I stayed there for a long time and fed on what life there was, but mostly...mostly I wanted the darkness to end. I may have spent years there or decades just staring at the light."

Cassidy had gone slack-jawed, unable to utter a sound, drowning in the terror of being trapped in an alien world—alone—and only wanting it to end. Not unlike her present situation.

"Eventually, I regained the will to keep going, and when I found land at last, I would have crawled ashore in the middle of the day if the sun had allowed it. Of course, I traded one hell for another. I found nothing but sand in every direction."

He paused, losing himself in those memories for so long, she wondered if he had forgotten about her, and not minding if he had. Eventually, he said, "I could travel a little faster there. Much faster after I followed the smell of water and found a Bedouin caravan camped at an oasis."

She sucked in a breath. No need to ask what happened to them. "Why are you telling me all this?"

"Because you asked. Because it has never been told before, and...because my chosen one chose to share his tale with you. Now you have heard mine."

"And I'm ever so grateful you shared it in words," she said. Had he made her relive those experiences, she might have gone mad. "I'm impressed that you're living on a boat, given that history."

"The sea has always been my home. But there are precautions; I do not intend to dwell on its floor again."

She thought for a moment before speaking. "It's not the physical darkness you want to end now, is it?"

This time, he replied silently, flooding her with a longing so ardent it made her eyes sting with tears.

Know me. Accept me. Love me.

These were all that mattered to him—everything this timeless man asked of Dominique—to vanquish unimaginable loneliness. Forever.

Tears spilled down her face as she scooted closer and placed a hand on his sunken cheek. "I know you, Kambyses. I accept you. And if you let him, Dominique will, too. But love...freely given love...that has to grow on its own. That takes time."

He raised his hand to brush a lock of hair out of her eyes and touch the moisture on her cheeks. "You weep for me. How exquisite."

One finger traced her jawline to where it joined with her neck. His eyes locked with hers, dark and deep and questioning, but exerting no power over her. It was of her own free will that she bent her head and exposed her vein, accepting him despite all she knew of him. This is why she wanted to meet this being—for this singular connection. So it didn't happen right away and not in the way she imagined, but it was happening. Her heart flooded with warmth and relief. This would be all right.

A sigh escaped her when his teeth gently found her vein, almost loving. So unlike the last time he fed from her. Or was that the time before? Her eyes snapped open. Just how many times *had* he taken her blood?

How long had she even been on this boat?

Why couldn't she remember these things?

Cassidy shoved at him, but his arms tightened around her. "What are you hiding from me?" she demanded, gasping for air. When had she become so weak? What was wrong with her? "What are you...?"

Know me, he thrummed against her mind. The darkness came for her again. *Know all of me.*

Cassidy jerked upright in her bed. The room tilted crazily, but daylight filtered through the sheer blinds lining both sides of the cabin. She dropped back into the pillows and concentrated on breathing. The circulating air still held a tinge of cedar smoke, bringing events of the night slamming home, unfiltered and undiluted.

At least as far as she knew.

During every other day aboard *Apokryphos,* she never re-membered the nights. Sometimes she didn't remember her name. The ancient bastard saw to that. And during the nights, he made sure she didn't remember the previous nights. Not this time. This time, he repaid her compassion with the gift of knowledge. About himself—and about her.

She crept to the side of the bed, but trying to sit up had her reeling with vertigo. Together with the gentle pitching of the ship, the effect was overwhelming. She flopped back and panted, then tried again. Grunting and clutching a chair, she heaved herself upright and willed her legs to straighten and bear her weight. She *had* to get off this ship today. Even if she leapt over a rail and dog paddled.

Two steps. That was as far as she could stagger before crashing to the floor in a retching heap. *Crawl, Chandler,* she commanded herself. *Go. Now.*

On hands and knees, her progress was wobbly. Her arms refused to work in a coordinated fashion and her knees kept tangling in the ridiculous red slip. Her vision contracted into a flickering gray tunnel. None of it mattered. So long as she was conscious, she would move. If she was still here by sundown, her life was over.

"Freaking bastard," she cursed. Of course, he wouldn't let her know what he was doing to her while she was still strong enough to fight. "Know me, accept me, love me, my ass!" Her legs tangled in the slip, pitching her over again. She yanked the fabric up around her waist and crawled on, bare-bottomed. "And you wonder why nobody can stand being around you of their so-called free will, you sick, two-faced, murderous viper!"

Her heart knocked against her ribs, and a hazy veil closed over her tunnel vision. Gasping, she dropped to the ground.

Stay conscious, stay conscious, stay conscious, she chanted over the roaring buzz in her skull. *If you faint, you're dead.*

She was about to hazard moving again when the door opened.

"Cassie!" Monica cried. The dishes on the breakfast tray rattled as she hurried to put it down. "What happened? Are you all right?"

Cassidy rolled to her back and looked up at the other woman's face, which was convincingly lined with worry. Monica was Kambyses's minion. Trusting her would be insane. Yet, there was no one else she could ask for help.

Also, that coffee smelled awfully tempting. She had the whole day to get away. Maybe there was time to regain some strength.

"I don't feel so great."

"No, I'm sure you don't. Come, let me help you up." She scooped an arm behind her shoulders. Cassidy struggled to her feet but held on to Monica with the little strength she had left. "Let's get you back to bed and fed. Maybe not so much hot tub time today, huh?"

Cassidy bit her tongue until she was settled back in bed with pillows propping her up into a seated position. "You know what he's doing to me, don't you?"

Monica placed the bed tray before her and smiled. "I do." She poured a cup of coffee from the carafe. "I take it you now do as well?"

"Now that it's too late for me to do anything about it, yes. Yes, I do."

A splash of cream went into the cup as well, just the way Cassidy liked it. "It's a great honor he's paying you. It's the first time he's brought someone over since I've known him." On a wistful note, she added, "I was so hoping it'd be me."

After several fortifying swallows of coffee, Cassidy picked up a fork and dug into the enormous, fluffy omelet, gourmet hash browns and crackling crisp bacon. "Hungry" didn't even begin to cover it. Every cell in her body screamed for the calories required to replenish the blood she had lost these past three…nights.

She stopped chewing, searching her memory. No, not three. Not even four. Icy fingers gripped her belly. Dear God. It was five. *Five* nights in a row that she had felt his canines pierce her vein. She must be pickled in serum. Her immune system likely teetered on the verge of collapse. It wouldn't take much more before she would need to be turned.

Or die.

Not that Kambyses would be the one to give her his blood. He had shown her how that would kill her before it would transform her, and there were more expedient ways of getting rid of her. No, he let her know—with no small amount of anticipation—that Dominique would have to make that choice for both of them.

Whatever Dominique decided, his fate, too, would be sealed. Whether Cassidy died or transformed, his humanity would be destroyed once and for all. He would always be Kambyses's shadow.

"I don't want this. I never wanted this," she said, swiping at fresh tears in between forkfuls of what might be her last meal ever. "I'll gladly trade places with you."

"Oh, sweetheart." Monica touched Cassidy's arm. "I know this must be a bit much for you to take in right now. You haven't had time to think this through, but you'll be all right. I'll help you all I can to get through this, and we'll be great friends. Maybe forever."

If Cassidy hadn't been so ravenous, she would have pitched the tray at the woman. "Would you mind helping me today?"

"But of course. Anything you want. You know the ship is our playground," she said in a conspiratorial tone.

"I'd like to get off it."

"Water sports? Are you sure you're up for that? We have a big dinner planned for tonight. You wouldn't want to wear yourself out and fall asleep in your plate, would you?"

Dinner? Seriously? "How about a ride in a tender? Just, you know, a trip to dry land or something. I'm going stir-crazy on this tub."

"Oh, I see." Monica nodded thoughtfully. "We might be able to arrange something. Sure."

"That'd be great," Cassidy said, wary. Too easy.

"Why don't I go see if I can get that organized?" Monica got up and headed for the suite's double-doors. "You eat your breakfast and save your energy."

Cassidy finished her meal and washed it all down with the tall glass of fresh-squeezed OJ, her favorite breakfast staple. It wasn't as sugary as usual, but calories were calories. She settled back against the pillows, her eyes falling shut. Just a couple of minutes to collect herself before tackling a voyage to the bathroom and getting some clothes on.

Just a couple of minutes. Then she'd be good to go.

Maybe.

28

DINNER WITH JOHN

"Wake up, Cassie. Time for dinner."

Cassidy sighed and turned over, buried her face in the pillow, and let herself sink back into the lazily rocking bed.

A touch on her shoulder. Gentle shaking. "Cassie?"

Who the hell was so persistent? A woman, but it didn't sound like Samantha. She opened her eyes to the cabin that was her prison. The windows she faced were dark with night. No, that couldn't be. A minute ago, it was morning. Adrenaline shot through her, blowing away every bit of sleep. "No. No, no, no."

"Yes, yes, yes. You slept all day. I bet you feel much better now."

"I'm going to die," she moaned.

"No, we're actually going to have a nice dinner with our guests. So, c'mon. I'll help you get ready. We can't leave them waiting."

Cassidy sat up and waited for the waves of dizziness to stop sweeping over her. "How did I sleep through the entire day? I'm not that far gone."

"Well—" Monica averted her eyes. "I may have added a little something to your juice this morning to calm you down. I had a feeling you might be upset."

"You didn't have a freaking 'feeling'. He told you to do that."

"Does it matter? Look what good all that rest did you. You've almost got some color back in your cheeks."

"I'm almost strong enough to hit you, too," Cassidy lied. She could have slapped that patronizing smile off Monica's face right now, but that would have wasted precious strength she might still need tonight.

Monica pulled the comforter aside. "I know you don't mean that, so I'm going to let it go." She held out a hand. "Shower?"

Cassidy allowed Monica to help her across the cabin, but was adamant about privacy in the bathroom. After relieving a painfully full bladder, she wobbled across a tile mosaic of some Greek mythological figure and stepped into the shower to let the hot water beat her limbs until she stopped shivering.

The translucent gray reflection in the mirror frightened her. Purple bruises marked the sunken, haunted eyes staring back at her, and the lips were as cracked and flaky as those of a corpse. She was running on empty in so many ways. What she needed was an IV, not a formal dinner with—wait.

"Did you say we have guests?" she said when she emerged, swathed in towels.

"Yes, I did." Monica beamed. "Which do you think? The blue sequins or the green chiffon?" She held up two cocktail gowns, the former strappy, the latter with sleeves. "We're about the same size, so either should fit you fine."

"The warmer one. Who are these guests?" Had Kambyses captured more innocents to toy with? Was there a chance they could help each other? For this possibility, she would make herself join a formal dinner on her deathbed. Under no circumstance could she allow Kambyses to feed on her again.

"I don't know. I think the green clashes with your coloring. Blue it is. I have a wrap to go with that. You'll be fine."

"Bitch," Cassidy said under her breath.

Half an hour later, hair neatly pinned, makeup applied, and slinky, blue-sequined dress draped, she hugged a thin, black shawl around her bare shoulders and followed Monica, similarly attired in shades of red and orange, down the pitching hall. Past the little elevator lobby, the doors to the dining room stood open. Male voices engaged in animated conversation issued from inside.

"No way," one exclaimed.

A more seasoned voice replied, "Better believe it. So what was I going to do? I told your father they were all round."

Uproarious laughter.

Cassidy knew these voices, she was sure of it, but she couldn't place them with faces. Not in this alternate reality. Then she stepped through the door—and into a nightmare.

"Good evening, gentlemen," Monica said as she swept into the lavish dining room. "I hope we haven't kept you waiting too long."

"Not at all. We were just reminiscing. Hey, Cass, is that you?"

Cassidy reached out to the nearest wall for support, but her fingers slid on the polished wood. That couldn't possibly be Jackson leaping up from his chair and heading toward her with arms flung wide? He engulfed her in a bear hug. "Finally. I was wondering where you were hiding."

She held on to him, clutched at the too-small blazer he wore, and inhaled his familiar aroma of sun and soap. It was him. Dear God, Jackson Striker, vampire hunter, was aboard a vampire-owned yacht. Having wine. With his uncle!

"Miss Chandler," Garrett Striker said brightly when Jackson released her. He, too, wore an ill-fitting gray dinner jacket over...cargo pants and boots? She locked her knees to prevent them from caving and struggled to breathe as the man who had bounced a bullet off her skull the last time they met now embraced her like a member of his dearest family. "Good to see you again."

"What the—what the—"

"Your surprise seems to have succeeded," Monica said with unabashed delight. "You are surprised, Cassidy, aren't you?"

She could only nod in numb horror.

"They joined us yesterday evening and have been enjoying themselves ever since while you were resting."

"Come sit with us," Jackson said. Tucking her hand into the crook of his arm, he lead her to a chair at the oval table where five elegant place settings were laid, three on one side, two on the other.

"You did enjoy your day, didn't you?" Monica asked as she rounded the table and took her seat opposite Cassidy.

"I don't think I've ever had so much fun," Garrett announced. "Those jet skis are something else."

"And the gym is top-notch," Jackson added.

Cassidy's head threatened to explode. "I don't understand, Jackson. What are you doing here?"

"Oh, we were way overdue for a vacation. Here, try this wine. It's an exceptional Montracht. I think you'll like it."

She looked across the table to Monica, who sipped her own glass. As was Kambyses.

Another shock.

Had he been there a moment ago? He slouched in the chair with one elbow casually draped on the seatback. Red silk shirt, black blazer, hair gathered at his nape. Civilized. Except for that glass. That wasn't wine he was drinking. The liquid coating the crystal was far too dense and red. Cassidy's stomach flopped.

"Jackson, listen to me." She put her hand on his arm and squeezed hard until he met her eyes. "I need your help."

"I know you do, babe. That's why Nick suggested we take this cruise. To keep an eye on you."

She blinked. "Dominique sent you?" The shocks just kept on coming. She wasn't sure how many more she could take at this rate.

"He sure did," Garrett agreed, picking a roll from a gilded breadbasket. "And I daresay we found you."

Cassidy cast a hesitant glance at Kambyses, who was, of course, not surprised. He would have learned of his youngling's plot against him when he fed on Jackson and Garrett, which he certainly would have.

"Jackson," she tried again. "Listen to me. You're compelled."

"Not hardly. Nick knows better than to try that shit on me."

"Stupid risk you took there, trusting him," Garrett put in.

"It all turned out fine. Just like I told you." Jackson raised his glass and looked straight at Kambyses. "Right, John?"

"John?" her voice rose with incredulity.

Kambyses raised his goblet of blood in silent acknowledgement and sipped. Over the top of the cup, his eyes cut back to Cassidy. Beside him, Monica smothered a giggle.

In the recessed ceiling above, a crystal chandelier tinkled with the vibrations from the vessel's engines, casting bright shards of sound like shrapnel into the dark silence.

"John," she said, dazed. "Right. Okay. Jackson? Garrett? Listen to me, both of you. You've been compelled by the strongest vampire you've ever met." No reaction. "You're fucking compelled out of your fucking minds," she intoned, using language she knew had a better chance of registering with them.

They sobered and exchanged a look. Was she getting through to them? They had trained themselves to resist compulsion. There had to be a way to break this spell. Not that she had any idea what they could accomplish if they snapped out of it.

Kambyses was in their heads, privy to every thought, just as he was in hers, but not trying—not fighting—was unthinkable.

"You two are vampire hunters and *John* over there is the badass vampire you're here to...to—"

Kambyses's eyes were a physical weight on her. "Just get us the hell out of here," she finished.

The hunters regarded "John" thoughtfully. Garrett took a bite from his buttered roll, Jackson another swallow of wine. "Aren't you going to have some?" he asked, nodding at her untouched glass.

"Did you hear anything I just said?"

"Did you say something?"

She gaped at him. There was nothing in his cool, gray eyes beyond genuine confusion.

A crew member came in, balancing a tray of dishes across the shifting floor.

"Oh, good. Food," Garrett said, rubbing his hands together. "About time."

She began to shake. Her last, best chance of making it out of this as a living human being was so close she could touch it—and so far away it might as well have been at the bottom of the deepest sea. "No."

The server placed a steaming bowl before her.

"Did you say something, babe?"

"I said no."

"No soup?"

"No. No, as in 'no, I'm not accepting this lying down.' Damn you, Jackson, you said if I ever needed help, you'd be there for me. Remember?"

"Yes, of course."

"I need your help now. Right now." She grabbed his face hard with both hands. "Look at me. I'm sick. I'm being turned into a vampire right in front of you, and you're too compelled to see it. Listen to my voice. Listen to me. Find yourself. Help me. Help us all." Tears again. Damn it. She didn't care. This was her life she was fighting for. All their lives. She'd beg without shame. "Snap out of it, Jack. Please, please, *please wake the fuck up!*"

For breathless seconds alarm flared in Jackson's eyes, a recognition of the true situation, a glimpse past the illusion.

Then Garrett said, "I heard grouper's on the menu tonight. Cayman style. Have you ever tried that, Jack?"

The apprehension drained away. He gently pulled her hands from his face and turned to his uncle. "No, I don't think so."

"Well, let me tell you. The secret is all in the sauce. The peppers and onions are mixed with…"

Cassidy couldn't look at them any longer. She stared at her soup, stunned, a drone filling her ears as if a jet engine were howling right behind her. Slowly, she pushed back her chair and stood on legs as clumsy as stilts. Both Monica and Kambyses watched her, the former with concern, the latter with calm curiosity and darkening eyes.

Anger rattled in her voice. "Do you really think that playing these sick games is how you're going to get all those things you want so badly? To be known? To be accepted? Even loved?" She spat the word at him and leaned forward, both hands splayed on the table. "No one in their sane mind would want to know you. They would sooner loathe you than accept you as anything other than the freak show you are. And love? You're not worthy. I'm guessing you never were. Even all the way back in ancient fucking wherever-you-came-from!"

Silence.

The Strikers stopped spooning their soup. Monica blanched. Kambyses didn't move. No expression on his face. Only his eyes had gone full black, aroused no doubt by her unbridled emotional outburst. Like a skittering mouse might arouse a cat. Something trivial, to use and dispatch at will.

That thought kicked her rage up one final notch. Seizing the bowl of soup, she pitched it across the table. Kambyses caught the flying dish with a lightning-fast reflex. The same could not be said for its contents, which hit him square in the face. Monica yelped when veggies and broth splashed on her shoulder. He put down the empty bowl but made no move to clean himself.

Cassidy was as close to snarling as it was possible for a human to get. "Rot in hell!"

Lowering his head, Kambyses closed his eyes—and disappeared.

29

CHOICES

Every night Dominique woke to dig himself out of the dune, he grew more certain that something had gone terribly wrong. Kambyses still lived. The hunters had failed.

The first night, he called Jackson's phone and even Garrett's. Both went to voice mail immediately. Samantha inquired about them with her stepfather, who paused long enough before hanging up to accuse her of being complicit in luring his son and brother into an ambush they were unlikely to have survived. She cried in Dominique's arms until he took pity on her and compelled her into believing that all would be well.

Too bad he couldn't compel himself. Every time he thought of Cassidy alone with Kambyses yet another night—and he thought of nothing else—impotent fury boiled his blood.

More rage filled him when he realized that his oblivious houseguest—Cassidy's fickle, selfish father—had abandoned her yet again. Her absence was too long, his business too urgent, explained the note he left behind with his phone number. The man wouldn't know how much danger his daughter was in, but his disappearance now felt too much like another betrayal of her, another piece of Cassidy slipping from Dominique's grasp.

Serge had nothing to say about any of it, not even when Dominique tried to force the matter. Even slammed to a wall, the old pirate fidgeted and squirmed and quivered, wide-eyed, terrified, and silent. That prophesied glorious new world of night had clearly taken a detour into the unspeakable.

Powerless to do anything but wait, he took up a desperate vigil at the most likely place for *Apokryphos* to reappear—the last place he had seen Cassidy.

Near dawn, Bijou joined him on the sloped roof of her mansion. She hesitated at the sight of his swords, but didn't comment as she squatted down and joined him in staring at the sea.

"Did you know he is the source of us all?" he asked without looking at her.

"I do."

"You might have told me."

"I told you we all belong to him, *cher*, but you don't hear what you don't want to."

"I belong to no one." No one but Cassidy.

Bijou sighed, and pity touched her voice. "Spare yourself the grief and heartache of this struggle, young one. Accept his will and find your peace."

His nerves bristled, but he remained silent.

"*D'accord*," she sniffed and got up, the impeccable green silk pantsuit whispering around her curves. Her face and hands gleamed in the morning gray. "But you will only have yourself to blame for your misery. You are welcome to spend the day. You will be safe here."

When he still made no reply, she vanished. He didn't leave to sink himself and his misery into the dune until several minutes later, when the looming sun threatened to overwhelm his newly enhanced tolerance.

The next night, the fourth following the Strikers' disappearance, Dominique hunted, unleashing his anger on all the dealers and petty criminals he could find. He managed not to kill anyone, but he was unapologetically gluttonous with their blood and less than scrupulous about what he allowed them to remember of the encounters. Some of his prey would be in therapy for the rest of their lives. No matter. He needed all the strength he could get for whatever Kambyses had in store for him next.

He didn't have long to wait.

As he returned to the mansion, shortly past midnight, *Apokryphos* gingerly sidled her enormous dark bulk up to the dock. Dominique didn't hesitate. He strode across the dock, skirted the crew scurrying to secure lines, vaulted aboard, and burst through the first available door into the main lounge.

There he stopped.

The cozy scene before him, set to soothingly classical music, almost defied description. Jackson Striker hunched forward in his chair, studying a chessboard in the mellow light of a reading lamp. Sitting in the shadows across the table from him and swirling a crystal tumbler of dark amber was none other than Garrett Striker. They both wore an odd assembly of baggy, wrinkled black pants and scuffed boots, along with pastel polo shirts and dark blazers that fit too tight across their broad shoulders.

Garrett spotted him and broke into an affable grin. "Well, look who's here."

Jackson tore himself away from his strategizing. "Oh, hey Nick, how you doing? Good to see you, man."

"We've had a blast, haven't we, Jack? Best vacation ever. Thanks for the tip, Nicky. We wouldn't have found this trip without you."

Dominique stared at them. They stared back at him, not quite as blank as the crew, but close to it. "You incompetent fools," he burst out. "How could you allow yourselves to be caught aboard after dark?"

"Well, don't look at me." Garrett pointed at Jackson with his glass. "It was his idea."

Jackson nodded. "Yep. Didn't want to miss losing this baby after finding her."

"Ingenious," Dominique said on a slow exhale. He'd never seen a compulsion quite this sophisticated. Instead of locking their minds into a box, Kambyses had derailed their sense of reality to flow around inconsistencies like a river flowed around boulders. Undoing this would be a challenge. A challenge he didn't have time for. "Where is Cassidy?"

"Probably in her cabin," Garrett replied. "Poor girl's been battling seasickness for days now."

"Would you like to see her?" asked a familiar voice, resonant with power.

"Oh, hey, John," Jackson greeted. "You up for a game?"

Half-turning, Dominique saw Kambyses lean against the door frame, hands in his pockets. Their eyes locked as Jackson went back to pondering the board, probably forgetting they were even there, obeying a silent command without question. When Kambyses retreated from the lounge, Dominique reluctantly followed, apprehension mounting.

They passed through the dining room, a small elevator lobby and down a hallway he knew led to the yacht's suits. Cherry-wood wall panels provided a backdrop to Greek-themed paintings and busts. He inhaled to seek her sweet scent, but only caught traces of polishing oils, upholstery, machinery, and the ever-present forest fire stench of Kambyses. Terrifying memories of his early blood-drinker nights threatened to overwhelm him. He had sworn he would never set foot aboard this vessel again.

Yet, here he was—for Cassidy, the center of his existence, and the key to a destiny which seemed bound and determined to beat them both to death.

And she was just about there.

The moment Monica swung open the doors, Dominique was by Cassidy's side, whispering her name, hands hovering over the brittle husk that remained of his brave lioness. Still and pale, she lay beneath a red satin sheet, sunken eyes closed, the bones of her skull sharp beneath tight skin and a web of blue veins. Fevered heat radiated off her in waves...along with the scent of fire.

She reeked of Kambyses.

Dominique gasped with the shock of realization. If he weren't already crouched down, his legs would have given out. What a fool he was. Had he truly not seen this coming? Or did he turn a blind eye to the possibility because he refused to even contemplate it? He knew his sire, though. He should have known Kambyses wouldn't take Cassidy on a pleasure cruise for a week without a calculated reason.

"Why? Why would you do this?"

"To help you, Nico," Kambyses murmured.

Dumbstruck, Dominique looked over his shoulder at the ancient fiend watching with casual interest from a seat by the starboard windows. "*Help* me?"

"To find your true self."

He got up in a rush. "My true self? *Fils de putain*, my true self died the night you first took me."

"Did you not take life when you were mortal?"

"In defense of my sister. Whom I later killed because of you." He kept his voice low in the presence of Cassidy, but it trembled with suppressed rage.

Kambyses nodded and smiled, indulgent. "You took pleasure from both acts and all the ones since. And now...now you will take pleasure from drinking this life as well."

Dominique bared his fangs in a vicious snarl. "I. Will. Not."

"Then you can leave her to suffer and perish on her own. Or"—he heaved an almost human sigh—"you can give her your blood. The choice is yours. Either way, Nico, you will be true to yourself, and I will have you. You belong to me."

"*Brûle en l'enfer!*" This "choice" was no choice at all. Whatever he did, the Cassidy he knew and loved would be gone, and without her, he would be as cold and callous as every other blood-drinker, because they *all* belonged to Kambyses. They *all* secretly danced to the drumbeat of his madness—as would Cassidy, if she became one of them. For a while, with her help, Dominique had triumphed over the madness.

So much hope and promise in their love.

Gone now, all of it, reduced to smoking cinders.

He turned his back on Kambyses and returned to Cassidy's side. Lying there with the beast fighting to claim her, she looked frail enough to float away. Her chest rose and fell with shallow breaths, and he heard her heart stumble along, moving the last of her blood.

Lowering his head, he closed his eyes against hopeless tears. Of all the fates he could imagine for her, only one was worse than becoming a blood-drinker—becoming a blood-drinker enslaved to Kambyses.

"Cassie, *mon amour,*" he whispered, his heart quietly breaking as he took her into his arms one last time. "Forgive me."

———————

Cassidy's eyes snapped open.

That goddamned, bloodsucking jerk was at it again. She struck at him. Her hand connected with a less-than-satisfying slap, but it did have the desired effect of making him jolt upright. Surprise registered on the face that looked like Dominique's, but surely wasn't. "Get the hell away from me."

A wave of vertigo tangled her limbs as she tried to roll away, gasping with the effort. "Haven't you toyed with me enough?"

Every night, he took more. Every day she became sicker, but she held on and held on. Held on for Dominique. No matter what, she would find her way back to him.

The illusion of Dominique blinked, perplexed. No condescending smiles. No vague words. "Cassie," it said, reaching out but not touching her. "It is me, Dominique."

She hesitated and then grew angry with herself for wanting to believe him. "Leave me alone."

He glanced over his shoulder and spoke in harsh French. Another voice responded. She focused her reluctant eyes on the far end of the cabin. Kambyses? But then—

With a cry, she threw herself into the real Dominique's arms. He caught her, clutched her tight, and murmured her name over and over while her eyes burned with tears that would not come. They had dried up along with her blood supply. Delirious, she held on to him, soaking up his strength and inhaling his brisk winter smell. Kambyses never faked Dominique's scent for her. He only made her not notice its absence.

It really was him, her one and only Dominique. Desperate to merge with him, she pulled his face against her neck. Let him take what he wanted. If it would be the end of her, at least she would die happy.

"*Non*. No, Cassie *amour*," he whispered, stroking her grimy hair. "You have too little, and you can take no more serum."

A stifled sob returned her to an awareness of the moment, of the others hovering around her. Monica stood by the door and dabbed at watering eyes. "That is so sweet."

Cassidy collapsed against Dominique. He may be here at last, but their predicament was only getting worse.

"What will it be, Nico?" Kambyses mused. "Will you release her? Or will she join us?"

Dominique's arms tightened a little more around her. "Join us? You know you could never pit us against each other. We will not play your games."

The eternal vampire rose to his feet and slid his hands back into his trouser pockets. "No games. Of cowering servants, I have many. Of companions who will challenge me, I have none but you. By your defiance, you have proven yourself worthy of me and have succeeded where two thousand others have failed. If sharing you with her is to be the price of your acceptance of me, then it is a price I will pay."

A violent shiver ran through Dominique's body. Cassidy trembled and closed her eyes.

"You have until dawn to consider your choice," Kambyses said. A moment later, the door opened and closed. The silence that descended was the silence of a world standing still.

Neither Cassidy nor Dominique moved. "It is not my choice," he finally whispered against her temple, voice heavy with misery. "It is yours."

She stirred in his arms until he released her to sink, exhausted, into the sheets. He stretched out on his side, one hand on her belly. She grabbed it, threading her fingers with his as she collected her thoughts. "I've had some time to think about this." Over the past two days, she had done nothing but. "Your perspective changes when you're up against a wall like this."

He remained silent, watching her, listening.

"Yes, I want to be human and feel the sun on my skin. But more than that, I want to...want to—" Live? Given her options, that didn't sound right. "—continue. I want to continue, Dominique." He squeezed her fingers, but whether in warning, encouragement, or despair, she couldn't say. "I want to continue as long as I know you'll be there with me. Even if...even if I never see the sun again."

"All that is good in you will be destroyed, and with you, all the light that is left in me," he said in a low, harsh tone. "We will both be bound to him for eternity. We'll be monsters just like him."

"We'll be monsters together. Doesn't that beat being a monster alone?" Or would she be an eternal reminder of all he had lost? It was obvious Kambyses preferred her dead. Just as obviously, the bastard understood he would lose Dominique if he just killed her now. Which didn't mean he wouldn't get rid of her later, whether it was next week or next century. "Besides," she added and licked at her cracked lips, "there's the prophecy."

His expression narrowed and darkened.

"Kambyses is old and powerful," she went on. "What better way to influence him and the world of night than by being with him all the time? Maybe we can show him a better way?"

"He is not merely old." The words emerged in a croak. "He is the oldest of them all. The so-called hunters I sent to end him have told me so. His destruction will end us all. Including you. If you join us."

"The oldest?"

Brief nod.

"And you...you sent the Strikers to kill him? Even though that would destroy you and...*every* other vampire out there?"

"The price for your survival."

She tried to comprehend such an inconceivable sacrifice full of desperate brutality—and desperate love. "I'm glad you failed," she said, dazed, only her lips moving. "I'm glad you're still here. I'm glad I have this choice to join you rather than mourn you for a lifetime."

"Serge has said that those who want to be turned never survive long. What they expect never matches reality."

"Has he?" She almost smiled. "I've lived in your head for months. And your—make that *our*—esteemed sire has shared plenty of his darkness with me. If I don't know what I'm in for by now, I never will." Hell. She was in for hell. But as long as Dominique was there with her, she could deal. "You've taken nothing else Serge says seriously. Why this now?"

His eyes widened. Her words had found their mark. "You never cease to amaze me," he said. "I will never cease loving you."

"Even if I'm a monster?"

"Never in my eyes."

Cassidy rallied a smile. "So. Are we going to do this?"

Anguish filled his gold-flecked eyes. Human eyes, not a trace of vampire in them. The beginnings of a beard shadowed the hollowed cheeks, and an unruly shock of hair fell across his forehead. He had never looked so human, or so vulnerable.

She almost didn't hear him. And then she wished she hadn't.

"I cannot."

30

ONE LAST DAY

It wouldn't take much. Just a little, not even quite a sip, and the beast would triumph, taking her from the world of day. Within the hour, the darkness would rise from the cobalt depths of her eyes and turn her into a raging, blood-thirsty beast that would not recognize him for many nights to come. And when she resurfaced, the woman he knew and loved and needed above all else would be irrevocably altered.

All of this would happen—if Dominique gave her his blood.

He couldn't.

She looked at him for a long time, surprised, exhausted. Disappointed. Finally she said, "You would prefer I die?"

He shook his head. There had to be another way. There *had* to be. But what? His mind careened wildly between the only three options before him.

Turn her.

Let her die.

End her misery.

He stroked her brow, felt her fever burn against his palm. She still fought, her mind still clear. She would survive another day, if not the next night. That would have to be enough.

"I will not let you die, *mon cœur*, but will you live one more day as a mortal for us both? Live it knowing that it will be your last?"

"If you think I can make it that long, you've got more faith in me than I do right now."

"I know you will." He went to pour a glass of water from a crystal pitcher on the table and brought it to her. "I have seen this process play out more times than I care to remember." Lifting her upper body in one arm, he held the glass to her lips.

She licked at the moisture and made a face. "I'm going to be sick."

"Drink it anyway. You'll need it to keep your mind clear."

Grabbing hold of the glass, she bravely swallowed half the contents. He settled her back into the pillows. "Rest now. I need to speak to our lord and master," he said with a soft sneer. "But I will be back and not leave your side again until dawn."

She closed her eyes. "Hurry."

He found Kambyses back in the lounge, seated at the table with Jackson and Garrett, his attention riveted on the chessboard. The redhead lazed on a sofa nearby and flipped pages in a magazine. All four turned to Dominique expectantly when he entered.

"She will join us," he said to Kambyses. "Tomorrow."

Monica sighed, a sound of dreamy contentment.

"Lucky girl," Garrett said while reaching to advance a black knight. "And I believe that's checkmate, kid."

"Fuck," Jackson said.

Dominique looked between them and sensed something skirt his awareness. Something he should seize.

Kambyses steepled his fingers, waiting, and Dominique returned his attention to him.

"I will remain with you, but only so long as Cassidy is with us. If anything happens to her tomorrow, next week, next century or a thousand years from now—I will destroy us all. Do you understand this, old man?"

He inclined his head. "She challenges me almost as much as you do, Nico. Nothing of my doing will ever befall her. Like you, she shall always enjoy my protection. On this, you have my word."

These were admissions and statements Dominique could never have imagined from his sire, and he didn't know how good this creature's "word" might be. Maybe Cassidy's presence really was influencing him? Maybe they really could help him change? Maybe this was their joint mission in the world of night? The prophecy?

Maybe.

Dominique nodded. "Then give us the rest of this night, and you can have all the ones to come."

"As you wish."

Jackson sat back in his chair. "This sounds big. You guys getting married or something?"

Kambyses graced him with a dry smile.

"What will you do with them?" Dominique wondered, tucking his thumbs into his pockets to appear relaxed despite his nerves twanging with tension.

"They are hunters. What do you think should be done with them?"

He considered the two men who were oblivious to the fact that their deaths were being discussed. Such tender mortal beings. Their only crime was to secure the world for their kind—and to avenge their loved ones. A half-formed idea rolled around in the back of his head. "Ineffective hunters," he said. "They only catch the young and stupid."

"And?"

"And I think you can easily compel them to give up that mission. Release them to enjoy their brief lives with their families."

Kambyses tilted his head as he regarded him. Dominique met the naturally coal-black eyes steadily. The formidable mind behind them seemed to slide through his flesh and bone like a fine sword. "You are a wonder, Nico. They almost destroyed you, and yet you would show them compassion?"

"Be honest, old man. That's one of the things you love about me."

The ancient blood-drinker flashed a rare bright smile and got up in that way that looked like he levitated out of his chair. Stopping by Dominique's side, enveloping him with cedar smoke stench, he spoke in sultry French. "Do you know that you seduced me the moment I laid eyes on you?"

"*Oui.* I do," he said with a slow nod. Only now did he fully grasp the events of that night. Kambyses had seen him snap a man's neck without hesitation. Dominique knew exactly what he was doing to the brute who had raped his sister. It was this instinctive act of controlled rage that had bewitched Kambyses with the possibility of a blood-drinker companion who was as compassionate as he was unrepentant.

It hadn't quite worked out that way, of course. Not with Dominique's compassion tormenting him over what he had become. The regrets would have destroyed him—if not for Cassidy.

Kambyses actually laughed now, delighted, and a grudging warmth stole over Dominique's heart. Didn't this man only want to be known and loved despite what he was? Perhaps. But Dominique still wouldn't let him have Cassidy without a fight.

And he was nowhere near done fighting.

"Do with them as you wish, Nico," his sire said, looking as pleased as Dominique had ever seen him. "Enjoy your night."

The moment Dominique was sure Kambyses had gone ashore, he turned to Jackson and Garrett. How far dare he go with them? How deeply buried in their psyche was Kambyses? If he wasn't very careful, he would condemn them to a swift death and Cassidy to an eternity of night.

"The cruise is over. Time for you two to go home." Using all the compulsive power he could muster and keeping his voice just within human hearing range, he continued, "Find all in your family you have not seen in too long. Cherish them. Tell them you love them."

"Absolutely," Jackson said with all the conviction of a parishioner confirming a pulpit proclamation.

Garrett nodded. "Best idea I've heard all week."

Dominique crouched down between them and put a hand on each of their shoulders. When he had both their attention, he finished with a monumental punch of compulsive energy that would have knocked them unconscious if they had any fight left in them at all. "Do it tonight."

31

DEFINITELY NO VAMPIRES

"**W**ake up, golden one. Wake up!"

Samantha didn't need much prodding to rouse from her fitful doze. She sat up on the sofa in a tangle of blankets, sweater and skirt. "What? What happened?"

"Someone comes."

Pushing her hair off her face, she tried to gauge Serge's vibe on this observation. The apprehension rounding his eyes was not encouraging. She reached for her phone on the coffee table. Wednesday, four-twenty-seven in the morning. Her brother and step-uncle had been MIA since Sunday, and the last she heard from Dominique was a terse text of "they r back" several hours ago, with no response to her requests for clarification.

"Well? Who is it? Do we need to run for our lives?"

Serge shook his curly head.

"Oh, good. I think."

A car door slammed outside. A second one followed. She went to the window, peered between the blinds, and wondered if she was still asleep. A figure jogged up the driveway and came into the circle of light cast by the porch lamp. "Oh. My God."

The visitor rapped sharply at the door, and she rushed to open it. Jackson scooped her up in his arms. "Sam! I can't tell you how much I've missed you. But I'm sure going to try."

She squealed with surprise. Baby brother was back and happier than she had seen him since before losing his twin. She held fast to him, feeling his joy wash over her.

"I love you so much," he said, and she all but melted. Whatever may have caused it, she liked this new, more relaxed version of him.

"I'm so glad you're back, Jack. We were so worried."

"Oh, nonsense," someone else said from the door. She angled her head and felt her face drop when she saw Garrett standing there, hands on hips, sporting a fresh tan and an ear-to-ear grin. "Can't a guy take his nephew on a cruise?" he asked jovially. "C'mere, girl. You're a sight for these sore, old eyes."

Before she could comprehend what was happening, Garrett had pulled her away from Jackson and smothered her in his arms. Garrett, her stepfather's brother, hunter of vampires and calculating killer. Garrett, the man who had made it clear that she was nothing to him but a pretty piece of fluff that kept getting in the way.

Her relief evaporated in an instant.

Something was wrong. Horribly wrong.

She gingerly backed out of the embrace, all her senses now awake, most of all her sense of unmitigated alarm. The whiff of smoke she caught clinging to their frumpy jackets made her flesh crawl. That had to be the smell of him, the one, the ancient vampire they went to find and put down. So they had found him—and failed.

Jackson waltzed into the kitchen, which was separated from the living room by a counter and two bar chairs. "You got any beer? We need to celebrate."

Garrett looked around. "Nice place you got yourself here. Oh, hi there." He waved at Serge, who sat ashen-faced and statue-still in the sofa.

"What is happening?" Samantha mouthed at the vampire. Serge shrank back. His eyes glazed over into that disconnected look he got when he was checking into his own reality.

"Apple juice? That's all you've got? Okay, whatever. That'll have to do." Jackson took the bottle from the fridge and began rummaging for glasses.

She fisted her hands by her side and forged ahead. "Jack, can you tell me what happened to you?"

"Best cruise ever," Garrett said.

"Cruise? Which line?"

"*Apokryphos*," Jackson said. "New, small, totally exclusive. Great food. Super amenities. Nice crowd."

"Really?" she said faintly. "A crowd?"

"Yeah, John was a lot of fun."

"Nicky needs to chill, though," Garrett said.

"Cassidy seemed to have a good time, too, before she got seasick. Which reminds me. Is her father around? We should probably let him know she's okay."

"He...he left days go." Samantha's head spun. "What about Kambyses?"

Jackson finished pouring juice into three glasses. "Who?"

"The vampire you were going to kill?"

Garrett gave her a have-you-lost-your-mind look. "The what?"

"Do you have any munchies to go with this?" Jackson asked, opening random cabinet doors.

"Oh, good idea, Jack. I could use something to eat."

"Corner cabinet," she whispered and backed away several steps. When she reached the sofa, she spoke out of the corner of her mouth. "Serge, what's happening here?"

His saucered eyes remained riveted to the men in the kitchen. "Such power," he said with unabashed wonder.

"What? Them?" She glanced back, and an army of dread swarmed over her skin on needle feet. The duo amusing themselves in her house at four-thirty in the morning looked like her baby brother and no-good step-uncle, but they were strangers. Terrifying strangers. "They're compelled, aren't they?"

"Yes. They are. In a way I have never seen before."

She grabbed hold of his arm. "Can you undo it?"

"Me?" The question was a squeak lost in the sound of a Mylar bag getting torn open.

"Veggie chips," Garrett said, fishing around inside. Both he and Jackson still had their backs turned to Samantha and Serge. "Don't think I've had these before."

"Knowing Sam, be glad it's not straight-up celery sticks," Jackson countered and grabbed a handful of the chips.

Samantha lowered her voice to a hiss. "Of course, you. Do you see any other vampires here?"

Serge shook his head. "No, I cannot."

"Try."

The fearsome pirate shrank deeper into the cushions. "What must be, will be."

"Are you freaking serious? This is my brother you're talking about. You can't leave him like this for—what?—'til the end of next week? The rest of his life?"

"I am but a witness. Never a part of anything. Don't you see?"

"That didn't stop you meddling when Garrett nearly tortured Dominique to death, did it?"

"That was different. The blood-child asked for help."

"Well, now *I'm* asking."

"You all right there, Sam?" Jackson called.

She looked over her shoulder. The two men watched her and Serge with casual interest. Their jaws crunched through chips in a way that reminded Samantha of cows standing in a field. That simple. That blank.

Back to Serge. "They wouldn't be here if they hadn't been compelled to be here. *Here.*" She jabbed a finger at the floor. "With me. And *you.*"

"Sam, calm down, honey," Garrett said. "If he doesn't want to join us, leave him alone. We came to see you."

Serge rolled his eyes between everyone while his fingers fidgeted.

"Think about it," Sam tried again. "Who else but Dominique would compel them to come here? At this hour?"

"Compel?" Garrett inquired.

Serge's bushy brows gathered over the bridge of his nose.

She turned and marched toward the party in her kitchen. Fine. If the vampire was too cowardly to take a stand, the damsel in distress was about to. "Compelled," she told them straight out. "You two are not in your right minds."

"What are you talking about, Sam?" Jackson said.

"You've been compelled by Kambyses, the first and oldest vampire on the planet."

They frowned, exchanged dubious looks. "Don't think we met anyone by that name," Garrett said.

"And definitely no vampires," Jackson agreed.

"But you know they're real, right, baby bro?"

"Sure. I guess. Maybe?"

Suddenly, Serge appeared by her side, making them all jump.

Jackson raised his hands so fast, the chips he held went flying across the kitchen. "Whoa. Take it easy."

"You are correct," Serge told her. "They can only be a message for me."

"Finally. Gentlemen? There you go. A vampire."

"Not very subtle, are you?" Garrett asked.

Her heart tripped when she saw Serge's eyes flash to pure black. This was her vampire pirate at his best, swinging out of the virtual riggings for a surprise attack.

"Not for the likes of you," he growled and went for Jackson's throat.

32

REMEMBER

Jackson often dreamt he ran alone in the dark, toward a light that kept retreating beyond his reach. Over the years, he had learned to recognize the nightmare and wake himself up. This was different.

This time, he was in a place full of light and peace.

This time the dark came looking for him.

It pooled on the tiles around his feet and oozed from the outlets in the walls, dimmed the lights and clogged the air. Darkness covered his eyes and filled his lungs.

He ran until it swamped around him. Fought until it deluged him. Screamed until it choked him. The sound of his banging heart thundered in his skull.

Remember...

The pounding became the rhythmic beat of helicopter blades. The darkness coalesced into a sleek shape on the ocean surface. A cruise ship. No, a yacht. It belonged to...

Cassidy was there and desperate. "Jackson, I need your help. Get us the hell out of here."

Help her. He had to help her. Why hadn't he? She was so angry, throwing things at...

The darkness shoved at his back, pushing him through a thick veil that grabbed at him with vicious hooked claws. He had to get through, had to get out. Had to get them all out. Had to...

Nick! Where did he come from? He was angry, too, and so wretched when he spoke to...

Jackson gasped for air that wouldn't come. The darkness kept pushing, kept crushing him. He disintegrated against it. If he could only breathe. Then he could scream.

The veil thinned. Through the fog, he could just make out a new face, heard an unfamiliar voice, defining the world in wordless whispers. The voice of God...

The devil! wailed the darkness.

At last, the veil cracked, then shattered, the jagged edges tearing flesh off his bones as he fell through, screaming.

As the agony subsided into a dull throb, a new reality formed around him. True reality. He gasped. His stomach churned, reacting to what he already knew, but had yet to acknowledge.

Someone hovered over him. Tangled curls. Dark eyes, pools of night in a face as round as a moon with bright red lips. The copper smell of blood.

Jackson rolled over and retched.

"Is he okay? Did it work?" his sister asked, sounding more anxious than he had ever heard her.

"It is done," said the darkness that had chased him from the light, the vampire who had just fed on him. "He will need a moment to adjust."

A moment? Jackson was on hands and knees on Samantha's kitchen floor and drowned in memories. He'd lived under a compulsion—in an illusion—for days. An illusion spun by a predator without equal. Both he and Garrett should be dead. They had been captured and subjugated with terrifying ease. Cassidy saw it, knew it, and had fought to reach him.

"You're fucking compelled out of your fucking minds..."
The naked fear in her voice had been the lifeline he should
have known he needed, even if only by instinct. This was
what he had trained for, this skill of recognizing when his
own thoughts failed him. But his moment of recognition
had come and gone in the space of half a heartbeat, a ruthless
monster's power over him complete.

His jaw clenched as he stared down at his sick, splattered
on the tiles between his hands. Helpless anger punched his
solar plexus. They had been taken so easily—by humans, no
less. He had broken his promise of protection to Cassidy,
and on top of it all, he had to be rescued by yet another vampire. Not just any vampire, no, but the fucking bloodsucker
he had killed, and who would not stay dead. Jackson wanted
to howl with it all.

"Yes," Serge said, drawing the word out into a menacing
hiss. "How fortunate you failed, isn't it?"

"Fuck you. And get the fuck out of my head."

"Yep. That's the baby brother I know and love," Samantha
said. "You did it, sweetie. You fixed him."

The vampire drew the back of his wrist across his mouth.
"Not a simple thing, undoing that."

"You all right there, Jack?" Garrett asked as if inquiring
about nothing so much as a stubbed toe. He stood at the
counter, compelled—as Cassidy had rightly claimed—out
of his mind. It was like looking at a happy zombie. A zombie
like he had been.

He choked down the need to throw up again and instead
got to his feet. As he moved, the too-tight jacket he wore
wafted a smoky stench. He tore it off, balled it up, sloppily
wiped the floor with it, and tossed it in the trash bin. The
rest of him stank of sweat and exertion.

Calmer now that he took at least a minor step toward righting the world, he poured himself a glass of water and gulped it, while hyper-aware of the vampire in the room with him.

"Kid, what's going on?"

"Shut up." He turned to his uncle. "Not another word out of you until you're fixed."

Garrett's brow furrowed in confusion, but he said nothing, as ordered.

Jackson shot Serge a look. "Any time."

The vampire shrugged as he considered Garrett. "Maybe I like him better this way."

"You fucking little—"

"Jack," Sam cut in. "Why don't you tell us what you remember now? Where is Cassidy? And did you see Dominique?"

Cassidy. The memories rushed in, ridden hard by guilt and fury.

"I don't know where she is. Last I saw her, she was sick and getting sicker on that yacht. That was a couple of nights ago—" Another memory. "He's turning her. She told me so. I wouldn't listen. Fuck." His hands balled into fists on the countertop.

She wasn't compelled. She knew damn well what she was dealing with. Still, she fought and spoke her mind with a courage that now took his breath away. "You're not worthy!" she had told the most dangerous vampire in history. She might as well have been talking to Jackson.

Sam came to his side and put her hand on his hard-as-rock shoulder. "You didn't have a choice. You were up against way more than you knew how to handle."

He shook his head. "I should have—"

"Where is the blood-child?" Serge demanded.

"Who?"

"Dominique," Sam translated, and more memories crystallized.

"He's aboard. He...he sent us here, I think." Jackson shook his head to dislodge all the tattered cobwebs. Just how many vampires had messed with his head? Even Bijou added her compulsion when she ushered him and Garrett into a hired limo and sent them on their way. She had made her vow quietly, sweetly, and with her green eyes as hard and cold as emeralds. "Never let me see, hear, or smell you again. If I do, you, your family, and everyone else you know and love...will be dead."

They had smiled and nodded.

Now he groaned.

"He sent you to me," Serge confirmed.

"We were there when he spoke to Kambyses about something." He remembered the ancient vampire clearly now, a striking presence that eclipsed his short stature. Nick, too, his shoulders hunched, beaten, as he spoke to his sire, who looked inordinately pleased at what he heard. "Fuck no. Nick agreed to give Cassidy his blood. He's committed them both to stay with that demon."

"No, that can't be right," Sam said. "He would never do that."

Serge backed away and tugged at the front of his Hawaiian shirt. "Tomorrow night. He will do it tomorrow night."

"No," Sam said again as tears pooled in her eyes. "That can't be the destiny you saw for them, Serge. It can't be."

"Together they will change the world of night forever." His voice dropped to a hushed whisper. "So many ways to do that. So many ways"

Jackson slashed the air with a flat hand. "Okay, enough. I don't give a shit about what you two think is going on here, but I'm guessing that if Cassidy doesn't get the blood tomorrow night, she'll die." Though that would be preferable to being turned into a vampire. "We'll get her back." If it killed him, he would get her out of this, human and alive. He'd promised. "We'll get her back."

Everybody, vampire included, looked at him, hushed expectation on their faces. Even his uncle, bemused though he was, uncrossed his arms, leaned on the counter, and waited for Jackson to continue, to speak, to spell out the plan. To save the day. Jackson felt the mantle of responsibility settle on his shoulders with an unaccustomed weightiness.

Taking a deep breath, he gathered his thoughts. "We have this one day to get our shit together, and we're going to start right now. You. Serge."

The vampire blinked as though coming out of a trance.

"Fix that mess masquerading as my uncle."

Serge didn't hesitate. As he passed Jackson on his way to comply, Jackson grabbed him by his shirtfront. "Then do whatever you have to do to be there tomorrow night. You're the backup plan. Got it?"

The vampire gave a dazed nod.

"You think you can save her?" Sam asked and swiped at her eyes. "If you get to her in time?"

Could he? There was no record of anyone coming back from a turning gone as far as Cassidy's probably had. Jackson was willing to gamble that this was only because no one had tried.

Garrett, pinned up against the stainless steel fridge with Serge at his throat, cursed vehemently as he fought the darkness chasing him out of his happy place. The scene brought to mind another memory for Jackson, this one of his twin brother fighting, just like that, in a vampire's clutches.

He turned away and tried to tune out the sounds. "I'm going to do everything I can to save her, Sam. Everything." And he wouldn't hesitate to use every tool at his disposal.

Every last fucking one of them.

33

GAMBLING MEN

Just before noon the following day, Jackson pulled the rented, single-engine Sea Ray away from the Riviera Beach Marina dock. As he headed south, he did his best to stay focused on Cassidy and what they were about to do rather than the new turmoil rattling in the back of his head.

He glanced back at his uncle prepping for the next phase of the operation. Beneath the "disguise" of a ball cap and sunglasses, Garrett's face was all business. There was no trace of the usual feral grin of anticipation, not even now, this close to the target. Jackson's gut squeezed. Their plan was haphazard—more of one giant gamble, really. Success had never been less assured. Or more critical.

"This is one hell of a game you've got us caught up in over this girl," Jackson's father, Warren Striker, had declared this morning when they met in his study.

"It's no game. She—"

"Of course, it's a fucking game," Warren exploded out, and slammed a hand on the surface of the antique desk. His face flushed dark red around a neat gray beard. "They've manipulated you into believing you actually have a chance of taking them all out. You are both pawns, and what's worse, you've made pawns of the rest of us! If you weren't my only surviving heir, I'd deliver you to them on a platter myself!"

Jackson had stood, hands clasped behind his back, and waited for the familiar taste of failure to fill his mouth. True, since he first encountered Nick, everything in his life had gone off a cliff. But that wasn't the biggest disappointment his father lay at his feet. In Warren's eyes, Jackson's greatest failure was that he survived his first mission while Justin, his twin brother, had not.

And now this. They were all at risk—his family, the mission, everyone important to him—because of his miscalculations. Maybe it was just because he was in so deep that going back was no longer an option, but he had to believe that Nick wasn't playing him. He had seen too much of the youngling vampire's unguarded emotions. Nick was a pawn right along with everyone else, and if there was a game, Kambyses was the only one playing.

But none of this would ever convince his father. To the imposing, flint-eyed man seated in front of him, there were only two sides to any issue—human and vampire, life and death. He would never understand, much less tolerate, the gray in-between world that had swallowed his less favored son.

The silence stretched, and the taste of failure remained absent. Something else took root in Jackson's chest instead. His father had trained to hunt along with Garrett, but his clandestine work had been cut short by a random car accident that left him crippled and office-bound, and, Jackson realized, incapable of understanding the realities of the hunt. It left him perpetually angry, too, with far more than his disappointment of an heir.

Jackson continued to meet Warren's accusing glare and watched the older man's expression shift from anger to surprise and finally suspicion. Of course. Not cowering before his father's wrath could only be evidence of a compulsion. Jackson twisted his mouth into an ironic line. There was no winning here, there never had been, but for the first time, that was okay.

Garrett shifted beside him and propped both hands on his hips. "Be that as it may, we really don't have a choice. They've been inside our heads. They know everything there is to know about Foundation business and the family. If we don't take care of this today..."

No need to spell it out. There would be no tomorrow for any of them. Bijou's parting promise of total annihilation still sat heavy in the back of their heads. They could not afford to trust her not to make good on that threat, regardless of what they did.

"We have the advantage today," Jackson said. "They won't expect the compulsion to have worn off this fast."

That set Warren off again, raging about how that compulsion had "worn off," in the first place, and culminating in, "Get the fuck out of my office, both of you, and get this clusterfuck cleaned up." He heaved his bulk out of the oversize chair and leaned on his cane, grimacing in pain. "And Gerry? If anything happens to Jack, you make damn sure it happens to you, too, because I won't want to see your useless dick in this house ever again. You hear me?"

Jackson knew better than to interpret that dire warning to his uncle as anything like concern for him. No, if Jackson died, Warren would have to do what Garrett was incapable of—start another family—and do it for the third time in his life. Assuming he stayed clear of avenging vampires and, given his temper, heart attacks.

While Jackson and Garrett cleaned up, prepped gear, and grabbed an hour of much-needed rest, Warren launched the evacuation of the house and the offices of Striker International Capital Investments, the Foundation's public face and financing source. Jackson's mother, Lillian, was blissfully unaware of all things supernatural, but she knew not to argue with her husband's orders any more than his staff did. Together, they, all domestic personnel, and key management, met two SICI jets warming up at the municipal airport, departing for destinations unknown to Jackson and Garrett. If they got caught again—which Warren clearly believed they would—they wouldn't be able to compromise anyone but themselves.

Last they heard, the jets had been wheels-up twenty minutes ago. Jackson wished Samantha were with them, but she had dug in her heels. She wanted no part of such a pessimistic plan, though she did eventually agree to stay away from her cottage tonight.

Even at a distance and in the light of an overcast day, *Apokryphos* was cloaked in menace. Kambyses, the most powerful target in Foundation history, would be aboard. Right there, out cold, and an easy target—if not for the armed human slaves compelled to defend him to the death.

Normally, when they expected serious daytime resistance like this, Garrett had security pros and militias around the world on speed dial to provide the muscle and firepower required. Today, everyone he called was already on assignment or too far away to act on short notice.

They were on their own. Jackson couldn't shake the sinking feeling that it wouldn't be the last thing to go wrong today.

A "disguise" of ridiculous Hawaiian shirts flapped over their new Kevlar vests as they impersonated hapless tourists out on a pleasure cruise. They motored up to the sprawling Palm Beach mansion fifteen minutes past noon. This first gamble was that the guards would be preoccupied with lunch—either preparing, consuming, or digesting—allowing random boaters to approach under relatively little scrutiny.

With a slow, deep breath, Jackson let the icy calm of the hunt settle over him. Drifting them past the estate, he tried to spot all the surveillance cameras blanketing the property. That would be the day's second great gamble. According to a text message just before sunrise, Nick had hacked into the estate's system and programmed the cameras to go down right about—he checked his watch again—now.

From the bench behind him, Garrett scanned the area through a pair of military-grade binoculars. "Well, well, well. Looks like baby vamp came through."

"They're down?"

"The lights on the ones I can see just went dead." The binoculars pivoted to the yacht. "Can't tell if anyone's on the bridge. Let's stay out of the direct line of sight."

As they were about to pass the vessel's stern, Jackson turned in sharply and threw the motor in reverse before cutting it off entirely. The Sea Ray coasted up to *Apokryphos's* landing platform in silence. While Garrett took the wheel, Jackson grabbed a line, hopped aboard, and tied off on a cleat.

So far, so good.

All remained quiet as they shed their disguises and collected their gear. Taut lines squeaked as the yacht shifted in the currents sloshing beneath the dock. Brine and fresh-cut lawn soaked the damp air. No hint of smoke.

Garrett activated one of the small signal jammers he brought and stuck it to the side of the hull facing away from the dock. He activated another one in his pack. The radius was limited, but it would render any nearby mobile or radio device useless.

The gamble of their timing faltered the moment they started creeping up the short twin flights of stairs to the main deck, and the sound of a door slamming froze them in place. Clearly, someone was not occupied with lunch. Unhurried footsteps, along with a rolling clatter, approached. The clatter stopped, but the footsteps continued moving off toward the dock.

The would-be invaders looked at each other. Garrett, crouched on the port side of the platform, signaled Jackson to hold position.

Fuck that. Stretching his body up the narrow starboard stairway, he slowly poked his eyeballs over the edge. A large rolling bucket bristling with cleaning supplies sat in the middle of the open deck. The bucket's keeper, a lanky young man in crew-standard black slacks and T-shirt, was busy wrestling a hose from the dock.

Jackson glanced at the expanse of salt-smeared windows and decks apparently slated for a scrubbing. This kid would be busy for hours. Or he might be the first of several crew on this task. The landing platform was likely part of the cleaning project. It was only a matter of minutes before the Sea Ray was discovered—along with Jackson and Garrett—and the alarm went up.

If they didn't move fast, they were fucked. Ditto if they stayed where they were. Another gamble.

He scanned the windows, deck, and dock for a solution. Still only the one guy, dragging the coiling, ornery hose toward the bucket.

It was now or never.

When he turned his head to alert Garrett, he found his uncle already hovering behind him, silenced gun in hand, impatient expression on face. "Go!" Garrett mouthed.

Jackson scrambled, Garrett on his heels. Under the covering racket of water blasting into the bucket, they bolted up the stairs and across the deck behind the crewman's back. As they hustled down the starboard promenade to the main entrance, Jackson drew his own gun. His belly roiled as he took it off safety. If this turned into a gunfight, they were fucked every which way.

Garrett took the lead going through the door, moving like the trained commando he was, silent, alert—ready to kill. Muted kitchen clatter greeted them in the small lobby, but no crew. Gun pointed at the deck in a two-handed hold, Jackson monitored the stairway and door to the salon while Garrett tucked another jammer into the coat closet.

They slipped down the corridor to the suites. To the right was their cabin. Ahead lay the door to Cassidy's prison. Four nights and days they had spent here like college kids on spring break while she suffered. All those missed opportunities. The thought made his jaw clench with fury.

With his fingers, Garrett counted down three. Then they burst through the unlocked door. Rumpled sheets covered the bed, towels piled on a chair, and a tray of uneaten food filled the stale air with fetid rot. But there was no Cassidy.

While Garrett opened the small closet, Jackson headed for the bathroom. It, too, was empty. "Shit." This operation was unraveling at a record pace. He had sworn to help her, save her. Instead, she was closer to death—and worse—with every minute he wasted. Maybe his father was right. Everything Jackson touched, he bungled. "Shit!"

Garrett joined him in the extravagant bathroom. He had holstered his weapon and pulled another jammer from his pack. Activating it, he handed it to Jackson. "Under-sink cabinet."

Securing and holstering his own gun, he knelt and did as told, even as frustration and panic raced each other up his spine. Most of the yacht, including the bridge just above them, was now in a bubble of signal silence, but that wouldn't be much of an advantage if they had to search this ship of nightmares deck-by-deck. Eventually, someone would spot them.

A second later, he realized it was already too late.

34

SHAMBLING BEARS

The unmistakable sound of the cabin door clicking open made the hunters freeze in place.

"Fuck," Jackson mouthed, envisioning one of the addled and brawny crewmen seconds away from trapping them in a bathroom with nowhere to hide. Was nothing going to go right for them?

Garrett pivoted to the door. His hand reached for the Glock, but he kept the weapon in its holster as he stepped back into the cabin.

"Mister Garrett?" a surprised female voice said. "You still here?"

"It looks that way," Garrett said amiably. Jackson stood and looked over his uncle's shoulder.

The maid gawked, confused but not alarmed. She smiled when she noticed him, apple cheeks coloring, and Jackson stifled a groan as he remembered how recklessly his compelled ass had flirted with this girl. Her hands clutched before her. "I sorry I so late today. They say you check out."

"That's alright, Carmen," Jackson said as he pushed past Garrett, who was wearing a terrifying caricature of a dopey smile. "We just stopped in to check on Cassidy. Do you know where she is?"

"Oh, Miss Cassidy gone for the day with Miss Monica."

"So she'll be back?" Jackson asked, forcing a buoyant tone. Garrett shot him a warning glare over the death grimace.

The maid frowned. "I think so?"

"Okay, thank you, Carmen. We'll check back later," Garrett sang and dragged Jackson out of the cabin by an elbow. "For the love of God, don't waste a stroke of luck with small talk," he hissed under his breath. In the lobby, he headed for the stairway.

Jackson grabbed his shoulder. "She won't be down there. They must have moved her to the house."

"Or she could be dead," Garrett snapped. "That maid only knows what she's told to know."

"We can't risk getting trapped down there until we've searched everywhere else."

Garrett's mouth pinched with banked anger. "Down there" was Kambyses along with about ten or twelve armed crew who were likely compelled to kill them on sight. But Kambyses was not their first priority. Getting Cassidy medical care was. Jackson had insisted, and Garrett had grudgingly agreed. Once that was done, there would be plenty of time to separate Kambyses from his head and bring the apocalypse down on every bloodsucker in existence.

"I'm going to the house," Jackson said and turned to the exit. They had also agreed that they wouldn't split up this time, and he counted on his uncle not to risk both their lives by arguing about it now. He didn't.

The plan had been to secure Cassidy on the Sea Ray and get her to an ambulance before dealing with Kambyses. Instead, they walked down the dock, fully exposed in the middle of the day, on their way to break into a mansion. They walked as quickly as they dared while also looking like they belonged there, gambling—again—that at a distance, their black clothing could be mistaken for crew uniforms. If someone aboard saw them go and thought otherwise, the jammers they had left made it impossible to notify anyone else.

Once on the property, they veered off the paved path and hugged the shadows of the box-trimmed hedges up to the main house. With soft pops from his silenced Glock, Garrett knocked out every camera they spotted—just in case—reminding Jackson of his own less-than-stellar marksmanship skills. With his right hand crippled, and training with his left lagging, he was far from sharp shooter material.

He followed his uncle across the spongy green lawn to a side door. Beside it, hidden in more manicured greenery, was a large Briggs and Stratton generator. While Garrett picked the lock, Jackson located the generator's propane line and twisted the handle to the closed position.

Once inside the garage, they broke open the circuit breaker panel and threw the master power switch. The generator outside sputtered briefly before falling silent again, starved of fuel. For good measure, Garrett fired a round into the panel and the transfer switch. The house would be powerless for the foreseeable future—and all surveillance equipment along with it, hacked or not.

Most of it, anyway.

A human surveillance system was already tromping down the hall the moment they cracked open the door to the house itself, a beefy brute in jeans and a shirt tight enough to show off enormous pecs. Probably coming to see why the generator had failed. Coordinating with quick gestures, the hunters flattened against the wall to either side of the door and waited for their prey to step through.

Before Pecs realized he wasn't alone, Jackson landed a right hook with devastating force. Garrett took it from there with a chokehold. Two minutes after that, Mr. Security lay in the trunk of a BMW, hogtied with FlexiCuffs and gagged with duct tape. One eye looked puffy. The other blazed fury.

Jackson swiped the radio from the guy's belt, set it to low, and clipped it to his own vest. "So, Uncle Garrett. You do know how to play well with others, after all."

Garrett slammed the trunk on their catch. "Let's keep these incidents to a minimum, shall we?"

Jackson took point as they advanced into the house. His nose caught the scent of food cooking before he heard dishes clattering through an arched doorway up ahead. Risking a peek around the corner, he spotted two unfamiliar men and a woman eating wordlessly at a table. Mr. Security's cohorts, judging by their prime physical conditioning and sidearms. Probably Bijou's enslaved daytime security detail.

Other noises came from areas of the kitchen not visible from his vantage point. Impossible to say who was there or even how many. Before he could over-think it, he soft-footed past the entry. Garrett followed.

They encountered no one else all the way through the grandiose foyer and up the pompous staircase. The dead eyes of the security cameras did not see them, and the radio remained silent. On the second floor, a single small window at the far end cast a gray gloom over a hallway, lined by four doors on each side. With Garrett covering his back, Jackson, gun back in his hand, moved quickly and silently from door to door. Each room featured a different decorative style, catering to a variety of sensual proclivities. All were empty.

Doubt nudged Jackson. Could she still be on the yacht after all? Had she died? Or...? No, he refused to entertain that possibility. He would *not* find her in a dark corner somewhere in a vampire's daytime coma, never to wake again because she, too, would die when Kambyses met his end.

He opened the second to last door. Heavy brocade drapes, wide open, revealing a bed and—

"In here!" he called softly.

Garrett, who had been moving down the hall backward, keeping an eye out for pursuers, turned and slipped through the door with Jackson. While his uncle canvased the room and the adjoining bathroom, Jackson holstered his gun and leaned over the gaunt body on the bed.

His relief at finding her drained away at the sight of her bloodless face. He probed her neck. Found only a thready pulse.

Behind him, Garrett muttered a curse. "For the love of God, Jack. The only place she's going is the morgue. There's nothing you can do for her."

The pulse ticked harder against his fingers as her eyes fluttered open deep in their sockets. Those eyes. Glazed with exhaustion, but clear blue as the sky. Her spirit was still in this shell of a body, still alive and fighting.

"Hey, Cass," he said, taking one of her flaccid, fever-hot hands in his. "We're getting you out of here. Hang on just a little longer, okay?"

Her cracked lips barely moved. "Jack?"

"Yes, babe. It's me. The real me." He nodded at Garrett. "Him, too."

"About...fuuugin time."

Jackson grinned. "That's my girl."

The radio clipped to his vest crackled quietly. "Status check."

He held his breath. No reply. No follow up.

"That's our cue, Jack. Time to go."

Jackson pulled back the covers and paused in shock. She was skin and bones, dressed in nothing but a slip, her movements feeble as a newborn kitten. "Garrett, grab that blanket over there. Help me get her wrapped up."

"Jack—"

"Just do it!"

Garrett cursed under his breath, but complied. Together, they bundled her emaciated body into Jackson's arms, her head lolling against his shoulder. Gun muzzle leading the way, Garrett carefully opened the door...and stopped.

"Well, if it isn't the special one," he drawled and let the door swing wide.

Monica stood in the hall, hands clasped. "You can't take her. Don't you understand? She'll die if you take her away." Heedless of the silencer pointed at her sternum, she stepped toward them. "Please don't do this. If you care for her at all, let this process conclude. There is no other hope for her."

Jackson hated himself for the renewed doubt bubbling in his belly. Cassidy, a boneless weight in his arms, gave no sign she even heard the conversation. He tightened his hold on her.

"Why don't you explain it to us some more?" Garrett gestured "come in" with the Glock.

Monica, dressed in a fluttering white tunic over a pair of blue jeans, advanced, her anxious eyes locked to Garrett's. "The process can't be reversed now. She should have received the blood last night, but she wanted to witness one more sunrise."

"Stop right there," Garrett warned.

She didn't seem to hear him. "I pray that won't cost Cassidy her life. I pray she survives to sunset."

"She'll be fine if we get her out of here now," Jackson said to convince himself more than anyone else.

"No! You're killing her." Tears now. Wild gesticulation. The tip of the silencer almost touched her sternum.

"We don't have time for this." In one fluid motion, Garrett holstered the Glock, grabbed Monica's wrist, pulled her around against himself and clamped a hand over her mouth. She didn't protest, though Jackson realized a moment too late that her quiet had nothing to do with surprise and everything with intention.

Her free hand flashed beneath the drapes of her shirt. Then the unmistakable electric snapping of a stun gun filled the air before it went silent against its target.

Teeth clenching, eyes bugging, hands flailing, Garrett jerked from head to foot in a violent, uncoordinated dance. Finally, he crashed to the floor, curled into a fetal position, and lay still.

"What the fuck," Jackson said before he could stop himself.

Monica retrieved Garrett's firearm and tossed it aside. Then she studied her handiwork. Gone was the desperate woman of moments ago. A fire-haired warrior savoring victory stood in her place. "What a pity that fancy vest of yours doesn't cover those tender bits."

Jackson's mind reeled. Just like that, he was on his own and up to his eyeballs in alligators. Again. He spun on a heel to put Cassidy back on the bed, but by the time he reached for his gun, it was already pointing at his forehead.

"No sudden moves," said the man holding it, one of the two he had just seen eating downstairs.

Jackson slowly raised his hands and tried to think. He'd have to lull them, bide his time until he saw an opportunity to act. Until Garrett got over his fried balls. He glanced at his uncle and ground his back teeth in frustration. The second male guard was there, too. He had pocketed the Glock, retrieved a pair of FlexiCuffs, and reached for Garrett's wrists. When Garrett tried to struggle, Monica stuck him with the stun gun again, this time in the neck. He collapsed, moaning, perhaps unconscious, judging by how limp his arms were as they were secured behind his back.

Jackson bit back a blue curse. How the fuck was he going to overpower one cunning chick, two trained guards, and two loaded guns all by himself?

Without getting anyone he cared about killed?

Before sunset?

"Don't blame yourself," Monica said, advancing on him. "I've had my master's blood. I heard the two of you breathing like bears shambling past the kitchen." She cocked her head at him, her smile as empty as her eyes. "And since you're so obsessed with helping Cassidy, I think I know just what to do with you."

35

Would-Be Assistants

Dominique returned to consciousness with a profound sense of doom. His plans hadn't been more than a pale hope, but hope nevertheless. Now this, too, vanished in the encroaching night.

He still lived, which meant Kambyses did as well. The hunters had failed yet again. And if Cassidy wasn't dead already, her fate was sealed.

Merde.

He leaned his head against the equipment rack in the cramped little wiring closet and felt despair circle like a hungry shark. Then he realized he was hearing heartbeats. Two of them, human, and close.

Tension rippled across his shoulders. He had chosen this closet for his daytime refuge for its proximity to Cassidy and its relative remoteness to the rest of the house, *Apokryphos,* and Kambyses. For once, being discovered while he slept hadn't figured into his calculations. If either Kambyses or Bijou wanted him dead, they would do the job themselves, not delegate it to their human slaves.

He flared his nostrils to taste the air and cursed.

Outside, the heartbeats escalated.

Dominique slammed the door open and stepped into the moody light of a small home theater. Fifteen leather recliners in three rows faced him, all empty except for two at the front. He barely kept his voice down. "You useless pieces of shit!"

The Strikers stared up at him, bug-eyed and disheveled, mouths plastered with duct tape, tied hand and foot and lashed to their seats by sturdy rope. Dominique scraped up the edge of Jackson's gag with a fingernail and yanked without mercy.

Jackson gasped. "Fuck, ow!"

"You will get worse yet for this latest blunder, which is sure to be your last."

"Maybe if you stop talking and get me untied, we can still get something done."

"Imbeciles. Mere mortals keep getting the better of you during the light of day. Now that night has come, you are as good as dead." Dominique snapped off the plastic ties around Jackson's ankles and reached for the rope across his chest. In the next seat, Garrett grunted with impatient fury.

The door at the back of the room opened. "What's going on in—"

Recognizing the situation, the woman, a security guard judging by her outfit and weapon, spun on a heel. But before she could do more than draw breath to shout, Dominique clamped the discarded piece of duct tape across her mouth and hauled her to the front of the theater.

There was no time to waste on trying to overpower her existing compulsion. The impulse to kill her flickered in his mind, an impulse he now understood to be his sire's. Dominique quickly squashed it, disarmed his captive, used Jackson's rope to truss her up snug as a chicken for the oven, retrieved his swords from the electrical closet, shoved in the chicken, and latched the door.

Not quite ten seconds had elapsed since the door opened.

His audience stared.

Jackson recovered first. He wormed out of the recliner and turned to present his bound hands to Dominique. "Any time."

Dominique snapped the tie. "Did you find Cassidy at all?"

"Yes. Around noon. Very weak, but still coherent. We had her, Nick. Then Monica—"

"Excuses? Truly?" When he freed Garrett, he took special pleasure in tearing off the gag with a violent flourish that ripped up a day's growth of beard along with it.

"Son of a bitch," the old hunter cursed and wiggled his jaw.

"Monica says Kambyses gave her his blood. She heard us breathing, for fuck's sake."

Dominique barely stopped to chastise himself for that unexpected development. This concept had never even crossed his mind outside of the actual making of a blood-drinker. He had dismissed the woman as inconsequential from the beginning, a potentially irrevocable mistake. "Regardless, she is human. As was everyone else here today." He slung the swords across his back. "You have one last chance to get Cassidy out of this house alive. If you fail—"

"Don't you dare threaten us, too, you punk," Garrett snapped. "Your friends are way ahead of you there."

Dominique arched a brow.

"Bijou made it clear she'd come after everyone we know," Jackson said.

Of course she would. "So much more motivation not to fuck up this time, *non*? Go get Cassidy, run, do not look back. I will do all I can to keep your path clear."

Garrett put up a hand. "No. Jack and I are done risking our lives for a girl that is more than likely already dead. We're leaving and revisiting this in the morning."

Jackson's eyes widened, but before he could speak, Dominique had Garrett by the front of his shirt. "You are mortals in a blood-drinker house after sunset. The only way you leave here alive is with my help. Which you will not have unless Cassidy is with you," he finished on a low growl.

Fury flashed in Garrett's eyes, but he said nothing. Message received. Dominique let him go.

From a seat in the next row, Jackson collected two small backpacks, and secured the loose roll of duct tape into one before slinging it over his shoulder. "I'm here for Cassidy," he said and tossed the other pack at his uncle. "With or without you."

Garrett cursed. "We have no weapons, no Kevlar, nothing. Just how far do you think we're going to get past that door with nothing but utility gear?" He brandished the pack before throwing it aside.

"You have me," Dominique said. "And you have this." He handed the captured guard's pistol to Jackson without looking away from Garrett. "Now shut your ugly face and let's go." He sped to the door.

"Hell's freezing over," Garrett said under his breath.

Jackson scoffed. "Took you long enough to figure that out."

Outside the theater was a study, richly appointed in tones of green, red, and gold. A gas fireplace hissed, and a small Christmas tree filled one corner, adding a festive glow. In the adjoining living room, a TV was on. Beneath the prattle of a newscast, he could also hear a pair of human hearts.

Dominique hugged the shadows and waited for his would-be human assistants to creep their way to his side, which took enough time for ugly doubts to nip at him. It had been a week since he drank the fire-blood, and the effects were fading quickly. It would take more than physical strength to hold off Bijou, much less Kambyses. Their best chance lay in distraction and subterfuge.

"Be ready to move," he told Jackson and Garrett, then blurred away into the next room. To the two men—both armed—catching up on the headlines, he appeared out of nowhere. Before they could do more than register surprise, he touched his voice with compulsion and said, "Your mistress requires your services outside. Now."

As they hustled out the nearest door, something shattered back in the study. Dominique flashed back in time to see Garrett pull an antique dagger out of a display case he had crushed underfoot. Raising his new weapon, Garrett gave Dominique a narrow look as though calculating how best to use it on him.

Dominique signaled impatiently. "*Allez.* Go."

The humans moved with as much speed and stealth as they could, which wasn't much. The temptation to pick them up and carry them to Cassidy's room made his fingers twitch. Their breathing and rushing blood roared in his sensitive ears, so he wasn't surprised when he caught Bijou's woody fragrance only a moment before he emerged into the foyer.

Make that an arena.

With its tall, black walls, elliptical shape, and dramatic sconce lighting, the entrance hall took on shades of the Roman Colosseum. There were even spectators. The two guards he sent scurrying moments ago hung over the second floor rail, their faces gleaming with blood lust. Stone Aphrodite and her pillar had been moved to the side. Taking her place in the spotlight at the arena's center, clad in leather and gathering her chains, was the defending champion.

Bijou smiled with malevolence. "Your pitiful mortals were warned not to venture here again. Their lives are mine."

"Chains? Against 'pitiful mortals?'" Dominique replied in English for the benefit of said pitiful mortals behind him.

Bijou also switched to English. Her doll face distorted into something fierce and ugly. "Perhaps I suspect you will be foolish, young one."

Dominique moved into the arena, aware of every infinitesimal movement she made with every heightened sense at his command. "Or perhaps you doubt yourself against me now."

Unlike at their last encounter, he spotted the twitch in her small, white wrist an instant before the chain came flying his way. He ducked the moment it would have wrapped around his neck. Instead, it whistled past his head with millimeters to spare. The other chain hurtled over the floor, coming for his feet. Tucking into a tight ball, he launched over it sideways.

He hadn't yet landed when the sharpened weight on the end of the first chain flew at his head. He twisted in mid-air, letting a scabbard take the brunt of the impact and then pushed off the floor, rolling in the opposite direction at lightning speed. The feint earned him a precious instant of clear access to his target. As he reared up and rushed forward, he pulled the short *wakizashi* sword from its sheath and brought it down in a flashing arc of lethal intent.

Shock registered on Bijou's face. Her arm jerked, directing the chains. It didn't matter. His blade was about to split her in two from head to groin.

Or it would have—if all the power didn't suddenly drain out of his arm.

Shattering pain radiated through his shoulder, and the sword fell from his numb fingers as Bijou vanished.

The chains found him an instant later.

36

WINGING IT

"Aren't you done trying to get us killed yet?" Garrett raged. "You hit the wrong bloodsucker!"

Jackson lowered the gun he clutched with both hands and watched, horrified, as the chains whistled around Nick like steel whips. Shooting the vamp bitch to give Nick an advantage had been an insane gamble, given the phenomenal speed of their combat. An insane gamble that would have paid off—if Nick had just stayed the fuck down. Now their only hope for getting out of this disaster alive was a bloody rag doll lashed near the top of a marble pillar. *Fuck, fuck, fuck!*

Vamp bitch stood before her captive with hands resting on leather wrapped hips. Blood oozed from a gash across her forehead, stark red against the porcelain skin.

"Foolish, foolish boy," she cooed in a voice that was both terrifying and seductive.

Nick strained against the chains, grimacing and snarling. Only his legs had any wiggle room, and he slammed his heels into the pillar at his back. Above him, the Greek goddess wobbled. Stone gaze never wavering, graceful arms never flailing, Aphrodite dove to the floor. Her head cratered into the glass tile and snapped off, exploding away like a bowling ball flying for a strike.

"*Vous êtes des imbéciles!*" vamp bitch shrieked. "Is nothing sacred to you?"

Nick spat a gob of blood in her direction. She sidestepped it in a blur and just as quickly backhanded him across the face so hard Jackson heard bones crunch. More blood gushed from Nick's nose and filled the air with the cold metal smell of youngling blood. He was no match for these primeval forces. Yet, he railed against them, seeming to wing it more often than not, and somehow he got further than all of Jackson's careful plotting ever did.

Jackson moved before he could think about that one too long.

Garrett grabbed his arm. "What are you doing?"

"Winging it. It's all we've got left."

For once, his uncle had no argument. The only thing that stood between them and certain death was one outmatched youngling vampire.

The Foundation's field operations standards continued to plummet.

"God in heaven," Garrett muttered, but fell in behind Jackson, dagger at the ready. As they hustled forward, Jackson remembered the small flashlight no one had considered important enough to remove from his pocket. Retrieving it, he thumbed it on and held it clutched in two hands together with the gun.

Nick saw them coming and redoubled his efforts to get free of the chain, which, thanks to gravity, was already unraveling. He also began hurling what must have been choice French obscenities, capturing the vamp bitch's full attention and giving them the slimmest of advantages.

Vamp bitch, according to Foundation records, had last seen sunlight in the fourteenth century. She was a super predator to be tracked, trapped, and dispatched during the light of day only.

Yet, here they were, charging her wide-awake and infuriated self with nothing but a gun and a pocket light—and their veins full of serum. His steps almost faltered as he recalled that last bit. All the anger in the world wouldn't cloak their intentions in a direct psychic link.

And it didn't.

Bijou's platinum-blonde head snapped around, her face the horrific blank of an aroused vampire.

Jackson pulled the trigger, the shot like an explosion in the confined space.

A plume of red exploded on her bare shoulder—as opposed to the head he had targeted. The next instant, she came at him, black-eyed and bare-fanged—straight into the full-spectrum beam of his flashlight. Her obsidian eyes shut, and she screeched with hellish fury, but she did not retreat.

Jackson pumped the trigger again, this time at close range. Not that it made any difference. Between the adrenaline, his crippled hand, and pointing the light, he had no aim to speak of. Also, his target was gone.

More gunfire erupted from two different directions, turning the elliptical foyer into the inside of a giant gong, vibrating with the blows of sledgehammers. Shards of glass blasted up from the floor at his feet, and heat seared his right shoulder. Fuck, how could he forget about the armed guards? Winging it was going to get them killed long before the vampires could catch them.

Jackson dropped and separated his hands, keeping the light trained on Bijou, and pivoting the gun up at the security detail on the second floor landing. He squeezed off several rounds, sending them diving for cover, before swinging toward a doorway where two more guards held position. One of them was the female guard Nick had stuffed in the closet. So much for the youngling's success rate at winging it then. *Fuck!*

From the corner of his eye, he saw Garrett lunge toward Bijou with the antique dagger. At the same time, the flashlight and pistol tore out of Jackson's hands.

Garrett stopped in his tracks, eyes going wide.

All the guns fell silent, leaving only the gong to vibrate inside Jackson's head.

Bijou stood close enough to touch, her skin glowing bright red across her blood-smeared face and shoulders. A swarm of blisters on her forehead melted away, along with the gash Nick's blade had left there. With a dark growl, she raised Jackson's gun and leveled it at his left eye.

Jackson lifted his hands in surrender, as though carrying a fifty-pound weight in each. The anger he depended on to carry him through trembled. The terror was far too close to the surface, his options by far too non-existent.

She watched his face, took his scent. Her hyper-dilated eyes reverted to their jewel green color and narrowed. "Oh, but you are a brave fool, are you not?" Her small mouth puckered. "And such a fine male specimen. I believe I have a use for you, after all."

Jackson wanted to hurl at the implication. Garrett coughed beside him, then wheezed, but Jackson refused to look away from the vampire with the gun until Garrett sagged to his knees.

"Not so much use for that one," Bijou mused.

"Garrett?"

His uncle looked up, bug-eyed and slack-jawed with wonder or shock, or both. Blood edged his pale lips, and his hands...his hands clutched at the ornate hilt of the dagger protruding from his ribcage.

"No!" Jackson put his arms around the man who was more of a father to him than his real father had ever been, but the best he could do was brace him, keep him from a hard landing on the glass floor. He touched the hilt, hesitated. The blade wasn't near the heart, but it obviously pierced a lung. No telling what kind of damage removing it would do.

Garrett's breathing labored, rattled, and bubbled as he collapsed all the way to the floor. "Wing it. Great idea...kid."

Rage overwhelmed Jackson as suddenly as the fear had earlier. First his brother, now his uncle. Tomorrow, his parents? Samantha? No, never, not without a fight, no matter how hopeless. Roaring at the top of his lungs, he bolted to his feet and threw himself at Bijou.

Streaks of silver flashed through the haze of red before his eyes. She lowered the weapon, her expression amused, but didn't otherwise move, not until he closed his hands around her neck. He squeezed with all his strength, knowing logically that this would accomplish nothing, yet feeling absurdly satisfied when her head popped off her shoulders anyway.

Her head.

In his hands.

Smiling.

The rest of her lay prone beneath him. Thick blood oozed from the stump of her neck. The aroma of wood shavings enveloped him.

"What—what the—?" Jackson dropped the head and willed himself to see the truth beyond this hallucination. He couldn't. Nothing changed.

The bloody tip of a sword flicked Bijou's head away. Still she smiled, frozen as the stone head she bumped up against. Grubby bare toes curled to avoid the lake of blood spreading across the white floor. Jackson looked up to find a sand-encrusted wild man grinning at him. The backup plan. Serge. That was Nick's sword in his hand. Nick's sword he had used to cut down Bijou an instant before she might well have stopped being amused and killed Jackson. The same instant he had distracted her with his irrational attack, giving Serge the opening he needed.

Jackson doubled over and heaved. His entire body shook with the adrenaline pounding through him, the realization of how close he had come to dying, how close Garrett still was.

Nick untangled himself from the last of the chains and sped to Serge's side. He was blood-smeared and disheveled, but he moved without hesitation, recovered from his battle and from that unfortunate bullet.

Jackson turned to his uncle, who was anything but recovered. His breathing sounded like the drowned end of an air hose and his face had gone gray. His eyes rolled with wild panic.

"Is this how you do not interfere with almighty destiny?" Nick asked of Serge, holding out his hand for the sword.

The other vampire handed it over with grave reluctance, but there was a note of pride in his voice when he said, "My services were requested."

"A minute sooner might have been nice," Jackson said. He scanned the area for new threats, but the guards were all gone.

In a blur of speed, Nick wiped the short sword on the leather skirt adorning Bijou's headless corpse.

Garrett coughed up more blood.

"He's drowning," Jackson said.

"Obviously," Nick replied, and slammed the blade home into its scabbard.

"Can't you do something for him? Or do I really need to call 911? He's not going to make it."

Garrett groaned and closed his hand on Jackson's forearm in unmistakable warning. He'd return from the almost-dead and crawl out of here under his own power before he'd let a bloodsucker play doctor on him. Too bad.

Nick opened his mouth, but hesitated when he caught Jackson's look. "He is not my priority."

"He needs to be, blood-child." Serge's gaze emptied as he stared at Garrett in a way that gave Jackson an involuntary chill. "You will need him greatly."

Nick spewed a volley of passionate French, followed by, "Then you see to it, old fool. I *request* it of you."

Serge squeaked in surprise, but Nick was gone. Jackson only caught a dark blur at the top of the stairs because he knew to look for it there. The hand clamped around his arm turned into a steel vise. For a dying man, his uncle's grip was impressive.

Serge knelt beside his patient, eyed the protruding dagger hilt, and cracked his knuckles. The patient tried to roll away. Jackson pinned Garrett to the ground by the shoulders and glared at Serge. "One wrong move and—"

"And nothing."

Jackson shut up. What an idiotic thing to say. There was nothing he could do. For once, he had zero control. Or maybe control had always been an illusion. Or at least since the moment he let Nick out of that cage all those months ago. Right there was where the line between mortal enemy and ally began to blur, and his reality took on new shades of gray.

Serge shrugged. "Besides, I don't know what the right moves are."

"What?"

"I can—" Suddenly, he pinned Jackson with a panic-stricken stare. "You didn't tell the blood-child what you intend."

"What?" he said again.

"With the sweet one." Hyper-quick glance up the stairs. Back to Jackson. "You must go. Now. Before he changes everything the wrong way."

"I'm not leaving my uncle, you nut job. Help him. Now."

The vampire's bushy brows pinched together, his anxiety cresting into snarling impatience. "He will transform her, and murder the light within her if you do not follow your destiny!"

Between them, Garrett began to convulse and turn blue—and dropped out of view. Jackson reached for him, but he was gone. The entire world morphed away in a rush of sound. He couldn't even think to flail until he was put back on his feet in the upstairs hallway that flashed into existence around him. Serge grabbed him by the biceps and spun him around to face a door that stood ajar.

"Do what must be done," the vampire whispered, and abruptly released him.

Jackson turned around, staggering to keep his balance. The hall was deserted. "Son of a bitch."

He stuffed the urge to run back to his uncle's side. He'd never get there in time to do anything for him. Vampire blood really was Garrett's only option, and Jackson would have to trust in Serge to provide it in time.

Movement caught his eye through the open door. Monica stepped into view, her attention riveted to something Jackson couldn't see but could well imagine: Cassidy. This was her room.

And her, he knew he could save.

37

The Evening's Business

Dominique found Cassidy where he left her that morning, laid in a bed under a brocade comforter and facing a window. Out there, over the sea, the last of the day's light faded from the sky.

The last of her light wasn't far behind.

"Finally," Monica said and rose from the bedside where she had dabbed Cassidy's forehead with a cloth. She wore blue jeans, a black turtleneck sweater, and sensible shoes, clearly prepared to be agile and unattractive to a newborn blood-drinker with no control.

"What is going on down there? Were those shots—" She faltered when she caught sight of his face, completely healed but still covered in the gore of battle.

He pushed past Monica and took her place at Cassidy's side. Her breath came in shallow sips, and her heart made weak and erratic thuds, faltering every few thumps. The fighting spirit of the night before was gone. A corpse-in-waiting lay before him. His dying soul.

Cradling her face in both hands, he caressed her chapped lips and delicate jaw with his thumbs. Her skin felt clammy cool, her fever broken, the beast fading, taking her with it. "Cassidy. Cassie, *mon amour. Mon tout. Écoute-moi.* Listen to me."

When she didn't react, he dared a gentle shake. "I am here. Wake up. Please, please wake up."

Nothing.

Too long. He had waited too long, his gamble lost. It was more than his desperate need to see her human spirit shine in her eyes one last time, to see her understanding and acceptance of what was about to happen to her. She also needed to be conscious to swallow the blood he would give her.

His insides convulsed in a sob.

"She was awake only an hour ago," Monica said softly behind him. "She asked for you."

He slumped forward and touched his forehead to Cassidy's. Shattering grief threatened to pull him under.

A rush of breath against his face. A sigh.

"Cassie," he said, voice breaking.

Her eyes opened into thin slits, filled with recognition and alarm, and opened wider. "I...ready."

Relief seized him, followed hard and fast by bitter resolve. Yes, he would do the unthinkable. And he would do it to the absolute best of his ability. He would give her his blood, all the blood she needed and wanted. Now, all night, the next night and beyond. He would hold back nothing.

His vision shifted, rendering her a husk barely dusted with the spark of life. Her once-vibrant golden aura was a mere wisp clinging to her skin. His fangs emerged, and he ran his tongue over one sharp point hard enough to split the flesh clean through. As his mouth flooded with the blood he would feed her, he leaned forward for the kiss that would deliver it and bind them for the rest of time.

"No. Don't interrupt!"

Dominique's head snapped up at Monica's strident order. There came Jackson, a bull charging across the room. Impossible. He'd just left him downstairs. Before he could puzzle it out, Jackson barreled his shoulder into Dominique's side and tore him off Cassidy's prone body. No sooner did they hit the mattress beside her, then Dominique gripped Jackson's shoulders and rolled him beneath himself. Blood flew from Dominique's snarling lips and splattered over the human's face...and into his open mouth.

Jackson stared up at him, his eyes bugging from their sockets. He coughed and spluttered, swallowed, then sucked in a violently deep breath. His back arched like a drawn bow, but his limbs trembled.

Dominique sat back, straddling Jackson, watching with his enhanced vision as the human man's muddy red aura gained a cold, silvery sparkle. Jackson had serum in his system from both Kambyses and Serge. Two doses wouldn't be enough to start the process...would it?

Long seconds later, Jackson stabilized. His eyes dilated like those of a strung-out junkie. "Oh. Fuuuuuuck."

Dominique wiped the blood from his mouth with the back of his hand and moved off Jackson, who sat up and looked around with a sort of apprehensive wonder. The effect was obvious, but he wasn't turning. His immune system was still strong.

But Cassidy's immune system—and life—was all but gone. She had turned her head, watching them. "Got some...for me, too?"

"*Oui, chérie.* All you want and more."

"Wait." Jackson grabbed his arm with a speed and force that surprised them both. "We can save her. Keep her human."

Dominique hesitated. He didn't dare hope. Nor was there time to discuss this. She was too far gone to dally. Still, he couldn't stop himself from asking, "How?"

"We have to get her to a hospital. No, listen. I've thought about this, Nick. This is a viral infection that's overpowering her weakened immune system. There's no reason she can't recover if she gets enough blood and gets her strength back."

"How certain are you of this?"

"I haven't seen it done, but—"

"Heard of it being done?"

"No, but—"

"If I give her my blood now, I *know* she will continue to exist."

"The infection takes hold because of the anemia. Reverse that and it has to clear up." He gestured for emphasis. "Think about it. It's a wimp of a virus. You know that. Every time you get near a bit of daylight, you know that. You really think this thing's got a prayer if we flood her with fresh blood?"

This gave him reluctant pause. Jackson's theory felt like a gamble with only the slimmest chance of success. Of course, there was a less-than-zero chance of getting her out of there at all. He had no sense of Kambyses anywhere near, but assuming his sire didn't already know what was going on was the most dangerous gamble of all. Kambyses would never permit them to take her away while she still lived.

Yet this was their only chance.

This was Cassidy's only chance.

Dominique took her hand in both of his. Wilted and chill, skin-covered bone in his grip. "*Mon amour.* Will you fight a little while longer? For me? For us?"

"I don't want...to die." More than a whisper, not quite a whimper.

Jackson scooted up beside Dominique and put his hand on her forehead. "I won't let you, babe. You hear me? I won't let you die. This time I won't let you down."

Her slender fingers tried to curl around Dominique's. Her efforts felt as insubstantial as butterfly wings. She said nothing, but her eyes told him everything. She dared to hope Jackson was right. She dared to gamble.

And so would he.

"You have until midnight," he told Jackson while still holding her gaze. "If she hasn't improved by then, I will do this thing. She will not survive another day otherwise."

"Let's go then. We have a van parked nearby."

"I really can't let you do that."

They looked up to see Monica at the far end of the room. She aimed a pistol at them in a steady, expert stance that said she was likely to hit what she shot at. Her expression was all business and held no doubt.

"Don't you have anything better to do than be difficult?" Jackson said before Dominique could decide if he wanted to risk that weapon going off anywhere near Cassidy. With his new, vampire-blood-enhanced abilities, Jackson had no such reservations. He went for the firearm holstered on his hip with what, for a human, amounted to stupendous speed.

Stupendous, but not sufficient.

Monica pulled the trigger an instant before Jackson.

Dominique used his own new strengths to focus on the bullets crossing paths in slow-motion. The one heading for them was on a collision course with Jackson's head. The slug moved too fast to catch and hold, but not to deflect. It seared through his hand and streaked away at a new angle to crash into the vanity mirror.

The other bullet smacked into Monica's thigh, causing her to stumble and cry out. Dominique ripped the pistol from her hand and slammed her against the nearest wall. The smell of her spilling blood hit him between the eyes like a rusty nail. The beast shivered just beneath the surface of his skin.

She stared at him, open-mouthed. Human. Weak, frightened human.

Prey.

A pawn in his sire's games.

He stepped back from her, from the brink.

Monica slid to the floor, clutching her leg. Blood squelched between her fingers. "Please. You can't do this." Tears burst from her eyes. "My lord will never permit it."

"He can go fuck himself," Jackson said as he bundled Cassidy in a blanket with brisk efficiency. "Let's go."

Dominique engaged the safety on Monica's gun and handed it to Jackson, then carefully gathered the blanket cocoon in his arms. Cassidy's head flopped against his shoulder. The look she gave him was one of utter trust and surrender.

"I will not fail you," he vowed. He *could* not fail her.

She closed her eyes.

In the hallway, Garrett Striker bounded toward them, hair askew and blood smeared across his chin and neck. His dark-gray aura sparkled with an even stronger silvery energy than his nephew's. "We're about to outstay our welcome."

Jackson pulled at the soggy gash in his uncle's black shirt, revealing unblemished skin. Not even a scar. His shoulders slumped with relief. "You're okay."

"That loon forced his magic juice on me before he pulled the dagger out," Garrett said, resentment soaking his voice.

"That loon saved your life."

Dominique continued carrying Cassidy toward the stairway. "His judgment is often suspect."

"Wait," Garrett called below his breath. "Your daddy is down there, and he's not looking happy about that mess."

Dominique's steps slowed, but he didn't stop until he caught the first whiff of cedar smoke.

Jackson came up beside him. "Back stairway? Window?"

"Futile," Dominique whispered as though Kambyses could not hear him anyway, didn't know every thought in the minds of the humans from whom he so recently fed. "We can't outrun him. The only way out of this—"

"Is through," Jackson finished, echoing Dominique's thoughts.

He exchanged a look with his erstwhile enemy, who now stood by his side with an uncanny understanding of the situation. This realization struck him as both comforting and disorienting.

"*Exactement.*" Dropping a kiss on Cassidy's brow, he deposited her in Jackson's arms. She was unconscious and fading. "Follow me down at a distance. Whatever you see or hear, keep moving. Get her out of here. No matter what."

Jackson nodded.

Garrett shook his head. "You've both lost your minds."

Dominique blurred away to the landing, overlooking the foyer. Bijou's body still lay where it fell on the white tile. Kambyses stood over her, his crimson silk shirt and ebony slacks crisp, unbound hair falling in a sable curtain from his bent head.

Serge cowered on his knees at the room's far end and hugged himself against violent shivers. The look on his face was more crazed than ever. With his eyes locked on the ancient vampire, he muttered and mumbled, whined and gasped, buffeted by whatever future he perceived in Kambyses's aura—or maybe just overwhelmed by the sheer, ancient power.

The front door stood open to the night. Dominique could be through it in a flash, and it still wouldn't be fast enough. So he strode down the stairs with no misguided attempt at stealth.

He hadn't yet reached the bottom when Kambyses turned to face him. He steeled himself for wrath. What he got instead was...disappointment.

For two brief steps, he slowed, then resumed with a confidence he far from felt. He kicked one of the loose chains and a block of broken statue across the floor, purposely making noise. Rounding to the far side of Bijou's body, he forced Kambyses to turn away from the door. "Her temper was bound to get her killed event—"

He stopped, stunned.

Bijou's severed head lay pushed up against the stump of her neck in a still-growing pool of red. Still, she smiled. Dead. The trick that had saved Serge at Samantha's hands wouldn't work here. Too much time had passed. This death was final.

But Kambyses had tried. The old, selfish bastard had cared enough to try.

Kambyses's casual tone made Dominique's flesh squirm with dread. "I wonder, Nico. How many more will have to lose their lives before you acknowledge the truth?"

On the stairs, Jackson and his uncle did their best to transport Cassidy with quiet haste, though they were neither silent nor swift.

"You might have kept her on a tighter leash, if she meant that much to you." Dominique spoke slowly, buying time with every syllable. The humans reached the bottom of the stairs, picked their way around the broken statue, and hustled for the open door. "Perhaps you should ask how many more you will sacrifice to get your way?"

Kambyses graced him with an acid-edged smile. "As many as it takes."

The ancient vampire tilted his head to the side, maybe to indicate the men behind him, maybe in contemplation, maybe both. "Or perhaps I should ask how many you would ask of me?"

All of them. That's how many Dominique would sacrifice to prevent Kambyses from getting his way. Or it had been. If Cassidy would need to receive the blood before this night was out, tethering her existence to the dark web Kambyses ruled, he would have no more treachery to fear from Dominique. Even now, with her teetering at the edge of death, Dominique knew he couldn't risk his sire's destruction, not as long as she might still need the blood to survive.

Dominique said none of this, but neither did he hide it from his face. Resignation shadowed Kambyses's coarse features.

The mortals reached the door with their burden, but inexplicably slowed.

Kambyses looked at Serge, who trembled so hard the sound of his shirt rubbing against his skin hissed in the stillness. The old pirate whimpered and clutched his arms over his head.

Jackson's face flushed with the effort to set one foot before the other, but the closer he got to the door, the more he seemed to battle against an unseen headwind. Garrett stood with fists balled, jaw clenched, and eyes blazing fury.

Hope died in Dominique's heart like a candle in the storm. Kambyses bent the humans to his will with nothing but a passing thought. Should flames engulf the house, they couldn't have escaped without his permission. That they had any fight left in them at all was by his whim alone. That and perhaps the vampire blood they had both ingested.

When Dominique turned back to his sire, he found him waiting.

"Shall we see to the evening's true business now, Nico?"

38

MONSTERS

Kambyses held out his hand toward Jackson and Garrett, inviting them to approach. They did, unhurried, their faces stoic masks, though their eyes still contained clarity and reason, watchful for any opening. Dominique felt a pang of unexpected pity for them. Their fates as dispensable humans present at a siring was a foregone conclusion. Cassidy's new-born beast would tear them apart. Their deaths would be her eternal burden to bear.

"Her time draws near, Nico. I would see her made this night. With or without you," Kambyses added with a pointed look at Serge.

Serge stilled against the wall.

It took Dominique a moment longer to comprehend the warning and its implications. Serge still lived because, terrorized as the old pirate was, there was no question he would follow Kambyses's every command—including giving Cassidy his blood if Dominique continued to refuse. Once linked to Serge's unhinged reality, her mind would be as closed to Dominique as it had ever been, and her personality undoubtedly changed.

Perhaps Serge would be allowed to live for his cooperation. Perhaps not. Maybe Dominique would want to kill him to free Cassidy from his madness. Maybe she would want to free herself. As Serge would not be her serum sire, his fate would not dictate hers.

Only one thing was certain—Dominique would lose someone dear to him. And just how dear his mentor and only blood-drinker friend had become occurred to him only now.

Kambyses turned to the motionless, wrapped body draped in Jackson's arms. "She is a creature of rare spirit. Worthy of our kind." He stroked the tip of one finger over her brow. She stirred a little, but didn't open her eyes. Kambyses tilted his head and grew pensive. "Much like the one you took from me tonight."

Suddenly Jackson burst out, "Get your filthy hands off her!"

In the same instant, Garrett acted with near-superhuman speed. In a single motion, he pulled the pistol from the back of Jackson's waistband, unlocked it, swung it up, and fired the instant the muzzle cleared his nephew's shoulder.

The bullet popped Kambyses in the throat, exited the back of his neck, and zipped past Dominique's shoulder. He felt it rip at his jacket, felt the ageless blood spray his face, smelled the smoky stench of it explode in the air.

Kambyses flickered away and reappeared behind his assailant. The blast still echoed in the foyer when the weapon itself flew off in one direction while Garrett jerked into another. He catapulted up and back, arcing across the room like a misshapen cannonball and, with the wet crack of bone, smashed into the wall of the second floor landing. He bounced off and tumbled to the floor right in front of Monica as she limped out of the hall.

Jackson and his burden bolted for the door.

Or tried to.

Three steps into his flight, he hit that invisible wall again. His shoulders hunched, and panic etched his face as he turned back.

The indignant anger he cultivated with such care drained out of him faster than wine from a broken bottle.

Kambyses stood before Dominique, bristling with displeasure. Dark blood smeared the ashen neck, but the wound itself had finished knitting back together. Garrett had fired too early. Half a second later and the bullet would have struck Kambyses's brain and disabled him long enough to gain a true advantage. As it was, all the hunter accomplished was to stoke the powerful blood-drinker's twisted temper.

Useless. Everything they did to save Cassidy had been useless. Wasted efforts that risked her life over and over again. Bijou had advised him to stop fighting and find peace in accepting the inevitable. He glanced at her body. Had she taken her own advice, she might still live.

And nothing else would have changed.

Nothing at all.

Dominique's fate settled on him with the weight of a world. Slowly, he sank to his knees.

Cassidy would be made tonight as Kambyses commanded. The only choice that remained to Dominique was whether this would happen with his blood or Serge's. From the corner of his eye, he caught sight of his mad friend, who stared at him as though watching a ghost.

It was no choice at all.

It never had been.

Dominique stared at his sire's spotless leather loafers and waited. The shoes moved aside, momentarily replaced by Jackson's combat boots. Then Cassidy floated into view, unconscious and swathed in a blanket. Jackson took care to settle her head, which looked as fragile as an egg in his strong, tanned hands. Hands that belonged to a man who loved her still. A dead man walking. A man who had nothing to lose—and knew it.

He made only a passing note of the little device he saw hidden in Jackson's grip, but his gut tightened with both anticipation and apprehension. He met Jackson's blank look. Whatever the human was thinking of doing, he didn't think about it much at all. He felt it, moved by instinct, kept the idea away from the menace controlling his mind. But that instinct would also tell him he couldn't survive such a gambit. Not without help.

Dominique inclined his head in unspoken agreement. "*Merci.*"

After that, everything happened both very fast and in slow-motion. His heart drummed in his veins, providing the rhythm, beat by frantic beat, for the macabre dance that followed.

Jackson got up...stepped back...raised his hand.

Dominique reached over his shoulders...found the handles of his swords.

Jackson pointed the full-spectrum pocket light...activated it.

Kambyses roared.

Dominique hooked his fingers under the guard of the *katana* and, with a flick of his wrist, shot the blade straight up toward the ceiling.

His other hand curled around the *wakizashi's* hilt and freed it from its sheath. He could almost feel the embedded dragon rise to meet him.

Kambyses rushed blindly toward the light, toward Jackson, eagle talon hands outstretched.

Dominique launched forward over Cassidy's prone body, twisted in mid-air beneath Kambyses, and swung the razor-sharp blade up and around, hard.

The impact of honed steel against primeval bone vibrated through his hand and elbow and into his shoulder.

Shimmering sheets of blood fanned into space.

An explosive kick to Kambyses's midsection sent him flying away from Jackson.

As the thump of Kambyses's impact reverberated in the walls, Dominique reached for the whistling sound of the katana returning. He caught the hilt without looking at it, instead watching Kambyses drop to the floor, nearly on top of Serge, who darted away with a yelp.

When the ancient blood-drinker hit the floor, he tried to get up, but...his legs were gone, reduced to stumps squelching blood.

Jackson sucked in a ragged breath and turned off his tiny light.

Silence.

Then Monica realized what had happened and screamed.

Kambyses put his hands to the tile, raised his body up on his arms, and sped toward Dominique. Or rather, toward his severed legs. Dominique leapt to kick the limbs away from Cassidy. With a bestial growl, Kambyses scurried after them. But walking on his hands was far from natural for him. While he still moved superhumanly fast, Dominique had no trouble keeping track of him.

The *katana* hummed as it slid through Kambyses's left shoulder and sent him crashing to the floor. Dominique kicked the arm away. Without missing a beat, Kambyses rolled across the floor in a flurry of motion and tangled hair. This time Dominique waited until he reached for one of his legs before he struck, taking the other arm as well.

With the toe of his boot, he rolled the dismembered body onto its back. Then he slammed his foot on the torso and set the long sword's razor edge against Kambyses's throat. Through the shroud of hair covering his sire's face, he saw the glint of the beast's tar-black eyes and the ferocious fangs that had ended countless lives.

One flick of his wrist. That was all it would take to destroy five-thousand years of misery. That was all it would take to destroy potentially hundreds of thousands of blood-drinkers—and himself.

A shudder rippled his flesh. Dominique removed the blade and swallowed hard. The spilled blood's cedar smoke smell choked the air, his lungs, his mind. All around him, an invisible forest stood engulfed in flame.

The beast craved to live, and just like it wouldn't let Dominique remain exposed in the light of day, it would not allow him to end the source of them all.

"Let go of me, you waste of space!" shrieked an outraged female.

Dominique became aware of the room and its inhabitants again. Garrett Striker had captured one of Monica Sol's wrists behind her back and kept her pinned against himself with an arm locked across her shoulders. In her free hand, she clutched one of Kambyses's severed arms. Burgundy splatters covered the tiles at her feet. Fat streaks of burgundy also crisscrossed the room—and Cassidy.

He froze, terrified that the potent blood could have hit her just right—as his own hit Jackson earlier—to cause her to ingest it and finish her. She wouldn't be strong enough to survive the fire-blood, but she didn't writhe in agony as she surely would have if that were the case. She moved only a little with the encouragement of Jackson, who bent over her.

"I've got this," Garrett announced and then gasped as Monica elbowed his no doubt injured ribs. He cringed and doubled over, releasing her. Off she went, hobbling away to retrieve the dropped arm and return it to Kambyses. She paid no attention to Dominique until he snapped up the *katana* in front of her, and she stopped just short of running herself through.

Her eyes shimmered with impotent rage. "You unspeakable monster. How *could* you do this?"

This, Dominique could not argue. It was monstrous. But it was hardly the most monstrous thing he had done on account of this ancient beast that had stolen his life, caused him to murder his family and lover, hunted him, and manipulated him at every turn.

"Step away," he commanded in a soft growl. If any of the limbs strewn about found their way back to their rightful place, they would reattach in moments, gaining Kambyses an advantage Dominique could ill afford.

Monica took a step back, her sense of self-preservation at last overriding the hold Kambyses had on her, but she wasn't done.

Dominique saw the move coming a second before she tossed the arm in Kambyses's direction. He sent it flying with the side of his sword. Beneath his foot, Kambyses arched his back and trembled, fighting to free himself and move a body which could do neither.

"Release me!" he roared. "Restore me! Now!"

The compulsion surged in the air. Dominique took his boot off Kambyses before he knew what he was doing. Monica scurried for one arm, Garrett stumbled toward the other, coughing and holding his side. Jackson climbed to his feet and turned toward the legs.

"Restore him and you all die," Dominique shouted, letting his rising panic fly like an arrow in a compulsion of his own. He had no desire to kill these mortals—except perhaps Garrett—but if that was what it would take to prevent Kambyses from being made whole again, that was what he would do. Jackson's step faltered as his head swiveled toward Dominique.

Then he ran again, but with a different purpose. He tackled Monica and pinned both her wrists behind her back. She shrieked tear-soaked venom at the top of her lungs.

Garrett shook his head as though trying to shake loose from a sticky spider web.

"Some fucking help here?" Jackson called as Monica, fueled by her master's blood, thrashed like an enraged leopard, pulling them both to the floor. One of her hands got free and went straight for Jackson's eyes. With a yelp, he released her.

Garrett ripped open the small utility pack on his nephew's back and pulled out the roll of duct tape.

"No," Kambyses said, and a fresh wave of vertigo rippled through the room. Before he could utter another word, Dominique ground his boot heel into his sire's voice box, silencing him. That wouldn't stop Kambyses from casting psychic webs of compulsion, but at least he couldn't reinforce them with his resonant voice.

Monica slipped in a smear of blood, and stumbled back to her feet when the vampire hunters caught up with her, each grabbing one arm and duct-taping them together behind her back. They did the same for her ankles. Her screams were worthy of gruesome torture, but they fell silent when Garrett slapped one last strip of tape across her mouth.

"Victorious at last," Dominique said. "I was wondering what it might take for you two to accomplish anything other than disaster."

They turned to face him, and something about what they saw gave them pause. He couldn't blame them. A blood-drinker armed with bloodied swords standing over a dismembered body would have made even Dominique reevaluate his odds of survival.

"That thing's still alive, isn't it," Garrett said when he rediscovered his voice.

"And will remain so until Cassidy has recovered," Dominique countered with more certainty than he felt.

"Cassidy," Jackson said, jogging back to where she lay.

Garrett propped both hands on his hips. "In the meantime, you'll be keeping watch, will you?"

"We can argue about it, if you like." Dominique's lips pulled back in a toothy grimace intended to stop a heart with fright. Garrett shook his head in disgust.

Jackson scooped Cassidy off the floor. "We don't have time for a pissing contest. We need to get her help. Now."

"Yeah, right. We all know how this is going to end, but here. You might need this." Garrett lobbed the duct tape at Dominique, who speared it in mid-flight with the tip of the *katana*. Grabbing Monica by an arm, Garrett hauled her upright and slung her over his shoulder. "C'mon, Red. The humans are clearing out of this hellhole." She made a series of strangled noises. "I don't give a shit if you ever thank me for this. Really, I don't."

"I'll let you know how it goes, Nick." Renewed distrust hardened Jackson's eyes before turning to the door.

"Jackson," Dominique called, causing the man to stop and glance over one shoulder. "I made you a promise. I intend to keep it. You have until midnight to keep yours."

The muscles in Jackson's jaw twitched. He nodded once and left.

Dominique stood and listened to their retreating steps. He didn't move until he heard doors slam and an engine start, rev, and race away. Only then did he allow himself to release some of the tension knotting his body. For now, there was nothing more he could do. He might still have to turn her before the night was through, but not now. Now he stood over his sire's desecrated body, in a creeping lake of blood. There was a great deal of work to be done to clean up this house and remove all evidence of the supernatural.

Not just physical evidence would have to be erased. The security team would need their memories altered. He could hear them in the depths of the house, their frantic, uncertain whispers as they attempted to escape notice. After witnessing Bijou's death, they feared for their lives, but their compulsion not to leave the property was stronger.

Serge had emerged from hiding, as had his nerve. The barefoot pirate vampire bent over the scattered limbs, poking at them, as if assuring himself that they truly wouldn't move on their own. "Clever, blood-child. Very clever."

Dominique let the duct tape slide off the *katana* and land on Kambyses's chest. Putting the blades aside, he peeled off several strips and plastered them across Kambyses's mouth before moving his foot off the neck. There was no reaction. No struggle. Only that hellish stare skewering him.

Dominique straightened. "No, I cannot end you," he told the ancient beast, the source of them all. "But the hunters can. And if Cassidy survives the day, tomorrow night you belong to them."

Serge approached the edge of the blood pool and peered down at the grisly scene. His head bobbled to the side. His eyes lost their focus. "Ah, blood-child," he said, tone solemn as a preacher's, "that is one promise you will not keep."

39

O-Negative

Every minute ticking toward midnight was both a hope and a fear for Cassidy's life. To distract himself, Dominique tackled the cleanup operation with vigor.

Most of the blood and chaos to be cleared was in the entry, so that is where he stayed, working around the cracks and bullet pockmarks with buckets of soap and a hose running from the yard through the front door. Serge, he tasked with disposing of Bijou's body some place hidden where the sun would find it. After that, the pirate was put to work dealing with the humans—the security staff and *Apokryphos's* crew—clearing their minds, replacing their memories.

Kambyses, they rolled up in a rug.

That rug, shoved against a far wall, stuck in his awareness like a barbed thorn. Dominique hadn't replied to Serge's presumably informed opinion of what he would or wouldn't do with the contents, but dread about the possibilities loomed ever larger. There was no hope of Kambyses regaining his compulsive voice or becoming whole again on his own. His limbs sat in a trash bag on the other side of the room, beside the headless Aphrodite statue. Come dawn, their re-attaching to his body would be impossible.

Regardless, as long as he lived, Kambyses would have his mind—and the power to influence perceptions with his thoughts alone. This was a prospect Dominique remained on guard for as he rinsed and polished the glassy tiles and scrubbed at the walls, but there was no sense of strangeness, no evidence of Kambyses wielding his silent influence. Which left Dominique stewing over how he might break his promise to Jackson. The only way that would happen was if Cassidy became a blood-drinker before dawn.

He glared at the rug. If that happened, would he make that beast whole again? Or would he just leave Kambyses like this, stashed in a crypt somewhere, providing him with just enough blood to keep him going for—what?—decades? Centuries? Forever? As an eternal vegetable? What would that mean for the blood-drinkers of the world? Would they be free? Or just zombies?

Dominique cursed under his breath and pulled his phone from his pocket. Eleven-oh-four. Close enough. Done waiting, he called up Jackson's number.

The hunter answered in two rings. "Nick." No joy in that greeting. Only exhaustion.

Fear crawled up Dominique's chest. He strangled it. "How is she?"

"Stable."

"But?"

"But...I don't know for how long."

"Explain."

Jackson hesitated. Dominique imagined him slumping forward in a waiting room chair somewhere, massaging the back of his no-doubt tight neck, choosing his quiet words with care. "She's burning through the blood almost as fast as they can get it into her, and—"

"They're running out of blood," Dominique finished. He could feel his own blood drain from his face. "It is a rare type."

"Yes," Jackson confirmed with a sigh. "They can only give her O-negative, and she's currently getting the last pint they have."

Blood being a critical part of their relationship, Cassidy had shared her blood type with Dominique long ago—as well as how she came to have it. "Her father."

"What?"

"Her father has the same blood type. Get him there."

"Yeah, I know. We tried. Sam called him, but he's not answering his phone."

Dominique opened his mouth to berate Jackson when he recalled that Gil Chandler no longer conveniently resided in Dominique's lair.

"We have no idea where he is," Jackson elaborated into the silence.

Dominique didn't so much lean on the stair railing as he deflated over it.

A chlorinated haze wafted from the hall below. The rest of the house still waited for him to scour it for supernatural evidence.

The rolled rug lay motionless. Waiting.

"*Putain,*" he murmured, then said it louder, and finally, straightening, screamed it. His voice echoed off the curved black walls. Several light bulbs shattered in their sconces with plaintiff pops and tinkles, thickening the shadows.

Jackson said nothing.

Serge sped in from the back of the house, his human projects abandoned. His eyes bulged in his round face, mouth hanging open.

Regaining a measure of control, Dominique said, "Always when she needs him most, that man abandons her. And this time it will cost Cassidy her life."

"We don't know that yet," Jackson said. "There's still a chance she'll pull through."

"That is not a chance I'm willing to take." He pressed a hand to his forehead and thought hard, riffling through his near-perfect memory for any shred of information he had on Cassidy's father, why he had come and where he might have gone.

The answer was not in his memories but in Cassidy's, or rather the bits and pieces that had come his way the night Gil Chandler first arrived. He came to assist the wife of a friend with a business. The friend had died suddenly—Dominique's head snapped up—because he, Dominique, had scared him to death in a sleazy motel room the night he had met Bijou. The night his life began its latest downward spiral.

The night that wasn't done with him yet.

"*Merde.*"

Jackson was speaking, but Dominique paid no attention. "I will find him," he promised, and disconnected the call.

Not quite an hour later, he rocketed his bike down the quiet, neatly manicured street of a gated community in Boca Raton, home of the widow Iris Horner. According to a quick search of online obituaries, it had been her husband, Horatio Horner, who, wearing nothing but a hat and boots, dropped dead at Dominique's feet.

Discovering his widow's residential address and personal contact information was simple. But she, too, didn't answer her phone, which left Dominique to compel his way past the guard gate to her neighborhood and appear in person. If anyone would know where to find the man who had rushed to her side in a time of need, it should be the widow Horner. And maybe, just maybe, that otherwise useless man was still in the area.

The house, one of a long row of cookie-cutter mansions, lay in near-darkness. Only a soft glow from a back room was visible through the etched glass surrounding the front door. Dominique rang the bell three times in short order. A polite *bing-bong* reminiscent of church bells resonated inside.

Seconds ticked by with no other sound and no motion. Dominique punched the button again—continually—until angry shouting inside overpowered what sounded like a church steeple gone mad. Footsteps raced, accompanied by terse voices. He stopped ringing the bell when shadows moved toward the door and another light came on.

"What the fuck do you think you're doing?" bellowed a bearish male voice just before the door tore open and the muzzle of a shotgun emerged.

The weapon pointing at him didn't surprise Dominique nearly so much as who was holding it. Unshaven and red-faced, Gil Chandler looked a furious mess in his boxers. He also reeked of sex. As did the blonde forty-something woman—presumably the widow Horner—standing behind him in an askew silk robe.

"You," Gil said, deep blue eyes narrowing. Cassidy's eyes. Cassidy who was fighting for her life and desperately needed her father's blood while he was busy screwing his next conquest. Every time his family needed him, whether on purpose or by accident, Gil Chandler checked out. The man was a plague.

Impatient anger shot through Dominique's veins, rousing the beast. His fangs thrust out, and his vision shifted, turning the humans into figures of aural light and webs of glimmering blood. "Your daughter—"

At the sight of Dominique's transformation, the widow blanched and screamed.

Gil jerked in surprise and pulled the trigger.

40

GIFTS OF THE AFTERLIFE

Something was missing. Something Cassidy was on guard for. Something...smoke. The sweet bite of flaming cedar. Gone. It must be daytime again.

Or she was dead.

Opening her eyes felt like pouring wet sand across her eyeballs. The afterlife slowly came into focus. It looked an awful lot like a hospital room.

Her thoughts stumbled around her skull, looking for answers to questions she didn't know how to ask. She blinked several times and scanned the details of her surroundings. A window with drapes drawn, subdued lighting. The colorful bouncing lines of a vital stats monitor, a mechanical chill in the air. A TV suspended near the ceiling was tuned to a muted football game.

She started furrowing her forehead in confusion, but even this tiny effort bordered on too much work.

"Baby girl? You awake?"

No. It couldn't be.

But it was.

Her father, the large, boisterous coward of a man who couldn't handle illness, much less hospitals, leaned over her. The recessed lighting above her head highlighted the worry lines in his round, unshaven face. His presence was so incongruous she could only stare.

His smile beamed like a full moon. Was that moisture glinting in his eyes? He took her hand and squeezed. "You're going to be fine, Cassidy. You're at a top-notch hospital. They're patching you up." He swiped at his eyes. "You'll be good as new, baby girl. Good as new."

Cassidy was more disoriented than ever. She had been held hostage by a vampire, brought within kissing distance of death, was certain she would be an immortal blood-drinker by the time she could string two coherent thoughts together again, and now it was her father—her father who couldn't possibly know what happened to her—who was telling her she would be all right?

She licked her lips and swallowed. "Where...where is—"

"Jackson? He went to get us some coffee. Should be back any minute." He tapped a half-collapsed bag hanging off an IV hook with one finger and chuckled with obvious relief. "They told me you'd probably come around with this one. Wasn't gonna chance missing you wake up."

A dark-red tube ran from the bag. She followed it with her eyes to the other end, where it was attached to an infusion needle embedded in and taped to her left arm.

"That's right, baby girl. Take as much as you need. Even if it's my last drop." Another swipe at his eyes. "Yeah, that's mine." He turned his free arm to reveal a bandage in the crook of his elbow. "By the time I got here, you had cleared them out of O-negative just to pull you back through death's door, so I said 'plug me in'. I'm the reason you're stuck with this blood type, after all. Besides, I owe you."

She pulled her hand out of his. "What you owe me, a pint of blood will never make up for."

He inclined his head, pushed out his lips, and nodded. "I know that, too, but maybe...it could be a down payment?"

Cassidy closed her eyes. Exhaustion pulled at her. She couldn't think about this. Not now.

The awkward silence grew so thick it squeezed all the air out of the room. It all rushed back in when the door opened to admit Jackson.

"Any change?"

"She's awake. But she still hates me."

Jackson put down two steaming paper cups and cellophane-wrapped muffins and came to her side. Dressed in blue jeans and a polo shirt, he looked like his typical deceptively casual self, but something about his movements made her head hurt. They were smoother, easier, more efficient than was usual for his tightly wound, muscle-bound frame.

"Cass? Babe? How are you feeling?"

"What is he doing here?" she said, shooting a narrow glance toward her father.

"I'm your father, and you need me. Of course, I'm here."

She gaped at him. It looked like her father, but certainly didn't behave like the man who couldn't be bothered to show up for his wife's chemo treatments. Maybe she really had died. Too much felt off here.

Jackson softly cleared his throat. "Gil's blood saved your life." His hand settled on hers. "Cass, you were halfway turned. The serum annihilated everything we put in you until we finally drowned it out. With your dad's blood." His Adam's apple bobbed. "It was close."

She opened her mouth but stopped. Her sluggish thoughts connected the dots a little faster now and the picture they painted felt ominous. Being restored to humanity was a bonus, true, but that hadn't been the plan, especially not this late in the game. Dominique was going to give her his blood. Kambyses would have allowed nothing else short of letting her die—certainly not her getting carted off to a hospital. Yet here she was. And no vampire in sight...

The bouncing lines on the monitor sped up. Her voice sounded strangled. "Did you kill him? Did you kill them all?"

Jackson hesitated a moment too long. Cassidy tried to sit up, but he put a hand on her shoulder, pushing her back into the pillows. "Easy. Kambyses lives. But he won't be bothering you again."

"I don't understand. How is this possible?" She followed Jackson's glance toward her father.

Gil still only looked relieved to see her awake and recovering. No hint of worry, much less confusion about their odd exchange. "Dominique took care of everything, baby girl. You're safe now."

She felt like she did back on *Apokryphos,* when people spouted perfectly reasonable nonsense at her. Jackson and Garrett were compelled then—as her father must be now. The noxious panic bubbling at the back of her mind ebbed a bit. There was only one vampire who would have an interest in compelling Gil Chandler.

"Where's Dominique?"

Jackson's face soured. "He's got a few more hours of night left. I'm sure he'll be here before dawn. I texted him earlier that you'd be pulling through."

She blinked, incredulous. "You two are on *texting* terms?" What sort of drugs had they doped her with?

"You're very lucky that they're both crazy about you," her father said, startling her again with his presence, which she continued to tune out. "And they're men enough to put aside their differences when it counts."

"Their *differences*? Do you understand that they're mortal enemies?"

"Yes, I do. Makes them working together for you so much more special, doesn't it?" He shook his head and let out a rueful sigh. "I only wish I hadn't shot him."

Cassidy stared. She hadn't heard right, had she?

"What?" Jackson said, sounding as lost as she felt.

"I shot Dominique. By accident, I swear," he added, hands raised in defense.

"You *what*?" Cassidy croaked, trying to struggle upright again. This time, Jackson didn't stop her, but she ran out of steam anyway and flopped back into her pillows.

"Iris scared the ever-loving shit out of me when she screamed. I had my finger on the trigger." He shrugged, chagrined.

She glanced at Jackson. There was not a shred of comprehension on his face. "What do you mean, you *shot* Dominique?"

Gil rubbed at his face, more uncomfortable than she had ever seen him, but stayed put. No shrugging it off, no shouting, no turning his back in disgust. Was this part of Dominique's compulsion? Or a side-effect?

"He shouldn't have rung the bell as hard as he did," Gil said. Blame the victim. Nice touch. "We thought it was a home invasion or a prankster. Iris pulled a shotgun out from under her bed, and I grabbed it, thinking I would scare them off." Another shrug. "She didn't tell me the damn thing was loaded."

Cassidy's jaw dropped. No words. She had no words. Not for any part of what she was hearing.

Seeing her reaction, Gil raised a placating hand. "But, look, it all worked out. He healed up quick enough, then told me what was going on and brought me here. That bike of his can really move, let me tell you."

"Oh. My. God." Never mind Dominique getting shot—she had seen him survive far worse—but the imagined visuals of her bear of a father hanging on to the feline vampire while speeding through highway traffic on a high-performance motorcycle were beyond bizarre.

"Ditto," Jackson murmured. He eyed Gil with a grim, unreadable expression.

"Now you tell me what happened, Jack. If Kambyses still lives, why am I here?"

He unfolded his arms, face softening. "Don't try to wrap your head around everything right now, Cass. Too much has happened. Concentrate on getting better. That's the only thing that matters."

"No. It's not. Tell me what happened."

He didn't want to. She could tell by the way his mouth went as hard as his eyes. She mustered the most determined glare she could, her hands fisting around wads of the thin blanket. His only recourse was to walk out of the room, or tell her.

He told her.

The tale that emerged was a harrowing recounting of Bijou's death, Garrett's mortal injury, Serge's insistence on saving him, and the effects of ingesting vampire blood on both him and Garrett. Together with Dominique, through a combination of serendipity, cunning, and accident, they'd cornered the oldest vampire on earth. All while she lay unconscious on the battlefield.

"Nick and Kambyses came to an...agreement, I guess." Tight smile. "The important thing is that we got you to an ER in time to save your life," Jackson concluded.

She met his eyes evenly. Something about how he inclined his head all but commanded her to not ask any more questions.

"You know he's going to tell me when I see him, don't you? What really happened?"

He shrugged. "He'd be the one to ask, yes."

Her energy flagging, she let it go. At least for now. Her fingers picked at the edge of the blanket. "What do the doctors here think is wrong with me?"

His shoulders visibly relaxed at the change of subject. "You have a very rare genetic disorder that periodically causes your body to destroy its own blood supply."

"I do?"

"You do," Gil agreed. "Sad but true. Runs in the family. I told them how poor cousin Clive kicked the bucket because of it." The melodramatic expression on his face melted into a twinkling smile. Clive Chandler had died of stupidity while under the influence.

"Garrett has a doctor in Sweden in his pocket who called and confirmed the condition as well."

"Gee. Feed that man vampire blood, and he turns into a human being. Figures."

"Then you give him too much credit, *chérie*," a new voice said, soft and warm as a summer wind caressing her battered heart.

Sweet relief rushed through her. "Dominique."

He was a tall, dark vision melting out of the shadows by the door. Black leathers, jacket unzipped, no swords, ebony hair tucked behind his ears except for the curl that always insisted on falling over his forehead. A gentle smile softened his clean-shaven angular face and danced in the depths of his hazel eyes.

Gil stood. "Hey, it's the man of the hour. Or should I say, man of the night?" He chuckled. "How'd you get in here?"

"I have my ways," Dominique said. He accepted Gil's offered hand and then leaned forward to peck quick kisses on the man's flushed cheeks in a familial French greeting that made Cassidy's brows shoot up.

Her father was too caught up in his own sentiments to be more than mildly surprised. He clasped Dominique's elegant hand with his beefy paws. "I can't thank you enough for what you've done for Cassidy, Nick. And I apologize again for shooting you."

Dominique retrieved his hand and grasped one side of his open jacket, pulling it away to reveal a slug-sized hole in the leather. "You weren't the only one who shot me tonight," he said with a pointed look at Jackson, who had neglected to mention this particular detail to Cassidy earlier. Dominique turned back to Gil. "But it was a small price to pay for you being here when she needed you. Finally."

The quiet sarcasm wasn't lost on Gil, who dropped his gaze and nodded to himself, lips pursed. A moment later, he swiped at his nose. "Yeah, well. She's my daughter. Right?"

Nice of you to remember, Cassidy thought, but the words didn't find her tongue. She didn't have the strength to pick over these old bones now.

When Gil met Dominique's gaze again, the vampire's eyes had darkened along with his voice. "You should go get some rest now. When you wake, you will remember nothing unusual about tonight. Only that your daughter lives and you helped save her."

"Oh, you're doing that thing—" Gil broke off. The finger he pointed at Dominique hesitated, curled, uncertain. He scratched the back of his head. "You know, you're right. I am kind of wiped. Think I'll go find a place to stretch out. You mind, baby girl?"

He didn't wait for her to reply before yawning hugely, grabbing his windbreaker off another chair, and ambling out the door.

"Oh no, you don't," Jackson said when Dominique turned to him. "Don't even start with me."

Dominique tipped his head, raised an inquiring brow.

For several more seconds, Jackson glared, his cheeks twitching with his clenching jaw. "Fine. I'm leaving." He scooped up a coffee and muffin and headed for the door. He was halfway through it when he turned back and said, "No biting."

"No biting," Dominique confirmed after a brief hesitation.

Pulling off his jacket, he dropped it into Gil's vacated chair. His shirt was clean and unmarred, obviously not the one he had gotten repeatedly shot in tonight. He settled on the side of Cassidy's bed, leaned over, and placed a kiss on each of her cheeks. Then he gathered her close so gingerly he seemed to expect her to break into pieces. She answered with all the strength she could marshal, winding her arms around his bunched shoulders, pushing her fingers through his thick hair, drowning in the distinct, familiar smell of him: ice and snow, leather and night. His sigh caressed her shoulder as he inhaled her in turn, both of them delirious with relief.

No words passed between them. No thoughts hummed in their non-existent link. There was only this embrace, as raw as it was tender, suspending them in a singular moment of gratitude and love—and uncertainty.

Whispers in the back of her mind. She pushed them aside again and again. Yet they continued to rise with every slow stroke of his thumb along her neck, and with every breath that didn't culminate with his lips against her skin.

The whispers became a buzz.

"No biting?" she ventured. Much as she hated being separated from him like this, she could understand it. Her body had only just triumphed over a heavy serum load. A bite now might upset a delicate balance. Dominique could have given this possibility as a reason, but he didn't.

He said nothing.

She loathed breaking the silence, but for this answer she could wait no longer. "Where is Kambyses?"

Dominique raised himself up far enough to peer down at her with sad human eyes. Even the gold flecks she so loved to watch dance with mischief were muted. "He lives."

"Obviously. But he didn't just let me go, did he?"

He tucked in his chin and looked away. "No. He did not."

The building anxiety threatened to eat up all that precious fresh blood in her veins. "Jackson said...Jackson said you and Kambyses came to an...agreement."

"Of a sort." His mouth twisted with irony. His eyes glistened when they met hers again. "I...I have accepted what I am, Cassidy. I will fight no more."

Chills raced up her arms. "What...what does that mean?"

"It means...that my place is with my sire. Allowing you to remain mortal is—"

"The bribe?"

"No. It's...it's his gift to me."

"Allowing you to turn me was supposed to be his gift." Her voice wobbled. Sobs gathered beneath a hard lump in her breast. "We were going to be together. Forever."

"*Oui.* Forever with him. And he could have turned on us any time. We would have existed in constant fear of his whims. You deserve so much more."

"Now I'm human and even more vulnerable." A strange ringing filled her ears, along with the sound of her heart slamming hard enough to bruise her ribs. She almost didn't hear him.

"Not if you never see either of us again."

She moaned, a primal sound of denial. This could not be happening.

"You deserve a *life*, Cassie." He captured her hand and squeezed, as if that would persuade her of his argument.

With her free hand, she grasped his forearm, the hard muscle and tendons achingly familiar beneath her fingers. She gripped hard, holding on to him, to life. "I can't live as half a soul. I can't."

"Serge could com—"

"No, don't you dare. If he makes me forget, all I'll have is an emptiness in my heart I won't even know can be filled. I'll be hollow until the day I die."

The shimmer in his eyes swelled and broke free into glistening tracks down his face.

Questions tore from her body in raw, bleeding chunks. "Why didn't you give me the blood? Why didn't you turn me? Why didn't you give us the time to figure this out? Why?"

He drew an unsteady breath. "Because, *mon amour*. We were doomed from the beginning. An immortal and a human. It was madness. Madness," he repeated in a terse whisper, his French accent thickening.

"It's the only true thing I've ever known."

He pressed his hand to the side of her face. "For all the rest of my nights, I will never forget the gift of your love, of this magical light you have brought into my lonely darkness. You, Cassidy, allowed me one final, precious glimpse of the life I loved. For this, I will be forever grateful. But I know now what I am, what I must do. Kambyses has shown me. There can be no going back."

She sobbed without reservation now. Her entire body shook with grief. Her fingers clawed into his arms as though she could keep him there with her mere mortal strength alone. Forever. "You should have turned me. Why didn't you turn me?"

He scooped her up, lifting her into a sitting position, pulled her close. Tremors chased each other through his bunched muscles.

His whispers brushed her ear, words from another reality. "You deserve to live the life I will never have, Cassie, *mon* cœur. That is my gift to you."

41

Gray Reality

Jackson ate the stale muffin, drank the lukewarm coffee, and did his level best not to think about what might be going on behind the closed door of Cassidy's room.

He hated leaving her alone with the vampire. Barely back from the threshold of death, she was more fragile—more tempting?—than she had ever been. But then, Dominique Marchant wasn't just a random bloodsucker. The youngling had more strength and discipline than many who were centuries older. He also had more integrity than all his bloodthirsty kind put together. More than most humans Jackson knew.

Maybe more than Jackson had himself.

That last thought made him shift in his seat. Nick could have killed him and his entire family countless times, but except for Garrett—whom he let live in the end anyway—he had never laid a fang on any of them. In contrast, if not for the much greater prize of Kambyses in his sights, Jackson would have finished Nick the first chance he got by any means of deception necessary.

At least in the beginning. Back when his world was still black and white. When he worked alone—and screwed up more times than he could count.

Remembering how close he had come to bungling Cassidy's rescue tonight and what it had taken to pull it off in the end made his nerves jangle like Christmas bells. The "game" had run its course, the end imminent, and he, Jackson Striker, vampire hunter, had trusted a vampire to seize the sliver of a chance to save them all. No, more than that. He had worked together with the vampire to accomplish what neither of them could do alone.

Now that he wasn't fighting for his life anymore, Jackson didn't know what to do with that.

He stuffed the last of the muffin into his mouth and wadded the cellophane wrapper into the half-empty cup, then got up to toss it into the trash. Gil lay prostrate on the next bench over, snoring, a whale of a man and accidental vampire hunter at peace. Jackson envied him. Nothing was so simple anymore in the gray morass of his new reality.

The blood he ingested wasn't making things any clearer. It was only a few drops, but they had hit him like a shot of adrenaline straight to the heart. The effect was already waning, but he could still see with a clarity that cramped his brain. There was, for instance, an ant marching toward a box of donuts sitting on the nurse's station counter—fifty feet away. He felt stronger, too, and wondered what times he would clock on his morning run. Also, if he concentrated, he could hear Gil's heart...

Jackson settled in the seat farthest away, propped his elbows on his knees, and scratched the stubble sprouting on his chin. His fingers found the two small St. Christopher medallions hanging below the hollow of his throat. One had always been his, the other, the one with the notch in its side, had been Justin's. Jackson remembered finding it amidst the gore of his brother's savaged body and marveled at the fact that he didn't end up the same way tonight. Not only that, he even walked away with a taste of the supernatural strength that had murdered his brother. His skin twitched with unease.

Garrett was a good deal less conflicted about his enhanced abilities after receiving far more "magic juice" to repair his stab wound. Jackson would have sworn his uncle's canines looked longer than usual.

"If it hadn't been so damn inconvenient, I would have rather died," Garrett said after they had delivered Cassidy into medical care and could catch their breath. "This better wear off by tomorrow night. I want to be completely human when we finish this mess."

What would happen if it didn't? Would the vampire blood in their systems die with its source? What would that do to them?

He wished Garrett was still there to discuss it, but his uncle had headed for home soon after Gil walked into the ER, asking for Jackson and demanding to donate O-negative blood for his daughter. Getting Monica Sol—if that was even her real name—away from any opportunity to instigate disaster was Garrett's top priority.

On the way to the hospital, Jackson had stopped her from working herself into a stroke by dosing her with a tranquilizer from the van's emergency kit. He was relieved to see that she required no medical attention for the gunshot wound he had inflicted. The bullet had passed clean through her thigh, and there was potent vampire blood in her system. The damage was as good as healed. Later, Garrett had arranged private transportation and took her semi-conscious self back to the house for safe-keeping.

How they were going to deprogram her was anybody's guess.

The door to Cassidy's room opened, pulling Jackson out of his thoughts. Nick's elegant form slipped ghost-silent into the hall. He closed the door without a sound behind him, then leaned his head against it, shoulders slumped. One hand splayed on the surface as though he considered pushing it open again. The other hung by his side, leather jacket clenched in his fist. Under the overhead fluorescents, his bare skin glowed white.

Jackson didn't move, though not out of fear of being spotted by a predator. No, it wasn't his vulnerability that riveted him, but the vampire's. Whatever Nick told Cassidy about the night's events and their consequences, she would not have taken it well. Whatever the vampire felt in response was very real—and very human.

When Nick collected himself, he walked toward Jackson, putting on his jacket as he went, his boots squeaking on the linoleum floor. Unguarded heartache etched his ridiculously handsome face. The face Jackson once thought of as the unblinking mask of a viper. Though he knew that creature was still in there, there was no sign of it now.

Nick sat on the bench opposite him, leaned back, and closed his eyes, the picture of exhaustion.

Jackson clasped his hands together where they hung between his knees. "How is she?"

"Alive."

"You didn't—"

"No. I did not taste her blood." Nick opened his eyes and stared straight ahead, gaze unfocused. "This is difficult enough without being so closely bound."

Jackson knew what the vampire meant on both counts, but only one reference seemed safe to question. "So it's true, what she told me? About you two reading each other's minds after—" He made a small circular gesture, then, unsure, rejoined his hands.

"*Oui.* We become one," Nick said softly.

"I've never heard of anything like that before."

"It is rare, and unspeakably precious. Like her."

Jackson said nothing. There were no words in the face of what he heard in those hushed tones. If Cassidy felt even half of this, she would be an unspeakable mess without Dominique. These two were willing to die for each other.

One of them actually would.

"Will you make sure she will be all right?"

With a start, Jackson realized the vampire was now focused on him. He sat up. "As far as that will be possible, yes. You have my word."

"You can start by keeping her away from the cottage today."

"I'm sure the staff here will want to keep her for another day of observation. If not"—he lifted one shoulder—"I'm even more sure I can convince them."

The corner of Nick's mouth tilted up. "Careful, hunter. I almost like you."

Jackson's face pulled into a grudging smile. "I might almost not hate you, vampire."

"But when I bring Kambyses to you tonight, you will finish him, *non*?"

And here was the other thing. This bloodsucking menace was nothing if not blunt. When they discussed this before, it had somehow been too remote a possibility to be real, this destruction of Kambyses and all his monstrous spawn. Nor had Jackson ever envisioned it at such a leisurely pace, or with such cooperation from one of the casualties. Could he do this now, knowing he'd also destroy—no, kill—someone he had come to respect, however reluctantly? He didn't know, but thinking of his uncle, he nodded anyway. "Someone will."

"Then I will ask one more favor of you, *mon ami*. I will need to borrow your van."

42

Forever Change

Dominique spent his last day on earth in Cassidy's empty bed. The hunters wouldn't come for him during the day. Or if they did, they wouldn't destroy him. It was Kambyses they would want, and Kambyses they wouldn't find. For that, they would need him. To make sure this was clear, he penned a note to that effect and taped it to the bedroom door.

Dying while oblivious had once been his wish, but no more. He wanted to know the exquisite delight of being fully alive when death found him. He wanted to welcome it with arms thrown wide. Above all, he wanted to feel the beast's panic and laugh in its face.

All of this would be his. Tonight.

Tonight, five-thousand years of terror would end.

With only the shades drawn, the upstairs room was far from light-tight, but even this he was willing to risk. Wrapped in blankets saturated in his love's fragrance and zipped head-to-foot into an old sleeping bag that still carried a touch of his father's earthy aroma, he was content as he slipped into unconsciousness.

The feeling still suffused him when he woke and listened, as he always did, for her heartbeat. Silence. Jackson had kept his promise. She wasn't here. Dominique would never see her again.

He stayed where he was, lying still, letting his mind wander over his life. Memories of sunshine and laughter were countless, but others of darkness and horror soon overwhelmed them, weighed them down, obliterated them.

Know me.

No one would. Not ever again. And that was all right. That was as it should be. What he had told Cassidy was true. He was done fighting.

A footfall approached the cottage. He recognized the quick, staccato cadence of a not-so-stealthy blood-drinker. The source came inside, hesitated in the living room before it moved up the stairs, and paused again in front of the bedroom door. The accompanying heartbeat thumped in his sensitive ears. Then the knob turned.

With a sweep of his arms, Dominique ripped the layers of his cocoon open and sat up. Serge stood at the foot of the bed, wringing his hands, trembling. "It is happening, blood-child. Do you feel it?"

The solemn whisper slipped around Dominique like an icy draft from a crypt. Suppressing a shiver, he got up and pulled on his gym pants. "What happened?"

"The prophecy is upon us."

"Not yet. He still lives." He raised the shade on the window that overlooked the front porch roof. Kambyses's limbs had met the day out there. The sun should have reduced the arms and legs to a shimmering ash residue on the brittle tar shingles. Instead, they lay withered and gray, but solid.

Kambyses was the oldest of their kind. How different did that make him? Dominique had left him buried in a shallow grave, safely out of the sun's reach. Since his limbs would have burned in the sun today, had he died anyway? Since part of him burned in the sun today, had he died anyway? If so, how long before his death pulled the rest of them under?

He scrubbed his face with both hands and turned to Serge, whose mouth wavered somewhere between a bare-toothed grin and white-lipped apprehension. "Is this what you meant when you said I would not keep my promise to Jackson? Is Kambyses already dead?"

Serge shook his head. The sandy curls sticking out all around his head quivered. "You won't deliver him. That is not your future."

The ire he typically felt toward his contrary friend sputtered out before it fully flared to life. He refused to spend his last hour on Earth debating nonsense.

Serge dropped onto the side of the bed as though his knees caved in. He stared at Dominique, the light in his eyes more mad than ever. In an awed tone, he pronounced, "You are about to become the lock, blood-child. She will be your key."

Leave it to the madman to make it impossible to have any sort of meaningful farewell. Nonsense to the very last of his existence. So be it. He reached out and squeezed Serge's shoulder in mute appreciation of their too-brief time together.

Serge grabbed his hand with ferocious intensity. "You can do it, blood-child. With her." His voice dropped further, beseeching. "You *must.*"

Dominique waited for the mad fire to ebb from Serge's gaze before he pulled his hand free. "Of course," he murmured. "Of course, I will." Everything he did of late, he did for or with Cassidy. Delivering his sire to the executioner would be no exception.

On his way out, he pocketed the keys to the Striker van from the kitchen counter. That vehicle had proved invaluable in transporting both Kambyses and Dominique's bike this morning. Now it waited in the driveway for the next and final leg of their journey.

A figure with bright, unbound hair swirling around her shoulders hurried up the driveway toward the cottage. Dominique suppressed the impulse to vanish before Samantha noticed him. It would be the last contact he would have with her. He owed her a farewell.

She didn't spot him on the porch until she was halfway up the stairs and pulled up with a small gasp. "Dominique. Have you seen Serge?" When he didn't respond right away, she continued. "He acted strange this morning—well, stranger than usual—and didn't tell me much of what happened last night. I think he's still having visions. Bad ones."

She drew her fringed shawl tighter and hugged herself as though bracing for something unseen. An unexpected new sorrow pricked at Dominique. Samantha cared deeply for the old pirate and would grieve his death. Through Serge, she had touched eternity. Without him, she would never be the same—because of what Dominique was about to do.

Unwelcome doubt welled as he held her troubled gaze. How many humans would discover their blood-drinker friends and maybe even lovers mysteriously dead tonight? And how many would find themselves free of cruel blood-drinker masters? What was it he would deliver to the world of night? Overdue justice? Unspeakable anguish? He knew why he was breaking Cassidy's heart—it was the only way to keep her safe—but what about all the others and the mortal lives they affected?

Samantha's tentative touch on his forearm brought him back to the moment. "Dominique? Where is he? What's going on?"

On impulse, he pulled her into his arms, this gentle, courageous woman, his erstwhile enemy's sister. She went stick-stiff with surprise. "*Merci*," he whispered. "Thank you."

She relaxed a little. "For what?"

"For your faith in us. Serge and I don't deserve it, but we are better for it." He pressed a kiss to her forehead and released her.

"You don't deserve to suffer," she said, gathering her shawl around her, along with her rattled composure.

"Our suffering will end soon."

"That sounds...not good."

He dragged a small smile to his face. "Serge is inside."

When she glanced at the door, Dominique silently vanished.

At the beach, a cold winter wind blasted from the northeast. Dry sand flew across the ground like swarming snakes, and the sea, blacker than night, boiled with silvered foam beneath a full moon. He didn't have far to go. The gnarly old sea grape that marked the spot shivered in the wind as he dug into the soft soil underneath.

It wasn't long before the rug lay exposed, quietly oozing a smoky scent. Dominique knelt over it, contemplating. All he had to do now was pick it up and carry it away, the same way he had carried it here this morning. Put it in the van, drive to the airport, hand it over. That was it. The end. He had seen the last of Kambyses and his world of horrors.

Also, the last of life.

And the last of hope.

His hands fisted on his thighs. Becoming a blood-drinker had not been his choice. Countless times since then, he tried to end his nightmarish existence, but the beast never allowed it. So, instead, he had dared to hope. Hope for some small measure of redemption, and of seeing the sun again.

This time, the choice was his. Nothing would stop him. This time, he would succeed. His life would end, and with it, all his hopes.

For so long, Dominique had been sure about this decision he no longer believed was his. Now that it was at hand, the finality of it reared up before him with staggering power. For himself, he thought he was still sure—maybe—but what of the others he was about to condemn? The untold thousands who would never know what happened and had no choice at all? Would he, in death, be the monster he fought so hard not to become?

A dizzying wave of fury blasted through him. Dominique's entire body vibrated with a deep growl as he seized the edge of the roll and ripped it open, fully intending to do the same with the contents. A simple death at the hands of mortals was too good for this creature who had taken his body, gutted his soul, and made him his puppet.

Then the head appeared, and he stopped, uncertain again.

No black-eyed glare met him, nor cold indifference. The eyes were closed and sunken, and the face...the face was gaunt as an old corpse, the web of dark veins beneath the translucent skin denser than ever. Was this how ancients died slowly? Desiccate the way the arms and legs had desiccated in the sunlight?

Dominique tore more of the rug, revealing the chest. This, too, was thin, almost birdlike, with ribs and hide wrapped in a fine silk shirt. His anger ebbed further, replaced by a new sense of nameless dread. Kambyses's blood was a fiery sludge. It didn't flow, and hadn't left him in great enough quantities to explain this. Not last night, and not since, judging by how little of it marred the rug.

Hands shaking, he ripped the thick fabric all the way across, and had his answer. Kambyses hadn't wasted away so much as redistributed himself. This was how blood-drinkers recovered from severe injuries. Tissue in one part of the body dissolved and re-formed elsewhere in whatever form was required. He had witnessed this several times, but never like this.

The ancient body had healed the "injury" of his missing limbs.

New matchstick arms and legs extended from the hacked-off shirt sleeves and abbreviated pant legs. They looked impossibly delicate, these new appendages, but they would be more than enough. Kambyses was essentially restored.

Dominique scrambled out of easy reach. How foolish not to bring his blades. By the time he went to fetch them, Kambyses would be long gone.

Of course, Kambyses could have been long gone before Dominique ever got here to dig him up.

The withered body lay still in the dappled shadows cast by the moon. Fingers of wind teased at his thick hair and torn clothing. He seemed to listen, entranced, to the crashing waves.

Alive.

Dangerous, Dominique corrected himself, but there was no conviction behind the thought. Stealing over him was the same serenity he felt earlier, freedom from all doubt and struggle...and complete certainty about what he intended to do.

No, that wasn't quite right either. He tipped his head as though he could hear what he suddenly knew had always been there, just beneath his conscious mind. The heart of the beast, his vampire soul. It was this that now surrendered to peace.

Exactly like the living corpse lying before him did.

Know me. You hear my call every time you pierce a vein...

"It is your will we obey when the beast takes control," Dominique murmured as he comprehended the mind-numbing true extent of that fact. "Your will, your...soul. These are what we are. You are...the beast in us all."

No reaction.

Dominique reached for the duct tape still stuck across the mouth, pried up an edge, and pulled. There was nothing Kambyses could do with his voice now that he couldn't already do without it. His mouth opened a little, and his wasted ribcage rose in a deep, savoring inhalation of the salty-wet air, but he didn't speak.

The eyes of the beast met Dominique's, but not as he had ever seen them. The desperate hunger receded. In its place, something like gratitude emerged. It hummed in the telepathic web holding them bound to each other—and all their kind. A web Dominique noticed only now that it was changing.

One of those bony arms extended across toward him. Kambyses's mouth moved. The voice that emerged was as dusty and strained as the wrappings of a mummy and sounded just as foreign. The words bore no resemblance to any language Dominique could name. Yet, he felt their meaning as if they were his own thoughts.

You are the chosen one, Nico. You always have been.

With a small shock, he realized Kambyses no longer blocked him from his mind. The one-way link established when Dominique fed from him over a week ago was weak, but it was far from gone.

"To be your eternal companion?" Dominique could summon no rancor. Only curiosity.

Companion. Lover. Prodigy... Heir.

Heir? The implication of that one word flat-lined his mind.

A thousand years of searching has brought me to you. You are the most worthy, my ultimate champion. You are...my better.

He said nothing, trusting neither his voice nor his thoughts as he experienced what Kambyses had felt the previous night. Dismembered and pinned beneath his youngling's heel, he was outmaneuvered and more thoroughly defeated than he had ever been. Defeated, but not defenseless. Spinning illusions that would have tricked them into restoring him would have taken little effort. Ending them all after that, no effort at all.

But after that first attempt, he knew there was no point.

Nothing would have changed.

Nothing ever...changed.

Kambyses inhaled again, savoring the air, the moment, in utter contentment. This time, he spoke in French. "I would have liked more time with you, Nico. I would have liked to become the man you would have been proud to call your sire." Another breath. A smile weighted with regret. "But I am so very tired of the darkness. I can bear it no more." Switching to English, he finished, "Dominique, you never accepted me as your master because you have none. You bow down to no one, and you never will. My brave young one. I cede you my kingdom. It is yours to tear from my body at will."

Dominique's mouth was dry as the sand flying over the ground in ribbons. In his mind, Kambyses showed him exactly how this incredible thing was to be done—the way it had been done before, so long ago. He felt the fire-blood burn through him just thinking about it. Not merely in his gut this time, but in the deepest caverns of his being. His canines lengthened at the very idea of drinking such blood to the death.

"I want nothing of yours," he said, though he couldn't deny the horrified anticipation stealing over him. It belonged to the beast. It belonged to Kambyses. "I never did."

"But it will not be mine once you claim it, will it? It can be anything you want it to be."

The words were a lightning strike down Dominique's spine. Without Kambyses at its center, the world of night would no longer thrum with the fear and desolation of his insatiable, lonely spirit. Without Kambyses, the world of night could truly be anything Dominique wanted it to be—anything he and Cassidy wanted it to be. It would be changed as Serge had prophesied.

Forever.

He moved closer. His hands shook. If he was compelled, he didn't care. "What if what I want is for it not to exist?"

That would be a forever change, too. All he had to do was deliver Kambyses to the hunters as agreed. Or he could finish him himself now with his bare hands. This time, the beast wouldn't stop him.

"If that is what you choose, then so it will be," Kambyses said with a sigh of reluctant acceptance. In his heart, he had already abdicated his throne of blood and darkness. He no longer cared. "But I don't think you will."

Fiercely cold wind swept over Dominique's bare chest and back, but the promise of the eternal blood warmed him. The last of it—the very last blood he could pull out of Kambyses before he died—would be the most potent blood of all. It would brand his soul...and reshape it.

The beast as he knew it would be no more.

He leaned forward, eyes fixed on the sinewy neck and the fat vein he had tapped there before. He inhaled the ancient one's scent. The smoky essence sparked only the barest memory of fear. Something new held him captive now, something quiet and considering. Something waiting. Waiting for him.

"Why is that, old man? Why do you believe I won't end us all?"

Kambyses caressed Dominique's cheek with bony fingers, the tender touch of a father. Millennia of ghosts haunted his smile. "Because you want to live, Nico. You want to live...for her."

"*Oui*," he whispered. A simple truth. The only truth that mattered. Gently, he cradled the old one's head in one hand. "I do." His lips slid over the paper-smooth skin, mouth throbbing with hunger. "I want to live."

And he knew that he would.

Forever.

43

DARK LORD

Jackson's phone vibrated. Seeing who it was, he hesitated. He still hadn't decided if he wanted to take the call by the time it dropped into voice mail.

Beside him, stretched out on the overstuffed sofa in the Striker mansion's palatial living room, Cassidy remained oblivious. Exhaustion claimed her halfway through the movie. Before that, she had stared at the screen, blank-faced, reacting to nothing.

Though all but catatonic with grief, physically there was nothing wrong with her anymore. The hospital cut her loose late in the afternoon, and he had braced for a fight about where she would go from there. He didn't get one.

"I can't deal with the cottage yet," she said on the ride home, her quiet voice flat. "Too many memories."

Unwelcome memories also greeted her at the house, where elaborate holiday decorations were on full display. The sight of garlands, lights, and glitter made Cassidy's face pinch. "It's Christmas already?"

"Next week." He stopped himself from adding that her recovery from a near-death experience was his best Christmas present ever. She had lost her mother in December, and now she would have another heartache to associate with the holiday season.

"Well, ho, ho, freaking ho," she muttered and tuned out for the rest of the day.

So much for turning to Jackson in her time of need. She was running from pain, not toward the safety he offered. He tamped down a prickle of bitterness. This would take time, he knew it would. Even if she never learned what really happened to the vampire and the deal he'd struck with the hunters to save her, losing Dominique could shatter her. That much was painfully obvious.

He would keep his part of the bargain. He would be there for Cassidy for the rest of their lives in any way she would permit—friend, lover, husband, foe. Anything. Whatever it took. It was what he owed her for dragging her into this mess and all the lies he spun for her. It was what he owed Dominique for the sacrifice the vampire made for her. And it was what he owed himself for the love he still held for her.

All around him, the house felt like an enormous set of steel and concrete lungs holding a breath. His parents and the domestic staff weren't due back until late tomorrow at the earliest. This morning, their houseguest, a hollow-eyed Monica Davis—formerly Sol—informed them calmly that she wanted to go home. All the fire and venom had left her, all compulsions mysteriously released. Garrett bought her a first-class ticket and drove her to the airport himself. Her family would meet her at the gate in Seattle, eager to embrace the daughter and sister who had vanished months ago without a trace.

Samantha had brought over some of Cassidy's clothes but didn't stay. She was impatient to get back before sundown for Serge, her vampire buddy. How much did his sister know of what was about to happen? Would she hate him for the rest of their lives?

The phone vibrated in his hand. Uncle Garrett again.

End credits scrolled on the muted TV. The clock on the fireplace mantle read well past midnight. Plenty of time for Garrett to meet Dominique in their facility at the municipal airport, take delivery of his incapacitated sire, and put an end to them both.

Put an end to them all.

Everywhere.

Jackson had bowed out of being there, telling his uncle that Cassidy was too frail to be left alone. Also, as the Foundation's senior hunter, Garrett should have the honor of this ultimate kill. But was there more to Jackson's reluctance? After all, his whole reason for being would disappear when the Foundation shut down. There would be no outlet for his grief and anger over his murdered brother, and...

The phone. Again. *For fuck's sake!* Was Garrett so thrilled about what he'd done he couldn't wait until morning to share all the gory details? That didn't sound like his cold-blooded killer of an uncle. Jackson's brow gathered in doubt. He took the call.

Garrett was talking before Jackson could open his mouth. "Talk to me, kid. What's going on there?"

"Nothing."

"Why are you whispering?"

"Cass is sleeping."

"Is anyone else there?"

"No."

Silence. "I don't like this. Something's wrong."

His gut lurched. "Why?"

"Your new pal Nicky hasn't shown up yet."

The lurch morphed into a twist. "It's still early."

"He's had plenty of time to get Daddy here. He also had plenty of time to put him back together again and head out on a killing spree."

Jackson's right hand curled into a fist. Had he really misjudged Dominique and fallen for a ruse after all? No, he decided. He hadn't. He let out a long breath. "If he did, you don't think they would start with you?"

"Wise ass. Check the house systems. Call me back."

The call disconnected. He hesitated a moment before thumbing to the house security app. When he touched the icon, his phone froze. "Fuck."

Cassidy shifted and sighed. She lay with her head on a pillow propped against his thigh. He straightened the blanket around her and waited for her breathing to return to the even rhythm of sleep before gingerly extricating himself from his seat. "I'll be right back," he said in a bored tone. Something to inform her unconscious mind that all was well. Another lie. When would he stop?

The puzzle pieces added up to nothing good. Only a week ago, Dominique hacked Jackson's phone. Now the vampire was MIA, and Jackson's phone was hosed. Coincidences were rare bitches in his world.

His bare feet were silent on the cool marble floors as he headed for the operations center. He only got as far as the foyer when the back of his neck prickled. There seemed to be a hum in the air so low only his skin could hear it. Following it, he rounded the lavish Christmas tree and moved toward the front door. His senses, still keener than usual, told him nothing was amiss. Yet, on an instinctive level, he knew that he and Cassidy were no longer alone.

The little flashlight grew heavy in his pocket, but he didn't reach for it. That feeble weapon would no longer surprise any vampire he was likely to encounter tonight.

When he opened the door, damp, chill air swirled in like a swarm of ghosts. He peered into the night. Nothing more ominous than landscape lighting and...a shimmer. Something out of sync, half-formed. Something he couldn't see with his eyes so much as feel in his gut.

The shimmer became a blur and then snapped into vivid, 3D focus.

"Nick?"

The vampire stood not even ten feet away in the mellow glow of the entry lights. He looked as cavalier as Jackson had never seen him. Jeans and a simple blue T-shirt. Sneakers. Hair semi-neatly tied back. Both hands stuck into his pockets. Eyes as still and dark as mountain lakes. And just as deep.

"*Bonsoir, mon ami.*"

"How did you...where...." Jackson's mind tumbled. The van was there too, sitting by the garage, Dominique's motorbike next to it. Had they been there a second ago? He would have sworn not.

"*Pardon.* I didn't mean to startle you."

Jackson swallowed the impulse to scoff. The words held no hint of smugness. If anything, the vampire looked almost as confused as Jackson felt. He willed his hand off the massive brass door handle, took a step forward, and tried to look casual despite the adrenaline pumping in his veins. "So, what brings you here?"

Dominique nodded at the van. "This was useful. Thank you."

Jackson hesitated to think about what might be inside. "You could have left it with"—no, better not mention Garrett—"at"—or the facility—"the airport."

"I could. If I planned to go there."

He crossed his arms. "You changed your mind?" Surprise, surprise.

"In a way."

"Nice. And you hacked my phone again and took down the security system?" A shrug. "Well, fuck me for ever trusting you then." Still trusting him. Had no choice but to trust him. With the system down, Jackson had no way to defend himself.

Odd how that didn't bother him nearly so much as the fact that he had ever believed this creature's promises. That he had spent even one second giving this bloodsucker credit for anything that remotely resembled humanity. That he had—yes, damn it—started to care. He could see the burgeoning amusement now, the glint of interest in the eyes. A cat gearing up to pounce on its prey.

"I need to speak with you," purred the cat.

Jackson glanced at the van. "You want me to end your sire? Is that it? Right here? Fine. Let's do it." He rubbed his trembling hands together. "Did you bring your swords? Should I get mine?"

"There is nothing to be done. I just need you to listen." He held Jackson's gaze for a long moment. "Kambyses is already dead."

Jackson stared. "Then how are you still standing there?"

"Only his body is dead. His essence survives...in me."

Jackson felt his mental fuses fry and pop. "I don't...I don't understand."

Dominique came closer with breathtaking predatory grace. "I consumed all his blood, and with it...everything he was."

Another pause. "That was his ultimate plan for me. To be his heir. To take his place as the lord of us all."

Jackson opened his mouth, but no words would come out. *My God*, he thought. *My God*.

"I have his gifts, too." The tentative look said he wasn't sure how he felt about this. "There is a learning curve."

My God, Jackson thought again, the impulse to laugh out loud instantly at war with an urge to flee. He did neither. That was what he saw earlier: Dominique using new abilities to erase himself from the awareness of those who looked right at him. Like Kambyses had done. Maybe on purpose, maybe by accident. It was also what Jackson had felt, what compelled him to open the door. Dominique wanted him to—or maybe only thought about it.

That simple. That powerful.

A nuclear bomb of psychic power in a being who had only just mastered the equivalent of a slingshot.

Petrified calm settled on him, even as his heart stampeded through his chest. He tried to summon the protective smokescreen of anger, but there was not a wisp to be found. Fear oozed out of his every pore, and judging by Dominique's flaring nostrils, the vampire didn't miss it. Jackson's life was over.

Yet Dominique regarded him with only mild curiosity. "Did you know such a thing was possible, hunter?"

Jackson shook his head a tiny bit, all the motion his tense neck muscles allowed.

"Neither did I." Dominique sounded distracted—by the stink of fear, no doubt.

Jackson swallowed his rising gorge. "Don't play games with me, Nick. You owe me that much. Whatever you came here for, get it over with."

The vampire's gaze sharpened. "No games. I returned your property. And you should know what I intend to do."

"Meanwhile, I'm standing here marinating." Jackson ground his teeth to keep them from clacking. "Do I need to piss myself, too, before you rip off my head?"

The bastard actually smirked. "Very good, *cher*. You are proving the very point you need to understand."

Next thing he knew, a vice grip seized the back of his neck. A mere inch separated their faces, if that. Slamming his hands against those rock-hard shoulders was a foolish impulse, but he did it anyway.

Dominique's words drowned in the panic storm screaming in Jackson's head. His knees shook and his insides turned to water. He gasped, sucking in the vampire's tang of winter ice…and mud. Wood, too. First thaw in the mountains, a whisper of spring.

"You have nothing to fear from me, *mon ami*. You have nothing to fear." The soft, repeating murmurs finally penetrated. "Even when you are like this, you have nothing to fear from me. The hunger for fear belonged to Kambyses. Without him, it no longer exists."

Jackson trembled. He was alive. Still alive. Might even stay that way? The red fog of terror thinned into a pink haze. "Let. Me. Go."

Dominique did. Jackson jerked back and fell against the open door, his legs awkward like putty sticks. He wiped the back of a fist over his mouth, not daring to look away from the vampire, who now stood several paces away, hands back in his pockets. "Asshole. You couldn't have just said so?"

"Would you have believed it? Or would you have taken it for a lie? Or a game? Because that is what you expect from my kind?"

No point in answering that. It was true. He willed his knees to lock and hold him as he pushed away from the door. Adrenaline still seethed in his system, but in anger now, not fear. "Terror doesn't give you a hard-on anymore? Congrats. What about the rest of your sort?"

"I don't know."

"You're the fucking top of the line now. What do you mean, you don't know?"

A flash of impatience. "I will conduct a survey for you as soon as I determine how."

"What about Serge? Did you ask him?"

"No need. He tells me things whether I ask or not." Dominique shook his head. "He claims to feel a difference, but he is close to me and actually expected this madness. He is not a typical blood-drinker."

Jackson cleared the knot out of his throat, almost able to draw a full breath again. "You're supposed to be connected to them all."

"According to thousands of years of legend, yes, perhaps. But all I sense is that they exist, and that Kambyses never tried to direct them. His fears controlled him, and so they controlled all of us. How long it will take for that to change, I cannot say."

"Change," Jackson repeated. "Are you planning to convince the world's vampires to stop killing?"

Dominique spread his hands, palms up. "A better solution than condemning them all to death, *non*?"

"Like they've condemned their victims?"

"Often not by choice."

Jackson rubbed a hand over his face, trying to stop his head from reeling. "That's why you're here instead of at the facility. Now that you're the one with all the power, you won't let us wipe you all out. Is that it?"

The vampire gave him a long, unfathomable look. "I would like to try this first."

"Oh, by all means." Jackson made a grand, sweeping gesture with one arm. "How long do you think you'll need? A week? A month? A year? Uncle Garrett will want to know how long to hold off coming after you." Not that he would. By Garrett's standards, the only thing Dominique had inherited was a bigger bull's eye on his forehead.

"He will not hold off. He relishes the hunt too much," Dominique said, echoing Jackson's thoughts. "Nor will I stop him, or you."

"Come again?"

Tiny, rueful smile. "The only blood-drinkers you can track are the inept and insane, the truly dangerous ones. I have not tolerated these in the past, and I will not tolerate them now. You are welcome to them." The smile widened a little. "Their numbers are inconsequential compared to those you have no hope of finding."

Jackson swallowed. "Nice. Just how many of you are there?" The smile didn't budge. "I see. Well, I doubt you can just erase part of their psyche like that. Something will have to take the place of your sire's insecurities. So let me ask you, Nick—what are *your* fears? What rules you?"

The vampire tilted his head, his sweeping brows drawing together in contemplation. "Love rules me," he said. "I fear a world without love."

"That is a fear you will never know," Cassidy said as she emerged from behind the Christmas tree. "Not as long as I'm around." The vacant husk he had left on the sofa was gone. In its place stood a sleep-rumpled woman in an oversize sweater, PJ bottoms, and socks, blue eyes sparkling and freckled cheeks flushed. She had never looked more beautiful.

The vampire seemed to agree. At the sight of her, his face lit as though fired by an inner sun.

Without hesitation, she walked up to the most lethal supernatural creature on earth and fisted both hands in his shirt. "But you better be done trying to save me from yourself by leaving me, because I can't do that again. I just can't. Do you hear me?"

Dominique kissed her forehead and folded her into his arms, as if trying to absorb her into his being. "Neither can I, *mon amour*. Neither can I."

Jackson felt like an intruder on his own driveway, but he was spellbound, unable to look away from the quiet embrace that bordered on the erotic. Every tender caress, every relieved sigh, every shift to cleave closer together, conveyed two souls coming home to each other.

Not even at their most familiar had Jackson and Cassidy shared a moment like that. Strange how his resentment seemed to crumble before it was half-formed. If this was what the new lord of the vampires would flood his subjects with, there might be a chance, however remote, that he could persuade them to change their murderous ways.

This audacious plan might just work.

But if not, if it failed or even stumbled, Jackson and the Striker Foundation would still be there to sweep up the refuse—and scatter it in the sun.

44

WORLD OF NIGHT

Three months later...

Secrets.

Cassidy hated them. Always had. Always would. Secrets had destroyed so many things in her life. Dominique knew better than to keep them from her.

Or at least he should have.

She lay in his arms, staring up past the enormous spinnaker sail swollen with moonlight and wind. They had made a nest for themselves in the webbing suspended between the catamaran's twin hulls. Stretched out on a quilt and pillows, they watched the stars sway overhead as a steady wind carried them across long, lazy Atlantic swells. Beneath them, black water hissed against the twin hulls. Above, lines creaked in the rigging.

If not for the mysterious new secret looming over them, this outing on Serge's new pride and joy, the aptly christened *Sunseeker*, would have been perfect. The forty-one-foot sailing catamaran was a gift from Dominique, who had purchased it with cash thanks to the wealth he inherited along with his power and title.

He had presented Cassidy with a gift as well—a new home. All she had to do was find it. He wasn't picky. Anywhere, any style, any price was fine with him, so long as it contained a bomb-shelter-grade room for him to spend his days. She took her time researching the options in the high-end real estate market, an arena in which she never imagined herself as an active participant, much less a money-is-no-object buyer. In the meantime, the beach cottage worked fine as a cozy place to hide away in. Even if that meant the vampires in her life spent their days buried in a dune.

Another gift was a new job. She had left the *Gazette* six weeks ago, not just to tackle luxury house hunting, but also for a challenge she couldn't refuse—coordinate the launch and operation of a new online service catering exclusively to the blood-drinker community. A more-than-generous salary came with the position, which took hefty chunks out of her student loan debt and nicely padded a personal savings account. Her heart and soul might be bound to a vampire, but her ability to be self-reliant was growing by the day.

Dominique interrupted her mental inventory of events and blessings by brushing stray hair out of her face. When he slid a fingertip down the bridge of her nose, she met his eyes. They were soft and warm and alive with mischief. Moonlight cast the planes of his face and bare torso in a magical glow and made blue highlights shimmer in his wind-tousled hair. He looked every inch as suited to the night as dolphins were to the ocean—and twice as graceful.

Lord of Night.

It was how Kambyses had thought of himself, and Dominique warmed to the title soon enough. Not that he actually lorded it over anyone but Serge yet.

A soft cough pulled Cassidy from her reverie. Annoyance flitted across Dominique's features, but was gone by the time he turned to face the intruder.

"Am I interrupting?" Samantha asked.

"Delaying the inevitable," he said, earning himself a quizzical look from Cassidy. God, how she hated not being in his head. Surely he meant to remedy that tonight? Surely that was at least one reason he had suggested they accompany Serge and Samantha on this outing?

Samantha didn't look convinced. "Uh-huh. I see an awful lot of canoodling going on up here and nothing that looks like meditation practice."

He flopped on his back with a groan.

She squatted down and placed a wide-bottomed thermos cup on the solid deck beside Cassidy's pillow. "I brought you some hot tea, sweetie."

"Thank you." Cassidy extended an arm from her blanket cocoon and reached for the blessed promise of heat. The early spring day had been hot enough to qualify for summer, but she underestimated the chill of the sea air at night. Her sun dress might as well have been nothing, and the sweatshirt helped only a little. Samantha herself was as-ever attired in yoga pants topped by a bulky sweater.

"I have refreshments for you, too—" She stroked the thick blond braid draped across her shoulder and glanced at Serge, who manned the helm only a few feet away. He nodded vigorous encouragement. "My lord, Dominique," she finished.

Cassidy rolled her eyes at the title Serge insisted on using and at Samantha's continued efforts to get Dominique to feed from her. These two were so made for each other. Space cadets, both of them.

"Do you?" The Lord of Night sounded intrigued by the proposal.

Samantha licked at her bottom lip and tucked a fluttering strand of hair behind one ear. Her fingers trailed down the side of her neck, drawing the eye. "It's all right with Serge—and me, of course—if you want to."

So, it was true. There was nothing Serge wouldn't agree to if he thought it maintained his lordship's good humor. And for good reason. Based on one of his visions, he had talked Dominique into a mutual exchange of blood. While the resulting telepathic bond dissipated as usual, other effects appeared to be permanent. Serge was now profoundly susceptible to Dominique's moods—and the age-old instinct to terrorize his meals had been replaced by a craving for affection. In short, Serge proudly considered himself "re-sired" by the new Lord of Night.

Dominique appeared to give the offer of "refreshment" serious consideration. "Will you serve your vintage to me in a wineglass?"

Samantha looked scandalized, but Cassidy heard the teasing undertow in his voice. "Will you mind if I throw my tea at you?" she countered sweetly, though she would have been loath to lose the warmth nestled in her hands.

Dominique burst out laughing with infectious delight. In the cockpit, Serge chortled right along with him.

"Ah, *mon amour*," he purred. "Promise me you will do exactly that if you ever see me taking blood from anything but a vein."

"Promise," she said, and sipped more tea.

"*Je suis désolé*," he told Samantha. "I have all the...refreshments I need tonight right here."

"Could have fooled me," Cassidy said into her cup, knowing only Dominique would hear her. A dimpled, lopsided grin full of promise was her reward.

With a sigh, Samantha deflated. "Oh, well. Can't blame a girl for trying."

"But of course," Dominique concurred with exaggerated smugness.

"So. Any luck tonight?" she prompted. Serge sounded like he was clearing a boulder from his lungs. "My lord," she amended.

"I have not tried to reach out to them yet, no. I have been distracted." He smiled seduction down at Cassidy bundled in her blankets. "I would like to keep being distracted."

"Do you?" she said, using the same words and tone he had used with Samantha. His smile grew dazzling. Moving as fluidly as a cat, he snuggled into the blankets with her.

"Well. Okay then." Samantha sounded uncertain. "Guess three's a crowd."

"It is," Dominique agreed, nuzzling closer to Cassidy.

"All right. Let us know if you need anything." She turned, and Serge harrumphed again. "My lord," she tossed over her shoulder with an agitated huff.

Cassidy put the cup aside, its contents now radiating warmth in her belly. She kept her voice low even though with Serge's supernatural ears aboard, privacy was an illusion. "Promise me you'll never make me call you that."

"It is his choice."

"You're not exactly discouraging it."

He considered. "It feels right coming from a blood-drinker, but you... The only thing I want to hear you call me is by my name. Or lover," he amended with a suggestively cocked brow.

The shiver rippling through her had nothing to do with the cool air. She reached to caress his face. He captured her hand and pressed a kiss into her palm.

"*Je t'aime, ma reine,*" he whispered. "I love you." Desire darkened his gaze, rousing his vampire nature, and her breath caught, as it always did, at the golden glow flaring in the back of his eyes. She thought of the surreal luminescence as a beacon of life and passion. He claimed it was the part of her soul that had become an intrinsic part of his being, his humanity.

Dominique's mouth struggled to subdue a smile, the dimple in his left cheek quavering with effort.

"Your queen, am I? Pretty words." She sniffed. "Are you willing to back them up?"

The smile almost broke free. "You are a difficult woman to please."

"And you love that about me, *non*?"

His eyes danced with merriment. His obvious delight with whatever he was keeping from her almost made up for him keeping it from her in the first place. He'd nursed this secret with care, even letting their precious link fade away so she couldn't discover it in his mind. It was a good secret then. Nevertheless, Cassidy had about reached her limit of putting up with it.

"An impossible woman to surprise."

"I don't like surprises."

"Maybe I can change your mind about that."

"All you have to do is taste my blood." Then nothing would surprise her unless it surprised them both.

"Or—" He reached into the pocket of his jeans and wiggled out a small, velvet cube. "I could give you this."

She knew a moment's resentment. Dominique's most disquieting new talent was influencing the minds of others with his thoughts alone, making them see—or not see—whatever he wished. He wielded this skill with an increasing casualness that reminded her far too much of his sire. While their link was strong, however, he could not muddle her mind, not on purpose nor by accident. But with their mental bond non-existent, he had muddled her into not seeing that suspicious bulge in his pocket. The bulge which was the box he opened and held out to her. The contents glittered in the moonlight.

It took her a moment to switch mental gears. Then the surprise hit her over the head. Her jaw dropped.

The ring glinting in its satin pillow was a work of art. Ribbons of silver and diamonds swirled around an oval central stone. Dark-blue embers winked in its depths. A sapphire. She could only look a dumbfounded question at him.

He tucked his chin in a little, uncertain. "Do you like this surprise?"

All the air rushed out of her, incredulous. "*Like* it? Are you kidding me? It's gorgeous." She took the box, admiring the ring, while her thoughts whirled. Theirs was not a relationship requiring gifts. After all, such tokens could never be more than superficial symbols of what they truly were to each other. Why would he spring this on her now?

At last, his smile burst free, a fizzing manifestation of pleasure. "The color matches your eyes. Like the Caribbean Sea at noon. That was the first spell you ever cast over me." When he extracted the ring from the box, she held out her left hand, allowing him to slip it over the finger that once hosted Jackson's pink diamond brick. Unlike the Striker family heirloom, this ring appeared to be made for her. It wrapped around her finger like a frothing wave.

"But it's silver. How can you touch it?"

"Platinum," he corrected.

Priceless, she thought. Not that money would ever be an issue for him again. Among the things he learned in his sire's blood was how to claim the wealth Kambyses had amassed over the ages. Dominique's personal net worth now far exceeded that of the Striker billions, as befitted the Lord of Night.

"Dominique," she said carefully, her heart squeezing into her mouth. "Are you...are you...proposing?" She knew the answer because she knew him. But for once she needed to hear him say it, too. This possibility was too overwhelming to leave open to interpretation.

He took her hand in his, thumb rubbing over her fingers as he met her eyes. "If you thought that performing such a ritual would give us anything we don't already have, then yes. I would find a way for you to wed a man who is legally dead."

She heaved a tiny sigh of relief. She'd been leery of marriage since her father's betrayal, and accepted Jackson's proposal only because at the time he was her best friend. Though he, too, betrayed her trust soon enough.

No, marriage hadn't been part of her life plan since she was too young to know better. Maybe not even then.

Plus, this was Dominique. He was a reality onto himself. By being with him, she was part of a world where human standards didn't apply. In their world, they were already joined until death do them part. Nothing would ever change that. Nothing could ever make their relationship stronger than it was. Certainly not a piece of paper.

Nor jewelry, no matter how breathtaking.

"Then why give me this?"

He touched her cheek with the back of his fingers. "Because I love you. Because you are my lady and my soul. Because you are my queen of the night. Now more than ever, you are my reason for being, my anchor to all that is true. You belong with me, Cassidy Chandler, and I want there to be no doubt about this in anyone's mind when they see you, regardless of whether I am by your side under the stars or you walk alone in sunlight."

With him. She belonged *with* him. Not *to* him. Emotion swelled her heart. A pure, heady mixture of trust, love, and desire. She was as free to leave him and return to a mortal life as she ever was.

And she knew she never would.

Cassidy squeezed the ring on her finger. The metal warmed and radiated into her skin, almost as though setting invisible hooks. "You are my home, Dominique. You always will be."

Joy. It beamed from his face to pierce the night in countless ways. She could feel it in his strong, confident touch when he pulled her close; taste it in his deep, passionate kiss when he took her mouth; and heard it in his playful, guttural growl when his teeth found their mark.

Within moments, her mental edges dissolved as she tuned into the blaze of light that was his natural state of being. Life, passion, love, all amplified a hundredfold and radiating out into the collective vampire psyche.

Well, maybe.

As far as they knew, no one had yet tuned into the change of programming. Except Serge, of course, who basked in Dominique's presence like a cat in a beam of sunlight. But Serge knew what was happening from the beginning. Without that, ancient habits apparently died even harder than merely old ones.

They heard him cackle from the cockpit as he picked up on the emotional surge flowing from his lord.

Cassidy sighed her bliss into the star-spattered sky beyond the ballooning sail while Dominique finished taking his "refreshment." She shivered with anticipation when he closed the tiny injuries with sensuous strokes of his tongue. Burying her face in his thick hair, she savored the fresh notes in his scent, wet and dark with hints of earth and spring to come.

So much yet to come. One thought, echoing in two minds.

He settled deeper into her arms beneath the blankets, his groin swelling against her hip, inviting. She shifted her legs, accepting. Some things were unstoppable. Such as this moment right after their telepathic link re-ignited. They would always make love. Now was no different—even with an audience. Her hunger for him overruled all of her normal inhibitions—as did her French vampire lover's exhibitionist tendencies. With his new gifts, they could have rendered themselves invisible, but by the time he moved as deeply in her body as he moved in her soul, neither of them cared enough to bother.

Samantha's breathless murmur rode the wind. "They're such a tease."

"Hush," Serge replied, entranced.

As much as Kambyses's power had changed Dominique, one thing remained the same—his heart still beat, his blood still flowed, allowing him to function as a man. He could indulge in lovemaking for the rest of her mortal life, and a thousand years beyond that.

So much yet to come.

Rocked by the sea and cradled by night, they moved together in a slow, primal rhythm, emotions and sensations ricocheting between them. In her awareness, a familiar glowing, crystalline spiral formed around them. It twisted out of the sea and into the stars, and pulsed in time with their escalating passion. Dominique never saw this. The spiral was Cassidy's alone, her perception of his vampire essence, the beast, coming for her. Any other mortal lover, unaware, would have been swept up and killed at this point. Instead, she reached for it, whispered to it her love, and felt its sepulchral breath the moment the ecstasy crested over them, turning their bodies as liquid as their minds.

The spiral shattered, untold shards of fading light whirling away, disappearing, undone. Undone as they were undone. Undone and reassembled into a new and glorious whole.

As she lay, catching her breath, Cassidy tried to imagine a thousand years of making love with this magnificent man who wielded unspeakable power with such heart-stopping vulnerability. She didn't think it would be enough. What would it be like once she, too, became immortal? Now that she had decided to join him once, she knew she would again—when she was ready. When they were both ready to leave the sun behind forever. Maybe in a year. Or five. Maybe more. Maybe less.

Then she would taste his blood.

So much yet to come.

He kissed his way up her neck, along her jaw and chin, then brushed her lips with his. She nipped at him, questioning, demanding. Rapture when his mouth melted into hers.

Blood. There was blood in his kiss.

Cold and sharp, like a shard of ice steeped in starlight and time. It was just a drop, but it burned all the way down into her belly and from there out through her arms and legs into the tips of her fingers and toes.

His eyes snapped open. "*Non.*"

"Ohhh," she moaned and broke into a broad, giggly smile. "*Ouiiii.*"

He had raked his tongue over a sharp canine and given her the blood in a kiss as he had almost done before, as he would do again some future night. Their joined mind had envisioned this, anticipated it, and so he had done it.

Her immune system was robust, and his blood wouldn't harm her. But, oh, how it reacted with his fresh serum in her system! Every artery and vein warmed, becoming a web of light holding her suspended in the dark. She could feel every inch of her skin, every tiny hair on her body. Saw every nuance of darkness in the water, every fiber in the sails. Heard every squeak and groan in the hull, and...and... *What the hell?*

Dominique stared at her with his mouth hanging open, blood on his lips, the epitome of fascinated horror.

It was a sound, but not one she heard with her ears. Her whole body—or rather Dominique's body—seemed to act like an antenna tuning into something that swelled out of the sea and the sky, from everywhere and nowhere at once. It was a warbling, high-pitched alien drone that felt desolate and eternal and juddered in her body with tangible force.

"You hear it," he whispered.

She nodded. "What—?" But she already knew. This was the web, the psychic fabric of all the blood-drinkers in existence. From the moment Dominique had taken Kambyses's place within it, he had sensed it like this, but Cassidy never had, not until now. Now that his blood bound them on a deeper level than his serum alone ever could.

He closed his eyes and dropped his forehead against hers. *Do you also see what it means?*

She did, and it left her reeling. *The Strikers underestimated your numbers a bit, I think.*

Oui. A bit.

Holding on to him, as though hanging over a precipice, she stared out at the psychic expanse and listened. This web of the collective blood-drinker unconscious, perhaps half a million strong, vibrated with the desperate energy of pain and eternal isolation. The wonder was not that Kambyses had yearned to end himself. It was that he had lasted so long.

Dominique curled his body around hers more tightly. The only reason he could face this was that, unlike his sire, he didn't face it alone. Through her, he was anchored in the mortal world in ways Kambyses never was. *What am I to do with this? It's like trying to stir a world with a teaspoon. And I'm the only one who knows that it even exists.*

Cassidy contemplated this world, the world of night. *It seems to resonate with itself. Like a feedback loop.*

Oui, exactement. *I try to disrupt it, but no matter what I do, the loop is always stronger.*

"Maybe..." The drone oscillated, becoming louder for a moment before settling down again, as though disturbed. "It's not a world, Dominique."

He plucked the thought from her mind. "A...swarm?"

She raised her brows. "It lives in each vampire's heart."

"The beast."

"Yes. The beast. As a whole." *Formed in Kambyses's image.* "You can't subdue the whole thing at once, because it wasn't born all at once. You have to change it the way it grew."

Revelation lit his face. "One blood-drinker at a time."

Find one, she challenged silently. *Find one right now. Just one.*

He glanced at Serge, who didn't even pretend not to be listening to the verbal portion of their conversation. The old pirate's face shone in the moonlight. "The key," he said, eyes flashing gold with giddy excitement. "The key is turning."

"The prophecy?" Samantha said, breathless.

"Yes, yes, yes! Cassidy is the key and Dominique is the lock. At last! They have found a way to make it so!"

The key prodded the lock. *Never mind him. You can hear them all. Try to hear only one.*

Dominique stretched out on his back beside her, clasped one hand with hers, and closed his eyes. Then his awareness expanded exponentially. Cassidy's sluggish human brain tried to keep up, but it was like riding a bolt of lightning through a flickering strobe effect of impressions.

The boat. The sea. The beach. People. Talking. Traffic. Horns. Accident. Restaurant. Party. Drugs. Plane. Police. Birth. Shouting. Gun. Laughter.

Silence...shock.

Close to the coast that slid past on the western horizon, a single member of the swarm paused in his nocturnal habits and felt warmth crawl over him like the touch of a sun he hadn't seen in more years than he cared to recall. The invisible sun sought him out, enveloped him, stung his flesh. He overturned tables and chairs as he bolted for the hotel bar's exit. Outside, tires screeched in his wake. A speeding pickup hit him, sent him flying across the pavement, tearing a fine suit, skinning knees and elbows.

Cassidy cringed, but the Lord of Night wasn't about to let the first blood-drinker to sense him get away. He focused harder.

Terrified, his target ran, speeding down alleys and up walls, over rooftops and across freeways. The heat pursued him, relentless. Finally, he stopped, far out amidst the vast fields of a commercial grower. He spun around, seeking what his eyes could not see. Strawberries crushed beneath his feet, their fruity sweetness rising around him. He was alone. The sensation of sun-fire thrummed deep in his trembling flesh.

Dominique and Cassidy sensed the panic rise once more and reached out before it could overtake him again. *Do not be afraid. I mean you no harm.*

Out in the field, the other vampire fell to his knees, sliding along the razor's edge between terror and relief. *What are you?*

Their joined hands tightened in silent triumph. They drew a mighty breath with their lungs and with their hearts, and set out to change the world of night forever.

I am your lord and master. Hear me. You are not alone.

THANK YOU FOR READING

If you enjoyed this book and have a moment, please consider leaving a brief review wherever you purchased this book or on Goodreads to help others discover this series. Thank you!

If you would like a free eBook, sign up for my mailing list and also be the first to find out about new releases and special offers.

Mailing list signup: https://skryder.com/mailinglist

For a bonus short story, turn the page...

Bonus: Ancient Hunger

A Dark Destinies Tale

1

The attack came inconveniently close to dawn. With the night's tasks complete, Kambyses had just turned his attention to his most promising acolyte in centuries, when strident alarm shot through the mental links he maintained with his crew. In an instant, he was off and racing for his lair, turning into a ghostly smear against the city lights.

At the San Juan Bay Marina, the cause of the turmoil was clear even before he reached *Apokryphos*. Four helmeted humans, encased in heavy gear to protect their fragile mortal bodies, huddled behind the facility's maintenance building of the marina. Their weapons were pointed toward the far end of the dock.

One jerked a gun barrel toward Kambyses before he remembered to will them not to see him. He'd been momentarily too astonished by those weapons of war to think clearly. Fully automatic, highly portable, and more efficient at taking lives even than he was. What in the name of all that was eternal was this firepower doing here?

The mortals exchanged brief words of suspicion and warning in Spanish. The man who had gotten a glimpse of him was breathing harder than the others. All their hearts pounded in Kambyses's sensitive ears, and their auras glowed like colorful prisms in the predawn darkness. Wafting in the sultry air, shading the stench of sweaty bodies, was the heady, unmistakable aroma of fear.

Kambyses's canines lengthened in anticipation of a satisfying feed.

A shout pulled him back to the crisis at hand. It came from *Apokryphos*, the yacht that was his lair. More warriors bristling with weapons could be seen moving around the outside decks. His crew's anxiety escalated. There wasn't time to gain thorough control of the warriors here. Instead, he shifted his voice into the resonant register of a mere compulsion. "Remain here, no matter what."

Leaving them as good as shackled for the moment, Kambyses sped the rest of the way to the yacht. There, he found all eight of his crew on their bellies in the salon. A few were dressed in their standard uniform of black slacks and shirts, but most were rumpled with sleep and clad only in their underwear. Four more human warriors stood over them, assault rifles at the ready.

The scene was so unthinkable he stopped, gaping, beset with an unfamiliar sense of shock.

Banging and crashing noises echoed from every one of the vessel's five decks as men systematically ransacked her. Violated her. His home. It felt like an attack on his very soul. The low growl in his throat escalated into an outright snarl as he allowed himself to be seen.

Every gun swung toward him. Orders were shouted in both Spanish and English. One weapon discharged.

Kambyses saw the stream of bullets coming, and he flashed inhumanly fast out of their way. By the time the tiny instruments of death thudded into a sofa, splintered the cherry-wood-paneled wall, and shattered a window, he had torn the offending weapon out of the soldier's hands.

"Stop," Kambyses roared, voice throbbing with power. "Drop your weapons. There is nothing to do here. Sit down. Shut up."

The three remaining weapons thumped onto the rug. The four warriors followed, dropping to their haunches on the spot.

Kambyses tossed the rifle aside, his hands shaking.

The more alert crewmen leapt to their feet, immediately resuming their primary compulsion—to serve and protect *Apokryphos*. They collected the weapons without a word. The others got up more slowly. As one, they turned their empty faces toward him, awaiting his command.

"Wait here," he snapped.

He found twelve more intruders in various locations on the ship. On the bridge, checking navigation computers. In the cabins, splitting open mattresses. In the galley, emptying cabinets. With each assault he saw, his blood seethed hotter. When he caught the last two rooting through the mini-sub in the engine room, he came closer to losing control than he had in a thousand years. The only thing that stayed his impulse to tear them limb from limb was the certain knowledge that these men—and a woman!—could not be working in isolation. Others would know where they were and why, and one—or all—going missing would be associated with *Apokryphos*. If not for that, he would drain them all and drop their bodies overboard into the darkest depths of the sea.

Instead, he corralled everyone in the salon.

The hurried compulsions he had placed were minimal and fading. Some of the soldiers looked around, questions in their eyes. Others appeared conflicted as they received hails on their communications devices that the compulsion to keep silent prevented them from acknowledging. Two of the crew, programmed as diligent servants, circulated with trays of refreshments.

Everyone focused on him when he followed the final two offenders as they and their gear clattered into the spacious room like cattle going to slaughter.

"Who are you?" Kambyses growled in Spanish.

No one answered.

"Who is your commander?"

A sharp-eyed man of medium build raised his hand. Kambyses was at his throat before he could utter a sound.

Hot and creamy, the blood slid through Kambyses's mouth, delivering knowledge along with sustenance. Within seconds, the commander's thoughts burst open in Kambyses's awareness. He rummaged through them as though they were a pile of scrolls, unfurling one memory after another, casting them aside until he found the thread he was searching for. These were members of Puerto Rico's elite narcotics division, and they were acting on a lead they had received this very night from a nameless, faceless informant. They believed *Apokryphos* to be filled with contraband, and had expected to be met by fierce resistance.

He let his saliva seal the wound he'd made before letting go, leaving the commander to sway on his feet. Kambyses's hand no longer trembled as he pulled the back of it across his mouth, but his belly contracted into a hard knot. It was rare to know a mind and end up with more questions than answers. But that wasn't his only concern right now.

The sun, due to rise soon from where it lay just beneath the eastern horizon, thrummed against his bones. Consciousness was a limited commodity, and his lair was infested with hostile mortals. He had to act fast.

His silent commands were simple and temporary, allowing him to hide in plain sight and alter impulses on a small scale. Spoken compulsion was deeper and lasted longer. But to seize permanent control, something more was needed. In this situation, nothing less would do.

Seventeen and a half interminable minutes later, the deed was done. Kambyses had tasted the blood and bent the minds of all twenty assailants, including the four on the dock. They each recalled the same non-event now—a false lead with no contraband found, no resistance encountered.

All had dutifully wiped their personal recording devices as well.

None would remember him.

His awareness of their buzzing minds faded as they marched away, the first rays of sunlight glinting off their gear. The familiar sluggishness crowded into his skull. Every fiber in his eternal body screamed to retreat into the darkness, to close his eyes, and to let go.

But where was Nico? Kambyses reached out for his cherished youngling. He sensed his presence nearby, but not on board where he should have been. Newborn and fragile, Nico would have succumbed to the day many minutes ago. If he had seen the chaos aboard *Apokryphos*, he might well have sought shelter elsewhere. It would be easy to retrieve him, return him to the safety of their lair, and Kambyses staggered into the morning brilliance, intending to do just that.

Daylight found his eyes with the intensity of red-hot daggers. Painful tears streamed down his face as he held up a hand to ward off the harsh rays. Heat seared against his palm and fingertips and the top of his head when he doubled over in agony, his long hair dragging on the concrete pavement. The world turned into a blazing white blur in which he spun wildly as his most basic survival instincts took hold and redirected his steps.

It was too late. Oblivion was coming for him. Nico would have to stay where he was.

After Kambyses slipped into the mini-sub, he slammed the hatch shut and secured it. Burrowing into his nest of velvet pillows and blankets, he slid into unconsciousness, his last thoughts of Nico. Wherever he sheltered for this day, Kambyses beseeched the fates that the youngling had chosen wisely.

2

The sun's howling presence had barely faded to tolerable levels the following evening when Kambyses left *Apokryphos*. With the coming of night, his own strength and power regenerated. He could feel it radiate from his bones outward to his skin—and beyond.

His will alone rendered him invisible as he moved through San Juan, part of the wind, the shadows, and the cacophony of pounding life in the streets. A sprawling shipyard lay before him, piled with neat rows of stacked metal boxes. Along the waterfront, several freighters lay tethered as cranes like spindly giants moved the transport containers between their crowded decks and the jam-packed dock.

It was here he had last sensed Nico. Of this, Kambyses was certain.

Also certain was that he sensed nothing of the youngling now.

He pivoted slowly, expanding his senses. It was still too early for Nico to be conscious. He could not have woken up and moved beyond Kambyses's reach in the past few minutes. But moved he had. Somehow. Because Kambyses could not detect him anywhere. He didn't even sense any other blood-drinkers. For a hundred miles around, Kambyses was the only one.

Had Nico been discovered? Exposed to the sun? He sniffed the air, seeking any hint of the cold ash that would have remained. Diesel, rot, and the lingering briny heat of day filled his nostrils. No ash. Which meant nothing, really. Too much time might have passed. The spot might not be here exactly.

Unease stole over him. He was alone. Only him and countless fleeting mortal nothings. And the eternity that stretched before him was far greater than the past stretching behind him.

Again, Kambyses turned, using his keen eyes this time, seeking any structure that might have hidden the vulnerable young vampire. There were none. At least none that wouldn't have been used during the day and therefore risked discovery. Only...

His gaze swerved back to the crane giants, to the multitude of forklifts and carriers moving the shipping containers. What if Nico had been desperate enough to take shelter in one of these?

What if it had been moved?

Onto a ship?

That had already set sail?

If there had been breath in his ancient body, it would have left him in a rush. The unease erupted into the sort of panic he hadn't felt since... His mind shied away from that time, the darkest of all his dark centuries. He would have to find Nico. That was all there was to it.

For the next several hours, he methodically fed on—and plundered—every dock worker he could find. After the fifth, he no longer fed. He only bit and then healed the wound right away, which was all that was necessary to seize a human mind. At the thirty-fifth, a night-shift worker who had just come on duty, Kambyses finally found what he was after.

Nico.

The memory in the worker's mind was vague, almost dreamlike, muddled as it was by Nico's apparent compulsion of the human. But Nico's striking beauty was unmistakable. Tall and pale, strong and graceful, with perpetually tousled wild dark hair and piercing hazel eyes that danced with gold and rebellion. Dominique. His Nico.

The worker had been hypnotized by the young vampire's strangeness, compelled by his French-accented Spanish words. "You see nothing but this open door. Lock it and be on your way."

Nico had disappeared into the container.

The man had locked the door.

And left.

Kambyses stood, staring at the empty pavement where the container had been. Nico should have returned to *Apokryphos* despite the mayhem there. He should have had faith that Kambyses would keep him safe. He could even have helped wrap that incident up more efficiently.

Instead, he'd hidden in a shipping container.

"Foolish, young one. Very foolish."

Finding Nico would be an exercise in patience, and it wouldn't happen tonight. But happen it would. A youngling vampire without a sire to restrain him could be relied upon to kill—and kill often. Reports of disappearances at sea would be a given. Perhaps even a ghost ship would be found with no one left alive aboard.

All Kambyses had to do was wait.

While he waited, his priority had to be *Apokryphos*. What had caused the local authorities to suspect her? He had only compelled the warriors themselves, not those they answered to, any one of whom could move against him again.

It took several hours of ghosting through police stations, command centers, and private residences, avoiding twenty-first-century surveillance—or destroying it when he couldn't—and tasting enough blood, pillaging enough minds, and murmuring enough compulsions to fill a year of nights. One by one, he worked through the chain of command, erasing all traces of the action against *Apokryphos* wherever he found it, then compelling those who had access to erase it from the official records as well. Kambyses's silent heart thrilled with this challenge. It was a hunt such as he had not enjoyed in many decades.

Near dawn, he approached his final target, a simple house in a crowded suburb. Inside, the lights were on, the occupants preparing for their day. He counted four heartbeats, a family. Only the male interested him. Daniel Ramos, inspector with the Puerto Rico drug division, was the original source of the information that had launched the attack. Why? That was a question only the inspector could answer.

The sky was turning light, and there was no time to waste lying in wait. Kambyses rang the doorbell. A woman in a bathrobe answered, but he willed her to see nothing, compelling her to wait by the open door as he entered her home. Seconds later, he was in the bedroom with Daniel Ramos's muscular, half-dressed body in his arms. The inspector's memories flowed along with his blood.

They were full of Nico.

Nico melting out of the night. Nico greeting him, speaking to him. Nico...

Kambyses reeled.

It was Nico who had convinced this man that *Apokryphos* was a plum prize ready for capture. He'd even told them exactly when to strike.

The knowledge landed like a hard blow to Kambyses's gut. Many of his younglings had plotted against him, but none had ever come this close to succeeding.

Kambyses barely remembered to erase all knowledge of Nico and *Apokryphos* from the inspector's mind before he bolted from the house and back to the marina. For the second morning in a row, he saw the sun's first greedy rays flashing off *Apokryphos's* shining black hull and superstructure. As he staggered inside and hurried down to the engine room and safety, waves of heat washed over his body.

But they could not touch the nameless chill sinking roots into his soul.

3

A week passed, and every night when Kambyses visited with the mortal who captained his lair, he received the same news. Nothing out of the ordinary had occurred during the day. No one had gone missing at sea. No ships had gone off course. Nico had vanished. Had he reached another shore? Or...?

Kambyses cursed under his breath in the ancient tongue of his people, which was no longer spoken—or even remembered—by anyone but him. Never had he known betrayal of this magnitude. Without an understanding of Kambyses's true power, Nico might well believe that a multitude of modern-day firepower could cripple or even kill him. It was the vilest of treachery, one that deserved the most severe of punishments. Even death.

Every night, he stalked along the beach where Nico had committed his duplicity, where he had compelled Inspector Ramos to launch an armed human horde at *Apokryphos*. Palm trees, hotels, tourists...but no vampires.

Eventually, Kambyses's fury cooled enough to acknowledge a grudging respect. To the end, the willful youngling surprised him as no other. Despite his crime, the possibility of Nico reduced to a pile of ashes left an uncomfortable heaviness in Kambyses's chest. There was no other, and no others he would make. Only humans crowded his awareness now, beings as plentiful and temporary as flies—and mostly useless beyond their blood.

In a desperate moment, he returned to his most recent prospect, and considered trying to complete the process himself. However, it had been three nights since the would-be convert had last felt his bite, and the man was now well on his way back to health. Even if not, even if a transformation attempt hadn't been doomed to failure, there was no point. This youngling would have been nothing like Nico and never could be.

Kambyses was alone.

His fingers twitched impatiently as this thought circled like a hungry shark. He, too, was hungry. Since the night after Nico's disappearance, he had pierced no veins and consumed no blood. It was time to remedy this, but not too fast. He needed the prey to be exquisite and marinated in terror, seasoned just the way he preferred. This would require time. It would force him to put his troubles aside to focus on the hunt.

In some ways, old San Juan soothed him. Much like himself, the cobblestoned alleys and colorful buildings with their narrow doors and cast-iron balconies were steeped in time and reeked of history. They, like him, remained unmoved by the tides of cheerful Latin music and laughter surging all around them. But unlike him, they became part of each age as treasured homes to generations of families. Kambyses was part of no time, nor any of the untold little lives swarming through the centuries. He was a still, immutable point among brilliant flashes of existence. And he was alone...

No, if Nico still lived and Kambyses found him, he wouldn't punish the wayward youngling. He would embrace him, cherish him, forgive him—so long as he was back by his side.

Kambyses was on top of his prey before he even realized he had made a choice. It was her hair that drew him. Thick and a deep auburn red, it gleamed in the ambient lights, bouncing and flowing across her bare shoulders as she strode down the street, absorbed in the handheld technology so prevalent in this age.

Entranced, he ghosted some distance ahead and tucked into the shadows of an alleyway. From there, he studied her at leisure. Willowy as a goddess, she didn't so much walk as glide across the cobbles on sandaled feet, her flawless young body on display in a frayed pair of jean shorts and a draping white sleeveless top. A pink glow on one side of her arms and legs betrayed the touch of the sun on delicate skin.

A tourist, then. One of thousands, but to his eyes, like no other.

Prey.

When she passed, he would call to her, compel her before she even saw him, bring her under his spell, alter her perceptions. Once she was in his arms, once his teeth pierced her skin, he would pour into her mind, let her know what was happening, stoke the horror of being fed upon. Her fear would rise like a fine spice to satisfy his jaded pallet.

It was what he always did. It was what always happened.

But then she looked up...and saw him.

Her stride faltered. A strange expression rounded her artfully outlined eyes. Kambyses couldn't recall the last time he had seen a look like that. Of course, neither could he recall an uncompelled human seeing him at all.

At least none he intended to let live.

She stopped at what she no doubt considered a safe distance, just past arm's reach, her gaze taking him in from the toes of his worn shoes to the crown of his head. The rest of him was covered in a charcoal-gray cloak, a comfortably obscure style he had adopted two or three centuries before.

"Oh. My. God."

Curious, Kambyses waited in perfect stillness. Whatever she did, if it wasn't agreeable, he could and would take control in an instant.

"Oh, my God. You're a…" Breath leaving her in a rush, she sucked it back before dropping her voice to a conspiratorial whisper. "You're a vampire."

Another first. No mortal had ever uttered those words to him with anything other than well-justified anxiety oozing out of their pores. This female's cheeks bloomed with color, her blue eyes glittery and dark. What oozed from her was nothing short of arousal.

Despite himself, Kambyses smiled.

"I knew it," she said, triumphant. "I've seen every movie there is. Read every book ever written. I knew there had to be some truth buried in all that. Please tell me you don't sparkle. Do you sparkle? No, forget I said that." She frantically waved the question away with both hands. So alive. So young. Barely a woman. "What a stupid thing to say. Please forgive me. I'm just so…I mean…I'm Monica." Rallying, she held out a long-fingered hand. A thin gold bracelet circled her wrist, matching the hoops in her ears.

Kambyses didn't touch her. She knew him. This human knew what he was, and she wanted to know more. In a deep, deep corner of his darkest heart, an invisible hand plucked a powerful chord.

"Um." She withdrew her hand. "What's your name?"

He recalled himself enough to cast a silent compulsion that made them both unnoticed by the mortals streaming past. "Kambyses," he said.

"Kambyses," she repeated, as though tasting the syllables. "I like that. It sounds…wise. And it goes with your rumbly voice."

Small talk was a human skill for which he had neither gift nor need. The temptation to compel her, enjoy her blood, erase her memories, and then send her on her way tickled the back of his throat.

"So." She took a small but firm step closer. Her pink tongue wet her glossy lips. One hand tucked a hank of hair behind an ear, the other, still clutching her phone, also tightened around the strap of her tiny bag. The beguiling aroma of sexual excitement wafted off her skin along with the warm vanilla of her blood. "Are you going to…I mean, did you want to…"

Kambyses arched a brow, encouraging her to continue. He had to tilt his face up to meet her eyes. People grew so tall now, even the women. This one—Monica—she was a long-limbed gazelle to his compact predator build.

"You know," she prompted, suddenly shy. "My blood?"

His mouth went dry. "Are you…offering?"

"Well, I wouldn't mind getting to know you a little first."

He tilted his head to one side, almost amused. "That is not the usual way of things."

She caught her lower lip between bright white teeth. "Maybe I'm not usual."

"That you are not," he agreed.

The girl fingered her phone for a moment as though considering using it to capture his image or communicate the knowledge of him to someone else. *No*, he commanded silently. The phone disappeared in her bag.

The moment she took her eyes off him, he retreated deeper into the dark alley, but allowed a distant streetlamp to touch him. She took a moment to spot him, and a sharp gasp followed. When she realized just how far he had moved in an instant without a sound, her heart rate spiked and her lips moved in a hushed exclamation. "Holy fucking shit."

Kambyses waited, resisting the urge to call her. What an unaccountably sweet pleasure to deny himself like this. How long could he draw this out?

To his delight, she followed of her own volition. Tentative at first, then with increasing resolve, she walked toward him.

Wonder lit her face. "How did you do that?"

"I like privacy." Not for mere feeding. That he could do in the middle of any crowd with no one the wiser. For this novelty, however, he wanted to focus on her alone.

The first whisper of apprehension colored her scent. "You should know I have friends waiting for me."

"You will return to them." He didn't add that this was not guaranteed, nor that if she did, she would remember nothing of this encounter, but for now, he would play her game just to see what rare delights might result. Even if it meant uttering the strangest words ever to pass his lips. "You wanted to...get to know me before you...allow me to feed?"

"Yes. Yes, I did. I mean, I do." She looked just a little dazed now. As if for all her earlier grand statements to the contrary, it was only now that she believed what he was. "It's just that I've imagined meeting someone like you for so long, and I'm not sure where to start."

"Try. I'm curious."

"Okay. Basics first then. Is it true you can't go out in the sun?"

"Yes."

"And you're...immortal?"

"Yes."

Her throat bobbed, drawing his attention to the pulse ticking there. "How...immortal?"

He met her eyes again.

She continued in a blur of words. "I mean, you look like you're maybe forty-something? But if you're immortal, that wouldn't be true, would it?"

"No," he said more softly. He didn't think he had been anywhere near that old when he last walked the Earth as a mortal, but time—if there was enough of it—had a way of wearing down all things. Even immortals.

"So, how old are you?"

"I am eternal."

He expected her to follow up this non-answer with another question about his age, and he was on the verge of being bored with the "small talk." Instead, she only studied him. He felt his skin squirm under her careful regard.

"You're alone, aren't you?"

She could not have stunned him more had she hit him across the face. That plucked chord in his heart thrummed so loud he heard nothing else, and he only mouthed his answer. "Yes. I am alone."

4

After her uncanny insights into his circumstances, there wasn't much Kambyses could deny this mortal enchantress. As he walked with her, he shielded them both from notice, letting her choose the path as he answered her questions the way he had been incapable of answering for his young ones. This, too, he told her.

"Maybe it's because I'm human," she offered thoughtfully.

"I rarely speak with humans at all."

"Because we don't rate?" No trace of derision threaded through her tone.

"Because you are mortal," he countered. "You are...food."

"Oh." Her mouth pursed tight before she nodded to herself, the gold hoops in her ears bobbing amidst her red tresses. It was the first thing he said that seemed to take her aback. The craving for her blood burned a little hotter. The anticipation of knowing her thoughts sweetened. He continued to wait, drawing out the moment into an exquisite, aching need.

"You are offended?" Not that this mattered, but without a link to her mind yet, he had to satisfy his curiosity by asking.

She shook her head, and she pushed her hair back behind both ears. The muggy evening thickened it into a dense, uncooperative mane, and coaxed from it a pleasing, bright mint scent. "No. You're right, of course. We are food to you." Another question welled in her eyes as they cut him a sideways glance, but instead of voicing it, she said, "I think you find it easier to talk to me because I'm like the person you'd meet on a plane or train. You feel our relationship is temporary. It doesn't matter what you tell me, how personal you get, because you know you'll never see me again. Not after a few decades, anyway. I have an end date."

Which might be soon at hand. The more he told her, the more difficult it would be to compel her into permanently forgetting, which made it easier to consider "ending" her. "Perhaps."

"No, I think I'm right. I mean, think about it. If you talk to other vampires, they're around forever, right? So who knows what might come back to bite you in the ass? But when you talk to me, everything you tell me...dies with me."

There was the slightest catch in her voice at this last statement, and he upgraded his estimation of her. She wasn't a complete ignorant. By engaging with him, she danced with the darkest, most dangerous of fires, yet dance she did. For reasons he couldn't quite grasp, Kambyses decided to ease her worries. "When we part ways, you will forget all you have learned of me."

One way or another.

Her eyes widened with astonishment. "You can do that?" At his raised brow, she hastily amended, "Oh God, yes. Of course, you can. Stupid question."

"Stupid question," he echoed, considering. Was she right? Was she an easier companion because she was mortal and at his mercy? Or was she more like a pet? Humans bared their souls to their pets, did they not?

They had stopped at the edge of another of the many tree-lined plazas dotting the old town. A fountain splashed at its center, and a handful of cars and vans, some blasting lively beats, flowed past. Pedestrians, too, though these gave him and his pet mortal wide quarter.

Monica watched several people dramatically alter their path when they unconsciously responded to the invisible psychic barrier Kambyses maintained. A small frown gathered her fine brow before understanding dawned. "Yes. Very stupid question."

"Do you think you know me well enough now, Monica?"

Her heart rate escalated again when she read the hunger in his face, deciphering his meaning. "What, here? In the middle of the street? What about..." Another quick glance around. Still no one paid them any attention. She cleared her throat, her hands coming together before her. "I guess I was hoping for something a little more...private."

"Were you?" It didn't matter. Once he had her mind, she would no more notice anyone else than he would. But, oh, this longing sliding in his entrails was beyond delicious. How much longer could he endure it? And as much as he had already shared with her, what was a little more? Or a great deal more? At what point would her fascination disintegrate into terror?

Resolving to find out, Kambyses dropped the barrier, caught the eye of the first driver to come their way, and extended a silent command. The boxy little black car squealed to a halt before them, making the girl flinch. He leaned into the open passenger side window, and spoke to the man at the wheel, who had a screaming skull tattooed on his bicep. The driver's only response was a familiar, empty stare.

Kambyses straightened before gallantly opening the rear door for Monica. "Get in."

"Where are we going?"

"You will know it when you see it." He pushed an image of the destination into her subconscious. With a touch of compulsion, he added, "Until you do, remember nothing of me."

5

Simple as it would have been to carry her, he knew, with surveillance systems so prevalent, that a young woman getting into a strange car alone before disappearing would be a far better mystery to leave behind.

Because disappear, she would. That was all but decided.

He sped back to the marina and melted into the shadows of the maintenance building straddling the dock. Interminable minutes of solitude drifted past before he saw her again, emerging from the late-night bustle at the marina's restaurant. With uncertain steps, she made her way past the dock gate.

Retreating to *Apokryphos*, tied up at the dock's deepest and most distant end, Kambyses waited on the aft main deck. From there, he overlooked the landing platform and most of the dock. Another minute passed before the prey eased around the maintenance building with a puzzled, anxious expression on her dewy face.

Then she spotted *Apokryphos's* black hulk in the distance, and the compulsion crumbled. Her eyes and mouth rounded as one.

For the second time that night, Kambyses restrained himself from willing her to come to him. The power he wielded to bring her here was far beyond the silent speed she had already witnessed. He had compelled a stranger to bring her here without comment, dulled her memory of the supernatural, and left her with an inexplicable desire to find a dark yacht. Now that she realized this, would she still want to be in his presence? If not... If she ran...

The girl swayed, undecided, but then seemed to brace herself and marched forward until she came to a stop on the dock before him. "How?" she exclaimed. "How did you do that?"

Kambyses almost smiled. "Stupid question," he murmured, gesturing at the platform. "Welcome."

Still, he was careful not to will her actions. Still, she moved forward. The moment her sandals touched the teak deck of her own free will, he all but came undone with need. She was now truly in his domain, her fate sealed.

"Wow," she said as she climbed up the narrow stairway to the main level. Her gaze traveled over the expansive deck space, stowed tenders, and sleek obsidian fuselage. "I'm not going to ask another stupid question, Kam. This has you written all over it."

"*Apokryphos* is my home."

Monica grinned. "Even the name is perfect."

He ushered her toward midship and into the foyer with its rich wood-paneled walls and fine Grecian busts. From there, he led her through the crystal-studded, never-used formal dining room into the staid silence of the main salon. If fire were one of his gifts, the intensity with which he watched her would have set her ablaze. For the first time since their meeting, her attention was not riveted on him. He felt invisible again, this time through no action of his own. Incredibly, he was being upstaged by a ship.

Monica prowled around the salon, admiring the fine furnishings, gilded fixtures, and alabaster statues. Her fingertips trailed over the polished woods and plush upholstery. "She's beautiful, Kambyses," she said, and his heart swelled. "Oh, the things I could do with this."

"What things?" he wondered, not moving from his spot near the door. One step, and he wouldn't be able to stop. He wasn't ready to lose her yet. Or rather, not ready to end this sweet, tortured longing.

"I'm training to be an event planner. This place would be perfect for all kinds of intimate parties." When she glanced at him, she seemed to recall where she was, and with whom and what she had said. Her lips thinned as she sucked at them, shy once more. Sexual arousal soaked the air. Intimate parties, indeed.

A crewman brushed past Kambyses, dressed in the standard uniform and carrying a tray with a single glass of burgundy wine. Like all the crew, this one was utterly compelled, his expression empty as he went about obeying Kambyses's silent command to offer the refreshment to his guest.

"Oh. Thank you," she said, accepting the glass.

The servant did not respond. He and the tray left as they arrived, with quiet efficiency.

What the girl thought of the servant's vacant manner was impossible to tell, but a small line creased her brow as she watched him go. The man would have already forgotten the striking redhead, and he would have never even noticed Kambyses. The crew's sole purpose was to serve *Apokryphos*. Beyond this, they had no ambitions, no memories, and no thoughts. They were trained tools and convenient blood supplies, nothing more.

Monica took a full-mouthed swallow of wine as though fortifying herself with the alcohol. The sweetly acidic scent mingled with her musky perfume, making his mouth water. "You're not having any? Or are you really limited to only drinking blood?"

"I enjoy it as a seasoning only." And the vintage in her glass was his current favorite.

"A seasoning...oh. I see."

He inclined his head in silent confirmation of her new understanding.

An uneasy smile flickered on her wine-shiny lips as she looked away. Her eyes fastened on the first available distraction. "Oh, what happened there?"

The window that had caught the bullet was patched with a tarp and tape. Finding and compelling the right craftsmen to replace it and repair the rest of the damage without asking questions was a project for another time in yet another port. As it was, he had lingered here too long already.

Monica stared at the splintered walls near the broken window. "Are those...bullet holes?" She turned back. "Kam? Why are there bullet holes in your ship?"

He allowed himself a tiny smile. "You are alone with a powerful vampire, but you are concerned by bullet holes?"

"Well...I'm..." Her hands clasped the glass more tightly, her cheeks blooming.

"They are from my most recent youngling's parting...gesture," he said before he knew he intended to. Not that it mattered. She wouldn't get to share his words with anyone else. Not anymore.

The girl blinked at him, owlish with unspoken questions.

Perhaps she was right. Maybe it was easier to talk to her because she was so temporary. Unlike Nico, who should have been anything but.

"So you're not totally alone," she ventured.

"I am now." And until he found another, he would remain so. For all his age and power—or perhaps because of them—the one thing he could no longer do was make a youngling on his own.

"What happened to this...um...youngling?"

Kambyses reached out into the void again, yet still found no sense of Nico. Just like there had been no reports of unusual deaths or disappearances at sea from anywhere. A bony finger of grief touched his still heart. "He died."

"Oh." Her brows knit together. "So you're not...I mean, he wasn't immortal? Yet?"

"He was. But we can still be killed. Usually by each other," he added more softly, vivid memories of the recent past roaring to the surface.

To prevent them overtaking him, he moved into the room, unclasped his cloak, and dropped it on a chair before inviting her to sit on the nearest sofa. He joined her there, not because of any social conventions of casual conversation, but because a great, invisible weight had settled onto his shoulders. "My last young one, Dominique...he was here only a few nights ago."

A beguiling hint of worry laced her scent now as she drew new conclusions. Lost in reverie, he ignored the growing temptation.

"He was beautiful and cunning and so very tormented. He was...the perfect companion." And what had Kambyses done to him? The same he did to all the others, the flawed ones, the weak ones, all the ones with so much promise who always disappointed him. While Kambyses roamed the night as a solitary shadow, seeking others to seduce, Nico was left to his own devices, struggling with what he had become while plotting bitter revenge. "I didn't see the truth of him until he was gone. I don't know if he is dead, but I have no reason to believe he still exists, either."

Monica pulled her knees up underneath her as she faced him. "May I ask what happened?"

"You may." He was about to add that he did not need to answer or explain anything to a human, but those weren't the words coming out of his mouth as he gestured at the bullet holes in the wall. "He tried to kill me."

This elicited a small, breathless gasp.

Kambyses continued, sharing how he had first found Nico, made him his, and kept him safe while the youngling's blood lust raged. He told her some of what came after, too, and the attack on *Apokryphos* and on him. As he spoke, he tried to find a reason for how it all ended. He couldn't.

Not so the human girl.

She listened with rapt attention until he fell silent. Then she nodded, eyes crinkling in thought. "I don't think he's dead, Kam. He ran away."

Too surprised to react, Kambyses said nothing.

"He didn't ask to be turned. You just dumped this life on him without explanation. He was pissed and desperate enough to try to kill you before. He couldn't possibly think a bunch of humans with guns could do what he couldn't. I think the attack was a distraction, a cover for him to..." She trailed off at whatever change she detected in his expression.

"Escape," he finished, feeling numb. When she didn't refute this, it was he who looked away. There was no denying this, not even to himself. He had known Nico's mind before the transformation, when he fed from him. Kambyses knew how Nico thought, what drove him, what he was capable of and why, and what he craved more than anything else. Nico's master he may be, but the youngling had never submitted. Not in his heart. And even though he would only add to his torment by taking more lives without a mentor to guide him—even risk his own immortal life in the unpredictable world of humans—Nico had not only chosen to flee into the dangerous unknown, he had also engineered the dangerous means to do so.

It would have been easier to believe Nico had merely tried to kill him again. Easier to think the attack resulted from nothing but a fit of temper. This was different, though. This was cold, calculated, and full of loathing, and it engendered a strange sensation behind Kambyses's ribs. Almost...painful.

He drew in a deep drink of air. No hint of a youngling's cool scent remained. Instead, the air was ripe with the girl's sweet warmth. Beneath her heart's excited hammering, he heard the activity of the crew all around the ship as they obeyed his silent, almost unconscious command to make ready to sail. Soon, he would be at sea again, free in the night—and filled with fresh blood. He would survive this disappointment as he had a thousand others.

No longer able to contain himself, Kambyses's razor-sharp canines appeared, aching to pierce this virgin flesh. His vision changed, too, shifting into a realm that allowed him to see her veins like a delicate web of pulsing light stretched beneath her skin.

"I wonder, Monica, do we have enough privacy now?" He made no effort to conceal his rampant hunger, and greedily anticipated the blind terror that would supply the final, most perfect ingredient. What a sublime drink this would be. What balm to his raw nerves.

Her jaw slackened, but her scent remained free of apprehension even as the radio chatter from the crew coordinating the release of the lines reached them from outside. Her body would be fed to the sea long before dawn. "Well, it is, but, Kam...I'm not ready to forget you."

He took the glass from her hands. Only half empty, she had drunk enough to flavor her blood and left enough to ruin the upholstery. His eyes did not leave hers as he leaned over her, reaching to set the glass down on the side table. She was prone prey beneath him, ready for the taking. Yet instead of tensing, she relaxed, lay back on the pillows, and opened like a flower.

Her hand burned against his cheek. "I don't think you want to let me go yet, either, do you?" she whispered.

On the contrary. Kambyses was more than ready to end this yearning for her blood, her mind, her life. He brushed her hair from her neck, hypnotized by the pulsing light of her blood, the clamoring of her heart.

"Please don't make me forget this magic, Kambyses. It's all I've wanted for so long."

The tip of his finger traced the thickest vein. Too plump. She would bleed out too quickly, the pleasure over too soon. He considered a smaller stream.

The girl shivered. "I'll be honest. I would love for you to turn me. But if that means you'd stop confiding in me...well, I can wait."

Startled, he met her glistening eyes. Make her a youngling? Even if he could, with all she knew of him now, he'd sooner turn her into a corpse. "You have belonged to me since the moment you set foot aboard my lair. I will do with you as I wish."

To emphasize this point, he nuzzled against her cheek, forcing his scent into her flaring nostrils. Fire lived in his blood. The smell of smoke and destruction shrouded him. Still, there was none of the terror he craved. Still, she believed she would live past the moment her blood touched his tongue.

Her fingers combed into his hair, her voice husky as she said, "I could stay with you. As anything you want. No strings. No limits."

The wet heat of her mouth on his, and the suggestive movement of her hips, made it clear what she imagined he might expect of her. Nothing could have been farther from the truth. With no heartbeat in his body, physical passion had long been a thing of the past. Blood was the only actual pleasure that remained for him.

"I could be your eyes and ears in the daytime," she said when he ignored her overture in favor of burrowing into her neck. "I could help you find Dominique."

This made him pause, then draw back. She gazed up at him, her face flushed but completely serious. The offer was genuine—free of compulsion or even accidental influence because that possibility had not even remotely occurred to him.

"I will never allow you to know of me during the day." What was he saying? She would never know of him again, day or night, and she might well be dead before she could utter another word.

Or not.

"Then compel me however you need to be comfortable. Anything. Just let me be with you. Let me be there *for* you. Since I'm willing, I'm sure you wouldn't have to make a zombie out of me like that guy who brought the wine. At least, I hope not."

This was true. Her mind would need only the lightest touch. But gods! An aware mortal for a companion? Was he as desperate as Nico now, to break all his own rules and risk his life so recklessly? He didn't think so. Not at all. Which didn't mean the proposition didn't intrigue him.

With his rising emotions, his vision expanded further, bringing the soft pink light of her life force into brilliant relief while darkening his eyes to the full black of his truest self. With no small satisfaction, he heard her breath hitch. She saw him. Monica knew as much about him as any living thing ever had, and her submission to him was as quiet and eloquent as the turning away of her face to expose her vulnerable neck.

The last thread of restraint snapped. Kambyses clutched her against him, drove his teeth deep. The blood came, rich with heat and wine and lust. In mighty pulls, he inhaled it into his starving body, and when he flowed into her mind, he inhaled that, too.

Not even a whisper of trepidation met him, no hint of deception, nor the touch of any other blood-drinker's meddling to account for her strange willingness to confront such lethal danger. Danger she was very much aware of. As *Apokryphos* shivered with the power of her engines rumbling to life, she knew he held her life in his hands, that life as she knew it was over. Yet, her faith in her ability to survive remained undaunted, worthy of any warrior.

She knew him—and refused to fear him.

So be it. Fear was not the only spice he enjoyed.

While he held her, drinking her life, he spun for her a new reality based on her most private fantasies. In her lucid dying dream, she knew passionate kisses and sweet caresses. Knew heat and moisture and penetration. She knew sure hands, hard strokes, and frantic rhythms, raw ecstasy that had her trembling and spasming and moaning his name.

His name.

Not the name of the human man she had bedded for months now. Nor the name of the friend's husband she had pined over for years. Not even the imagined name of some exotic, faceless stranger.

Him. Kambyses.

He was her fantasy.

And when Kambyses discovered he had stopped feeding but continued to hold her, adrift in the wordless rapture of her acceptance, he knew he would be her reality, too.

Acknowledgements

My biggest thanks must go to my family for the continuing support of—and patience with—the writer in the house. Your love means everything to me.

Many heartfelt thanks also go to:

Aleksina Teto, second-edition editor, for her continuing eye-opening insights about my own words.

Máirín Fisher-Fleming, first reader, dear friend, and my go-to French and motorcycle reference.

Sandy Parks, aviation expert, who took me seriously when I asked about landing a helicopter in strange places.

Carol Fridolph, yoga instructor extraordinaire, who bravely agreed to read about a vampire to make sure Samantha makes sense when she talks.

And, of course, thank you to all the writers who have encouraged and inspired me over the years, and all the readers who have ventured into my world. You are the reason this book exists.

About the Author

S.K. Ryder writes paranormal and science fiction fantasy featuring fish-out-of-water characters forced to deal with reality gone wrong. Her stories reflect her deep love of nature and are filled with adventure, suspense, humor, and romance. Though she currently calls South Florida home, she has lived in Germany and Canada and has traveled widely, usually in the hot pursuit of wild and scenic spaces. When not writing or working as a freelance programmer, she enjoys plotting her next scuba diving or river rafting trip, beach combing, or just getting lost in a book. Should push comes to shove, she can also bake a halfway decent cake and stand on her head, though not (usually) at the same time.

Find her online at https://skryder.com

BOOKS BY S.K. RYDER

DARK DESTINIES SERIES

Dark Awakening (Prequel)
Dark Heart of the Sun (Book 1)
Dark Lord of the Night (Book 2)
Dark Reign of Forever (Book 3)

For a complete list, visit:
https://books2read.com/SK-Ryder

www.ingramcontent.com/pod-product-compliance
Lightning Source LLC
Chambersburg PA
CBHW021405310726

48971CB00005B/1215